SKIRTING FATE

A REVERSE HAREM NOVEL

SALEM CROSS

Dedication

To anyone who enjoys a good smutty book

Chapter One

Gemma

I gag on the dirt caking the back of my throat as I wipe the sweat from my face. Thoughts like, w*hy am I doing this again* and *'cause you're a badass who wanted to see how hard you could push yourself*, war amongst themselves in the foreground of my consciousness as I grit my teeth and try to ignore the exhaustion beating at me.

The finish line is in sight. Had this been a normal race, I'd just sprint the last eight hundred meters and cross the finish line with a big old smile on my face. But this race isn't your typical race. I'm participating in one of the hardest mud obstacle courses in the United States. This means sprinting to the finish line isn't in the plan to win a spot on the podium. I have to finish this metal A-frame obstacle and then handle the army crawl.

Even if this were a normal race, I'm not going to win it. Sam Cannon, one of the best obstacle course runners in the world, is already towards the end of the army crawl. Any moment he will be on his feet and sprinting towards the end. Then there is Jackson Ellie, the second-best obstacle race runner, trying his hardest to close that small gap between them. Finally, there's Janice Backer, the top female obstacle course racer, who is right on Jackson's heels.

So, I may not come in first overall, but I can take first in my age group and second in women overall. That means money in my pocket. That is, as long as I can shake this bitch Elizabeth Gambit who is giving it all she has to catch up to me. To be fair, Elizabeth isn't really a bitch. I actually like her. But right now, she is a competitor, and all my competitors are bitches in my head. And if I don't pay attention, this bitch may pass me.

I throw my body over the top of the A-Frame before taking one cautious step down to the next metal bar. I risk a leap to get to the ground faster and then cringe as my knees take most of the impact. I don't stop though. The barb wire obstacle is next, and I'm already on the move to tackle it. The breath is knocked out of me as I throw myself onto my stomach. There is hardly enough room between the barbs and the hard, rocky ground for us to use to move, but I push forwards anyway. I ignore the cuts and scrapes from the stones, sticks, and barbs. I will tend to them later. I have a hundred more from earlier obstacles, so these aren't going to stand out amongst the others.

My foot kicks something, and behind me someone swears. Shit... Elizabeth is catching up. I move faster. The moment I'm free of the wires I am on my feet and sprinting hard. The small group of fans are cheering, the large timer is ticking, and the announcer is giving a play by play, but I shove all that far back so I can focus on that small, white line that will end all of this.

This time when I choke, it's from relief and success as I cross the finish line. The fans erupt into even louder cheering. For a moment, I scan the crowd for my coach before I remember that Aaron couldn't make it. Some sort of an emergency, he said over the phone.

Instead of worrying about Aaron, I whirl around to face Elizabeth who has stopped just behind me. Her hands are behind her head as she breathes heavily. When she sees me, Elizabeth flashes me a grin. I walk over to her and throw my arms around her shoulders,

"That was amazing! You just got your first personal record on a legit course!" I told her, grinning stupidly. My head is spinning, and I can't really catch my breath, but I had to congratulate my frenemy. Elizabeth laughs and throws her arms around me. Neither of us care about the sweat and mud we're transferring to one another. That comes with the territory with these kinds of races.

"I *almost* caught you. Next time," she says breathlessly.

"Yeah, yeah, like I'd let you overtake me," I tell her, and we laugh again. We both drop one arm but keep the other around each other's shoulders as we walk away from the finish line. Race staff rush over to us with some recovery drinks and protein bars, which we take thankfully.

We're ushered over to the winners' tent, and inside are a ton of photographers. The winners of each category from the paranormal race are standing around mingling with one another. I stare at the various non-human runners as they talk and laugh amongst themselves. Their race took place two hours ago, and most of them are cleaned up now. Watching them tackle the obstacles was absolutely mind-blowing. Seeing their speed, agility, and strength in action is humbling. No matter how fast or strong I think I am, I know I will never come close to what they have.

It's strange to think that it was hardly a hundred years ago that the civil rights act for non-human species passed. How had humans considered non-humans like shifters, vampires, and witches to be monstrosities? They are just like us, only way cooler. There are still a few factions here and there that harbor prejudices against those that aren't human. But me? There is something about the paranormal world that calls to me.

Elizabeth and I are ushered over to where Sam, Jackson, and Janice are standing and talking to one another. The three of them greet us with hugs. My body is shaking from fatigue and humming with adrenaline. The grin that splits across my face might be a bit manic, but hell, I worked my ass off to get into this tent with these people, and dammit if I don't feel good about making it!

"Great job, Gemma!" Sam says with a wide grin. He's a lean guy with lanky long legs and a short buzz cut. "Way to make it to the top! You definitely have come a long way since last year."

Oh, he knows who I am? I find myself pleasantly surprised. I glance down at my watch. Talk about a personal record from last year. I finished a full twenty minutes faster than last year's race. Thank goodness all my hard work has paid off.

"Thanks," I say, grinning like a fool.

We all stand around talking, waiting for the last few podium placers. As we talk, I glance around the winners' tent and catch the eye of one of the non-human athletes. He is incredibly attractive with piercing green eyes and short, messy dark brown hair. My mouth, already dry from dehydration, turns into a desert. My heart races as we stare at each other. Despite being utterly spent, a sudden zing of energy courses through me, giving me a second wind.

My cheeks warm in embarrassment. I really should look away, but I find that I can't. Finally, he lets me go with a wink before turning back to whoever was talking to him. I look away from him and try to gather my scattered thoughts. But they only seem to get more frazzled. Who is this man?

"Alright, everyone, let's get pictures on the podiums with your medals and then a few group shots!" the race director bellows over us.

Pictures are taken in small groups by categories: age group, male, female, then human and paranormal. The last picture is a group picture with all of us together. As Elizabeth and I head out of the tent she asks,

"Are you going to the dinner tonight?"

"Yeah, it sounds like fun. I wouldn't mind celebrating with everyone. I feel like finally making it to the podium deserves a celebration," I tell her. *And I might get to see Mr. Green Eyes again...*

***

I step into the fancy dining hall inside of the hotel where all the elite athletes are staying. After resting up after the race, I thought I would feel better, but my joints are screaming and a particularly large scratch along my hip is grating on my nerves. I sigh in relief when I glance around the room at the attire of the others. My cocktail dress is just enough. Any other time, I would be embarrassed to wear a dress this short and revealing with all the scratches and bruises, but everyone else in the room has the same wounds. There is no need to assure people I wasn't attacked here.

Live music is playing, people are dancing or mingling nearby, and the staff of the hotel is making their rounds with drinks and hors d'oeuvres. I take a glass of white wine offered to me by a staff member and make my way into the room. When I take a sip of the wine, I'm pleasantly surprised. It is pretty good. I'm not typically a drinker, but tonight I want to indulge.

My eyes search the crowd for the non-human who captured my attention earlier. That gorgeous man has been on my mind since I laid eyes on him this morning. My hands shake as my body practically hums with excitement and anticipation while I search for him in the throng of people.

It doesn't take me long to find a group to insert myself into. Elizabeth finds me not long after and joins the group. I mingle and laugh for a bit with people whose names I instantly forget after they are introduced. When dinner is served, I find myself grouped with Elizabeth and Janice, Sam and Jackson, and the third-place male, Conner Soors, and the third-place, woman Debra Thymes.

Sam leans in to talk to me a lot during dinner. At first, I'm pleased that such a famous athlete is showing me any attention and seems interested in my background. Quickly, though, that changes when I smell the alcohol on his breath, note the slight glaze in his eyes, and how he leans in just a little too intimately to whisper in my ear. Only after a flimsy attempt under the table to slide his hand up my thigh, which ends up with my elbow digging into his ribcage, does he stop his advances.

I won't allow him to ruin my night. Tonight is a celebration of all my hard work, and there isn't a damn thing anyone can do to ruin the mood.

Well… except maybe not show up. I continue to search the crowd, looking for that handsome man from earlier, only to continuously find myself further disappointed each time I realize he is not here. Each time that disappointment creeps up, I force it back down. Nope, I will not let anything ruin my mood.

After dinner, speeches are made by the race committee, coaches, and a few athletes themselves. Once the formalities are out of the way, the music starts back up. I'm not sure how many drinks I have had by the time Elizabeth pulls me out onto the dance floor, but I'm feeling good. Hands come around my waist, and I pause swinging my hips to look at the person behind me. He's a handsome guy with warm brown eyes. When he quirks one brow curiously, I smile and lean into his touch as I go back to dancing. I catch Elizabeth's wink before she spins around to disappear into the crowd, leaving me alone with my new dance partner.

I turn in his hands so I can face him, and immediately I note the fangs peeking out from his lips. A vampire. Ah, he must be one of the paranormal athletes. A zing of excitement shoots through me.

I grin up at him, and he twirls me around. We don't speak while we dance, but there's no need. I giggle as he bends me backwards during a song. I can't remember the last time I had this much fun.

Chapter Two

Christopher

I am the last one to arrive at the party. Dinner has already been served, the award ceremony is over, and now everyone is dancing. The noise is deafening, and my senses are overwhelmed with the smell of food, perfume, and body odors. Normally I avoided the after events. There are too many people all crowded together, and I always feel suffocated. I hate people. I do these events because I love the challenge. It is the mingling afterwards, talking about the same old things, that drives me close to madness.

But tonight, I am hardly in my right mind.

Ever since I laid eyes on that human woman in the tent, my wolf has been going nuts. It is taking everything in me to keep my wolf in check while I stand there in the doorway looking for her. After the group picture in the tent earlier, my wolf tried to go after the woman. I stalked her to the parking lot where the company that sponsored the race had buses waiting to shuttle us back to the hotel, but that is as far as I allowed my wolf to control me this morning.

Now, I'm driven on pure instinct to find her.

Typically, I am not interested in humans. I have made that mistake before. Luckily, I have learned from it. Humans are fragile, prejudiced assholes, the lot of them. There are plenty of non-humans to mingle with. My wolf is usually in agreement with me, but for some reason this human causes him to flip his opinion quickly. After she was out of sight this morning, he had tried to force his way out, fighting for control. His panic and the sense of urgency had become mine as well, but for the life of me, I could not and still cannot figure out what is wrong with the beast. When was the last time I felt so out of control? So out of sync with the creature within me?

Never.

After such a grueling race, my wolf should have been exhausted. Shifting from one form to another in the blink of an eye, while on the move, is a feat only ten percent of the entire shifter population, no matter the species, can master. But to be able to do it over and over while racing through obstacles is even more rare. I love the rush the race gives me, and my wolf basks in the competition with others. We both should be exhausted now.

But my wolf is determined to find this human. His sense of urgency and concern worries me enough to finally indulge his desire to find her. If my wolf is distressed, so am I. We are one and the same. If he wants to meet this woman so badly, then so be it.

On their own accord, my feet begin to move, pulling me into the ballroom. I grab two glasses of wine from a server's tray, down them both, and place the empty glasses on a nearby table. As my eyes search the crowd, my nose twitches, searching for a scent that will alert me to where this human can be. As I move around the room, I scold my wolf,

This is ridiculous. She's just a typical human.

Though my wolf cannot speak, I can almost feel him bristle at my words. His reaction confuses me. What is so special about this woman? A few people come to speak with me. Strange, since most of them know how I feel about chit chat. After the fifth time excusing myself, I find her, the woman who intrigues my wolf.

She is out on the dance floor with Marcus. The vampire is a fierce competitor, and he nearly won this year. If it weren't for some quick thinking out on the course, I would have come in second, not first. Marcus' annoyed huff as he crossed the finish line after me still echoes in my head. Yeah, a close one for sure. Out of all the athletes I compete against, Marcus is my favorite.

So why is the hair on my neck rising and my wolf angrily snarling in my head? Before I realize it, I am making my way through the crowded dance floor towards them. As I get closer, my wolf's anger increases until it is my own. My fingers curl into fists, and I grind my teeth together. Thank goodness there is music. Otherwise, my growl would be audible enough for most of the room to hear.

It is senseless to act this way. Somewhere in my consciousness, I know this. But that woman shouldn't be anywhere near another man. My wolf's agreement sends a shiver of anger down my spine. If it weren't for him, I wouldn't even be here getting upset over *nothing*. Marcus senses me before I even get the chance to tap him on the shoulder. Marcus whirls both of them around, and I have enough sense to relax, just as they turn to face me.

"Christopher!" he says with a wide smile. "You're not here to cut in and steal my dance partner, are you?"

The moment the vampire voices his possession over the human woman, my wolf's snarls louder in my head. I must swallow back a growl before I can speak.

"That's exactly what I am doing. You can't keep the prettiest lady in the room all to yourself," I say as charmingly as possible. There must be something wrong with my expression because Marcus' smile falters a little.

"I suppose I shouldn't bogart," Marcus says sadly and turns to the woman next to him. "It's been a pleasure dancing with you. Can I get your name before we split up?"

"I'm Gemma, Gemma Thomas."

"Ah Gemma, what a pretty name. I'm Marcus Bainford, and this here is my friend, and perhaps now my arch nemesis on *and* off the course:

Christopher Rogue."

I chuckle at Marcus' introduction.

"Enjoy your dance with Miss Thomas, Chris," Marcus says.

As Marcus steps away, Gemma says, "I hope you're as good as Marcus because I love to dance."

Her voice cuts through the music and infiltrates my consciousness. There the sound is permanently etched into my mind. I turn my head and give Gemma my full attention. Now that she isn't covered head to toe in mud, I can really take a good look at what my wolf finds appealing in this woman.

Her light brown eyes are the first thing I notice. They are large and wide, just a touch darker than honey. Next, I notice her full lips stretched into a wide beautiful smile. When I can pull my attention away from her eyes and lips, I take in the rest of her. Her skin is warm brown, and her dark brown curls are up in a messy bun with several strands breaking from their loose hold. Her figure is what I would expect from an athlete; slim with well-defined arms, and those long legs are ripped with muscle while remaining feminine. The only curves on this woman are from her breasts and butt, which are barely covered in that little black dress. If it weren't for the cuts and bruises all over her body, she would appear flawless.

Gemma is stunning. My wolf whines in agreement. In fact, I can feel his utter contentment as he gazes upon her. Strange.

Her words finally sink in after a beat. Dance? I hadn't really planned on dancing. Truthfully, I haven't really thought this confrontation through at all. But for some reason, her challenge sparks a little excitement in me. I give her a smile that feels tight,

"I think anyone can attest that I am the better dancer," I assure her.

Before she can respond, I step closer and take her hand. The idea *was* to spin her around and show her what I could do, but I am momentarily floored by the rightness the simple connection between us feels. I look down at her hand. It's small, but it feels so right in mine. Her knuckles are scraped up, and she has small calluses that gently rub against mine.

My wolf is howling with delight at the contact. I, on the other hand, am puzzled by the phenomenon.

"Everything, okay?" she asks me.

I glance at her face and find her giving me a perplexed look. I grin and, to cover up my sudden confusion, I say,

"Yeah, just amazed a beautiful woman like yourself would want to dance with a mutt like me."

She rolls her eyes, "Mutt? More like a show dog."

Her comment catches me off guard. My laughter is louder than the music, and people turn their heads to look at the both of us. I've never been referred to as a show dog before. Maybe a hound dog, certainly mutt, sometimes scoundrel but definitely not a show dog. Instead of responding to her compliment, I spin her around in my arms and show her how to really dance. Her squeal of delight causes my wolf to yip in my head. He likes it.

Oddly enough, I like it too. Maybe it's the alcohol hitting my system. I am not much of a drinker (the wolf in me doesn't like the taste), but it helps to take the edge off.

My hands slide over her body. I bring her close to my chest and then away. I envelop her into my embrace before twirling her this way and that. Somewhere in my mind, I wonder why I am finding it difficult to not rub myself against her. She would smell great with my scent all over her.

Gemma's laughter and the twinkle in her eyes are better than the music and the light show in the room with us. Her body moves to the rhythm with ease while her hands hold on to mine. I pull her close, wrapping my arms around her waist. I cannot resist leaning down and inhaling her scent.

The smell is heady. My body responds immediately, and I am thankful that the music suddenly comes to an end and she pulls away.

She looks at me and says, "I'm parched."

"Let's get you a drink," I say as I offer her my hand.

She takes it with a smile. We move off the dance floor, and I catch the attention of a wait staff carrying around drinks. As the staff woman approaches, she lowers her tray.

"Red or white wine?"

I glance over at Gemma next to me who answers, "White please."

After Gemma receives her drink and I take my own, I direct us further away from the dancing masses. My wolf is practically giddy now that he is near her. I almost roll my eyes at his excitement. I stop myself at the last second as Gemma turns around to look at me.

"You were right. You are a better dancer than Marcus," she says and sips her drink.

"I wouldn't lie to you," I tell her with a grin, weirdly pleased with the compliment. I'll rub this in Marcus' face the next time I get the chance.

"Do you want to go outside and get some fresh air? It's so stuffy in here," she asks, already looking around for the exit.

"Yes, *please.*"

My relief to get out of this hell hole must be more evident than I thought because Gemma gives me a knowing look before turning and heading towards the side doors. I down my glass of wine behind her back and place it on a server's tray as they walk by. I grab another glass of wine in the next move and half of it is gone before we make it outside.

What am I fucking doing?

I follow her outside where speakers are hooked up for the guests to still hear the music, but it is much quieter out here. I feel more than a little relieved to get away from the crowd, and from the heavy sigh coming from Gemma, I have the feeling she feels the same way. Out here, a fountain bubbles in the middle of the patio with cement benches placed in a circle around it.

"I haven't seen you before," I start, staring at her bare back. She turns around, and I find myself sinking into those eyes. "Is this your first year competing?"

"It's my first year competing as a professional. I've been racing obstacle courses for a few years but decided to take it seriously this past year. I had my friend, who's a coach, train me and managed to get a few sponsors to support me. I qualified at all the necessary races to get to this one, and now here I am, hanging with the pros." She gives me a proud, megawatt smile that stuns me into silence.

Even my wolf is stunned into a wordless '*oh.*' My answering smile feels awkward as I try to shake off the sudden stupor.

"That's quite a feat. Are you planning on going on to the race in Scotland in a few months?" I ask her. She shrugs.

"I don't know. I feel like I've been here and done it. I wanted to be a top athlete. Now that I am, I want to try something else," she answers then chuckles. "I'm not one to stick to much of anything for a long time."

"You like to try new things," I say this as a statement, not a question.

"All the time," Gemma confirms with a nod. "I get bored easily and… I know this sounds silly, but life is too short to just stick to one or two things you're good at. I want to try everything at least once."

I stare at her for a moment, taking a drink of my wine to prolong my next comment. When I pull the glass away from my lips, I tell her,

"I'm the same way. I can't stand the thought of being tied to one thing forever. The idea is stifling and depressing."

Most people who can say they know me know that I have few interests. My closest friends, which consist of only two people, know how hard it is for me to settle into anything for any length of time. So why am I telling Gemma this?

"I'm glad someone understands," she responds thoughtfully. "Some people call me flaky."

"Well, I call it adventurous," I tell her.

She takes a sip of her drink, and she closes her eyes to enjoy the taste. Her smile is soft and lovely. I bring my own glass to my lips and study the joy on her face. She is an expressive woman. For some reason, I like this. I like the idea of knowing how she feels just by reading it on her face. Again,

I wonder what I'm doing here. Who cares if this woman is expressive? A lot of women are.

Her eyes flutter open, and when she looks up at me, my breath is stolen. I clear my throat again. This is ridiculous. Why am I acting like a goddamn schoolboy? Yeah, she's pretty, for a human, but that's it. I don't care how expressive her eyes are or how pretty her smile is, none of that matters. I am here to appease my wolf. Once he gets his fill, I'm out of here.

"Are you staying tomorrow?" I ask her as I try to distract myself from her prettiness.

She shakes her head. "No, I have an early flight home."

"Why hurry home? I hear there is a tour to a winery tomorrow," I ask.

We walk around the fountain slowly. There are only a few others out here, speaking softly to one another.

"I just moved and started a business; I need to get back to run it."

So, we have just this evening together. My wolf hates this. He bristles and tries to fight against my hold on him. He wants to get closer, to stay near this woman next to me.

"So where did you move to?" I ask her.

"Boston," she says with a smile.

I'm surprised by her answer. After a year of drifting around the States, I am heading home to Boston, too. A strange coincidence. My wolf is nearly howling with delight, knowing that he'll be close to Gemma. I probably would have just headed back after the race this morning if it weren't for my wolf's need to find this woman. This is stupid. Why does my fucking wolf care so much? I certainly don't. The woman can up and disappear into the unknown for all I care.

So why is it, all of a sudden, have I stopped to face Gemma? She pauses and turns to me, curious why we've stilled in the shadows.

"Boston's a beautiful city to settle down in," I hear myself say.

"You've been?" she asks.

"I live there," I admit cautiously.

What would this human do with this information? Times are different from when we first came out to the humans, and most don't seem to mind us, but there are some crazy ones out there who would gladly find any excuse to kill us. I should be cautious around her. Around any humans. They are the worst. I never spend this much time talking to one if I can avoid it.

So why am I leaning towards her? Why is my hand reaching up to tuck a curl behind her ear? At some point, I must have put my glass down because while one hand is tucking that curl behind her ear, my other is sliding down her arm. Our fingers intertwine as her cheeks turn a soft pink, and she blinks in surprise.

Without warning, she takes a step towards me, closing any space that there is between us, and kisses me. So used to making the first move, I stand there stunned. My wolf howls in delight in my head, and my body warms up to the point where I feel like I have been set on fire. Just as I feel her sudden tension when I don't kiss her back right away, I stop what I know is going to happen. Instead of letting her step back I wrap my arm around her waist, press her close to me, and kiss her back.

Some sick and twisted thought whispers that this feels right. Too right. Too Perfect. No, no, it's the alcohol and a pretty woman. Nothing else. This isn't anything serious to worry about. I push the thoughts away and enjoy this moment. Gemma tastes of white wine and chocolate. She must have had a few bites of that chocolate mousse I saw on some empty tables earlier.

She is fucking delicious. I can't help it. I growl in pleasure as I pull away. My wolf and I are one as I open my eyes to stare down at Gemma. Her eyes find mine, and they go wide with surprise. I know what she is seeing. With the wolf so close to the surface, my eyes are glowing. Will she be repulsed like other human women? Will she run off? I brace myself, waiting for condemnation to coat her pretty features.

Instead of running, her pupils widen, and her breathing hitches in her throat. I can hear her heart racing, and I catch a whiff of her arousal. She reaches up to cup my cheek and stares back into my eyes without fear. Without disgust.

"I've never... um..." She pauses, and her cheeks turn pink again. "I've never asked anyone this before, so I'm sorry if it comes out awkward but, ah... Are you interested in going upstairs?"

There is no flirting or vague sexual suggestion. Her question is straight to the point. I like that. My wolf is grinning in excitement. He's practically humming with it.

"Let's go to my room," I tell her.

I can't be annoyed with my wolf any longer; his tenaciousness has led to getting me laid.

Chapter Three

Gemma

I should really slow it down. I don't know this guy from Adam. I should tell him I made a mistake, and I should be heading to my own room, *alone*, to go to bed so I can get up to catch an early flight home.

Instead, my body is humming with excitement, and all I can think about is seeing him naked. The moment Chris walked up to Marcus and me on the dance floor, my body went up in flames. He is much taller up close. Well past six feet. He's muscular, with wide shoulders and a thick chest. Since I saw him last, a thick dark five o'clock shadow has covered his chiseled jawline. It only makes his green eyes pop more. Jesus, he's sinful. His hair is tousled as if he hasn't bothered to run a comb through it. I itch to reach up and just run my fingers through it. That's not all my fingers want to touch.

After all that dancing, my body is alive with a fire that hasn't been lit in a *very* long time. Sex has never been an exciting experience for me. The few times I've done it with previous boyfriends was purely obligatory rather than for enjoyment. Their haphazard attempts to get me off just left me frustrated or bored. Usually, I finished myself off after they went to sleep.

But none of them set a fire in my stomach, causing me to feel so… *aroused* simply by touching me. And over the clothes at that! Chris's hands are large, and while I'm not a petite woman, I felt swallowed up by them as they slid along my body while we danced. So feeling emboldened by the alcohol and gauging Chris by his rugged player looks, I asked him to sleep with me.

Yes, I did that! If only Aaron could see me now… The thought causes me to grin.

Before I know it, we're suddenly walking down the hall to Chris's room. He swipes his key card against the lock, and the light flashes green. The anticipation is killing me. I'm excited. I'm nervous. And I'm horny.

Like, *really* horny.

He steps to the side to allow me to enter first, and I do so without hesitation. I want this. I'm feeling bolder than normal because of the alcohol, but I know I would have walked in here without it. I have hardly entered the room before the sound of the door clicking shut breaks the silence. Chris's hand wraps around my wrist and pulls me back towards him. I whirl around and bump into his chest. I am forced to look up due to our close proximity, and I find myself falling into his emerald-green eyes.

Earlier, when we broke from our kiss, they glowed bright gold. I have never been with a non-human, but I know that if they are shifters, sometimes when their animals are close to the surface their eyes change. Had Chris's animal been close to the surface? A shudder runs through my body as I think about it. Why does the thought of his animal's presence excite me?

Before I can dwell too much on the thought, Chris's mouth comes down hard upon mine. I gasp in surprise, and he takes that as an invitation for his tongue to enter. I press my entire body up against his and groan as I inhale his scent and our tongues clash together. He smells of pine trees and fresh air. It's wild and untamed. I love it. I grab his thick arms and hold on tight to the man in front of me.

He breaks the kiss and stares down at me. "Fuck, Gemma, you're delicious. I want to taste all of you."

"What—" I start as he grabs me by the waist and picks me up.

He walks me over to the bed and places me down gently on the edge of the mattress. My legs are spread wide. The only thing that covers me is just an inch of my dress. Chris's eye color shifts slowly until they are glowing. At the same time, he kneels before me. He grabs me behind the knees, leans forward and kisses my inner thigh.

My heart races as I close my eyes to enjoy the way his soft lips press against my skin followed by his rough stubble. He kisses up my thigh and stops at the junction right between my legs. I open my eyes to find Chris staring up at me. His eyes are glowing so brightly I swear I'm staring into two suns. When he grins, it's wolfish.

He places his hands on the outside of my thigh and slides them upwards. His hands are calloused and rough. I like it. He hitches up my dress so he can see my black lacy thong. His eyes are drawn to it, and unintentionally, I think, he licks his lips. The hunger on his face, so raw and primal, should be frightening, but it only excites me. He reaches up and pulls my thong down slowly. I already know, without looking, that it is soaking wet. I wiggle some so he can remove them completely. When he's done pulling them off instead of tossing them to the side as I expected, he brings them to his nose and breaths me in.

Instantly, I'm embarrassed and even more aroused than before. Chris fists the thong then slides them into his pants pockets before turning his attention back to me. Hm… I wonder if it should bother me that he thinks he can keep them. The thought disappears as he abruptly rises off his knees to tower over me. He leans forward over me and places a knee between my legs on the mattress. I lean back on my elbows, unsure what he wants but eager to do whatever it is. He crawls so he's completely on top of me, my back pressed against the mattress.

Chris reaches out to cup my breast with one hand while he holds my hip in his other. His head leans forward, and I arch up into him, loving how he fondles me through my dress. As he presses a kiss to my neck, his breath skates down my exposed skin and I shudder in delight. Is this how it's supposed to be? Should all my past sexual encounters have been this exciting? This arousing?

In a skillful move, Chris shifts our positions. Suddenly *I'm* on top, straddling him around the waist. The air is forced from my lungs in a huff of surprise, and he grins as if he knows that was impressive.

"Pretty Gemma, let me feast on you."

His voice has gone so deep and his teeth are clenched together so tightly that it sounds more like a growl than true words. Those eyes... They shine so bright I swear I could see the animal there, staring back at me. He leaves me no time to respond. He picks me up by my hips with an ease that no human could muster and suddenly places me *on his face.*

"Chris!" I shriek in surprise. "Oh! *Oh....*"

My groan is so loud it's embarrassing as his tongue dives between my folds. There are no words that can describe the mind-melting pleasure Chris is invoking in me. His tongue, his lips, even his teeth are involved as he does exactly what he said he would do: *feast.*

The pressure between my legs builds and carries outwards through my entire body. I can feel every muscle in my body beginning to coil. One of my hands grabs a fist full of his hair while I reach out to brace myself against the headboard.

"Oh, god..." I let slip as my pleasure nears its breaking point.

I can't stop my hips as they grind against his face. The stubble on his face creates even more intensity between my legs. His tongue circles my clit, once, twice, and then a third time, and suddenly, there's an explosion of colors behind my eyelids.

"Christopher!" I shriek as shock, ecstasy, and wonder crash over me.

Never have I reached an orgasm from a man before. Whatever pleasure I get is from myself and this... This is nothing I have ever achieved masturbating. My whole body shakes hard as I cum on his face. His fingers dig into my hips, holding me in place as he continues his ministrations until my body relaxes.

My body feels boneless in the best way possible. I lean to the side and roll off Chris so he can breathe as I try to catch my own breath. I sit up, leaning against the headboard panting. I turn my head to watch him sit up with a shit-eating grin on his face. From his nose down, his face is glistening with my arousal.

"You are fucking delicious, Gemma. Goddamn!" he growls through teeth that seem a little too big for his mouth now.

He sits up and grabs the bottom of his shirt, yanking it off in one fell swoop. As he rolls off the bed to walk over to a backpack sitting on a chair, I watch him. His back ripples with muscle as he moves. There are two dimples at the base of his spine that I have an urge to dig my fingers into. As he pulls a condom out of a pocket and turns to me, he says,

"Dress. Off. *Now.*"

His sharp command might have annoyed me if he were any of my past boyfriends. But his growled command causes my nipples to harden, and immediately, I want to do as he requests.

He unbuttons his pants and shoves them off his hips as if they offend him. His erection springs free, and I gape. Oh... He's nothing like my previous boyfriends at all. I peel my eyes off his cock and follow the happy trail up to his abs. Holy six-pack. I continue my gaze up his body to his wide, hairy chest. There's so much hair. My fingers itch to run through it.

Half-mesmerized by the sight before me, I slowly get to my knees and reach for the zipper behind me. Chris doesn't even let me attempt to get the dress off. He's there, kneeling on the bed and dropping the unopened condom onto the mattress between us before he reaches out to grab the front of my dress as if to rip it. Quickly, I place my hands over top of his to stop him.

"I need something to wear out of here! Don't go ripping my dress!" I tell him.

His dark brows come crashing together as he growls, "Wear one of my shirts."

I chuckle and then murmur, "How scandalous..."

Though, the idea doesn't sound awful. If I could bottle up his scent and wear it whenever I wanted so I could remember this night... Well, I'd pay for this smell. I take his hands and pull them behind me so he can unzip my dress himself. He does so, and I pull the strings off my shoulders causing the dress to drop around my waist. I wiggle the dress the rest of the way off and let it fall to the floor. Chris' expression goes from hungry to downright starved. He stares at my breasts with such fervor that I chuckle. I'm not huge, but I have enough to make a dress look good.

Chris growls, and this time I know he wasn't even trying to form words. He lunges at me, and I'm thrown onto my back. I laugh at his eagerness and run my fingers through his wavy hair. Chris takes one of my nipples in his mouth and sucks. I gasp at the warmth and the way his tongue twirls around the tip.

I wrap my legs around his waist, and he leans forward, pressing his erection against my entrance. I shudder with excitement. He lets go of my nipple and captures my mouth. It doesn't bother me that I can taste hints of myself as our tongues twirl together. I run my hands across his back, feeling and loving the muscles there. Chris leans his hips forward, pushing at my entrance. A sane thought creeps into the lusty haze that has settled over me,

"Hold up," I say, dropping my legs from around him. "Condom first."

Chris holds his position for just a moment, and I can almost hear the internal groan. I giggle and bat at his chest. He pulls back to sit up, and I sit up with him. He reaches over, grabs the condom, and rips it open. I snatch the condom out of his hands, and his gaze snaps to my face.

I smile and ask, "Mind if I help?"

His grin is wide, and I laugh. I lean forward, pinch the tip of the rubber, and slowly slide the condom down his erection. My fingers can't wrap all the way around him. His groan unfurls something wild in me. I grip him tighter and meet his gaze. Shuffling on my knees closer to him, I take my free hand to reach up and grab the back of his neck. I take his mouth possessively with mine while I stroke him with my other hand.

"Ah, Gemma, this feels… too… good," he chokes out as I pull my mouth away from him. "I need to be in you."

"What are you waiting for?" I ask him sweetly.

This time he snarls, taking the challenge and running with it. Next thing I know, he has flipped me around so I'm facing the headboard, his hands on my hips. How does he move me so efficiently? He places his hand in the middle of my back, causing my top half to fall forward. I catch myself on the headboard as he positions himself at my entrance from behind. I push my butt back against him, and he slaps it.

Then, he impales me.

The cry that escapes my lips is followed by the sound of Chris's hand slapping my ass again. This… this is heaven. I'm filled to the brim with a monster of a man, and it feels *glorious*. Chris doesn't give me a moment to adjust. He starts thrusting hard and fast. I love it. I spread my legs wider and push my butt back into him, wanting more. Wanting it as hard as he can give. He groans, and I echo it as he shifts his position ever so slightly, hitting a spot I didn't know existed inside of me.

Yes, I internally hiss as my body begins to tighten again. Chris leans forward and plants kisses down my spine. I like the scraping of his stubble against my back. His thrusts become wilder, and I can't stop the detonation inside of me. As I throw my head back, I grip the headboard tighter and cry out in delight. At the same time, Chris leans forward and bites my shoulder. The pain only intensifies my orgasm, and I cry out again. When Chris pulls his mouth away from my shoulder, he howls as he finds his release.

I'm floating on cloud nine. Two orgasms in one night? By a man and not a vibrator? Oh, what a lucky girl I am. I'm drifting on waves of bliss as aftershocks ripple through me as Chris withdraws from me.

"Fuck," Chris swears, pulling me out of my bliss.

I turn to find him staring at my shoulder in surprise. I look down and find that I am bleeding. It doesn't look bad. I shrug.

"No biggie," I say, but he scowls so deeply and pushes off the bed so aggressively I am taken aback. His expression turns thunderous.

"Fuck! Fuck!" Chris bellows, stumbling away from the bed and me. "What was I thinking? Damn wolf! Get out," he snaps as he scoops up his pants. As he pulls them on, I stare at him in shock. When I don't move, he yells, "Get out!"

"I don't under—" I start, confused and hurt by his sudden rejection.

I stop though because I realize in that moment that this is a quick one and done deal for him. If this is what one-night stands are typically like, it doesn't matter how many orgasms I get. The immediate crash is terrible. Embarrassed that I thought we were having fun and not just animal sex, I scoot off the bed and slip on my dress but don't bother to zip it.

Chris doesn't watch me get ready. He's too busy running his fingers through his hair with agitation and glaring at the bed. I shake my head and leave without another word.

Fuck men.

Chapter Four

Darion

Stop sending me chicks. It's not helping.

I glance at the message from Christopher as I straighten my tie. The naked woman lying on my desk is talking to me, but I ignore her as I pocket my phone and walk over to the mirror hanging over the drink cart. I check to make sure my shirt is wrinkle-free. The black shirt is free from any creases, and my black tie is centered perfectly over the buttons. I grab the black jacket hanging from the hook behind the door and turn to my guest.

She's still talking.

"You're still here?" I interrupt her string of mindless conversation. She stops talking and sits up.

"Oh, you're leaving? So soon? I thought—"

"Go to the address I texted you earlier. He needs some company," I tell her, not caring about whatever she has to say. I smile to myself. Chris will be pissed I'm sending another woman to the house, but his situation is amusing. How could I not find some way to rub it in? "I have business to attend to."

The woman sighs dramatically and moves around the room to pick up her discarded clothes. I wait until she is dressed before opening the door. She sighs again and walks past me into the hallway. Being the gentlemen that I am, I walk with her down the hall of my law firm. We pass the dark and empty offices of the other lawyers who work with me. It's a federal holiday, almost everyone else took the day off.

Not me. I never stopped working. I got to where I am today from hard work all day, every day. There are no breaks when you're working to get to the top. Now that I'm here, on top of the world, I'm certainly not going to stop. As we approach the last office before the elevator, I see its door slightly ajar. The lights are on, and I can hear a woman's laughter.

A woman? What is Phillip doing with a woman at... I glance down at my watch. It's seven-thirty. Phillip is usually home with his partner by now. A new client perhaps? I've been out of the office for a few weeks taking on special cases around the country. Maybe I missed an email from him about a new client he decided to take on this week. I push the button to the elevator and stand stoically next to the woman I just fucked, who is talking again. I ignore her chatter easily, but I know Christopher will not be able to, and this makes me smile slightly.

After walking her out to her car, I head back inside the old brick colonial. I bought the building ten years ago and have since gutted and renovated it to my liking. There is a perfect blend of modern and traditional elements through the building, but the lobby is my favorite. First impressions are always the most important, and the lobby is everyone's first impression of me.

As I stroll across the hardwood floors towards the elevator, my phone vibrates in my pocket. I pull it out and glance at the screen:

Fuck. I give up. I'm going to call her.

The text makes me chuckle. Ah, Christopher... What a predicament he has found himself in. His wolf has found his mate, claimed her while Chris was preoccupied, and now both the wolf and Chris are at war with one another. The wolf demands to be with his mate. Chris wants nothing to do with the human woman. For three weeks now, Christopher has been warring with his sanity as he tries to control his wolf and to no avail. He is too stubborn for his own good. He can hate the situation all he wants, but in the end, his wolf is going to win this. The animal won't let Christopher sleep with other women. The wolf refuses to run, eat, and sleep. It is driving Christopher insane.

Christopher Rogue is one of the only shifters I know that can compete with an incubus in sexual appetite, and he is stuck with one woman. A human no less. That is just icing on the cake. He hates humans. Can't stand them. Now he is tied to one. I knew he would cave, but I was sure it was going to take another two weeks before he completely snapped.

I laugh out loud and the sound echoes in the lobby. I look up from my screen to realize I haven't pushed the elevator button. I correct that and text back:

Good luck with that. Want me to bring home dinner?

Fuck you.

Again, I laugh. That's right. It's hard for him to keep anything down when his wolf refuses to eat anything.

It's not funny. I shouldn't laugh. The poor bastard is suffering. But really, this is a fixable situation. Not only does his mate live in the same city as him, but her graphic design company is just a block away from the firm. It is solely Chris's stubbornness that has made him this miserable for this long.

Thank goodness incubuses don't have to worry about mates. In the beginning of my existence, I served one woman, but those days are well behind me. Now, just imagining being forced to commit to one woman for the rest of my life… It sounds like a nightmare. I go through at least three women *a day*. Sometimes separately, other times all together while I feast upon their bodies. Orgies are a norm in my life. Incubuses feed through the sexual energy in a room, so the more people enjoying themselves, the more I can feed. While I can eat normal food, it does not sustain me like the sexual energy that flows around a room when sex occurs.

And I am an insatiable bastard. I love sex, as most incubuses do. I'll take it whenever I can get it. Since rising to my current powerful position, I have been careful who I sleep with. But that doesn't mean it has slowed me down at all.

I step into the elevator and push the button to the second floor. I shove the phone into my pocket and start flipping through my mental to-do list. The doors open again, and I head down the hallway. Laughter stops me mid-stride in front of Phillip's door. I glance at my watch. I have time to be nosy. Let's see who Phillip's new client is.

I knock twice as I push the door further open. Inside, Phillip is behind his desk leaning back in his chair, grinning ear to ear as he stares at the woman sitting perched in front of him on his desk. Phillip straightens in his seat as the woman turns to look over her shoulder.

Immediately, I am enthralled by a set of large brown eyes. The dazzling smile that accompanies the gaze is just as mesmerizing. The woman slips off the desk and turns all the way around to face me. In her professional, sleeveless dress, her body's curves are pronounced, as are her toned arms and legs.

Not only is this woman beautiful, but she is also familiar. The picture I saw of her three weeks ago did nothing for her. In person, she really is a beauty.

"Ah, Darion, I thought you had left a while ago!" Phillip says with a smile. He stands and walks around his desk, fixing his jacket as he comes around. "Let me introduce to you my good friend, Gemma Thomas. Gemma, meet the most powerful prosecutor this side of the States, Darion Nightshade."

At the sound of my name, I walk further into the room, keeping my eyes on Gemma's face, wondering how to play this. What are the chances that I would meet Christopher's mate in my own office? Do I tell her that I know of her? Should I tell Christopher she is here?

"Good evening, Miss. Thomas," I say as I take her outstretched hand.

Her handshake is firm. She doesn't bat an eye under my gaze as most people, men or women, do. Incubuses tend to make people nervous… or aroused, which only embarrasses them. That mixed with the lack of knowledge about my kind gives me a power that intimidates others.

"Please, call me Gemma," she says and grins. I'm momentarily stunned by how brilliant she shines. "It's a pleasure to finally meet the big, bad boss man. I hear you run a tight ship around here."

Her playfulness is disarming. I'm used to being flirted with or people cowering away from me. There are a handful of people who can handle being in my presence without being affected by the aura I give off, Phillip being one of them. Apparently, Gemma is another rare bird.

"I am but a humble businessman who likes to keep his employees on their toes," I admit. Phillip snorts and rolls his eyes.

"You want to go with humble?" he asks me skeptically. I glare at him, but he knows me well enough to know when there is no heat behind the look. "Alright, humble it is."

"What are you two up to? Have legal matters that need to be discussed?" I ask Gemma curiously.

I tell myself that I am not digging for information for Christopher. This is just personal curiosity.

"Not yet, but I'd like to make sure I have a foot in the door at one of the best law firms in the business… You know, just in case," she says with a wink. "Actually, Phillip promised me dinner tonight after work. After waiting for over an hour, I came here to find out what was keeping him."

Phillip visibly winces and says, "I told you I get lost in my work and to call me to interrupt me."

"I did, five times," she says sourly and sends him a dark look. "How Aaron puts up with you is beyond me."

At his partner's name, Phillip laughs. "Yes, well luckily, he has a bit more patience than you do." He glances at his wristwatch and sighs. "And unfortunately, I still haven't gotten what I need to get done for court on Friday, so I need to stay a little longer…"

"You're seriously bailing on me?" Gemma asks sharply.

Phillip grimaces but quickly recovers when he glances at me. "I can't go, but maybe Darion will take you if he isn't busy?"

Typically, I would decline. Unless I've run a background check on the person, I make it a point not to be seen with them. My reputation is paramount in my world. I would rather appear cold and mysterious; no need for people to assume I'm interested in dating or interpersonal relationships. Hang out with the wrong person, and I could get a bad rep.

I catch Gemma giving me a look that tells me she knows I'm about to make an excuse and wouldn't be offended when I did. For some reason, the placating expression rubs me the wrong way. It's as if *she* wants to get out of dinner with *me* and is giving me an out. I've never been turned away before. I don't like it. I decide to move out of my comfort zone for the evening.

"I certainly could eat. Do you have a reservation somewhere?" I ask her.

I glance at my watch; I highly doubt any reputable restaurant would allow a party to show up an hour after their reservation time. I could probably pull a few strings to get us in somewhere…

"Oh, no. The place the Gemma wants to go doesn't require reservations," Phillip says smirking.

Something in his expression tells me I'm not going to like where Gemma has plans to eat. Gemma rolls her eyes at him.

"You're so snobbish. Live a little, Phillip." She turns to me and asks, "Willing to be surprised?"

No. Not usually. I hate surprises.

"I'm willing to live it up for a few hours." I try, and fail, to keep the suspicion out of my voice.

Phillip laughs. "You're going to regret that decision, Darion."

Gemma glares at her friend again. "We'll leave you to slave away behind your computer screen. You just wait, Phil. Next time Darion sees you, he'll be raving about our dinner."

I highly doubt this, but I say nothing as Gemma grabs the blazer and purse hanging off a chair and walks over to me.

"Do you need to get anything from your office before we head out?" she asks.

I tower over her as she stands in front of me, but that's not unusual. Being 6'5, I have a height advantage over most. But just because I'm well over a head taller than her, that doesn't mean she's short. She must be around 5'7 or 5'8.

"Yes, actually. I'll meet you down in the lobby in five minutes," I tell her.

She smiles as she nods and slips by me to walk out the door. She pauses and looks over her shoulder at Phillip, "Good night, Philly. Give Aaron a kiss for me."

I look at Phillip, who chuckles.

"Good luck handling her," he warns me.

Handle a woman? Who does he think I am? I have handled all sorts of women. Gemma is no different from all the rest. Phillip must have seen my skepticism because he shakes his head with a knowing smile.

"Let me know how dinner goes."

"Will do," I tell him and then leave his office.

Exactly five minutes later, the elevator doors open, and I find Gemma waiting for me. She is looking around the lobby in appreciation. I expected her to be playing on her phone. People nowadays can't stand their own thoughts and purposefully lose themselves in their electronic devices. I find myself pleased to see she would rather take in the aesthetics that surround her.

"Have you called a ride yet?" I ask as I approach her. She shakes her head.

"We don't need a ride to get to dinner. It's just around the block." She pauses to glance down at my feet. She frowns and adds, "Unless you don't want to scuff those nice shoes."

I snorted. If I ruin these, I can just as easily buy another pair. Who cares if they cost a grand?

"I can do with some physical activity," I tell her but instantly regret it.

An incubus's sexual prowess is no secret. I'm sure her mind deduces another meaning to my words. Instead of becoming flustered or offended, Gemma simply smiles and walks towards the doors. My shoulders relax a little. When had they become stiff?

I follow her outside and note how low the sun is. The September days are slowly growing darker earlier. I wonder if a car wouldn't be the better idea. Gemma doesn't stop walking though. I take a few strides until I am next to her.

"Care to clue me in on where we're going?" I ask, genuinely curious.

In my head, I try to list all the restaurants in the area within walking distance that do not need reservations but come up empty handed. Here in the historic part of Boston, business and restaurant life is booming. Real estate is astronomical, and only the rich can afford this area.

"And ruin the surprise?" she asks with a false look of indignation. "Of course not! But, just to make sure you *can* eat there, do you have any allergies?"

"No."

"Good, then just wait and see," she says.

"So how do you and Phillip know each other?" I ask after a few minutes of companionable silence. We round the corner and walk past a few boutiques.

"I met him through his husband Aaron," Gemma tells me. She looks at me. "Aaron and I grew up together. When Aaron moved up here to get married and live with Phillip, I always planned to follow. Luckily, Aaron has great taste in men, and Phillip is incredible. We clicked instantly."

"Ah, I've met Aaron several times. He's quite the character," I say though that is an understatement. While Phillip is more reserved, Aaron has a thing for the dramatics. Gemma snorts as if she can hear my thoughts.

"He's ridiculous in the best way possible," she says.

I can hear the affection in her tone. I look down at her curiously.

"You uprooted your life to be a part of their lives?" I ask her.

She shrugs. "Like I said, we're inseparable. Also, there is a demand for graphic designers up here, so it was a win-win for me."

"How long have you been working for yourself?"

"How do you know I work for myself?" she asks with a frown.

Oops, I'm not supposed to know she works in the building over from mine.

"I saw you a few times in the next building over talking to the landlord. I just put two and two together," I lie easily.

"Oh, well, I guess it's been… five, maybe six weeks now," she answers after a moment of thoughtful silence.

Has she caught onto my lie or is her mind somewhere else? Mentally I shake myself. Why do I care if she caught me in a lie? Who cares where her mind is at?

"Ah, a new entrepreneur," I say. "Are you enjoying—"

I freeze as we round another corner. In a parking lot there are a plethora of food trucks. A live band plays nearby, and picnic tables are set up for customers. It's packed with young people, human and non-human alike. She wants to eat *here?* The words "unsanitary" and "mystery meat" flash through my mind. I balk at once. Gemma looks up at me with an amused half-smile.

"It's an international food truck festival," she says. "The reviews say the food is authentic and delicious."

Dear god, she is going to put me in the hospital. I open my mouth and then shut it, not sure how to respond. She laughs at me, and I pull my eyes away from the trucks to stare down at her.

"Not what you're used to?"

"No," I tell her. "But I suppose since we are here…"

"That's the spirit!" she says and beams up at me before taking off towards the trucks.

I follow her at a much slower pace. We check out each truck and their menu. Begrudgingly, I have to admit the food smells good. Once we both find something tolerable enough to eat, Gemma leads the way to the picnic tables.

"To answer your earlier question: Yes, I am enjoying running my own business. Going from working for someone else to working for myself has been a dream," she says.

She takes a bite of her food. I watch her face suspiciously to see how she likes the Ethiopian food she ordered. Her eyes grow wide before they roll into the back of her head. The soft moan after she swallows causes my dick to twitch to life. "Oh god, this lamb is delicious."

"Business is going well?" I ask. She nods.

"I stole some of my previous employer's clients before I left," she admits sheepishly. "And those clients have passed my name on to other people. I'm surprised how quickly things are taking off, honestly. I thought I would have a lull as I transition to this new location, but I've been pleasantly busy."

I look down at the Thai dish I ordered. Bracing myself for the inevitable food poisoning, I take a bite of it. I freeze as flavor bursts on my tongue. In disbelief that something this good could come from a truck, I stare down at the small cardboard tray that houses my dinner.

"Good, isn't it?" Gemma asks.

I look over at her, and her knowing smirk makes me chuckle. Despite the revulsion at our dinner location, I find myself enjoying this woman's company. Her sunny disposition is a change from the stuffy world of a lawyer.

"It's edible," I tell her, unwilling to admit that I may have judged a book by its cover. Her laughter causes a shifting in my chest. Uncomfortable suddenly, I take another bite of my food.

"So, what's it like being a badass lawyer?" she asks after taking a few more bites of her meal. Her candor is a pleasant surprise. I chuckle.

"A badass lawyer? I don't know. I've been a badass at everything that I have done, so I don't know any other way," I say. Her laughter, again, shifts something inside of me. I find myself enjoying the sound. "But I suppose being a lawyer has its ups and downs like any other job. I've been doing this quite a while... I just came back from taking care of a few different cases in other states. Working in other parts of the States has been a nice change of pace. There will always be criminals everywhere, so I'll always be working."

Gemma is silent for a moment. When she speaks again, she says, "You're bored."

Her statement throws me for a loop. Bored? "Why do you say that?"

She shrugs one shoulder and then turns her whole body to face me. "I can hear it in your voice."

"I had no inflection," I deny.

Being a lawyer is what I do best. How could I possibly be bored with it? Why do I suddenly feel exposed? I frown.

"The lack of inflection is what tipped me off. That and your expression... What's wrong?" she asks.

"I enjoy my job." I scowl, not liking her quick assessment of me.

"Why did you choose to be a prosecutor?" Gemma asks.

After taking a few more bites, I answer, "I enjoy putting criminals behind bars where they belong.".

I'm annoyed with her suddenly. I shouldn't have come. No wonder Christopher kicked her out of his room.

"Putting criminals behind bars... Does it come easy to you?"

"Yes."

"That might be why you're bored," she points out. "Do you not feel challenged? Have you ever considered fighting for the suspect?"

"Have you considered being a psychologist?" I snap. "Since you seem to want to dive into my psyche to figure me out?"

How dare this woman assume that I am unhappy in my work life. She doesn't know me. She doesn't understand what I do and why. Simpleton. I'm no longer hungry. I drop the plastic fork onto the table.

Gemma blinks in surprise and straightens. "I'm sorry. I put my foot in my mouth. I didn't mean to offend you or upset you," she says. She places a hand on my forearm and frowns. "Really, I am sorry. I just know how it feels to be unsatisfied, and I thought I heard a kindred spirit in you."

Her words take me by surprise… again. My mood shifts from annoyed to curious. "Kindred spirit? You just said you like what you do."

She sighs. "Yeah, I like it for now. I enjoy the creativity in my career field, but I… I find feeling content doesn't last long for me. Once I've done something, I am ready to move onto something else. I'm sure the newness of being a business owner will wear off sooner rather than later, and I'll find myself itching to do something else. I'm sorry if I misread you."

Some emotion flashes behind her eyes. Feeling guilty for snapping at her, I look away from Gemma and stare at the people around us. What is wrong with me? Since when do I care about someone else's feelings? And why did I get so upset at her assessment of me? *Am* I bored? Could it be possible that even though I have become one of the top prosecutors in the country that maybe that isn't enough anymore? Something like a light bulb seems to flicker in my head.

Am I bored?

The question swirls around my mind for a moment longer before I push it aside. Now is not the time to wonder about such things. I can mull it over another time. I look over at Gemma as she pushes away her empty cardboard tray. A woman that can eat… What a nice change. The women I know eat salads or simply pick at their dinners to make it look like they are eating.

"You did not offend me," I say with a sigh as I look back at her. "Are you ready to go?"

"Yes," she says.

We stand together. I take her trash and walk it over to the trash can. As I turn around, I hear Gemma's gasp before she cries out,

"Darion!"

Her cry of alarm is followed by her body slamming into mine. I stumble, unprepared for the sudden contact. The sound of gunshots echo around us, and chaos erupts. As people begin to run and dive for cover, I whirl around to see two gunmen running towards me, guns raised.

Familiar gang tattoos cover their faces. Their rough attire makes them stand out on this side of the city. Next to me, Gemma scrambles to her feet. I don't wait to make sure she is okay. My instincts kick in, and I snarl as I leap the fifty feet between us in two bounds, startling the two humans. They shoot at me, but I move too fast for them to hit me. I grab both of their heads and slam their skulls together. The satisfying crunch makes me smile. Both men crumble to the ground. Down the street an unmarked white van peels off. It whips around the corner, tires screeching in protest.

I debate running after it. I can probably catch it. There is still enough traffic in the city that could slow them down. But then I think better of it. I glance down at the two dead men, making note of their tattoos. These two were members of the gang whose crime lord I just put behind bars. I will use this to put him away for even longer unless he shares with me the name of the driver. If he cooperates, maybe I'll allow him to appeal for a parole hearing in thirty years...

So instead of chasing after the driver, I turn and search for Gemma through all the chaos. She is easy to find since she is the only one standing still as everyone else runs around. She watches me with wide, fearful eyes while clutching her arm. Even from here, I can see blood seeping through her fingers.

Shit.

I hurry back over to her, pushing people out of the way. I stop just in front of Gemma and grab a hold of her shoulders to study her face.

"Jesus, you just saved my life," I say, surprised and shaken by this fact.

This woman selflessly just stepped between me and a bullet. She doesn't even know me. Not even my partners at the firm, for whom I hold high esteem and vice versa, would have done that. None of the people within my social circles would have even dreamed about saving me. There are only two people in this entire world who would jump between me and a bullet, and one of them is this woman's mate.

Fuck. I am going to have to tell him about this.

"Let me see where you're hit," I demand.

She shakes her head frantically and tries to step away from me. I clutch her shoulders harder to hold her in place. In the distance, I can hear police sirens. They will be here soon. They'll have to take our statements, which will take some time, but they can call for an ambulance for Gemma.

"Let me see," I bark the order, not allowing her to defy me.

She shakes her head. "No, it's just a little graze."

Under my hands, I can feel her trembling.

"I'm fine," she says. "Are you okay? Are they...?"

"Yes, they're dead," I tell her firmly. "Let me see. You're bleeding profusely for a graze."

Gemma's expression is frozen in shock as she stares up at me. Her brown eyes are a little glazed over, and there is a lack of color in her cheeks, despite her warm complexion. After a few seconds, she pulls her hand away from her arm. I bend down to study the wound, and my stomach drops. Fuck. This isn't just a graze. There is an entrance wound in her bicep but no exit wound. Her body starts shaking a little harder. Is she going into shock?

"This needs to be looked at by a doctor. Let's sit down and wait for the police," I suggest, worrying about how much blood is pooling from the hole. Humans are a fragile breed of creatures. I have no medical expertise, but I am sure that this is a lot of blood to lose for her. I tear off a strip of my shirt and, as gently as I can, apply pressure to the wound. Gemma sucks in a sharp breath but otherwise doesn't complain.

She takes over applying pressure to the wound while I carefully lead her over to a picnic table. My mind is a whirlwind as I try to figure out the next steps. My heart races. It has been a while since I had a hit on me. In this field, I make a lot of enemies. It just comes with the territory. But I have people in low places who are supposed to keep me informed and ahead of hits. I pay handsomely for information. This attack has taken me completely by surprise. If it weren't for this lovely woman sitting beside me, I would be dead.

Seventy years on this planet and just like that, my life would have been snuffed out. My heart races as the police arrive on the scene. As I stand beside Gemma, my hand placed gently on her shoulder, I realize that as lucrative as my life is… the things I consider important and hold dearest to me might not be as important as I think they are.

Chapter Five

Gemma

Everything is happening too quickly. The cops take my statement as I sit in the ambulance. Once they're finished, I'm rushed to the hospital. I don't know where Darion is. Possibly still with the cops. He *did* just kill two people with his bare hands. That requires a few more questions from the cops I suppose. When I get to the hospital, they examine my arm to find the bullet lodged into my humerus.

Ah, that explains the pain.

How is this all real? One minute I'm kicking myself for putting my foot in my mouth, and the next I'm throwing myself between two angry looking gunmen and my best friend's husband's boss... What was I thinking? I could have just screamed and pointed like a normal person. Instead, I decided to become a human shield. The fear for Darion was so intense that rational thought disappeared. I just knew I couldn't let him get hurt.

Because somehow, I know we are kindred spirits.

Which makes no sense because I don't know the man, well, incubus at all. Maybe, because he is an incubus, I feel a pull towards the man. It is rumored that incubuses can make anyone find them attractive. He is easily one of the most handsome men I have ever laid eyes on, despite his unusual appearance. But it isn't just attraction I felt for the man... I felt... Well, I don't know what I felt. Now that he is out of sight, I can think a little more clearly.

By the time the bullet is removed and I'm stitched up, it's well past midnight. I am beyond exhausted and ready to leave. Unfortunately, it looks like I am going to be here a little longer while they complete the discharge paperwork. I am about to sit up on the hospital bed when I hear the commotion out in the hallway. Nurses rush past my room in a flurry of activity, and there is yelling echoing in the hallways.

"Gemma!" a deep voice bellows down the hallway. Who the hell...? I sit up straighter, bracing myself as the sound of stomping footsteps grow closer.

"Sir, you're not family, you can't be up here—"

"Gemma!" The voice sounds strangely familiar...

Christopher Rogue suddenly storms into my room. His dark eyebrows are slammed together in a dark scowl, his teeth are bared, and his nostrils are flaring. I gape, surprised to see my one-night stand stomping towards me, enraged. Embarrassment rushes over me as I recall our night together. How do I still feel so upset three weeks later? Maybe it's these damn teeth marks scarred into my shoulder. Like I need a visual reminder of the most insulting and humiliating night of my life.

Or maybe because ever since that night, something has awoken in me. I'm aroused almost every waking moment of my life, but when I masturbate, my orgasms are only a fraction of what Christopher was able to elicit. I always finish disappointed and needy. And I cannot finish more than once. I orgasmed twice that night, thanks to this asshole.

"What the hell are you doing here?!" I shriek as I scramble out of bed and he approaches me.

His eyes are glowing and wild. His shoulders heave up and down, and he's panting like he just ran a race.

"I'm so sorry, Miss Thomas," a nurse says, hurrying into the room after him. "He won't leave. Security is on its way. Sir, you can't be in here."

Christopher stands on the other side of the bed glaring at me.

"What are you doing here?" I ask again, staring at the man who caused me to vow to never have another one-night stand again.

He's just as attractive as I remember. He looks a little thinner, his face is a little paler, but he is still fiercely handsome. He has grown a thick, untamed beard now. I like it.

"You're hurt," he growls, through gritted teeth.

"I'm fine now," I snap. "That doesn't explain what you're doing here."

Christopher's whole body shudders hard. He hesitates and looks away from me as another shudder runs through him.

"Sir, you need to leave!" the nurse yells at him.

Christopher's whole body rises and falls as he takes a deep breath and lets it out. When he looks up, his eyes have changed from glowing gold to those handsome emerald-green eyes. He doesn't bother to glance at the nurse as he watches me.

"Gemma," he says, his expression softening. "When I heard what happened…" His voice trails off as he shakes his head.

"How did you hear what happened? It just happened a few hours ago! And why are you here? Get out!" I yell and point to the door with my good arm.

"No, I can't leave you again," he says with a defeated sigh. "Look, I need to talk to you about what happened a few weeks ago."

"We don't need to talk about anything," I snap as security hurries in.

They make a move to grab Christopher, but he whirls around and pushes them back.

"You're not family and visiting hours are over, sir. You need to leave!" one of the two guards tell him firmly.

"We *are* family," Christopher snaps at him before turning back to me. His expression becomes exasperated. "Gemma, you're my mate. I sealed our relationship together by marking you that night we were together. I lost control of my wolf, and in his persistence to claim you, he managed to bite you."

My mouth opens and closes like a fish. His confession is a jail sentence for him if I don't accept the claim in front of these people. It's against the law for non-humans to lay claim to unknowing or unwilling humans.

Oh shit. I'm a shifter's mate. I'm not sure that really means anything to me, but I know that changes things for non-humans. Like… It means life altering, irreversible changes for them. For Christopher.

"You, sir, have now broken two laws. I'm cuffing you," the second security guard says.

"I'm sorry, Gemma," Christopher continues as if the guard hasn't spoken. "I've tried to figure out how to handle this, and I should have come to you sooner. I just… wasn't ready. Fuck, I don't want a mate, and I certainly don't want a *human* mate, but damn if it matters what I want. When Darion told me what happened… I can't keep away from you anymore."

A guard tries to cuff him. I watch, too stunned, to say anything. Christopher turns to face the guard and snarls. The sound is so animalistic it snaps me out of my shock. As the other guard steps in to grab for Christopher, I storm over to them.

"Darion? He called *you?* Why? No, wait. You know what? I don't care how you two know each other. Do you know how fucked up this is?" I yell.

Even as Christopher grapples with the two guards, he turns his head and says, "Fuck, I know it is. I'm sorry! Please, just let me explain—"

"Chris, just let the man cuff you, and I'll bail you out when you get to jail," a voice drawls from the doorway.

I turn to see Darion leaning against the doorway as if he's been there the whole time. I take him in with a sweeping glance. Incubuses are a rare breed of non-human. With grayish-blue skin, a staggering height, wide stature, and jet-black irises, the incubus definitely stands out amongst the non-human species. There isn't much known about them except for their insatiable sexual appetites. None of them have been particularly keen on sharing whatever secrets they keep.

Darion's dark hair is gelled back, not a strand out of place. His coal-black eyes take in the scene before him, lingering on me before turning his attention to Christopher. When I first saw him back at his office, I noted his permanent smirk and sharp gaze. His expression was almost patronizing as he stood just inside Phillip's office. I can see people being intimidated by the confidence he oozes and the way he stands, the way he stares, and the way his aura seems to expand throughout the room.

But at dinner, I saw past the confident façade. I could see a loneliness in his eyes even though he seems to be unaware of it himself. Yes, I can feel the sexual pull towards him, but that isn't necessarily what made me so inclined to have dinner with him. I could have made up some excuse or let Darion out of it. But I didn't. I didn't because I wanted some company. Lately, I, too, have been feeling lonely.

Even now as he leans against the door frame to my room with that smirk and sharp gaze, I can see that shadow, merely a hint, of a loneliness that he hides from the world. Part of me wants to go to him, but another, larger, part of me is pissed.

If Darion knows Chris, then he probably knows what transpired between us. Which would explain why Darion called him. If Darion knows the whole story, then why would he think Christopher is someone I want to see?

Asshole.

Chris continues to struggle with the security guards, and I stand here fuming. Finally, the whole scene gets ridiculous enough for Darion to roll his eyes. He enters the room, passes the scuffle, and walks over to me.

"What are you doing here?" I demand and make a move to put both fists on my hips. The moment I move my arm, I hiss in pain and clasp it with my free hand.

"I'm here to thank you for saving my life," he says, pausing a few feet away from me, and eyes my arm. "And to drive you home."

"You're welcome, but I'm good. I'll call a car once I get my paperwork," I say dryly. Tired of all of this commotion I turn to the guards, the nurse who is yelling, and Christopher. "Okay, everyone out! Now!"

My shouting catches everyone's attention, and they freeze. Christopher straightens and turns to look at me. He opens his mouth to say something, but I hold up my hand to stop him.

"I'm exhausted, and my arm is killing me. Please, just go. I won't press charges on you... *tonight*. I just want to go home and pretend today didn't happen."

Christopher sighs and runs his fingers through his messy hair. "Can I at least take you home?"

"Absolutely not," I snap.

"Fine, but eventually we need to talk about this," he says.

I simply glare at him. I may not be able to cross my arms, but hopefully, he gets that I'm not about this nonsense. His jaw clenches when I don't say anything. He turns and leaves the room without debating this with me. The security guards chase after him, but the nurse turns her attention to Darion.

"You too, mister," she says.

Darion glances at her before turning his attention back to me. His smirk slips and is replaced with a slight frown. He opens his mouth to say something, but whatever he has to say isn't important to me.

"I'm glad you're alright, Mr. Nightshade, but I need you to leave now," I snap.

"Darling, your face is plastered all over the news and social media outlets. There are reporters waiting outside to speak with you about saving Boston's finest prosecutor," his smirk returns as what little blood remains in my face drains away. "I am here to sneak you out the back and take you home. It is the very least I can do."

I stop trying to argue with him. I'm exhausted, and the pain is intensifying. I sigh and take a seat on the hospital bed.

"I really must insist that you leave," the nurse exclaims with annoyance to Darion.

Her face is red with indignation, and she clenches her fists at her side. As I open my mouth to tell her it's fine, the doctor strolls in with my discharge papers. Luckily, the bullet didn't shatter my humerus, but it nicked it and caused some muscle damage in my bicep. I'll have to take it easy for quite a while until I mend. I'm prescribed some medication to help my pain and then given the okay to leave.

Against my better judgement, I take Darion's offer for a ride home. Darion is the gallant gentleman as he leads me through the hallway. Out back there is a black SUV waiting for us. Darion opens the back door, helps me in, and then comes around to sit in the back with me. In the car, it's dark and warm, and as we pull away, I can already feel my eyelids droop. I catch a glimpse of the front of the hospital as we drive off. Darion was right. There are a handful of reporters waiting just outside the sliding glass doors. I mumble my address to Darion.

I drift off not long after we leave the hospital. An undetermined amount of time later, I awaken as the car comes to a stop. My eyelids flutter open, and I expect to see my apartment complex. Instead, we are parked outside a large brick house. I try to straighten in my seat, but the pain medication I took at the hospital has me feeling woozy.

A car door opens and shuts. Then, my door opens. Darion leans in and lifts me easily from my seat.

"Darion? What are you doing? Where are we?" I'm not sure he understands me because my speech is slurred from sleep.

"Now that your name is all over the internet, it won't take long for Jacob's crew to find where you live and send men after you. You'll stay here until we figure something out," he says.

I think I protest a little. It wouldn't be like me to not object to staying at a stranger's house, but I'm too tired to know exactly what I am saying, and I find myself slipping off to sleep.

The last thing I hear is Darion snapping, "Down, Christopher! She's just tired!"

Chapter Six

Christopher

Gemma's steady breathing is peaceful to watch. A beam of sunlight has slipped into the room with us. It spills slightly to her left on the bed. Soon it will move and warm her face, but for now, it is still early, and she is left to sleep without the irritation of the warm beam. My tail wags, and I sigh, content to just lay at the foot of the bed and watch her sleep. It's the first time in weeks that I feel one with my wolf.

In my wolf form, everything is simple. My mate is here with me, which makes everything right in the world. His happiness overshadows all my anxiety and doubts. For the past three weeks, my wolf and I have been at war. He wants his mate. I want my freedom. We've both suffered for it.

Since I got back from the race, I've lowered myself to stalking this woman. I didn't have the gall to confront her yet, not while I've felt so indecisive. My wolf made a conscious decision to strip both myself and Gemma Thomas of any choice of a relationship. Once a wolf has claimed their mate, there is no other. Mates must be together, or the shifter will eventually wither away and die. But usually, a mate is another shifter.

Why did fate have to be so damn cruel? Shackling me to a human. Their prejudice against my kind never truly faded after we gained our rights. While she didn't seem perturbed by sleeping with a shifter once, I'm sure being practically married to one will really upset her. Perhaps disgust her.

Her feelings won't change the inevitable, though. While she may not feel the strength of our mating bond right away, she will eventually. It may take time for her to feel it, and she may believe she has free will to date or fuck whoever she pleases. Maybe she won't see the mating as a real union and believe that one day she'll have the ability to find a suitable man to marry...

Unfortunately, she does not have those luxuries anymore. My wolf will not allow it. His possessiveness won't permit her near another man to do such things. Hell, my own possessiveness, now that she is here, won't allow her to touch another man. I can remember the taste of her lips... the taste of her arousal. My wolf shudders in pleasure as he remembers too.

Fuck, I could have lost her yesterday. My heart beats wildly at the thought. The one night I'm able to talk myself out of stalking her, knowing that she is going to have a harmless dinner date with Phillip, and she gets shot. When Darion called and told me about what happened, my sanity was nearly ripped to shreds.

Darion... I don't understand my wolf's reaction to the incubus around my mate. My wolf allowed Darion to carry her into the house without fuss. Strange for a mated wolf to allow another man to touch his mate. When the two guards at the hospital entered the room behind me, my wolf wanted to kill them.

Gemma stirs in her sleep, and her eyebrows come together. My wolf whines softly, concerned for her. The sound rouses her further, and I stiffen in my wolf's body as her eyes flutter open. Her soft groan is the only sound in the room. I watch as confusion turns to surprise when she realizes she's not in her own bed. She tries to push herself up on her elbow but hisses in pain. My wolf whines again.

Gemma freezes. Slowly, she turns her head in my direction, and when our eyes meet, hers widen. She's holding her breath, as if that could stand between her and death should my wolf wish it. I brace myself for the disgust I know will follow her surprise. Humans believe they want to live peacefully amongst us non-humans, but I know differently. If they could, humans would exterminate us all.

Her eyes trail over my wolf form, still wide. When our eyes meet again, she slowly lets out her breath, her chest slowly lowering.

"Chr-Christopher?" she asks, her voice thick with sleep.

I nod my head, and she mimics the movement. She closes her eyes and groans. Abruptly, she sits up in the bed, her eyes shooting open in panic.

"What time is it? I have to go to work," she asks.

Gemma moves to get out of bed, but I growl. She looks at me nervously. I stand up on all fours and shake out my fur. Then, I jump off the bed and shift. Gemma gasps. When I look up at her, staring at her through human eyes now, her mouth is slightly open. Her eyes slowly trail down the front of me, and I warm under her open appreciation. She seems to realize what she is doing because her eyes abruptly snap up to my face as her cheeks color.

"What? Want to go for another round?" I offer mockingly but instantly wince.

As Gemma's face turns pink, I wonder why I am being an asshole to her. Is it because I expect her to do the same, and I'm just trying to beat her to it?

Gemma closes her mouth slowly, and her brows come back together. She attempts to cross her arms over her chest, and I see the moment she instantly regrets moving her injured arm. She gently places her hand over the bandages covering her wound and winces. My stomach twists in guilt. I should have been there to protect her.

"Are you done flashing me? I have to go to work," Gemma says through gritted teeth. I grin at her.

"You don't have to be ashamed to like what you see," I tease.

Her scowl covers up her pained expression. She slides the rest of the way off the bed and makes a move to walk around it, but she catches herself with her good arm on the mattress as she stumbles.

"Get back into bed," I order, storming over to her.

She glares up at me and opens her mouth for what I am sure is going to be a colorful response. I don't wait for her to speak, though. I scoop her up and place her back into bed.

"Cut it out, Christopher," she snaps sharply, pushing my hands away from her body. "I can't stay here... wherever here is."

She glances around the room with uncertainty.

"We're just outside the city limits in a house that Darion and I share," I tell her.

Surprise flickers across her face. I expect her to ask questions about the living arrangement, but she shakes her head and looks to the nightstand next to the bed.

"Where's my purse and phone? I need to call a cab," she says.

"You're not leaving here today. Darion is making sure your three employees have access to your office, has contacted the police to let them know you're staying here for a while, and if you tell me everything that you need, I'll make sure he gets his people to grab it from your office or apartment before he gets home this evening," I say.

She sputters, too angry to form real words. I can't help it; her outraged expression causes me to laugh, which only makes her angrier. Using her good arm, she reaches over and throws a pillow at me.

"You guys can't just kidnap me and force me to live here. I want to go back to my apartment! Where is my stuff?" she screeches as I let her hit me with the soft duvet pillow.

"You can't go back to your place for a while," I tell her with a frown. "The people that came after Darion will come after you. Since you took a bullet for him, they'll think you're someone important to Darion. I'm sure they have people at your complex, waiting for you to get home."

Gemma stills, the fight draining out of her. She clenches her jaw and shakes her head in defeat. "This can't be happening. Darion's an incubus for Christ's sake! I'm sure he usually has women around him all the time."

Jealousy swirls around in my stomach. I should have been the one out having dinner with her. It's a ridiculous thought since I have been fighting this union tooth and nail since that fateful night. After he put Gemma to bed, I cornered Darion to ask about their dinner together before the shooting happened. His unusually vague responses left a bad taste in my mouth. He is never one to let a good opportunity to antagonize me go. This situation should have been no different. But it was.

His silence this morning as he got ready for the day also worries me. Darion is hardly a sober person, but this morning it was like he was heading to a funeral. Is it because he is worried about another hit happening or is it… I stare at Gemma wondering if Darion finds her as appealing as I do.

Darion and I have shared women, *a lot* of women. I've participated in a lot of the orgies that Darion has hosted. I've never once cared if my dick went where Darion's had nor did I care if Darion picked up the women I left behind. But when it comes to Gemma… This is different. She is *my mate*. Not just some fuck. Darion knows to stay away… right? I wonder if this is a conversation I need to have with my friend.

A small part of me wonders why my wolf doesn't bristle at the idea of Darion near Gemma. Just the thought of her being with a random guy sends my wolf into a raging ball of fur. I frown. I'm pulled away from my wandering thoughts as the scent of Gemma's arousal reaches my nostrils. My attention snaps back to the woman in front of me who's trying awfully hard not to stare at my dick.

"Hungry?" I ask her innocently. When her eyes dart to my face in embarrassment, I laugh out loud. "Let me grab you something to eat so you can take your pain pills. I'll get your purse and phone too, but don't bother calling a cab. I'll just send it away."

"I'll just wait until you leave for work," she says with a shrug. I flash her a grin.

"I took the day off to spend time with my girl," I tell her.

My girl? Where the hell did that endearment come from? It's also the wrong thing to say. Her expression turns murderous.

"Fuck you, Christopher! You're an asshole. I'm not your anything. I don't care that you bit me, and now you think I'm yours. The minute I leave this house, I never want to see your face again!"

I try not to let the sting of her words get to me. She has every right to be upset after how I've treated her. I force myself to grin.

"Only my face? What, want to see my dick regularly? I can make that happen."

"Urgh!" she shrieks and throws another pillow at me, this time hitting me in the face. I catch it easily and carry it with me as I walk back around the bed towards the door.

"Be back in a few," I say and leave her fuming.

***

When I slip back into her room about forty-five minutes later, I'm dressed and carrying a tray full of food. I find Gemma standing and peering out the window. She looks over at me as I enter the room with a frown on her face.

"Yup, that's the paparazzi," I confirm, answering her unspoken question. "They want to know more about the mysterious Gemma Thomas and how she got so lucky to go on a date with Darion."

I roll my eyes although jealousy swirls around in my gut.

"This is ridiculous," she mutters. She eyes the tray of food in my hands. "You made all of that? For me?"

"Who else? Now get back into bed, and you can have it," I command. "You've only had a few hours of sleep since you arrived. Eat and then sleep."

She glares at me for a moment before finally walking back over to the bed. She climbs back onto it and makes herself comfortable.

"What time is it? And why am I wearing one of your t-shirts? Where's my dress?"

I glance down at the white shirt that falls halfway down her thighs. My wolf smirks. He's pleased to know that our scent is clinging all over her.

"Why do you think it's mine? Could be Darion's. And it's just now eight. You've only been asleep for a little over four hours," I say as I place the tray on her lap. Hash browns, scrambled eggs, and pancakes fill the tray. Her eyes roam over the food then rise to meet my gaze.

"I think I can tell your stench from Darion's cologne," she says sourly. "What's with all this catering? I don't need to be waited on hand and foot. It's an arm wound. It isn't life threatening."

I clench my teeth together, fighting off my annoyance at her comment about Darion's cologne. Of course, she was close enough to him to smell his scent. Instead of responding right away, I climb into bed with her. She grabs her phone that's lying next to the plate of food on the tray and swipes the screen to turn it on.

"It's my way of saying I'm sorry," I tell her, my voice coming out stilted.

When was the last time I apologized to anyone? Gemma looks over at me suspiciously,

"Sorry for what? For biting me? Or for kicking me out of your hotel room while I'm still in the throes of an orgasm?"

I wince at her accusations. I wipe my hand down my face and sigh.

"For both," I answer honestly.

Gemma glares at me but nods as if to accept that I am being truthful. She places her phone down and picks up the fork and knife. As she begins to cut into her pancakes, she says,

"Well, thanks for the apology. I still don't want to see you after this."

The smell of her arousal has grown stronger since I left for breakfast tells me her body isn't on board with the boundaries she's trying to set.

"Well, that's too damn bad. I've decided that I'm not going to fight fate any longer. You're my mate, and we're sticking together," I snap at her with a scowl.

She pours maple syrup onto her pancakes and plops a bite of it into her mouth.

"Remember, I can still charge you with forcing your stupid wolf mating thing on me. I'd watch what you say," she says after swallowing.

She reaches over, grabs her medication from the nightstand, and twists the top off before dumping two pills into her hands. She throws them back and sips on the orange juice I placed on the tray.

"You could have reported me weeks ago when you realized what those marks were," I snap. "You could have come to me—"

"I certainly did *not* know what your bite marks meant!" she interrupts angrily. "Or I would have decked you in the face right there in the room. And to tell me that *I* should have come to *you* is a cowardly thing to say when you're the one who put us into this situation. Asshole."

I take a deep breath. She's right. I'm getting defensive over something I started. When I'm calm enough to talk, I try this again.

"You're right. I'm sorry, *again*. This is a surprise for me, too. I never thought a mate was in the cards for me. I wasn't ready to handle the consequences when I realized what I had done. My wolf was hellbent on claiming you, and while I was distracted, he seized the opportunity to seal our fates together. I was pissed that I lost control, I was pissed that my future was stripped from me in a blink of an eye, and I was pissed that—"

"That you're stuck with me," Gemma interrupts with a frown. "A human."

I nod. Old anger flares up at the injustice of all of this, but it fizzles away just as quickly. At some point last night, as I watched my mate sleep, I decided I needed to accept Gemma as the human that she is. I need to be the mate I'm supposed to be. There is no use getting mad anymore. Gemma goes back to eating. I take a moment to collect myself before continuing.

"I've been a dick for staying away as long as I have. What I should have done was chase after you, after I kicked you out. I should have come to your apartment when I arrived back in Boston. Instead, I've been trying to pretend none of this happened. But my wolf won't let me forget. He won't let me shun my responsibilities. He doesn't care if you're a human or a squirrel shifter. He wants you and our animals always know what is best for us, so who am I to ignore him anymore?

"I've been, literally, killing myself by staying away from you, Gemma. I can't eat, I can hardly sleep, I can't focus on anything but you. Shifters need their mates or eventually we just kind of... wither away. We die because we can't focus on our wellbeing. I'm sorry, but you're mine now, and I have no plans on letting you just walk out of my life. This is more permanent than a wedding, so get used to having me around."

Gemma stops eating and puts down her utensils. She stares down at her plate and shakes her head slowly.

"Can you just go away?" she asks, her voice small.

"What did I just tell you? I'm not going—"

"Christopher!" she interrupts sharply as she turns to look me in the eyes. "Your declaration does nothing for me. You have just admitted that you still don't want this, but you have to cave to your animal instincts or whatever. You obviously have an issue with me being a human, and you're not ready to be in a relationship. None of that screams romantic to me. I don't want this any more than you do. We'll just have to figure something out where you don't have to be around all the time."

It's not that I don't understand where she is coming from. Replaying what I just told her, I realize that maybe I was a little too blunt. But nothing I said is a lie. I like women enough to want all of them, not just one. How am I supposed to be content with just one? Somehow, we are going to have to figure this out...

Suddenly, an idea pops up, and I grin. Maybe we aren't in love, *yet,* but maybe constant physical contact would help the both of us get there. Gemma notices my shift in mood, and her pupils narrow as her expression turns wary. I take the tray of food away from her and place it on the other side of me on the mattress. I scoot closer and take her chin in my hand.

"Look, we don't know each other very well—" I start.

"At all," she instantly corrects. I ignore her.

"But damn if we don't fit together like two puzzle pieces," I continue.

My thumb slides across her bottom lip as I stare into her eyes. Fuck, besides biting her, that night was one of the best of my life. I don't think I've ever had an orgasm that intense. I know she had had a good time, too. If she hadn't, she wouldn't be this upset that I kicked her out.

"Imagine this. We can replay that night every night, minus the bad parts. Multiple times, all over the house, all over your apartment. You're mine, but I'm yours too, Gemma. Whenever you want it, I'll be there to satisfy you."

Gemma's mouth pops open, and her pupils grow wider. The smell of her arousal clings to everything in the room and grows thicker. My dick stiffens, ready to answer my mate's call. My grin slips as I think about how those full lips would look stretched over my erection. I don't know if I want that right away or to bury myself inside her again. This time, no condom. No need. She is my mate, which makes her my wife. I'll get to feel everything this time.

"Think about it, have you ever felt that alive, Gemma? The way you came on my face… I could tell that isn't what it's normally like for you. You loved it. And god as my witness, I loved tasting you on my tongue," I tell her honestly. "I've dreamt about devouring you like I did that night. I know you liked it. The way you got wetter and wetter…"

Without meaning to, I lean forward and kiss her. She doesn't fight me. Instead, she instantly leans into the kiss. Her soft moan causes my dick to harden further. Fuck. At the party, she tasted like wine and mousse, but now she tastes like pancakes and maple syrup. I growl in delight. I nip at her bottom lip, and she gasps, inadvertently allowing my tongue to enter. Another soft moan from Gemma causes me to lose focus of my task to seduce her. I reach up with my other hand and cup her breast. I removed her bra while she slept, so now I have only a thin white t-shirt between me and her nipples. I want to taste them. The thought makes my mouth water.

Gemma's phone rings, snapping us both out of the moment. Gemma jerks away like she's been electrocuted. From the look on her face, I can tell we aren't going to finish what I started. I adjust myself; jeans don't really allow for comfortable erections.

"Hand me my phone, please," she says, a little breathless.

I grit my teeth in annoyance but reach over and grab her cell phone off the tray. The caller ID says Aaron with a little heart next to their name. Who the fuck is Aaron?

Before I give it to her, I turn and say, "I want us to get to know each other. Maybe we can just start out as friends. What I did… It's not reversible. We're stuck together, so let's try to make this work, alright?"

Gemma doesn't look at me, but I'm relieved to see her slight nod. Good, at least she is willing to *try*. I leave her to answer her phone call. It's time to call Darion to find out if he knows what's going on.

Chapter Seven

Darion

My day is a whirlwind of activity. Fighting off the press, contacting Jacob's lawyer to inform him that I know Jacob was behind the attack and that I will be coming after him, and then making sure Gemma's business is doing alright without her, which takes precedence over everything else. First, I hire security to stand outside her office doors so the press won't bombard her three employees. Then, I call a security company to install cameras at the front and back of her office. That done, I make a call to some off-the-books security detail to monitor her apartment for the next week to make sure no one else is doing surveillance on it.

This is probably all overkill, but something is compelling me to ensure that Gemma will stay safe. I've been telling myself that this is just the proper thing to do after someone saves your life.

The more I think over our conversation, the more I realize that I *am* bored. I am a big shot lawyer with money and power and only material things to show for it. The mundane routine of my days lacks the appeal it once had.

How have I not noticed?

Am I just noticing now because my life has been put at risk and I am seeing things in a new light, or is it simply because an outsider mentioned it? A beautiful outsider. Christopher snuck into her room in his wolf form the moment I placed her on the guest bed. If he hadn't, I'm sure I would have done something asinine… like watch her sleep. Instead once laid down in my own bed last night, all night I pictured her face in my mind. Her laughter, how her smile causes her eyes to twinkle, the way she sees straight through me…

By the time I walk into the house that evening, the press have given up trying to catch a glimpse of Gemma for the day. I'm sure they will be back tomorrow. It's late; a glance at my watch tells me it's ten o'clock. I stayed at the office looking over a few cases to quell the thoughts of our new guest. It helped a little. As I head up the stairs to my room, I realize that I have not had sex all day. Strange. Neither the urge nor the hunger have even crossed my mind.

I pause at the top of the stairs wondering when I last went a full day without sex. Years… It has been years since this has happened. I don't *need* sex every day, but I certainly never *don't* want to have it. The power of the activity is addicting, and it fills me with the nourishment that I need. Yes, a human can go a day without food and water, but do they want to? No. Same thing goes for an incubus and sex.

The soft sound of conversation carries down the hallway from Gemma's room. Curious to see what has kept her awake this long I wander towards her room. Her door is cracked open. Just as I go to knock, I hear Christopher's voice.

"You've been playing with yourself," he taunts.

"Go fuck yourself, Christopher," Gemma's voice sounds strained. Like she wants to sound firm, but even I can hear the husky tone.

"Why would I do that when you so obviously want to fuck me?" my friend asks his mate. "I can smell you. Do you know that? I know how I make you feel. You do the same thing for me, Gemma."

I hear the sharp slap of a hand across skin. I grin. Christopher has never been the one for sweet words. My grin slips though as Gemma's arousal hits my nostrils. Incubuses might not have a heightened sense of smell like shifters do, but we can detect and sense arousal from great distances. It's a beacon for us. I inhale her scent, and my dick hardens quickly. Too quickly. Alarmed, I look down to find myself standing completely erect and still painfully swelling. Gemma's arousal thickens in the air, and I hear a moan coming from her room.

I peer in through the ajar door to see Christopher and Gemma standing next to the bed. His hand is cupping the back of her head as he kisses her, and the other is at her waist. One of Gemma's hands is grabbing a fist full of his shirt while her injured arm rests at her side. Suddenly, she pushes him away. For a moment, I think it's because she heard me.

"I'm not doing this again!" she hisses at him.

Through the white t-shirt her nipples are erect and hard to miss. I stare at them, and my dick swells further. I reach down and cup myself, trying to calm myself down.

"Tell me to go, then," Christopher says, seemingly unperturbed by her annoyance. "Tell me, Gemma, and I'll leave for the night. But I'll just be here first thing in the morning. I told you, I'm not letting you go."

Gemma stands there for a moment, glaring at him. I'm sure she'll tell him to fuck off again. I can see the decision warring on her face. So expressive… What would she look like as she rode me? The thought sends another rush of blood to my dick. I'm almost lightheaded. Gemma closes the distance between them, her scowl deepening, and slaps him again,

"That's for doing this to me!" she shouts.

Then, she's on her tiptoes kissing Chris. From the way he's standing, I can't see his face, but I know him well. This wasn't the first time he's elicited this response from women. A shit-eating grin was probably plastered all over his face when she hit him. I'm sure he does it on purpose. He likes them feisty.

They start tearing at each other's clothes. Both too angry and too horny to worry about pant buttons or pulling their shirts over their heads. Gemma's arousal causes a haze to settle over my consciousness. The energy that sex creates is what an incubus feeds on; it's not the actual act of sex itself. As my friend and his mate paw at each other, their naked bodies slap together, and Gemma's arousal slips out of her room and hits me. I breathe it in, feeding on their energy. Gemma smells good; her arousal is sweet and intoxicating. Has any woman that I've met ever smelled this wonderful? As fog takes over me, I find myself quietly pulling the zipper of my pants down. I pull my erection free and stroke myself.

The sounds of her moans, her angry growls as she bites at him… I take it all in. I watch as Christopher, even in all of their madness, gently places her on the bed, carefully avoiding jarring her injured arm. It's strange to see him be gentle. He's not a gentle lover by any means.

That thought disappears though as he steps back for just a moment to admire what is his. I'm greeted by the same view, and I stifle my boyish gasp of delight. Her body is stunning. Her tits are large and perky, her stomach is flat, and when she breathes, I see a hint of abs. Her hips flare out, and between the junction of her legs, she glistens with arousal.

My hips jerk forward of their own accord, wanting to be the ones between her legs. I stroke my swollen cock faster. The hunger on Gemma's face as she looks up at Christopher is delightful. He pounces on her. As they kiss, grab, and nip at each other I watch, fully invested in what I am seeing. I lick my lips and bite back a groan as the energy in the room swells, feeding me. When Chris surges into her body, Gemma's cry of pleasure causes me to stroke myself even faster. Chris takes her rough and fast, and Gemma arches into each thrust angry and deliriously.

They both groan and grunt, and in my head, I'm making the same sounds. My balls begin to rise as my release nears. I'm close and so are they. Christopher bends down and nips at one of Gemma's breasts. She throws her head back and arches her breasts for him to get better access to them. Just as she throws her head back, Christopher's head turns, and he meets my gaze.

He knows I am here, watching them. He knows what I was doing. The gold glow in his eyes tells me his wolf knows, too. I don't stop stroking myself even as I meet his gaze, and he doesn't stop his thrusting into Gemma. He stares at me for a heartbeat longer before turning his attention back to his mate.

He pounds into her harder. The sound of their skin slapping together is music. Gemma cries out as her orgasm tears through her, and it heightens the sexual energy to a level I have never experienced before. I choke on it, bathe in it, and devour it just as I find my own release. Chris stills as he empties himself inside of her.

Thankfully, I am able to capture my own cum with my shirt before I make a mess. I am breathing hard, too hard. I stumble away from Gemma's door as I come down from my high. My body is shaking from the intensity of my own hand job.

As I am released from the heady haze that has taken over me, shock settles into my psyche. What the fuck was that? When have I ever been this aroused? When have I ever been this affected by a couple fucking? Sure, I have watched people fuck throughout my years. Many times, I just sit back and watch the women and men I've hired fuck each other. I feed off of it. But the need to pleasure myself has never been this desperate before. The energy the two people in that room just caused was astronomical. The smell of Gemma's arousal lingers in the air and doesn't allow the haze in my head to clear fully. Fuck. It's her. Something about her is making it hard to think straight.

I tuck my softening dick into my pants as I move quickly away from the door.

Chapter Eight

Gemma

When I wake the next morning, I know it's early. Really early. I turn my head and find that I am alone in the bed. I'm relieved and strangely disappointed. Christopher wants something between us, but I find myself alone after sex with him. Again.

Why couldn't I just say no to him last night? My body has been on fire since I awoke the previous morning, and the feeling only intensified throughout the day. When he caught me with my hand between my legs, I was mortified. Well… mostly. A different part of me wanted him to watch as I got off. The other part of me wanted exactly what I had gotten: frustrated, pent up, and angry sex.

I'm an idiot. I now know this about myself. I can't trust my body or my emotions. Where was my sanity when I needed it the most? I move gingerly off the bed. My body is gloriously sore in all the right places. I can still feel Christopher's hands and mouth all over me. I don't know what overcame me last night. I was so mad about everything. First, being shot and then, finding out that Darion and Christopher knew one another and that

Darion had called him thinking I needed some freaking knight in shining armor...

When Christopher strolled into the room and caught me masturbating, I should have gotten up and shoved him back out. Stupid, traitorous body.

Hating myself, I move around the bed. On the nightstand nearest the door, I find my laptop and purse. I pause. Darion brought my laptop home? I glance towards the door and see my dress hanging from a hook, freshly dry cleaned. Did he slip in when I was sleeping and put them both in here? Huh. I'm a light sleeper. I should have heard him come in.

Whatever. Doesn't matter. I throw off Christopher's t-shirt, slip on my dress, wincing as I move my arm into the hole, grab my stuff, and silently slip out of my room. I walk as silently as I can down the hall and stairs and order a car to pick me up. When it comes and I slip in without being detected by either Christopher or Darion, I feel victorious. If I never see either one of them again, I'll die a happy woman.

***

By mid-afternoon, I'm famished. After stopping at my apartment to shower and change, I went directly to the office, forgoing breakfast to catch up on work. As if the universe hears my stomach growl, Aaron comes barreling into my office with lunch in tow.

"How dare you only give me short responses after what happened to you! You were shot, and I have to hear about it on social media. Then, I have to wait ten hours before you answer any of my calls or texts! And then two not so good-looking goons at the door *frisk* me before I can even come in here!" he shouts at me, slamming my office door shut behind him. "Un-fucking-acceptable!"

My office has a window looking out into the rest of the small office space. I chose this office specifically so I can see the other graphic designers working at their desks and at the few seats where clients wait to be seen. All the designers exchange looks with one another over Aaron's dramatic entrance. He throws the bag of food on my desk as he glares at me.

Aaron is a lean, muscular guy with a thick head of hair and a well-trimmed beard. When he's not working, he typically wears a crop top and skirt. Now he is wearing workout gear. He must be meeting with a client after this.

I get up and come around my desk and throw my arms around him. Our friendship began when we were five, and ever since, we've been as thick as thieves. It broke my heart when he told me that he was moving to Boston, and when he demanded I come, I followed as soon as I could. Being in familiar arms triggers an emotional response and tears start to fall.

"Gemmie!? What the hell, you never cry. What's going on?" he asks, alarmed.

We sit down in the two chairs reserved for clients, and I tell him everything. I already shared with him my disastrous one-night stand, so I fill him in on everything else. When I am done, Aaron leans back in his seat and lets out a whistle.

"Alright, I understand the tears now," he says and sighs. "Well… Sounds like you made a good call getting out of there as soon as possible. You were bound to end up with Stockholm Syndrome if you had stayed any longer."

"What do I do? Every time that front door opens, I swear it's going to be Christopher storming in here trying to lay some wolfy claim on me," I say, wiping away the tears.

"If he does come in, I suggest *not* having sex with him if you want to set some boundaries," he teases. "Though, why you're so upset that he's marked you is beyond me. He's drop dead gorgeous. That man can claim me all night if he wants…"

"Aaron, you're married now. You can't talk like that," I tell him with a chuckle.

"Phillip would totally agree with me," Aaron says, waving off my scolding. "Okay, look. Why don't you talk to other humans who ended up being mated with a shifter? I'm sure there are support groups online you can join. There's a group for just about everything. See how everyone else adjusted to their new situation."

I stare at him, stunned. "Aaron, you're a genius!"

"Psh, I know. I'm so bewildered why you act so shocked when I give advice. It's like I've led you astray before," he says rolling his eyes.

"You have, like, a hundred times," I tell him pointedly. He shrugs.

"You win some, and you lose some. Oh, that reminds me, we need to make sure you stay in shape for Scotland's obstacle race. With that arm, I'm sure you won't get a place on the podium, but you can still get a good time, which will help in the following years—"

I groan. "I'm out for the season, Aaron. There's no way I can work out with this," I say and look pointedly at the bandages wrapped around my arm. "I can't take my medication without food, and I didn't eat this morning, so it feels worse now than when it did when I actually got shot."

"I brought you a salad, so eat up. Want to come over for dinner tonight? I'm finally home for a few days before I have to leave again," Aaron offers.

"No, I want to curl up in my bed, eat a pint of ice cream and watch *Penny Dreadful*," I say. He shakes his head,

"You and that dreary show… Fine. If you change your mind, let me know. I know Phillip's been worried sick about you too. He blames himself for all of this you know."

"Next time tell him not to bail on me," I say. "And maybe you should stop traveling for work so much. That way we can have dinner together more often. A traveling occupational therapist and trainer isn't as fun as it sounded when you first got the position."

"Tell me about it. But I'm making bank, so there's that. It won't be long before we can buy a house and afford adoption. So, I need to work hard now so I can have what I want in the future," he says with a sigh.

We talk a little more before he leaves. I eat the lunch he brought me and pop my pain medication. It helps take the edge off, but my arm feels swollen, and the medication makes me drowsy. By the end of the day, I have lost two potential, long-term clients due to missing our meetings from the day before. I manage to catch up on a website design for one client, but fail to make a deadline for a book cover with another. I have a pounding headache that I try to nurse by rubbing my temples. As I read through an angry email, a sudden flurry of activity erupts outside my office.

I glance up to my window to see Darion strolling through the office. My other designers are packing up for the night, and they all stop to ogle the incubus as he heads up to my door. He really is quite handsome. But he is also friends with Christopher, and I'm not in the mood to deal with him or the latter.

He knocks on the door and opens it before I can tell him to go away. He gives me a pleasant smile as he shuts the door behind him. Oh? No arrogant lawyer I'm-better-than-you smirk? A real smile? It makes his already good looks spike up to new levels, and I find myself warming under his gaze. But then I remember how he was the other night.

The looks he gave me and everyone around us at dinner spoke volumes about how he perceives the world around him. He held his nose high and quite literally balked at the thought of eating from a truck. I saw the way he adjusted his disgusted facial expressions to polite looks of indifference as he studied the menus.

Uptight and bored... What a combination.

"What can I do for you this evening, Mr. Nightshade?" I ask, coming to my feet.

"Please, call me Darion," he says casually as I walk around to stand in front of my desk. "I've come to see how your day went. You weren't bothered by the press or anyone were you?"

"No, the bodyguards you hired did quite a good job," I assure him while leaning my hip against my desk. "Thank you for doing that, but they can go watch over someone else. I don't need them here."

"They're for your protection," Darion tells me, his smile fading. "Someone sent out a hit on me, and now you're in the crossfire. It's an occupational hazard in my line of work, but it's not something you should have to worry about. You need to be careful. That's the other reason I've come here. I want to see if you want to grab something to eat before we head back to my house for the evening."

I raise an eyebrow in surprise. This handsome lawyer wants to take me to dinner? Is this an apology for last night, or does he actually want to hang out? I try not to ogle him as he stands there in that expensive suit with a devilish glint in his eye. A small, secret part of me wonders what it would be like to have sex with an incubus. I quickly squash the idea. Even if he weren't Christopher's friend, I don't do hook ups anymore, and with an incubus, that's exactly what it would be.

Darion misunderstands my expression and adds quickly, "*To sleep.* I know you have a... rocky situation with Christopher, but you need to consider staying at our place for a few nights. Just until my security is certain there won't be any attempts on your life."

I am already shaking my head before he gets a chance to finish.

"I don't need to consider anything. I'll be fine in my apartment, but thank you for the offer. Now, if you'll excuse me... I need to close up shop before I can head home," I say, looking pointedly towards the door.

Darion studies my face for a moment before that cocky smirk slides into place.

"What's wrong Gemma? Scared that if you come back to stay with us you won't be able to *not* fuck your mate?" he taunts quietly.

The heat that rises in my cheeks is blazing. Did Christopher tell him? Damn these two! How dare Darion tease me about this situation. He doesn't know me, and he doesn't get to make any presumptions about me based on my lapse of judgement.

"Excuse me?" I ask him, breathlessly.

Anger surges through me, but at the same time so does a rush of desire. The way those dark eyes are blazing, it does something to me.

Darion takes two slow steps forward, his black eyes pinned to my face. Those steps bring him directly in front of me, which causes me to have to tilt my head up to look at him. I can feel his breath on my face, and I breathe in the scent of his cologne and natural masculine musk. The soft burn of desire that seems to always be burning in me since my night with Christopher spikes hotter. I gulp nervously.

"Surprised I know about your sex-capades last night?" he asks with a quirk of a brow. "Oh, Gemma... I watched the entire thing. Can't say no and mean it, can you? You naughty thing..."

I gasp in surprise, and Darion takes advantage of my stupor. He dips in low and claims my lips with his. I freeze, too surprised and shocked to do much of anything. But my paralysis doesn't last long. The heat in my body skyrockets, and my mind stops thinking. My body relaxes ever so slightly, and I tentatively kiss him back.

The sound of a door opening and shutting knocks my sense back into me. I pull away from Darion and sidestep away, feeling shaken and confused. What is going on? Why the fuck did I just do that? My body is alive just like when I think about Christopher. I swear there is a soft humming under my skin. I can feel my pants dampening as I look back at Darion, who seems just a little baffled himself.

No. This can't happen. Whatever is going on here... I don't want any of it. I glare at the incubus and point, using my good arm, towards the door.

"Leave. Now." I snap.

"Gemma, I-," Darion starts but I cut him off,

"I said *leave*, Darion!" I snap. "Whatever game you and Chris are playing is sick. I don't want this from either of you. Go! Now, or I'll call the cops for trespassing onto private property."

Darion frowns and steps back away from me. "I apologize for my behavior. I'll see my way out."

He turns and leaves without another word. I watch as he pushes the front door open and heads towards the direction of his office.

Fuck online support groups. Fuck Christopher and fuck whatever game Darion is playing. I'm done.

Chapter Nine

Christopher

"Wait, so you're telling me the most powerful incubus in the States can't get a boner?" I ask my friend incredulously. I scoff as I lean back against the back of the chair in Darion's home office. "How's that working out for you?"

"How do you think, asshole?" Darion snaps. He's scowling at the window that looks out onto the front lawn. It's dark out, not much to see out there. "I'm wound up tighter than a ball of rubber bands."

My chuckle that follows his statement only pisses Darion off further. It feels good to see Darion frazzled. Not long ago, he was enjoying my dilemma with Gemma. Karma is a bitch, it seems. The laughter that comes from the speakerphone only angers Darion more.

"Cut it out, Tate," he snaps at our friend.

"Okay, okay, it's not funny," Tate agrees. Though, I can hear the laughter in his voice.

I chuckle again and then turn back to Darion. "When did you first notice this?"

"A week ago," he grumbles.

He clasps his hands behind his back. I know him well enough to know that is his tell. He's way more upset than he appears. I frown. Something is really wrong.

"A week ago?" Tate repeats with surprise. "I didn't think you could go that long without... eating."

I didn't think he could either. Why is he just now bringing it up?

"Alright, let's figure out what triggered this. A week ago was the shooting. You could have died if it hadn't been for Gemma. Maybe your body is too stressed or anxious to, you know, work properly," I say, thinking out loud.

"That's not it," Darion responds with a sigh.

"Darion's gone through a lot worse and has still been able to perform, no problem," Tate adds.

"Maybe you caught something from one of your broads that you ordered?" I ask. Darion rolls his eyes.

"Incubuses cannot catch diseases," he answers. He pauses before continuing, "I think I know the reason behind all of this, but... I have my reservations about it."

"Alright shoot," I say.

"I think it has something to do with Gemma," Darion says slowly.

My whole body tenses up. I lean forward as my wolf perks up at the sounds of his mate's name. It's been a full week without touching her or speaking with her. She's been avoiding my calls and texts. She hired her own security to stand in front of her office complex specifically to keep anyone who isn't a client out. She's even gone out of her way to enter at different access doors in her apartment complex to throw me off. I'm going insane all over again. My wolf is pissed he isn't with Gemma, and I'm beginning to feel the effects of going a long period of time without my mate. Something has to change.

But that change didn't have to come in the form of Darion. That night when I caught him jerking off to us, I tolerated it. Darion needs to eat, and if he wants to feed off the sexual energy my mate and I create, then so be it. But what is this about his boners and their connection to Gemma?

"Wait, Gemma? Like, Christopher's wayward mate, Gemma?" Tate asks, clearly confused.

Tate knows all about our situation. The three of us are closer than brothers. With Tate's top-secret jobs, though, he is gone a lot and most of the time unable to contact us. This evening when he called to let us know he's on his way home for good, we caught him up on everything. I'm sure his mind is reeling with all of this news.

"Yes, that same Gemma," Darion confirms grimly.

"Explain," I demand.

"That night I watched you two fuck…" Darion starts but trails off.

His whole body suddenly shudders, and he closes his eyes. There is silence in the room as I wait for him to speak again. He opens his eyes and looks back at me.

"I grew so hard I almost came before you two started. When I did it was… different, all-consuming, and it left me feeling… strange. The next day I found myself ravenous, but when I ordered a woman to my office, I couldn't get hard. I had to settle on fingering the woman to eat."

Darion pauses again and then turns his body so he's not facing me directly. He looks around his office. To my surprise when he lifts his hand, it's shaking, as he runs his fingers through his hair.

"After my order left, I thought about visiting Gemma for lunch to make sure all was going well, and the moment I thought about her, I got hard. *Painfully* hard. I decided against the visit but then after work, I saw her car was still in the parking lot. So I walked in to see if she wanted to get dinner and then come back to stay here for a few days until we're sure she's safe. Just being in the same room with her made me hard. Then I kissed her, and I almost came right there—"

I am on my feet and ready to fight in an instant. "You kissed her? What the fuck Darion? She's *my mate*!"

At the same time, I hear Tate say, "That's his mate, man."

"I know, I'm sorry. I just... I couldn't help myself?"

The statement is posed as a question as if he can't believe it himself. Darion's genuine uncertainty and worry on his face are the only reasons my fist isn't breaking his nose.

"No wonder she's completely cut me off. She probably thinks you and I are trying to play some stupid fucking mind game with her," I say.

"You were already cut off," Darion points out though he still seems lost in thought.

"Dude, you know this is messed up, right?" I tell him, scowling.

"Yes," Darion says and nods. "I don't understand it. This has never happened to me before. I didn't know it could happen. And the worst part is... I can't stop thinking about her."

"You better cut it out, Darion," I warn, a growl rumbling through me. "Gemma isn't like the others."

"If I could 'cut it out,' I would, Chris," Darion snaps. "Do you know how inadequate I feel? I'm a goddamn incubus! This shouldn't be a problem for me!"

"Shit..." Tate's voice carries throughout the room. "You got to eat, Darion."

"You don't need to have sex to eat, so go watch someone. Hell, order yourself a full orgy and get it out of your system," I tell him.

Darion turns to me, his dark eyes pinning me with a look of curiosity.

"What exactly are you mad at?" he asks softly.

"That you went behind my back and *kissed* my mate," I told him.

"The fact that I want to fuck her..." he pushes. "That's not more enraging?"

I open my mouth to tell him of course it is, but I hesitate. Am I mad that he wants to fuck her? Yes, she is mine, but my wolf doesn't seem too... upset. In fact, he doesn't really seem bothered at all. Curious, maybe, but not jealous or engaged. The tension in my body loosens as I think his question over. My wolf wasn't upset with another man jerking off as I took Gemma. I just figured it was because my wolf understood Darion's need, but now... Now I have to wonder: Is the wolf okay with sharing?

"Hello?" Tate asks after a long silence.

"We're still here," Darion answers, still watching me intently.

Before I can answer Darion's question, his cell phone rings. He pulls it from his pocket and scowls. He swipes his finger across the screen to answer the call and brings it to his ear.

"What is it?" he demands. There's a pause. "What? When? Where is she?"

My heart sinks. I already know who the "she" in question is. The growl that erupts from my chest is from my wolf, ready to spring into action. My body shudders as I fight the change.

"We'll be right there," Darion says and ends the call.

"What's going on?" I ask as panic washes over me.

"Someone tried to kidnap Gemma."

The blood drains from my face. I turn and rush out of the office. Behind me, I hear Darion say,

"We'll see you soon, Tate."

Chapter Ten

Gemma

I'm sitting at the police station in front of the desk of an officer typing with one finger at a time on his keyboard. He clacks his gum and continuously clears his throat as he uploads my statement. Behind me, one of Darion's security guys Alvin stands quietly. He was the one who intercepted the two men who grabbed me. A shiver runs through my body, and I pull the wool blanket someone gave me closer to my body.

"You're all set, Miss Thomas," the officer says and leans back in his chair. He looks at me. Well, leers at me. His gaze travels over me, and he licks his cracked, dry lips. I stand, glaring at him. He rises slowly and asks, "Can I call someone to pick you up, Miss Thomas?"

Before I can respond, Alvin steps forward. "My employer is on his way to pick up Miss Thomas. He should be here any min—"

"I'm here now," a cool voice says.

I turn to find Darion strolling towards us. His very presence commands the room. Officers, lawyers, victims, and the guilty all stop to stare as he walks by. He is dressed like the fancy upscale lawyer that he is. Not a hair out of place or a cuff un-shined. My heart flutters traitorously in my chest, and immediately, I remember the scorching heat of his kiss and how it warmed my entire body. The chill I feel now is a drastic difference between the moments.

He comes to stand next to me. His cool look of indifference shifts to worry as he looks down at me.

"Gemma, how are you feeling?" he asks.

He lifts a hand and to my surprise cups my cheek. For a second, I relax into the warmth his hand provides. His lovely expensive cologne envelopes me, and my mind begins to fog. Before I can do something incredibly stupid, like wrap my arms around his waist, I force myself to take a step backwards.

"I'm alright thanks to your security guard here," I mumble, glancing at Alvin, who nods his head in my direction.

I then turn my attention to the front of the police station, wondering where Christopher is. Strangely enough, I am disappointed to see he's not behind Darion. So much for being a mate…

"Mr. Nightshade," the officer who just moments ago leered at me says. He straightens and says, "I didn't realize you two were, ah, seeing each other. We were under the impression Miss Thomas was with, ah, Mr. Rogue…"

"I assume you were expecting him to pick up Miss Thomas so you could question their mating arrangement?" Darion asks, his look of contempt slides back into place as he studies the police officer. "I believe the police have bothered Mr. Rogue quite enough. The constant phone calls and visits to his work establishment and to the house are borderline harassment. If Miss Thomas has any grievance with their situation, I am sure she will file a complaint. Until then, if the police harass Mr. Rogue one more time, I will file a lawsuit against the city's police department."

So that's why all of this took so long. They were waiting for Christopher to arrive. I turn and glare at the police officer, who ignores me as he adjusts his utility belt. That also explains why Christopher isn't here.

"Oh, um, of course, Mr. Nightshade. We were just making sure that a shifter hadn't stepped out of bounds," the officer says.

"If there is nothing else, I will be taking Miss Thomas home," Darion tells the officer as he places his hand on my lower back. I am fiercely aware of each finger splayed against my body.

"Miss Thomas here is free to go," the cop says, flustered.

Darion nods and guides me towards the front of the police station. Alvin falls in stride on the other side of me.

"Good job, Alvin. Take the rest of the night off. Tell the crew I will be taking Miss Thomas back to my place, and their surveillance is no longer needed tonight. I will give you a call tomorrow to discuss a new schedule," Darion explains.

Alvin holds the door open for us, and Darion and I step out into the night. I pull the blanket closer to me. Is it colder out here, or is it because the dark seems so much more menacing? Across the street, Christopher is pacing back and forth near a familiar black SUV. When he sees us, Christopher darts across the street, ignoring the honking of a car he just stepped out in front of. When he gets to our side of the street, I'm swept up into his embrace. His woodsy smell is just as encompassing and welcoming as Darion's cologne, and I can't help but feel safe in his arms.

"Jesus, Gems, are you alright?" He asks, his mouth close to my ear.

"Yeah, I'm fine," I lie.

It sounds lame even to my ears. Christopher takes ahold of both of my arms, being careful not to touch my injury, and studies me with a frown. His concern is touching, and I find myself softening towards him. The sound of Alvin moving away from us reminds me that I am in this situation because of the two men surrounding me. I step back, out of his reach, and turn to look at the security staff making his leave.

"Thanks again, Alvin. You saved my life," I call out to him. Alvin turns, nods his head once, and then walks down the street and disappears into the shadows.

"Come, let's get you in the car and warmed up," Christopher says and takes my hand.

I look down at the contact and wonder if I should pull away. Even as I think it, I push the thought away. I kind of like that he has ahold of me. The contact helps me stay in the moment instead of thinking about what happened.

The three of us cross the street. Christopher opens the back door of the SUV for me, and when I slide in, he joins me in the back. Darion gets into the driver's seat and turns the SUV on. The heat immediately flares to life.

"I'm going to take us back to my place. Is that okay, Gemma?" Darion asks, turning around in his seat to look at me.

Our eyes meet in the darkness of the car, and for a moment, I'm lost in his. I should tell him no, that I can get a hotel. I'm certainly not going back to my apartment, at least for tonight. But the thought of being alone is terrifying. Instead of voicing my consent, I simply nod. Darion turns around in his seat and pulls into the street.

"What happened, Gemma?" Christopher asks after a few minutes of silence.

I bite the inside of my cheek, not wanting to talk about it. It was Darion's man who saved me. If it weren't for Alvin, who knows where I would be right now? I sigh. Darion deserves to know what his man did.

"I came home late from work and decided to use the side entrance of my apartment complex when I saw that someone was moving into one of the units and their furniture was taking up most of the space in the lobby. I didn't hear anyone come up behind me, but suddenly, there was a gun to my head," I tell them both softly.

I shiver as I remember the coldness of the barrel against my temple.

"He told me if I screamed, he'd just kill me right there. The second guy started to tie my hands behind my back. They told me to walk alongside the building, and I did. We cut down a smaller alley, and there was an unmarked, white van there waiting for us. Then, Alvin came charging out of nowhere. He knocked the gunman out and struggled with the second guy. Knocked that guy out, too…"

I look out the window and watch as Boston speeds by. Tears well up, but I try to hold them back. Christopher takes my hand again, and I'm startled by the touch. I look over at him, and I find his glowing eyes pinned to my face. He scoots closer to me and wraps an arm around my shoulders.

"I'm so sorry, Gems," he says sincerely. "You'll be safe at our house. We'll keep an eye on you."

"You guys don't have to do this… Maybe I should get out of town for a while?" I say.

In my head, I start creating a list of places that I can try to run to.

"You'll be safer with us," Christopher says firmly. "The house has the best security system money can buy, and we're out of city limits which makes us harder to find. Plus, no one can sneak up on us with the woods around us."

"Why do you think that?" I ask him with a frown.

Even in the darkness, I can see the flash of his white teeth.

"Because, Gems, the woods are a wolf's playground," he answers, his voice gravelly. I shiver.

"We both will be safer at the house for a while," Darion says softly.

I glance over at him. He is facing the road, but I know his attention is elsewhere. His grip on the steering wheel has his knuckles pale, and his jaw is clenched tight.

"Did they come after you again, too?" I ask him, surprised.

"They attempted to plant a bomb in my car," Darion admits. Christopher swears profusely.

"And you didn't tell me?" Christopher asks, shocked. "Darion, what the hell?"

"One of my men saw what was happening before it was installed and took care of the issue. So, with the threat dissolved, there was no need to worry," Darion says with a half shrug.

"Who's doing this? And why?" I ask.

"I *thought* it was one of the guys I just put behind bars," Darion answers slowly. "The men who shot at me, who shot you, wore his gang signs. He's supposed to be one of the top drug lords on the East Coast. But when he was interrogated on Wednesday about the hit on me, he swears up and down that it's not him."

Christopher swears again and tightens his arm around my shoulder.

"Maybe we should leave—" Christopher starts.

"No," Darion interrupts. "I'm not running away when things get hard. We'll lay low for a bit while I have my men figure out who's behind this and take care of the issue."

The car falls silent. For the rest of the ride home, we are all lost in our own thoughts. When we arrive at the estate, I stare at the house. It's huge. I'm more awake than I was when I first arrived here and can now appreciate the stunning aesthetics. It's beautiful.

The moment the car stops, Christopher is out and comes around to open the door for me. I murmur a thank you and let him lead me up the stone stairs and through the front door.

"Have you eaten?" he asks me softly.

When I shake my head, he leads me towards the back of the house. There, a kitchen massive enough for a classy restaurant lights up as we enter. I gape as I look around.

Christopher grins and says, "Wait until you see the rest of the house. You snuck off before getting a tour."

"Yeah, well… I needed to grab some Plan B. We didn't really think about the consequences in the moment, but I sure as hell did the next morning," I grumble.

Christopher's grin vanishes and his eyes widen. "Shit, you're right."

"I know. Besides, I do have a business that needs to be run. I don't know how I'll be able to do that here… but I guess I need to figure that out. Thank goodness, it's Friday," I say, walking further into the kitchen.

Christopher moves towards the refrigerator silently, lost in thought.

"We'll figure something out for you," he assures me a moment later.

I watch as he opens the fridge and begins taking out food. I sit down at the counter and watch him move around, pulling out different ingredients.

"What do you do for a living?" I ask him curiously.

He looks over at me and says, "I own a construction company. We specialize in skyscrapers and corporate buildings, but I like to branch out and tackle smaller projects, too."

I stare at him in surprise. "Oh, so you're not just a hot jock."

Christopher pauses what he's doing to throw back his head and laugh. "Nah, not me. I actually have a head on my shoulders. Winning races is just a hobby."

A head on his shoulders? Huh, who knew? Darion walks into the kitchen and glances over to Christopher, who is now seasoning a few chicken breasts. The incubus walks past him and opens the refrigerator to grab fresh vegetables.

"So how do you two know each other?" I ask, pulling the wool blanket tighter. I need to keep talking. That way I can't think about how close I came to being kidnapped. The two men glance at each other before Christopher speaks:

"We both worked for the government. Different branches, but we ran in the same crowd."

Hm… Vague but maybe their jobs were secret. Non-humans are an essential group in the government. They can do a lot more than normal humans, and in some cases, they are even handier than any piece of technology. I fall silent as I mull this over. It's a great distraction from what occurred, and I find myself slowly relaxing.

"Can I help?" I ask after a few minutes.

"Just relax, Gemma," Darion says softly as he takes the vegetables he has now chopped and sprinkles olive oil over them. I sigh.

"Okay. Well, can someone point to where your nearest bathroom is? I want to freshen up," I ask. Christopher turns his head and nods to the hallway.

"Down the hall, second door to your left," he directs. I leave the men to cook while I disappear.

In the bathroom, I relieve myself and then splash some water on my face. I don't bother to look at myself in the mirror. I know I have a bruise coming along my jawline. The barrel of the gun hit me when Alvin slammed into my attacker. I touch the spot gingerly. A rush of fear and adrenaline shoot through me as I replay that moment again in my head. I brace myself against the sink and squeeze my eyes shut, wishing to forget about the whole night. Instead, the entire moment replays in slow motion. I can see everything. I can smell the stench of my attacker's breath as he leans close to warn me not to scream. I can feel rough callused hands grabbing my arms backwards and together so they can zip tie them together.

I don't realize I'm crying until a tear trickles down my neck. I sniff as I wipe it away. I grab some toilet paper and blow my nose. After splashing water over my face one more time to hide any evidence of tears I leave the bathroom. As I slowly walk back towards the kitchen, I rub at my wrists where the zip ties were. Alvin cut them off immediately after the attackers were subdued. Still, they left a red mark.

As I approach the kitchen, I can hear whispering. I pause and listen.

"—does this leave us?" Darion asks. Someone huffs, I think it's Christopher.

"I don't know, man. I can't think about it right now," Christopher says.

"Well, I have to," Darion growls.

He doesn't seem like the type of person who needs to raise his voice to get what he wants or to get his point across. I make a note to watch some of his court cases online. If I'm going to live under the same roof with these two men, I need to know all about both of them. Especially if one is going to be glued to my hip for the rest of my life.

"Don't push me," Christopher warns.

I lean forward to listen for more, but I can hear my cell phone going off. Pretending I hadn't been eavesdropping on the two of them, I stroll back into the kitchen and pull my phone out of my purse, which is hanging on the back of my chair. Oh shit.

"Hey, Mom," I answer.

I walk away from both men towards the living room and lower my voice.

"Don't you 'hey, Mom' me, Gemma," my mom snaps. "Kidnapped, Gemma, you were almost *kidnapped.* When were you going to tell me?" Her shrieking causes me to pull the phone away from my ear a little.

"How do you even know this? It just happened," I ask her.

I wipe my hand over my face. I'm exhausted, and trying to calm down my mom is going to take time.

"I have an alert every time your name pops up in the news. Your face is plastered all over social media *again.* First getting shot and now almost kidnapped. What is going on? Did you get yourself involved in something you weren't supposed to? How are you? Where are you now?" Mom has hardly taken a breath as she talks.

"Mom, calm down. I'm fine. It's just a misunderstanding. It's being taken care of," I tell her.

"Why won't you tell me where you are? Are you in trouble now?" she asks, panicked.

I can hear Dad in the background trying to talk her down. I roll my eyes.

"I'm at a, um, friend's house," I say.

I haven't told my mom about Christopher or Darion. What can I say? I'm not sure of their role in my life, and I know she'll ask a thousand questions about them that I don't have the answers to yet.

"Well, that sounds suspicious. Aaron and Phillip are in Niagara Falls this weekend. They're your only friends in the city," Mom says warily. "We should have come up with a code word in case of situations like this. Shit, are you being held hostage now? Daniel, we need to call the cops."

I close my eyes and groan. Of course, Aaron would tell my mom where he's going this weekend. That's how close we are with one another. We talk to each other's parents like they are our own.

"I can make other friends, you know," I tell her.

"Gemma, if you don't tell me where you are, so help me God, I'm going to call the cops!" Mom yells.

Before I can respond, my phone is yanked out of my hands. I whirl around to see Christopher pressing it against his ear.

"Mrs. Thomas, I presume?" he says as he flashes me a wide smile. I gape at him in horror. No, no, no! All the questions I'm going to get bombarded with after this call will kill my phone battery. In the kitchen, I can see Darion's smirk.

"My name is Christopher Rogue. Gemma and I met a few weeks ago at the race in Pennsylvania. Yes, I am. First place in my age and overall, in the non-human category." His smile disappears. "Yes, ma'am, a wolf shifter. Is that going to be a prob—" Surprise flickers across his face. "Yes, of course. Thanks for putting your faith in me. Yes, she's staying with me for a bit. I haven't kidnapped her, and you're more than welcome to come visit whenever you wish just to check in on your daughter." He chuckles. "I'll be good to her, I promise. Yes, of course. You, too. Goodnight."

He hangs up the phone and tosses it back to me. I let it soar past me. It lands on the couch, safe and sound. I open my mouth to yell at him but then close it. I'm so furious, but I just don't have strong enough words to express myself properly.

"Don't fret. Your mom knows you're safe and sound. She should be leaving you alone for a bit," he assures me and heads back to the kitchen.

"You shouldn't have taken the phone from me. God! Now she'll ask if we're dating and want to know all the details," I whine and let myself flop onto the couch. "As if this day couldn't get any worse."

Christopher shrugs as he slides the tray of chicken breasts into the preheated oven. "If you tell her we're mated, then there's nothing to question," he says coming back over to me.

Quietly, Darion is pulling aluminum foil out and lining another tray. Christopher flops onto the couch next to me, his expression serious.

"Look, this weekend we'll have time to get to know one another. We can take this slow if you want. You were right earlier. I wasn't thinking when you were here last week, and we had sex. I want to get to know you before kids are even a question."

Behind him in the kitchen, I see Darion stiffen suddenly. He doesn't glance in our direction. Instead, he shoves the tray of vegetables into the oven and leaves the kitchen, and us, alone. I wonder if Christopher knows about what has transpired between the two of us. He must have seen where my attention has wandered to because he looks over his shoulder to see that Darion is no longer with us. He turns back to me.

"We'll all get to know each other this weekend. Afterwards, we'll just see where the wind takes us."

I study him for a moment. There is something he's not saying. I have a good guess about what it might be.

"You know about the kiss," I say softly. Christopher nods as his jaw ticks. He's upset by this. "I didn't go behind your back or anything. It just happened…" I tell him, though why I'm trying to assuage the situation, I'm not sure. I haven't done anything wrong.

"I know, Darion told me everything," Christopher says. This is a relief. "I'm not upset with you… or him, I guess. Don't worry about him right now. Let's just figure us out and go from there."

What is he saying? We'll *all* get to know each other this weekend? We shouldn't worry about him *right now?* As in, maybe in the future I'll have to? I wonder if I should question this. Immediately, I reject the idea. I don't want any more drama in my world. I shake off my curiosity and let the conversation of Darion drop.

"Can I ask you something?" I say to him, changing the subject. He nods. "You were going to ask my mom if it's a problem you're a non-human. Why would you think she would have a problem with that?"

Christopher turns away from me to look around the room. His long sigh signals his discomfort. When he looks back at me, he answers, "Humans and non-human just don't trust each other. I know we walk amongst each other like everything is all alright, but there are still prejudices out there. Humans fear non-humans and are willing to condemn us before getting to know any of our kind. I just assumed your mom, being from an older generation, would have stronger prejudices than most."

I am silent as I process this information. He is right of course. There are some humans that don't trust non-humans. But there will always be groups of people that don't like others that are different from them. Not everyone holds the same prejudices. The fact that Christopher immediately assumed that my mother would have a problem with him tells me that this has been a big issue for him in the past. I wonder if he'll share his story with me.

"Well, my mom has a big heart. She wouldn't care if you had three eyes and tentacles, as long as you're a good person," I tell him after a moment. "And the same goes with me. Though, I will admit when you were in your wolf form when I woke up here the first day, I was a little scared. Not that you were some evil creature, but wolves are so much *bigger* in person than what they appear like on television."

Christopher throws his head back and laughs. "Yeah, I could see how nervous you were. I'm glad you didn't run out of the room screaming, though."

"The thought crossed my mind," I admit, and he laughs again.

When he settles down, he says seriously, "You never have to be afraid of me, Gemma. My teeth can crush bone, and my claws can tear through muscle, but none of those things are ever something you need to worry about. Only my enemies will learn how dangerous a wolf can be."

He takes my hand and kisses the back of it. I look up into his emerald-green eyes, and my heart stutters at the sincerity I see there. Suddenly, I'm very aware how close he is sitting to me. Heat warms my cheeks and shakes off the shock that flooded my system. The oven dings, letting us know dinner is ready, disrupting the moment.

"Come on, let's get you something to eat," he murmurs.

***

Dinner is exactly what I needed. I am feeling much better as I climb into the same bed that I slept in a week ago. Christopher has graciously allowed me to borrow one of his shirts for the night. Tomorrow, I'll have to either go back to my apartment for more clothes or go shopping. I'll worry about that in the morning, though.

The lights are still on in the room, and my phone is playing music softly on the nightstand. Usually, complete darkness and silence is what I need in order to fall asleep. But when I try turning off the lights, the night's events overwhelm me, feeling even more real than when they bombarded me in the bathroom earlier.

So, lights on and music playing it is.

I pull the covers over me and stare up at the high ceiling. My body feels tired, and I know after a long week my mind should feel exhausted. Before the incident, I was ready to collapse into my bed. But right now, my mind is racing. I fear closing my eyes and remembering the barrel pressed against my head. The sound of zip ties getting tighter overshadows the music. My hands shake as I grip the comforter, and my heart starts to flutter. I glance towards the door wondering if I would feel better if I locked it.

Just as I sit up to do that, there is a knock at the door. A moment later, it opens, and Christopher strolls into the room. He's wearing just a pair of boxers. His abs ripple while he walks over to the bed, and his damp hair glistens in the light. He looks like a god. I can't help but stare as he approaches me.

He doesn't stop his progression, even when he gets to the bed. He climbs in without asking and crawls over to me.

"What do you think you're doing?" I ask.

I should be outraged or upset. Didn't he say let's take it slow? I'm not upset, though. In fact, I immediately feel safer with him here.

"I almost lost you today, Gemma. It scared the shit out of me when we got the call. I can't shake this fear that I could lose you again if I'm not careful. Let me hold you tonight." His expression is grave. "I haven't really explained to you how important a mate is to a shifter, but trust me when I say you're more important than my own life."

How can I tell him to leave when he says stuff like that?

"Fine, but I have to warn you about something," I tell him. He raises his brow, waiting for the threat. "I'm a cuddler. I can't help it. If you shove me off, I'll just come back for seconds, thirds, and fourths. So brace yourself."

Christopher's laugh shakes the bed. "I think I can handle a little cuddling."

I scoot in further under the covers and closer to him. I breathe in his woodsy smell, and I can feel desire begin to unfurl within me. Maybe this isn't such a good idea. I try to push away the feeling and close my eyes as I nestle my head against Christopher's chest.

I must have been more tired than I thought because suddenly I'm jostled awake. I blink, trying to figure out where I am. It takes me a moment to realize that someone turned off the lights and the music. Too tired to be annoyed or frightened, I close my eyes again. I take a deep breath and inhale the smell of a pine wood forest. I hum in pleasure and snuggle closer to the warm body the scent clings to.

"What are you doing?" Christopher hisses into the dark. At the same time, I feel a dip in the mattress on the other side of me.

"I need this… to be close to her. Especially after what happened," a deep, familiar voice whispers back. Darion? I must be dreaming. "I won't touch her."

"Fine," Christopher hisses back.

I feel his arm drape over me as I slip back to sleep.

Chapter Eleven

Darion

I awake feeling more at peace than I ever have in the past. As I slowly gain consciousness, I realize I am not the first to rise. My erection is pressing against Gemma's thigh. Sometime in the middle of the night, she threw a leg over me. The warmth of her core through her thin panties presses against my hip. They are slightly damp. The smell of her arousal hits me as I come completely awake.

I stare down at her. As I do, something unfurls in my chest. It is warm and followed by this overwhelming sense of utter contentment. Gemma is lying on her stomach and has one arm thrown over Christopher. Her mass of curls covers half of her face, but from what I can see a small smile splays across her face. Whatever she is dreaming of, it is pleasant.

It's strange to awake in bed with others. Usually, after sex I force everyone to leave, or I myself leave to sleep alone. But last night the sense of dread and loneliness swamped me until I could hardly breathe. Gemma's encounter played in my head in the dark until my fear for her safety overrode common decency. When I slipped into her room, I wasn't surprised to see

Christopher already there. I knew his wolf would get protective, possessive over his mate. When he didn't shift and attack me as I ventured further into the room, I grew confident his wolf doesn't mind me around his mate as much as we both worry.

This morning, the three of us are nearly piled on top of one another, and I find myself more comfortable than I ever thought possible.

Gemma stirs as she slowly awakens. I shudder under the intensity of her arousal as it grows the more she wakes up. Another strange phenomenon… Have I ever been so drawn to a woman's, or man's, arousal? Gemma's has a sweeter edge to hers. It's intoxicating. My mouth waters as I wonder what she tastes like.

My erection begins to pulse as more blood rushes in its direction.

Gemma's hand twitches on Christopher's chest. Her hips shift, and her core gently grinds, unknowingly, against my hip as she unconsciously tries to alleviate her physical discomfort. Her panties become damper, and I can feel them begin to soak the rim of my boxer briefs. I close my eyes and wonder how I ended up in this sweet hell. The ache to lean over to kiss her awake, roll her over, and ease my dick into her body causes my erection to grow more prominent.

I don't realize Christopher is awake until he shifts so he's turning to face Gemma. I glance over at him to find him gazing lovingly down at his mate. It is strange to see a softer side of my friend. Cocky pro-athlete, a hard-ass boss, and easily distracted pussy-chaser is the typical façade I've been privy to over these past few years. I wonder if Christopher is aware of how at ease he is around his mate.

Gemma hums, content, as Christopher strokes her hair. She turns her head towards him, and he takes advantage of her semi-unconscious state to lean down and kiss her. I fight back the black inky tentacles of jealousy that threaten to lash out at my friend. Gemma is his mate. Not mine.

"Did you have a nice dream?" Christopher murmurs to Gemma. There is a pause and Christopher chuckles. She must have rolled her eyes or made a face. "Don't try to hide it from me…from *us*." He shoots me a quick look before turning his attention back to Gemma. "I can smell how hot and bothered you are. Fuck, that's the best smell to wake up to ever. Tell me something. Was there much of this in your dream?"

Christopher leans forward again and takes Gemma's mouth with his. Her groan is loud, and she tries to bring her legs together to give herself some relief. But my thigh is in her way. Fuck. I go to cup myself. My erection is almost painful. She stiffens.

"Wait, *us?*" she repeats, her voice raspy from sleep. She starts to pull away from Christopher, but he chuckles.

"Oh no, darling. I want to know what you were dreaming about. If it wasn't about kissing, maybe it went a little something like this…" Christopher says playfully as he pulls away from her lips to reach down and grab her ass.

That perfect ass that peeks out from underneath the long shirt. Her thong that she has worn to sleep is no true barrier to the treasure that is just out of sight. Gemma's husky giggle is magical.

She pushes herself up onto her forearms and leans forward to kiss him again. His hand moves from her ass to hold the back of her head. Christopher pulls away, sits up and pulls her entire body on top of him. The moment her leg is removed from my thigh I feel oddly bereft. She straddles him now, laughing softly.

"Good god, you look like an angel in the morning," Christopher growls, his eyes beginning to glow as his wolf surfaces.

She leans forward and takes his mouth again, and his hands come up to her hips to hold her in place. Her hips grind against his, and through their kiss, Christopher moans. She breaks the kiss and looks over at me. Our eyes meet, and I see the curiosity in her eyes. It doesn't last long though, and those beautiful eyes darken with desire. Her gaze sweeps down my body, most likely taking in the scar-like runes that cover my torso. Gemma's gaze drifts further and notices my erection. Her eyes widen slightly, and she meets my gaze again. Her surprise disappears as her carnal hunger takes over again.

"Don't look at me like that," I warn her, my voice thick with desire.

Christopher glances over at me with an unreadable look. Then he turns, leans over with Gemma still on his lap to the nightstand. He opens the drawer and pulls out a condom.

"Take your top off, Gemma," Christopher commands.

Gemma pulls her eyes away from mine and does what she is told. She is left exposed, all except for what her thong covers. Her breasts greet us, perky and beautiful. Both Christopher and I suck in a sharp breath at the sight of them. Gemma chuckles at our response. Her breasts jiggle as she does. But her amusement fades as she looks between Christopher and I again. Her face twists with confusion.

"It's alright, Gems," Christopher growls through gritted teeth. "If you're okay with Darion being here, then… so am I."

Gemma studies his expression, probably wondering what he's thinking before again looking at me.

"It's up to you, Gemma," I tell her.

God, please be okay with this, I implore through my eyes. Even if I don't participate, at least I can feed off of the two of them. With her proximity, I can at least relieve myself… It's been a week since I had a chance to do so, and my body is aching for a chance to cum.

She looks back at Christopher and says, "Okay."

I let out a sharp relieved breath, and Christopher grins. She leans down and kisses him again. He cups her breasts and thumbs her nipples. I pull out my dick and begin to stroke it, wishing my hands were where Christopher's are. Gemma pulls her mouth away and pushes her breasts in front of Christopher's face. His mouth latches on to one of her nipples, and she moans in response. His hand comes between her legs and slips past the thong.

Gemma's gasp causes me to still. I grip my erection tightly and breathe through the urge to finish quickly. I am close already. I need this so badly that my body is not acting like a disciplined incubus but that of a teenager. No,

I'm going to last as long as these two.

"Jesus, Gems. So fucking wet," Christopher growls as he let goes of her nipple. He glances over to me and then up to her face. "Do you want to let Darion know how hot and ready you are?"

"This is insanity," she says softly to both of us, hesitating. "I've never… This is so new to me."

"It's okay if you're not open to this. Darion can just watch," Christopher assures her quickly.

"I-I want to as long as it doesn't mess things up between the two of you," she says slowly.

Christopher looks over at me, and we make a promise that whatever happens, we won't take it out on Gemma. It's a wordless promise, but the understanding between us is clear.

"We're good, Gems," Christopher tells her.

Gemma turns her head to look at me. She's excited. I can see how her chest rises and falls and how dark her eyes have turned. Fuck, I'm just as excited. She climbs off Christopher and, on her knees, crawls over to me. Curiously, excitedly. I grin. It spreads wide across my face. I cup her face and lean down to kiss her.

The way her soft lips mold to mine, the way her body arches forward so her breasts press against my chest, her nipples hard and erect… It causes my body to shudder with desire. A fire is ignited in me, and Gemma is the fuel, causing it to burn hot and fast. With one hand, my fingers reach up and take a handful of those wild curls. The other hand slides down her side and then dips into the front of her thong. My fingertips brush against her soft bud, and her achy gasp causes my erection to jerk hard.

My fingers slide through her slick folds, and I push two fingers into her core. Gemma's surprised and pleased cry is muffled as I slide my tongue into her mouth. She is wet, dripping wet. Her arousal drips into my palm easily. I curl my fingers that are inside of her in a "come hither" motion. Her hands grip my shoulder while her hips thrust forward. Her moan is lost in our kiss.

A haze falls over my senses, and I'm only aware of Gemma's pleasure. The spike of sexual energy in the air is a drug that I breathe in and feast on. It tastes like nothing I've ever indulged in before. I want more. I *need* more. I use my thumb to circle her swollen clit. She pulls away from our kiss to lean her head back. Her eyes are closed as she moves against my hand wanting more.

"Darion…" My name is a whisper as it slips past her lips.

Precum beads at the top of my erection. As if sensing it, Gemma reaches out with one hand, her eyes still closed, and takes a hold of my dick. Her warm hand causes my hips to jerk into her. She strokes me with slow, unhurried movements. It is torture. I am ready to cum now. The only thing holding me back is sheer willpower. I've never had to fight so hard in my life to keep from cumming. I hate it. I love it. I love how Gemma is pushing my limits. I've never been so close to losing it like this, and I like this new side of me.

Christopher comes up behind her, on his knees, and kisses the side of her neck. His arms come around from behind her, and he grasps her breasts, kneading them. His thumbs tease her nipples. I lean forward and take her mouth again, needing to taste her. Her body shudders, and I can feel her inner walls beginning to clench down on my fingers. I do not relent my attack on her body. Instead, I slide a third finger into her. Christopher nips at her skin, whispering into her ear. He scoots closer, pressing his body against her from behind. She's sandwiched between us, and we both feel it as her orgasm ripples through her.

She pulls her lips away from mine to cry out as her body shakes. Her hand stills around me but grips me tight as she arches her hips towards me while throwing her head back against Christopher. She is glorious. Her mouth is open, her eyes squeezed shut… The sexual energy in the room explodes to a new level, and I'm soaking it all in through every pore of my body. I almost cum as I savor it all. But again, I resist.

I slip my fingers out from between her legs, and Christopher pulls her away from me.

"We're not done with you yet, Gems," he tells her and pushes her front forward. She gasps in surprise as she catches herself on her hands on the mattress. Her butt is nestled at Christopher's hips, and my dick is less than an inch away from her face. Christopher slaps her ass, once, twice, and a third time.

"God, this ass is fantastic," he growls. He reaches over, grabs the condom package, and uses his teeth to rip it open. He slides the condom onto his dick then centers himself behind her. "Take Darion in your mouth, Gems."

Gemma looks up to meet my gaze. Hers is still slightly glazed over from her release. She smiles tentatively up at me before leaning forward. When she takes me into her mouth, I swear I have ascended to the heavens. She takes me slowly. Her tongue swirls around the tip of my cock before taking me deeper. My hips jerk forward on their own accord.

As Christopher eases into her, she is pushed forward a little, suddenly taking me further. Her moan vibrates against my dick, and I pant, trying to keep from embarrassing myself. Christopher slaps Gemma's ass again before beginning to move.

Christopher and I have shared women before. There is a technique involved, and after a few thrusts, we find our rhythm. As one pushes in, the other pulls out. She uses her tongue to play with me and reaches up to massage my balls. Behind her Christopher reaches around her waist and begins to play with her clit.

"God, you're dripping down my cock, Gems." Christopher rasps, staring down at the sight.

"You are a fucking naughty girl, Gemma," I growl. "I knew you were naughty…"

Christopher picks up the pace. I pick up mine, too, knowing that I won't be able to hold out for much longer. It only takes a few more thrusts before I can no longer hold back my release.

"Gemma, I'm going to cum," I warn her through gritted teeth.

She doesn't let go, and I take that as confirmation to find relief in her mouth. I let loose, and the force of my orgasm causes my whole body to tremble violently. Gemma holds me with her mouth and swallows everything that I give her. Just as I start to come down from my high, Gemma pulls away with a cry of pleasure and her body convulses.

"Oh, thank Jesus," Christopher grunts and stills as his own orgasm chases hers. When his orgasm fades, he pulls out of Gemma, who collapses on the bed. I collapse on the other side of her, and I hear when Christopher lies down, too. We're all panting and twitching as we bathe in the afterglow of sex.

"As good as whatever you were dreaming about, Gems?" Christopher asks.

I can hear his grin as I stare up at the ceiling, still bathing in my own bliss. Gemma's laughter makes me smile.

"It's exactly what I dreamt about."

Chapter Twelve

Gemma

Holy three way... My body is more relaxed than I have ever been. My bones have turned to mush, and my brain has followed suit. I drifted off back to sleep, and during that time, both guys slipped away. When I wake again, I'm by myself. This time I'm not waking to the overpowering smell of two incredibly attractive men. Though their scent lingers, it's not nearly as strong as before.

I sit up and wonder about what had occurred this morning. Was that real? I woke so horny that I was up for whatever they wanted to do, as long as they were willing to do me. My body shudders at the memories of where Darion's and Christopher's hands and mouth have traveled.

Darion and Christopher... My happiness begins to fade as reality starts to intrude on my mood. What the hell was I thinking? I've gone from regretting one hook up, to having multiple hook ups with the same guy, to having sex with his friend? What am I doing? My smile disappears as I wonder what the repercussions of this morning's event will be. Do they both think I'm easy now? A quick lay? *Am* I an easy lay?

I know who will tell me. When Aaron comes back home on Tuesday, I'll ask his advice on all of this. Not that I'll necessarily take it. I haven't taken the time to look into online support groups for humans who have mated with shifters. Not yet. This week has been crazy in the office, and honestly, I just wasn't ready to handle what being a mate means. But maybe now I should do some research. Did Christopher expect me to want to get with all his friends? Is this *typical* practice in a shifter world?

After using the shower attached to the room, I dress in my work clothes from the previous day. Once ready to face both men, I head down the stairs and wander around until I can find the kitchen. Christopher has his back towards the counter, leaning against it. His eyes are plastered to his phone's screen. He is wearing a snug black tee-shirt and jeans and looks every bit a model. He looks up as I enter and worry ripples across his face before he covers it with a smile.

"Hey, good morning again. How are you feeling?" he asks.

I stop a few feet from him, unsure how to respond to his question. He seems able to read my mood because he pushes off the counter, shoves his phone into his pocket and walks towards me. Christopher stops just in front of me and places his hands on my shoulders.

"Gemma, talk to me. Are you upset about what happened?" he asks with a frown.

His dark brows pull together with concern. I shake my head slowly as I think about his question.

"No... I'm not upset," I tell him after a moment. "I'm just..." I flounder for the right word to use. "*Confused.*"

Christopher nods his understanding. "I can understand that. What confuses you the most about it? Us? Us with Darion? Or that you enjoyed yourself?"

"All of the above," I admit. I can feel heat grow in my cheeks. "I've never done anything like that before. In fact, before you, I never just hooked up with someone. I'm not acting like myself at all, but honestly, I don't hate it… I just don't understand it, and that's what is scaring me a little. I'm not a slut or anything."

Christopher shakes his head hard. "I would never dream of calling you a slut. You enjoyed sex with two people you're attracted to and who are attracted to you. We're all consenting adults."

"I never dreamed that sex could be this good," I tell him, my cheeks burning hotter. "In my previous relationships, I thought sex was just a chore. I certainly didn't enjoy it, and it didn't last long."

Christopher's eyes brows flew upwards, and his eyes widened in surprise. "They never made sure you came?"

Finally, I have to look away from him. This is not a conversation I thought I would ever have with anyone else besides Aaron. Embarrassment rushes through me, and I have to take a deep breath before I can speak again. I don't meet his eyes.

"No. I usually just took care of myself afterwards. So, what we have… It's great," I tell him honestly. I look up into his face and find him smiling. "But we talked about going slow, and then suddenly there is a third person in this mix … That isn't slow. And yeah, I agreed to it, but now I feel like I'm being torn apart and being pulled in two different directions. Is this… normal? I thought that shifters didn't share their mates. Am I wrong? Do you guys share a—"

"No, we don't share. *Ever*," Christopher interrupts firmly, his smile fading. "Not in the wolf world at least. Wolves are possessive creatures by nature. Honestly, I'm as surprised as you are that this morning happened. I never thought my wolf would accept Darion touching you. Darion and I have shared women before, but those women meant nothing to us. You're different, Gemma. I don't know what you're doing to me, or to Darion, but trust me when I say none of this is normal."

He sighs and runs his fingers through his dark hair.

"Are you up for a walk outside? It's a nice morning, and I can let you meet my wolf," he offers.

"That sounds nice. Let me grab a cup of coffee first," I tell him and move away to make it. As I turn on the coffee pot, Darion strolls into the room with clothes in his hands. He places them on the counter and smiles at me.

"I found some clean clothes that look like they will fit you. There are some shoes by the front door," he says. I take in his business attire and how it clings to his body perfectly.

"Thank you," I say as I wonder where he would have gotten clothes that fit.

It only takes me a moment to figure out that the clothes are from his past sexual relationships. I try not to let the thought sour my mood.

Darion nods and looks at Christopher. "Tate said he will be in this evening."

"Tate? Who's that?" I ask curiously as Christopher nods slowly, a frown forming.

"A friend," Darion explains. "The three of us have been good friends for as long as I can remember. He's been out of the country for a few months, but he's home on an extended leave of absence."

"Oh, should I stay somewhere else so you guys can catch up?" I ask as I pour myself some coffee.

"Of course not, you'll stay here with us," Christopher says quickly. He comes over to stand near me and continues, "After this weekend, we need to discuss our future living situation, though."

My cup of coffee pauses halfway to my lips. *Our future living situation...* Is this a conversation we need to have now? Today? This month? This year? I try not to panic. I force the warm drink to my lips and take a sip of coffee.

"*What?*" Darion asks sharply.

I look over to where he is standing, and he's practically fuming.

"What?" Christopher asks, clearly confused by Darion's outburst.

With my cup in tow, I walk over to the clothes and grab them.

As I walk down the hallway towards the bathroom, I hear Darion ask in a mocking tone,

"A bit soon to be moving in together, don't you think?"

"What do you expect? It's not like anything is going to change. Gemma and I are mates…"

I don't stick around and listen. In the powder room, I quickly change into the jeans and shirt that Darion provided. They fit perfectly. In fact, I check the tag in the jeans to be sure; these are even my favorite brand. Well, finders keepers. I leave the powder room and come back out to find Darion and Christopher glaring at each other.

"They fit perfectly. Thanks, Darion," I tell him, pretending to ignore the stare off. "I'm going to put my other clothes upstairs, and I'll be ready to go for a walk, Christopher."

Without waiting for a response, I hurry upstairs. By the time I am walking back down the stairs, Christopher is waiting for me by the front door. He's scowling and pacing back and forth. When he hears me, he stops and watches me approach him. He opens the front door without a word, and I step out into the cool air. It's almost October now, and the colors in the trees are bright and lively as they die.

Christopher walks silently next to me as we head down the stairs. He takes the lead and walks us toward the tree line. I slow as I realize there is no trail in sight. Thoughts of being jumped in the shadows of the trees cause my heartrate to spike. I never used to be scared of the dark or being alone in the woods, but after almost being kidnapped, it appears I have a little bit of trauma left over.

Christopher notices my hesitation, and he stops to face me.

"Hey, don't worry about anything, Gems. I promise, I'm not going to hurt you," he says, his expression grave. I shake my head.

"I'm not scared of you," I assure him. I glance around us and say softly, "I think I'm just a little jumpy being in the dark after what happened."

Christopher visibly relaxes. He reaches out to take my hand, and I let him. "I can keep you safe. My sense of hearing and smell are better than yours are. I'll be able to sense anyone approaching us, no matter how quiet they are."

Taking a deep breath, I decide to trust him. I squeeze his hand to let him know I'm ready, and he pulls me into the woods. We walk together for a while silently. I can tell by the clenching and unclenching of his jaw that something is bothering him. Is he worried about us, or does this have something to do with Darion? Or is it work related? We don't walk far. When I turn around, I can still catch a glimpse of the house. When I look back at Christopher, he is disrobing in front of me.

"Oh!" I start.

"I don't want to shred my clothes or embarrass my majestic wolf by having him trip over the pants legs," Christopher says, chuckling.

Once he is completely naked, I take in all of Christopher. I don't realize that I am smiling until Christopher crosses his arms over his chest, bringing my attention to his face. I try to hide my enjoyment of seeing him naked, but I can't. I grin, and he mimics the expression.

"I want to say I'm sorry, but… I can't help that I like what I see," I tease him as I take his clothes from him. Christopher laughs.

"I'm flattered," he says. His smile fades, and he becomes serious. "Are you ready?"

"I'm not scared of you, or your wolf Christopher," I assure him. Scared no, excited? Yes.

Christopher nods and takes a deep breath. Just like the first time I saw him change the movement is fluid. His human form ripples and shifts. There are no jerky movements, cracking of bones, or grunts of agony. One moment he's human, the next a large wolf is staring back at me with gold eyes. His fur is almost black, but I can see spots of brown that match the hair on his head when he's human.

The breath exhales from me sharply as I stare at Christopher. I'm frozen but not in fear, just uncertainty. The wolf takes a cautious step forward, and I hold my breath, wondering what he is about to do. He takes one more, then another. Finally, he comes to stand directly in front of me. Slowly, I kneel so that we are eye to eye.

As I was taught how to act around a new dog, I raise my hand, palm facing up unhurriedly. Christopher's gaze never leaves my face as my hand sinks into his fur. Oh! It's coarser than I thought it would be. His fur is thicker and softer as I dig my fingers into it. I stroke his neck and scratch behind his ears, which elicits a rough moan from the wolf. I giggle as the tension leaves my body.

"Alright, this is awesome, Christopher," I tell him.

Chapter Thirteen

Christopher

My wolf loves his mate. His love radiates outwards, and it's overwhelming. Looking through his eyes, I can see him take in every detail about her, memorizing everything. He loves her smell, the sound of her laughter, and the look of surprise whenever he startles her. The way her hands run through my fur elicits such a burst of pleasure that I find myself almost drunk on happiness.

We walk for twenty minutes together. She eyes me with wonder, and my wolf preens under her gaze. She talks to me a little, but mostly it is a quiet walk. I see her occasionally eyeing the direction of the house, as if she's worried that we may move too far out of sight. My wolf whines when he sees this. He knows she is scared. Hell, I don't blame her. After what she's been through, being shot at, finding out your one-night stand is your mate, then almost being kidnapped... I'd be holding on to every shred of sanity I had left if I were her.

Finally, I shift back, knowing we need to talk. Gemma hands me my clothes, and I slip them on.

"So tell me something," Gemma starts.

"Anything," I tell her and that's the truth.

If we are going to make this work, there can't be any secrets between us.

"In the wild, wolves run in packs. From what little I know about shifters... I thought you guys stuck together like packs too. Are you part of a, um, pack of wolf shifters?" she asks tentatively. Before I can answer, she adds, "If I'm being rude or ignorant let me know. I don't know a lot of shifters, so I'm not sure what is considered PC..."

I'm struck by her willingness to learn about me and my world with an open mind. A lot of people are the exact opposite of Gemma. My heart swells.

"I'll correct you if something isn't right," I assure her. "This is your world now, too, so it's best to be informed about me, about shifters, heck about all non-humans now. Better to be educated with facts so you can face the prejudices of others head on."

She looks up at me confused, so I continue, "You know how people felt about interracial marriage?"

Gemma makes a face as she nods.

"It's even worse when it comes to a human and non-human union. A lot of people consider it bestiality."

"What? Really?" she squeaks in surprise. I wonder if this information will make her more reluctant to accept what is between us.

I nod. "Yes, but, as you know, being mated isn't something people can ignore. So those in inter-species marriages or unions find themselves facing a lot more issues than if they had just stayed within their species."

Gemma says nothing as she mulls over this information. I give her a few minutes before I circle back to her original question.

"As to if shifters run in packs, yes. Though they are called different things for different species. Flocks, herds, pods, whatever. Shifters tend to stick together because it's safer for us and is how nature intended for us to live. It's abnormal to find shifters who aren't part of a group. You can spot those shifters out because their last name doesn't match the pack's name. Shifters that go on their own are given last names that single them out from the rest," I explain with a frown.

Again, Gemma says nothing. She simply nods and stares ahead. I try to read her expression, but I can't. There is a faint bruise along her jawline that I assume she got during the attempted kidnapping. I frown as my stomach twists in guilt. This week I tried to give Gemma a little space so she could think about things. Look what good that did. I should have continued to hound and stalk her. Then maybe I could have been there when she needed me.

"Your last name is Rogue," Gemma says, piecing together the information I have given her. "So, does that mean you don't have a pack? Why? Wait... You're in construction, right? Are you the 'Rogue' in Rogue Enterprises?!"

I laugh at her excitement as she guesses who exactly I am.

"Yeah, that's me," I confirm with a half-smile.

Rogue Enterprises is stamped all over the buildings downtown. My company has the monopoly in the area when it comes to office complexes and skyscrapers. It took hard work to get to where I am today, but it was worth it in the end.

"Wow..." Gemma whispers, impressed. "Darion's not the only one who makes the big bucks in the house I see."

"Naw, I pull my own weight around here," I tease.

"Huh," Gemma says with a thoughtful nod. "Okay, back to my original question: Why aren't you part of a pack?"

"I used to be part of one, a long time ago," I tell her but pause.

It has been a long time since I have told anyone this. A long time since I have had to face the consequences. I take a deep breath and push forward. "I used to be part of a pack. Hell, it's been more than thirteen years ago, now. At the time I was seventeen years old, and I was one of the contenders to take over as Alpha. The Alpha at the time was getting sick; it was only a matter of months before I and another wolf shifter, Garrett Steelepointe, would have to compete to take over his position.

"But around that same time, I met a girl. A human, Alisson McFreely. She lived in the neighboring county. At the time I was in love, but my pack didn't want to bring in any humans, and because she wasn't my mate, I couldn't push the issue. Then our Alpha died one night. Pack law comes to a halt for three days after an Alpha dies, so we can lay him to rest and pay our proper respects before the fight for the position occurs."

I pause, remembering Alisson clearly. Her lovely blonde hair and clear blue eyes floored me. She was my first love.

"During those three days, Alisson and I spoke about running off together. Her parents were against our union completely, so we'd have to elope and live somewhere that was far enough that they couldn't come and drag her back home. We swore to each other that we'd be together forever. I just needed to ditch my pack, and she needed to ditch her family. So, when the third day after the funeral came around, Garrett and I were put into a ring and were told to fight."

I pause, stopping in my tracks as I think about that night. Garrett was my equal in size and strength. But he didn't have love to overshadow his thoughts. His mind wasn't elsewhere… Gemma stops, too, and turns to face me, her mouth turned downward.

"I didn't even put up a fight. I surrendered the position of Alpha, the coveted role in the pack, to Garrett. I shamed my family and received scorn from the rest of the pack. I didn't care though because I was going to run off with Alisson. Only… turns out that Alisson had been receiving payment from Garrett's parents. She was just *pretending* to love me. She made all those promises up just so I would be too busy with her to worry about taking over the pack. Even her parents had been in on it."

My hands curl into fists as my anger spikes. It's an old wound and picking at it proves that I'm not yet over the betrayal.

"Did Garrett kick you out of the pack or something after that?" Gemma asks when I don't continue with my story. I shake my head.

"No... I left. I was pissed at what Garrett had done, and I knew it wouldn't matter if I brought up what he did to the wolf council. I didn't fight, and it doesn't matter why I didn't. So I left. I struggled for a while until I got into the construction world after a lot of trial and error when it comes to careers and jobs. Turns out I can't stick to one thing very long. I got involved with a small branch of the government, and that's where I found some discipline that helped shaped who I am today."

The surge of anger that courses through me makes it hard to stand still. So I start walking again, and Gemma follows.

"Could you... I don't know, go back and try to take back the title of Alpha? Like challenge him or something?" she asks me.

I shake my head. "I don't want that."

"Why not?" she asks.

"I'm not fit to be an Alpha for a pack. You can't travel, you don't have time for hobbies which would mean no more racing, and really it's a lot of politics, which bores me," I explain. As I tell her this, I feel a weight lifting off my shoulders. I have never really thought about it like this before. I grin and my pace slows down. "I'm actually really happy right now."

Gemma raises an incredulous brow at me, and I laugh. "Yeah, there are some things I would change, but who wouldn't if they had that ability?"

Gemma frowns and looks away from me as her brows come together. Confused about her reaction, I replay what I said, and it hits me how she might have taken that. I grab her hand, pull her to a stop, and turn her around.

"I wouldn't change meeting you, Gemma. Meeting your mate is like receiving a personalized gift from our creator. How could I be upset with that? Yeah, it took me by surprise because I didn't think I was ready at the time to settle down, but my attitude about this has shifted. Honestly, meeting you has been one of only a few good surprises in my life," I tell her sincerely.

She nods, but I can tell she's not one hundred percent certain.

"So… Do you think Alisson is the real reason you're wary of humans? Why you were so against me being a human?" she asks me after a moment.

I think over her question. Is Alisson the real reason I was upset with my wolf when he chose a human as his mate? Does the betrayal run that deep in me that I was willing to attempt to throw away a perfect pairing because of how horribly it hurt me in the past?

"Most likely," I admit to both myself and her quietly. I haven't thought too much about it before.

Gemma nods slowly. There is a short pause between us before she asks, "You and Darion are obviously close. Do you consider him a… a pack mate? Pack? A pack person?"

I chuckle as she fumbles through the terminology.

"Yeah, Darion and Tate are probably the closest thing I have to a pack," I confirm.

"So close that you don't mind sharing…" she asks with confusion. I sigh.

"Gemma, if I had an answer to why I'm so comfortable with you and Darion together, I'd tell you. But my wolf isn't attacking Darion so…" I shrug.

"You keep saying your wolf, but what about you? How do you feel?" She pushes.

I huff and say, "Hell, I don't know. While it may seem odd because I've never heard of anything like this before when it comes to mates, that doesn't mean it's wrong… He's like a brother to me, and I trust him with my life, and I trust him with yours. So as long as you're okay with this, I am, too. Do *you* like Darion?"

Gemma clams up quickly, her mouth pursing. Her shoulders stiffen defensively, and she looks away from me.

"Hey, Gems, you can tell me," I say, stepping in front of her.

She gives me a guilty look then sighs, "I guess I do a little. I don't really know anything about him or you, though, except what you've shared right now so it's hard to say if I like either of you when I don't *know* you. And really, I don't know if I want to even consider liking Darion when I don't even know how he feels about this, too. This morning could just have been a one-time thing for him. He is, after all, an incubus."

I nod in understanding. "Time will help you get to know us and us you. But you'll find that our relationship, between you and me, may blossom faster than with him and that's because of the mating bond between us. You're my other half, and things will just kind of click into place for us. As for your relationship with Darion, you should talk to him to see how he feels. If he's not serious about you, then he's out of this. We don't have an open relationship, got it? Darion doesn't count because… Well, I don't know, I guess, because he's pack, but no one else."

Her honey-colored eyes stare up at me, studying my face. I want to ask what she's thinking, but I hold my tongue. This is a lot of information dumped on her, so I wait, hoping she's not feeling overwhelmed. Slowly a smile spreads across her face.

"Alright, deal," she says.

"Good, now it's time for me to learn a little about you," I tell her.

I take her hand, and we start walking again. I bombard her with questions. First, I start with her family and find out she's an only child.

"My parents tried for more kids, but after the fifth miscarriage they gave up. I like being the only child though," she tells me.

According to Gemma, she and her family traveled during summer and winter breaks. She is an avid skier, enjoys hiking and loves exploring historical sights. She loves the outdoors as I do. My wolf loves this. When I ask her about her education, she becomes flustered.

"It took me five years to finish a four-year degree," she says embarrassed. "Not because I wasn't smart. I had great grades; I just didn't know what I wanted to do. It was hard for me to commit to any one thing. Finally, I settled on communications with a minor in graphic design. I figured that I could freelance once I'm out of school so I can work from wherever I fancied. But it was hard to find a job when I didn't know exactly what I wanted to do, so I bounced around jobs for a bit until I found my footing in graphic design. Hell, I worked with a crime scene clean-up crew for a bit because I really got into serial killers and murders."

"Ah, you're one of *those* women who like listening to murder podcasts," I tease.

Gemma laughs as she nods. "I'm exactly one of those girls. The unsolved ones are the best. They're terrifying," she admits, but her amusement fades. "I could have been an unsolved case last night. I guess they're not fun when you're the victim."

The thought causes my blood to turn cold. I grip her hand tighter.

"We'll figure out who is behind this, Gemma. Then we'll take care of it. You'll be safe and so will Darion," I tell her. "I'll protect you."

Her smile doesn't reach her eyes.

"Can I confess something?" she asks me. I nod stiffly, wary about what she is going to tell me. "When Darion came into the police station, I was disappointed it wasn't you. It's weird, right? I hardly know you, and yet I wanted you there with me."

Guilt and happiness war in me as I say, "That's because subconsciously you expect your mate to look after you. I should have stuck close to you, Gems, but after being shot at and learning you had a mate who wants to be in your life, I thought that maybe giving you some space would be what was best for you. Then once you had time to adjust to the idea of a mate, like I have, we'd be able to go from there. I should just have just continued to stalk you like the creeper I am."

Gemma laughs and shakes her head.

"You know what? I'll take creeper stalker mate lurking in the shadows over scary drug lord goons any day," she tells me.

I smile, but again I'm gripped with terror. My mate's safety is something I really need to lock down.

"Our friend Tate is coming home today. He'll help keep an eye on you," I tell her seriously.

Tate is the only guy, besides Darion, that I trust with my life. I am excited to see him. Gemma rolls her eyes and says, "I'm sure he's looking forward to babysitting."

"He's one of the best guys for the job," I tell her. "Actually, I do need to tell you something before he gets here."

We stop walking, and I turn to face her,

"Tate is… special. He's human but… not," I tell her.

"Um… What does that mean? Is he another shifter?" Gemma asks, her brows coming together in confusion.

"I can't tell you much, government secret stuff, but he has a unique ability to, ah, for lack of a better word, disappear. Unfortunately, he can't always control it. So don't stare or make a big deal if he just vanishes in front of you."

Gemma scoffs, then shakes her head. "Kind of hard to stare at a man who isn't there, but I got it."

"It'll be hard the first few times, trust me," I assure her, chuckling. "It took me a while to get used to it. But he's a bit touchy about it and will lash out if he thinks you're staring too hard or whatever. So just try to be cool."

Gemma nods. "I'll try."

Relieved this information doesn't scare Gemma, I relax, and we start walking again. We talk for an hour as we wander through the woods. I make it a point to keep us near the house. As we wind down our conversation and head back towards the house, I find myself just as smitten as my wolf is for the woman whose hand I am holding.

Chapter Fourteen

Tate

It feels good to be on home soil. Almost a year in a foreign country spying for the country and seeing some horrible things has made me appreciate what I have here. I stare at the houses and buildings that pass by. It's almost ten o'clock, but I am wide awake. My hours will be off for a while until I get used to this time zone again. Usually, I don't bother trying to adjust when I come back. The week (heck sometimes only days) I'm home don't make it worthwhile to adjust my sleep schedule.

But this time, I'm home for good. I just completed my last job, and I'm officially free from the government's hold on me. Just in time, too. I swear I'm hanging on to my sanity by a thread. I plan to sleep in for as long as I want tomorrow morning. No alarms to awake to, no meetings I have to be present for, no special ops missions that require my services. Just sleep.

I rub my hand over my face, but the motion is unsatisfying. Currently, I'm a shadow. I have no real substance, so my hand has no feeling, nor does it have anything to touch. I'm the perfect spy. If I focus, I can shift myself into a partial shadow—a dark shape with physical substance. I can touch myself then. Or if I focus hard, I can look like Tate Granger: soldier, spy, killer. But rarely do I bother with my physical form unless I'm in the presence of my higher ups. It takes too much strain to keep myself like that.

What I'm going to do now that I'm out of the military is beyond me. Part of the condition to get out of my contract is that I remain inconspicuous. I'm a weapon, a secret weapon the government has spent hundreds upon thousands of dollars on. I honestly thought they would never let me go. But I guess they perfected the serum and have better, superior spies to use now.

Thank God for friends like Darion and Christopher. Brothers really. They always make sure I always have a place to come home to. I glance over to Darion, who is much more tense than normal. I know it's that fucking woman they're dealing with. He gave me the update that he and this, *Gemma,* have taken it to the next level. Apparently, Chris and his wolf are cool with it.

Like that won't cause any problems in the long run.

I've never cared who they fucked before. Hell, sometimes we all would fuck the same woman. This time it's different. There won't be any more women for Christopher now that he's found his mate. Darion sticking his dick where it doesn't belong is sure to cause some problems, but I'm sure this is a temporary situation for the incubus. Now that he's been with her, things will go back to normal for him. He hardly fucks the same woman twice. I haven't asked if, since his copulation with Gemma, he could get it up, but he hasn't complained about it since, so maybe there is hope for him yet.

The fact that this woman, knowing she owns Christopher now, thinks she can fuck whoever she pleases pisses me off royally. She should have shut down any advances Darion offered. Instead, she jumped at the opportunity to fuck an incubus. Already I hate her. She is going to tear us apart somehow; I can feel it.

"So, if Jacob didn't send out the hit on you, do you have any idea who did?" I ask, turning my attention back to the conversation at hand.

Darion's grip on the steering wheel tightens. "No, but I have my men watching all of Jacob's visitors and phone conversations within the jail. I'll find out soon."

"We should head west for a bit. Snow is probable just falling now in the mountains in Colorado. We could ski," I offer.

Darion could ski. I, on the other hand, would watch. Holding my form would be too much effort to be fun.

Darion says nothing, probably already concluding the trip would be more for him than for me. He won't go. I already know this. Darion and Christopher always sacrifice their time doing whatever to make sure I can be included or, at the very least, not alone. I appreciate it. Without them, my life would be incredibly lonely. But I do hate how much they have to change in their lives to accommodate me.

I should have never taken part in that experiment. I thought I could handle the consequences of the unknown. They sold me this dream of being a powerful, elite soldier. Better than all the others... The idea excited me. So, like the idiot that I was, I signed up for this top-secret program without knowing exactly what I was getting myself into.

"Have you given thought to my offer?" Darion asks, changing the subject.

I smirk. Darion is this hotshot lawyer who put criminals behind bars. Little did the world know he is a criminal himself. He's asked me to work for him. Blackmail and money laundering are his specialties. He has a handful of government officials in his pocket due to his ability to read a room... and seduce unhappy wives. Their loose tongues as they gripe about their marriage while fucking an incubus has been more than monetarily beneficial for my friend. All the other information he gains is from the people he employs who go undercover.

Screw over people in my own government after what they've used me for?

"Yeah, man, I'm in."

Darion chuckles. "Give yourself some much-needed time off before you jump into things."

"A week," I tell him. I can't imagine being idle longer than that. "I'll start next Monday."

We pull up to the house, and Darion turns off the car.

"I'm assuming this girl knows about my... condition, right? I'm not going to strain myself by staying in this form just cause she's hanging around," I say.

Darion shrugs and replies, "It's your house, too. Why should she care how you make yourself comfortable?"

"But she knows, right? I'm not going to have some fainting broad on my hands, will I?" I push, knowing that is exactly what will happen otherwise. Darion shrugs again as he unbuckles his seatbelt.

"I haven't spoken to her much today. I'm sure Chris has given her the run down. She isn't bothered by me or Christopher. Non-humans don't seem to bother her."

"But I am human," I remind him though it's not necessary.

Darion looks over at me, his hand on the car door, and says, "As long as you're not an ass to her, I'm sure she'll be just fine around you."

Darion is out of the car the moment he stops talking. While he's not running, the speed in which he moves to open the trunk tells me he's in a hurry. I get out slowly, watching my friend curiously. The cool, hard edged incubus is distracted, on the verge of frazzled, and raring to get inside. It doesn't take much to piece together that he is anxious to see Christopher's mate. I guess this morning didn't take the edge off him as I expected.

I clench my jaw. Nope, I don't like this woman at all.

I solidify and grab most of my bags. Darion takes a bag I don't recognize, and we head inside the house that has become the only place I call home. I can hear the TV blaring, and it smells like popcorn. Despite my eagerness to see Christopher, I'm not quite ready to meet the woman who is playing games with both of my brothers.

Instead of heading in the direction of the family room, I head up the stairs to my wing of the house. I shower, change, and finally make my way back downstairs. I walk into the open kitchen and living room space and take in the scene before me.

Christopher sits on the far end of the couch, one arm hanging over the armrest. His other hand rests on the ankle of the woman who is stretched out over the rest of the couch with her back facing me. Darion has settled himself into one of the leather armchairs and has one foot kicked up on the ottoman. I catch Darion's fugitive glance at Gemma before he realizes I've walked into the room.

Both men look over as I move further into the room. Christopher grins and stands up.

"Tate, it's good to see you again, buddy," he says as he comes over and throws an arm around my shoulders.

"You too, man," I reply.

And it's true. Christopher's sunny disposition and knack for mischief are always fun to be around.

"Flight okay? I heard there was a storm in Georgia," he asks.

He knows how much I hate flying. Flying during storms? I'm a nervous wreck.

"Yeah, it's all good. I survived, so I can't complain," I grumble. Christopher and Darion laugh. They're not fooled.

The woman who has caused so much drama for my brothers these past few weeks stands up. Christopher must have noticed my attention shift because his smile softens as he turns towards his mate.

"Tate, let me introduce you to Gemma," he says, and at her name, the woman walks over.

She is tall and lean. The jeans she is wearing hug her legs perfectly, and the shirt, while unspectacular in nature, clings to her body emphasizing her breasts and flat stomach. Her eyes are a striking light, warm brown, and her skin is flawless. The dimples that appear as she smiles are strangely endearing. Her curly hair is tied up in a messy bun that tilts to one side.

She's beautiful.

I hate her instantly.

"Gemma, this Tate Granger. Tate, Gemma Thomas," Christopher says.

He's beaming at Gemma as she comes to stand next to him. The damn wolf shifter is absolutely besotted by the woman.

"Hi, Tate, it's a pleasure to meet you," she says.

Her voice is low and alluring. She lifts her hand for me to take. I stare at it, decidedly ignore it, and look back up into her face.

"Hey."

My cold response causes Christopher to scowl, but he's not pissed. Gemma's smile never weavers as she drops her hand. Chris must have warned Gemma that I'm not great with people. It's only a matter of time before her eyes pop out of her head when I can't hold my form any longer.

"I'm not sure if you've eaten, but there is pizza in the fridge that I can warm up for you. We just started watching that new Viking movie," she offers.

I scowl. Does she think that because I can't hold my form I'm incapable of doing things for myself?

"I think I can handle feeding myself, thanks," I tell her.

"Hey, Tate, she's just trying to be friendly. Cut her some slack," Chris says with a frown. The two of them exchange a quick look, and I can almost hear Christopher's voice say, See? An asshole, just like I told you.

I find myself suddenly defensive. If he or Darion knew exactly what I go through on a daily basis, they would understand why I am the way I am. Maybe, to some extent, they do since I've shared a little bit of it. Seeing the fear and distrust in people's eyes, the open hostility I experience from the regular soldiers, and the torture and death that I have witnessed is enough to turn anyone hard.

But knowing that this woman has been warned that I'm a jerk suddenly rubs me the wrong way. Instead of trying to correct this image, though, I blurt out,

"Look, I don't know where this woman's hands have been. She seems to like to paw at any dick in her face, so only gods know what she's held. So, forgive me for not wanting my food contaminated."

I don't see Chris's fist in time to shift. The pain in my face is sharp and explosive. I can smell and feel the blood as it gushes from my nose. I deserve this. I know it. So I just laugh.

"That was the gentlest punch I've ever received. You're going soft, Chris," I tell him as I blink away the stars that are blinding me.

Gemma walks around me, her smile now gone. Chris has both fists clenched at his side as his body trembles. His eyes are glowing as he fights the change. Man, I have gone so far as to upset his wolf, too. Usually, his wolf side never comes out if we fight.

"It's late. I'm heading to bed," Gemma says behind me.

I turn and say, "Don't let me run you off." It comes out sarcastically, and I even add a mocking smile. "You need tougher skin if you're going to stick around."

She stares at me as if bored before turning to address the others. "I'll see you in the morning."

With that, she walks away. I watch for just a moment as her hips sway naturally and hypnotically side to side. I force myself to look away. As I turn back to face Chris, it's Darion's meaty fist that slams into my nose this time.

"Fuck, dude! What was that one for?" I demand holding my nose.

It's strange to see Darion look so enraged. Although much more imposing than either myself or Christopher, given his size, Darion isn't one to give in to physical retaliation. He is much too refined for that. Instead, he's much more calculating in his methods of revenge. So, to be on the receiving end of one of his punches, I really must have upset him.

"I misspoke in the car," Darion says coldly. His jet-black eyes bear down into mine as he continues, "What I should have said was: if you're not an ass to her, *we'll* be just fine."

He and Chris share a look before Darion leaves the room. I turn to

Chris.

"Talk to her like that again, and I'll be really pissed. Got it?" he growls.

I nod, and he storms off after Gemma. I'm left all alone on my first night home. Great, just fucking great…

Chapter Fifteen

Darion

After yesterday's blowjob, I thought that I would be able to get Gemma out of my system entirely. She is Christopher's… permanently his. To me, she's just a fling. A woman in a sea of women. It should be easy to move on.

Unfortunately, I awake this morning from a dream so intense and so real that I cum all over myself like a fucking teenager. I sit up astounded by my lack of discipline. The fleeting images of my dream of Gemma riding me are enough to keep me hard. Never, in all of my life, did I think that being able to maintain an erection for as long as I want would come around to bite me in the ass. I take a deep breath and try to will my erection to relax. Usually, this isn't an issue. This morning it refuses to listen to my command.

An image of Gemma throwing her head back as her tits bounce causes a wave of desire to pound through me. I grab my dick and stroke it, thinking of how I wish the hand belonged to the woman sleeping several rooms down from me. No, I don't. I shouldn't wish that. I try to picture someone, anyone else, but the moment my mind pictures someone else, my dick instantly, and painfully, softens.

What the hell?

That certainly has never happened before. I panic as I wonder what's going on. I'm still painfully aroused, but now I have my limp dick in my hand. Shit, shit, shit... I picture Gemma again. At once my dick comes back to life. I stare at it, fearful it will deflate once more. But as I stare, my hand begins to stroke myself. Gemma's moans float through my memory. Her eyes, sparkling with delight, cross my mind's eye.

It takes me no time to finish, and it isn't satisfying at all.

I get up and shower, too disgusted to try to go back to sleep. As I walk down the stairs after dressing for the day, I hear Gemma's soft voice drifting through the house. My feet begin to take me in the direction, but I force myself to stop. I could be catching up on some work. I could go work out in the gym. Hell, I could go drive the new Porsche that's in the garage. I haven't played with that yet. I could do almost anything else in the world right now other than to go see what this woman is doing.

My feet don't seem to be on the same page as my mind though. They move again, and I find myself in the kitchen. Gemma has her laptop open, and she's typing furiously as she listens to whoever is on the phone nestled between her ear and shoulder.

"Yes, I understand completely. I'll have the ad and color codes for them sent over to you later this morning," she says. She hums in agreement to whatever is said. "Yes, I'll send over a mock version for that as well. Once I get your approval, I'll start putting it together." She hums again, but this time she nods, a gesture that goes unseen by the other person. "Alright, wonderful. I'll get this started and send you what I have in a bit. Okay, thank you. You too, good-bye."

She hangs up and sighs. Her brows are pushed together in thought as she finishes typing whatever she is working on. When she's done, she sighs again before sitting up a little straighter. I walk further into the kitchen, and her eyes jump to me.

"Good morning!" she greets warmly. "Coffee is in the pot, and I'm just about to make some omelets. Do you like yours a certain way?"

I am momentarily taken back at how cheerful she is. Is she normally a morning person, or is she happy to see me? I find myself hoping it is the latter. I walk over to the coffee pot, taking great care that my growing erection doesn't catch her attention. Why won't my body heel?

"I like Spanish omelets, thank you," I tell her.

"Then you'll get one. Thanks for grabbing my stuff from the office and my apartment yesterday. I was wondering what I was supposed to wear while I was here. I wasn't sure how many more shirts or pants you had in my size," she says, teasing me.

I think about the whole closet filled with women's clothes. Items that have been left in my possession over the years after quick trusses... or long ones, depending on my needs at the moment. I am sure there are a number of things in there that will fit her. But the thought of Gemma wearing clothes from my past sexual conquests feels... wrong.

"I didn't know what type of clothes you preferred to wear, so I had my men get a few outfits from your closet," I told her. Her eyebrows rise in surprise.

"Oh, so it wasn't you who rummaged through my panty drawer to pull out my fancy ones? When I pulled them out this morning, I could have sworn you deliberately picked them out," she says, laughing.

Anger flares up in my chest. I sent my men to go through her apartment; I didn't trust myself to do it. If they raked through her underwear drawer, deliberately picking out sexy underwear, I am going to fire them. The lack of respect for Gemma in that manner will not be tolerated.

Gemma stands up, closes her laptop, and walks over to the refrigerator. She begins to pull out ingredients for breakfast, and I move out of her way.

"Do you usually work on the weekends?" I ask her as I walk into the living room to give us space. Gemma shakes her head.

"No, I'm just running behind on somethings and would like to be caught up by tomorrow when I get back to work," she replies as she begins breakfast.

It is odd to see a woman so comfortable moving about the kitchen. Most women don't stay here long enough to see this room, let alone become familiar with where everything is. Christopher talked about finding a place with Gemma. A logical step in a relationship as permanent as theirs. But why find another place when she can just settle here? In my shock to hear that Christopher is thinking about moving, I became deaf to his placating offer to look for a house nearby. I left after that, going to the office to get work done instead of dealing with this strange new position the three of us have found ourselves in.

Work. Her answer finally registers, and I'm snapped out of my musings. I shake my head.

"You can't go to work tomorrow," I tell her firmly. "That's why I had my guys pick up your laptop. You need to keep a low profile for longer than a weekend. You need to stay here until it's safe."

What if whoever is behind my hit tries to plant a bomb under Gemma's car? The thought frightens me so much I visibly shudder.

"I can't stay here forever, Darion. You're going to get sick of me eventually," she tells me matter-of-factly. Her back is facing me as she starts cooking over the stove, but I can hear her smile. "And there are others in the house that are already sick of me."

I scowl at her back. Tate… He has his issues, but usually he is slightly better behaved around women. There is something about Gemma that has really gotten under his skin. But whatever that was last night, it will not happen again. The offense I felt on behalf of Gemma was overpowering.

"But in the meantime, while I stay here, I need your Wi-Fi password. Also, do you have a printer?" she continues, not noticing that I'm suddenly shaking with anger again as I replay Tate's conversation with her last night.

"Of course," I say, forcing myself to calm down. "If you have any more to do, you can work in my office."

We talk for a bit as she cooks us breakfast. Once we sit down to eat, we discuss the trivial things we both deal with in our respective offices and laugh about some of our clients' predicaments. Well, more so Gemma's clients, but it is fun all the same.

Neither Christopher nor Tate appear as we eat. Gemma informs me that Christopher told her last night his wolf needed a run. If he left this morning, it will still be hours before we see him. It takes a lot of exercise for his wolf to settle. I tell Gemma this, and she seems content with the answer. And Tate... He is probably up but just avoiding her. This I do not share. I don't want Gemma to feel any more uncomfortable than she already is with him.

After dishes are done, I take Gemma to my office on the other side of the house on the first floor. I pull out the folding table I use sometimes when I need to spread my work out and set up her laptop so it is connected to the WiFi and printer. I pull up a small wingback chair, and Gemma settles in. I, too, decide to get some work done. It has nothing to do with spending more time with Gemma.

At least, this is what I tell myself.

We work silently for a while. There is a new case coming up, and there are plenty of previous charges against this perpetrator. As I study, I take notes. I scribble on a pad of paper, noting things that will help me put the guy behind bars. This will be an easy case.

Gemma is right, I think as I study what I have written down. This is easy. Too easy. I'm not looking forward to the court date as I once would have. Maybe it would be more exciting if the case were interesting. Something juicy and hard to crack. Like a serial killer. But when was the last time one of those happened around here?

I'm not sure how long we work, but the smell of arousal begins to saturate the air and distracts me. I look up sharply, perhaps a bit too eager and pleased to know who the scent belongs to. I lock eyes with Gemma, whose eyes widen in surprise and embarrassment as she realizes she's been caught staring.

My body responds immediately. I've been annoyingly semi-erect since breakfast, but now my dick springs joyfully to life. I lean back in my seat to study this new case. The case of Gemma Thomas. What do I know about her? She's beautiful, charming, and courageous. She's typically independent but leans on her friend Aaron perhaps a little too much at times. Heck, she moved to Boston to be close to him. She obviously takes her work seriously. Working on the weekends to make clients happy is going to become a bad habit to break if she isn't careful. One or two weekends here and there will eventually become almost every single weekend. I know this from experience.

But what is it about this young woman that makes my body react the way it does? I'm an incubus. I can control my arousal and can influence others. I can make everyone in a room become delirious with the need to fornicate. I can have sex with multiple women back to back without rest. My fingers and tongue are just more tools at my disposal when it comes to pleasure. I've had my share of women who range from high class women, models, beautiful escorts, all the way to simple maids. So, what is it about Gemma Thomas that causes all of my discipline to be thrown out the door? What is it about her that causes my body to shrink away from even considering fucking other women?

"Can I help you with something?" I tease quietly.

She looks quickly back down at her laptop.

"Nope. I just got… distracted," she says, her voice trailing off.

Her scent heightens in the room, and I close my eyes to savior it. When I open my eyes, she's watching me again, curiously. Even from here, I see her eyes have darkened. I should leave. Better yet, I should tell her to get out before it gets too hard to think. I know I cannot resist what her body is offering for very long.

Before I know what I am doing, I am standing up and coming around my large ornate desk. I walk over to her, and she leans back in her chair to watch my approach. Without seeming to realize that she is doing it, Gemma's tongue flicks out and wets her lips. Remembering the way her mouth slid over my dick only makes it harder to tell her to go.

"What are you working on?" I ask as I come to stand behind her.

On her screen is a long list of coding. I place my hands on her shoulders.

"I'm, ah, building the back end of a website," she answers. I feel the muscles around her neck contract as she gulps.

"Is it not interesting?" I ask her.

"I could think of a few other things that would be much more exciting than this," she says. Her comment causes my erection to harden. She must have realized the implications of her words because she sucks in a sharp breath and says quickly, "I mean, ah, job related things."

I chuckle at her nervousness. As my dick throbs, I try with all my might to attempt to not let things get too far between us. For Christopher's sake. I need to warn Gemma.

"Do you know much about incubuses, Gemma?" I ask her.

Her answer comes in the form of a head shake. Subconsciously, I realize that I have started to rub her neck with my thumbs. Gemma leans into the touch. I can't stop touching her, but... I should. I really do think about stopping, but I'm unable to. I push on with my warning.

"An incubus feeds through sexual energy created through sexual acts. While breakfast this morning was delicious, unfortunately my kind needs more than food and water to survive. The smell of your arousal right now is like blood in the water to a hungry shark. If you do not wish to feed me, I need you to leave before I cannot help myself."

Apparently, I already am slipping on the minimal control I'm holding onto. One of my hands has slid into the neck of her shirt, slipped under her bra, and I am beginning to cup her breast.

She looks up at me and says, "Darion, I... I do want this, but... I can't hook up with you unless I know where your head is at. I can already sense feelings for Christopher beginning to surface. He and I... Well, this is permanent between us. Feelings will come naturally between the two of us. But you and me? I don't know if I can hook up multiple times with you without catching feelings for you, too. That won't be fair to Christopher, to love another, especially if I'm just another hook up to you. I don't want to get bitter because you'll find someone else once you're bored with me. If you're not willing to be in a... I don't know, a relationship with us, maybe we shouldn't."

I pause fondling her breast at her declaration. Be in a relationship? Since when did incubuses commit to such monstrosities? They are too stifling. Too demanding. From what I've heard sex dwindles away to nothing after a while. That I cannot do...

But the thought of Gemma being mine... that is something that lights a fire in my gut. To ravish her as often as I wish, to spend time with her whenever I want without this cloud of doubt and hesitation hanging over me... Maybe, just maybe I can do that. Even if she isn't entirely mine, I could be content knowing that the man who also claims her is like a brother to me and will help take care of her. As I think this over, I feel how right the idea of being with Gemma and Christopher is. Yes... Yes, I could be in a relationship with both.

As that realization settles within me, I'm abruptly branded with a sheering hot pain that radiates from the middle of my chest.

I stumble and fall to my knees as I'm blinded with pain. Gemma yells my name, but her voice sounds far away. I clutch the middle of my chest and choke as the pain radiates throughout my body. Gemma screams my name at the same time I throw my head back and roar. I rip my shirt open, causing buttons to fly everywhere, and just as I look down at where the pain is coming from, it vanishes just as abruptly as it appeared. I gasp, taking in deep gulps of air as the shock wears off. But I'm not in the clear yet. The pain is gone, but a new fire washes through me. This fire is created from desire, and it's so intense I roar again.

I stare down at my chest. There, etched into my skin, are my typical markings. But now, branded over top of two and centered in the middle of my chest is a new one. While the other marks are slightly lighter grayish blue than my normal skin color, this new mark is inky black and stands out over all the rest. To the untrained eye and to the uneducated masses, the mark looks like a thick fishing hook. To an exceedingly small group of people, incubuses included, the mark means one thing: my fate has been sealed.

I jerk my head up to find Gemma staring at me with fear in her eyes. This woman... Gemma Thomas has just received a gift so powerful that people have died trying to receive it. Many have sold their souls, along with others' souls, for what Gemma has been gifted with. For me, I can almost hear the shackles of my new bindings. The rune that now marks me is a new sentence but of a familiar kind.

Unfortunately, or maybe fortunately, I don't have time to think about what has just happened. My consciousness is swamped with a haze of lust so thick that all rational thought is halted. The only thing in the world that matters to me right now is pleasing the woman in front of me.

Chapter Sixteen

Gemma

One-minute Darion's crying out in pain, ripping his shirt to pieces as if it's behind the attack; in the next, he's lunging at me. I launch myself out of the way, off my seat and on to the floor just in time. I scramble to my feet, alarmed by the intense hunger in Darion's eyes.

"Darion, are you okay? What happened? What's going on?" I ask as I take a step back, away from the incubus.

He takes a step towards me, and as he does, he lifts one arm. His hand reaches out above him, and his fingers curl, as if he is picking an apple off a branch. Suddenly, my body shudders as a wave of desire pools into every pore of my body. My breasts become sensitive, my skin feels too warm, and I can feel my pussy clench. My mind begins to drift, thinking of only pleasure. I raise my hands and cup my swelling breasts and squeeze. Oh… It feels good.

Darion steps forward again, a smirk spreading across his face. He's behind this sudden, unseen force that makes my body ache. I should probably be scared, but I've wanted him since he had walked into the kitchen this morning. So I don't care that he wants me to desire him more. I close my eyes as my hands slip over my shirt and my fingers begin to tweak my nipples.

In an instant, Darion's there replacing my hands with his. I lean towards him; his hands feel incredible against my breasts. I reach up, take his face in my hands, and kiss him. I need to taste him. I shove my tongue into his mouth, and he welcomes me. I groan into his mouth as his hands slide down my sides.

As he reaches around to grab my butt, through the fog that is descending over my senses, I remember what I had been saying just before Darion's brief episode. It takes all my will power to pull my mouth from his. I have to make sure where we stand before we do this. While my body has given up any resistance, my mind is only half lost, and my heart seems indecisive about the entire situation.

"Darion, listen to me," I plead softly. I look up into his eyes and find him watching me intently. His hands squeeze my butt, and he breathes heavily, but he's focused on what I have to say. "This can't just be a fling. I need to know if you, Christopher, and I can be a thing. If not, we must stop… I can't do this otherwise."

Darion's hands stop moving, but he doesn't let go of me. Instead, he yanks me closer to him so we're chest to chest.

"I am yours," he growls in an almost demonic octave. My toes curl at the sound. "This mark now branded upon me indicates to all that I serve you, and only you, in body and soul. I am committed to you, Gemma Thomas."

I should be confused and frightened by his words, but they have the opposite effect.

The fog descends over me completely now that there is no resistance on my end. I claw off the rest of his shirt, needing to feel and touch all of him. Darion must feel the same way too because my shirt is pulled off me and my pants follow suit. My hands run over each mark that is carved into his body. They look like scars, but that can't be right. As my fingertip traces the new mark that has appeared, Darion's body shudders. I grin and lean forward to trace it with my tongue, which causes Darion to let out a strangled cry.

He lifts me by my hips and carries me over to his desk. Holding me with ease with just one arm, he uses the other to push off everything on the desk. Everything falls to the floor, including his computer, but neither of us care. He lays me down the length of the desk and then nearly covers me with his body as he leans forward to take my nipple into his mouth. Both nipples feel as sensitive as my clit. The feeling surprises and delights me. Every twist and twirl with his tongue cause my pussy to spasm.

He slides his hand over my stomach and down in between my legs. His hand cups my mound, applying enough pressure to let me know he's claiming that space as his own but not enough to do much for my release. But I don't need any stimulation down there now because the impossible feeling he's eliciting from my nipples is intense, too intense. His tongue stops moving just as I am about to cum, and I cry out, only to scream his name a moment later when he bites my breast firmly, sending my body into an orgasmic spiral.

What the hell? How is that possible? There is no way I can cum like this… But I don't have time to think about it. That haze over my mind thickens until my thoughts narrow to the pleasure that Darion is giving me. His fingers slide through my folds, and he groans. His mouth comes away from my nipple before he kneels between my legs that dangle off the edge of the desk. He presses his mouth between my legs, and suddenly I'm being devoured. My back arches off the desk, and my legs squeeze Darion's head. I don't know what he's doing, all I know is that I never want him to stop. I can feel my pleasure building again. I don't know how it's possible to cum so quickly, but I don't think too hard about it.

Just as I'm about to cum the door to the office opens. Darion stops his ministrations, which causes me to let out a frustrated cry. I turn to see who Darion is looking at and find Christopher standing there. I wonder if I should feel upset to be caught like this with his friend. The thought fades away among the demands of that lustful fog. So instead of feeling embarrassed or ashamed, I reach out to him with a hand and beckon him over to us. I know in that moment I want both men.

Christopher's eyes turn gold as he studies us. I can hardly focus on his face when my mind is too busy recalling what he looks like under his clothes. Darion rises from his kneeling position. No, he can't stop! I need… I need… I reach down between my legs to try to give me some relief.

Darion points to the new mark on his chest, and in that same, demonic voice he tells Christopher, "I am Gemma's now."

Christopher's gaze lands on the mark on Darion's chest. I stare at Christopher, masturbating to his face. There is stubble along his cheeks again. I can remember exactly how that hair felt between my legs, and it pushes me closer to the edge. I call Christopher's name softly as I get closer. Christopher nods to Darion which sets off a chain reaction.

Darion suddenly reaches out to grab my working hand and pulls it away. I cry out in frustration again. But neither man pay me any mind. Christopher strips down until he's naked, his hard erection glistening with precum. The sight of it excites me so much that I gasp and reach out with my free hand for him. I need it. I want to taste it. I need it inside of me. My nipples bead painfully as I stare hungrily at the wolf shifter.

Christopher walks over to the desk, and at the same time, Darion lets go of my hand. I shift my position, rolling over to my stomach then getting to my hands and knees. My eyes never leave Christopher's erection. My body is hot and needy, and I swear it's getting worse every time I take a breath. Christopher stands opposite of Darion. I lower my arms until I'm in downward dog with my butt in the air for Darion to view and I am eye level to Christopher's waist.

Darion's slides his fingers into me, and I groan in pleasure.

"Gemma, take Christopher into your mouth," he says.

Yes, that's exactly what I want. The lust-filled haze hangs heavier over me as I lean forward and take my mate's erection into my mouth. I hear his sharp intake of breath. As I begin taking him deeper, Darion sinks his fingers further into me. His thumb begins circular motions over my clit, causing a hard shudder to run through me. Quickly, I find the harder I work on Christopher the more intense Darion's fingering becomes. Christopher's fingers weave through my hair. His moaning sets the fire in me to a blaze.

The heat in the room intensifies. My body grips Darion's fingers as I take Christopher to the back of my throat. It doesn't take either of us long to find our release. We cum together, our release vocal. I collapse onto my stomach, breathing hard. My body tingles as if I'm on the verge of coming again. I want to. I need to. When had I gotten so greedy?

"Fuck, Darion, cut it out," Christopher says, his voice strained.

"Not yet," the incubus snaps.

Christopher pulls himself out of my mouth, but he grabs his erection as if he's in pain.

"Come claim your mate. Then it's my turn," Darion orders.

Christopher doesn't hesitate. He comes around to stand behind me where Darion stood. Before I realize what he's doing, Christopher grabs my legs and yanks me back. I squeak in delight as he flips me over from my stomach to my back, understanding that I'm about to get exactly what I wanted. He wraps my legs around his waist, and in one swift movement he impales me. My arms shoot out, and I grip the sides of the desk to brace myself as Christopher starts thrusting into me.

I'm delirious. The fog in my head is so thick that I can't tell where I am or how insane this is. All I know, all I feel, is pleasure. Each thrust, each slap of our skin causes my body to wind back up. I'm on the brink of breaking again. I squeeze my eyes shut as my body snaps, and I'm on cloud nine. I cry out Christopher's name, gripping the desk so tightly my knuckles turn white. I hear him shouting, and I feel him tense.

"Thank God," he grunts as his body jerks inside me.

When he's come down from his second orgasm, I hear him breathing loudly. Christopher gently lowers my legs so now only my upper body is on the desk, my feet planted on the ground. I'm panting, but my body is ready again. How? My limbs feel weak despite the energy humming through me.

Hands grip my hips before I'm suddenly turned around and pulled up into a sitting position. Darion stares down at me.

"It will be the three of us," he says in this new deep, demonic voice. My toes curl, and my breath hitches. I lean forward and wrap my arms around his neck.

"Yes," I reply, though my voice sounds strange. It's deep and husky.

My nipples have beaded so tightly they're painful. I scoot closer to the edge of the desk where Darion's erection is waiting for me. I press my aching nipples against his chest where they find some slight relief. Darion lowers his mouth and captures mine. Our tongues dance. My nipples skid across his skin, the slight ridges from the strange markings on his chest give me a friction that sets my body on fire all over again.

"I am yours," he growls, pulling away from my mouth. Without any further preamble, he surges forward and sinks into me.

I've had Christopher between my legs before. I know how good it is with my mate, but this is my first time with Darion. And holy shit, it's much different. Darion's erection is thicker and longer. My whole body stiffens at the newness. Darion stills once he's all the way in, allowing me to adjust. My body is quivering. My arousal is so intense I hardly need the moment Darion is giving me. I lean my hips into his, needing him to start moving. As I lean my hips forward, I lean my head back and close my eyes so I can savor this new union.

Darion's lips skim across my neck, and I shiver at the contact. Then, he begins to move. His thrusts are different with much more control than Christopher's. When he surges forward, he does something with his hips that sends my whole body into a tight ball of sensory overload. My cry is strangled as he continues this strange new move. As I get used to this, one of his hands moves to my lower back.

Warmth shoots from his palm into my body, and I cum hard, unexpectedly, and wonderfully. My cries turn to screams as Darion continues moving. I haven't come down from this unexpected orgasm before more warmth shoots from Darion's palm into my body, causing another eruption. My body convulses with pleasure; my cries are incoherent now. This happens one more time before Darion stills as he finds his own release.

As his body begins to relax, the atmosphere in the room shifts. The heat begins to cool while the fog that has been hanging over my consciousness lifts. My body's demand for more pleasure, more attention, eases, and I find it easier to breathe and think. My limbs feel heavy and so do my eyelids. As my eyelids flutter shut, I sag against the incubus who holds me to his chest. He says something, but I'm not sure if he's talking to me or Christopher. I don't bother to try to pay attention because exhaustion swamps me, and I slip into unconsciousness.

***

I awake as hot water touches my skin. My overly sensitive skin. I hiss as the water slides over me. A chuckle from someone tells me I'm not alone. The sound is followed by the realization that I am in someone's arms being lowered into a tub. My eyelids flutter open as another pair of arms wraps around me from behind. When I'm fully submerged, I realize I'm in someone's lap.

I glance up to find Christopher stepping into the massive tub with us. It's big enough to fit five, maybe six people. I glance down to find a pair of gray-blue arms around my torso, keeping me from slipping under. Christopher scoots close to us before settling into his spot. I'm tense for a few moments longer before my body begins to relax. I hum, content, and allow my eyelids to droop halfway to enjoy the water.

"What was that?" I ask, knowing good and well that I don't have to specify what I'm talking about.

What just happened, the way my body was so greedy and out of control… I need some answers.

"A taste of the power an incubus has," Christopher says, staring at me through half-closed eyelids and a half-smile stretching across his face.

"Disconcerting, isn't it?"

Darion's chuckle vibrates through me. I turn my head and look up at him.

"You did that? You made me feel like that? How? Why? You knew I already wanted you," I ask him.

As I talk, I note how my throat feels raw. Actually, my whole body feels raw. It's uncomfortable, but the warm water seems to smooth the ache.

Darion says nothing for a moment, a frown tugging the corner of his lips down. His arms tighten around me. Christopher sighs with impatience when Darion doesn't respond.

"Tell her, Darion," he says, his amusement gone.

Darion remains silent. It is clear that he is warring over something. I can see the turbulence in his black gaze. I frown.

"Please? I won't be upset or anything," I tell him calmly. This time, it's Darion who sighs.

"I ah… lost a bit of control," the incubus says, his voice stilted with embarrassment. "But essentially that is how an incubus acts when he has found his new—" He stops talking abruptly. He swallows hard, and underneath me, his body tenses. "…master."

"*What?*" Christopher and I say in unison.

I shift carefully to turn my whole torso around to look at him.

"You said she's your mate. You didn't say anything about a master!" Christopher shouts in surprise.

His voice echoes in the unfamiliar bathroom. I say nothing as I stare at Darion. He stares back at me with a half-smile though it looks pained. When he answers, he is speaking directly to me,

"There is much the world does not know about the incubus, and it is for good reason that we do not write down our history or our source of power. This is not only because our power is tenfold what a typical non-human creature has but also because the way we are created is dangerous. We are born when a human woman has lost her lover to death and cannot bear the separation. The woman sells her soul to what many consider a devil, who then essentially places a demon into the body of the lost love.

"The possession is temporary because the human body cannot house a demon's soul for long. There is a change, a mutation of the dead body, causing the body to come to life, in a sense, change color, and gain some of the power the demon may possess. When the incubus awakes, it isn't the same person who has died. We are a new creature, whose life is tethered to the woman who wished her lover to return. She is our first master, and we live to serve her. Our job is to make sure that our woman always feels pleasure. We are the ultimate lover."

Darion falls silent, allowing us to process this information. So, Darion had once been a human… but not? Is he possessed by a demon now? I try to wrap my head around what he is saying, but it is hard to picture any of this.

"But a human only lives so long. Once the woman is dead, we are freed to do as we please. The markings on our body, which we refer to as runes, are the story of our birth. It is the ritual that took place. It names the demon who possessed us, and it indicates that we are enslaved to a master. They also warn that we can be enslaved again, but they mention that this time, it is a master of our choosing. Most incubuses never find, nor want to find, their second master. Who wants to be a slave to the one person when we can have whomever we please?

"I believe that before you gave your ultimatum, Gemma, I subconsciously already had one foot through the proverbial door to becoming enslaved. Since we met, I have been unable to have sex with anyone. The only time I can get it up is around you. My body had chosen you without me even realizing it. When you forced me to decide to commit fully to you and Christopher, everything clicked into place. When I made the conscious decision, my fate was sealed. Thus, the new rune, telling the world who my master is. It unlocked my more… demonic side, which only wants to please and claim. My power can enhance desire until that's all anyone can think about. I can cause you to cum on command."

Darion shoots Christopher a smirk and adds, "I can keep every male in the room hard, just on the verge of cumming even if he just finished doing so, which is why Christopher got his panties in a knot."

Darion pauses again. This time I'm not sure if it's to allow us to catch up or for him to get used to the idea that he is now tethered to someone else.

So, I have gone from one mate to two in the span of a month, both irrevocably tied to me. I'm extremely uncomfortable with Darion considering me his master, and I also don't know how I feel about Darion tampering with how he affects me. We are going to have to talk about boundaries.

"Jesus," Christopher whistles after a few minutes of silence has ticked by. I look over at him to see Christopher staring at Darion in amazement. "I didn't know any of that. So since you chose Gemma, she is still, like, your mate, right? It's just slightly different than what a mate is in the wolf world."

Out of the corner of my eye Darion nods his head cautiously.

"Yes, but this mating is different. There is a hierarchy," he answers. "Gemma can command me to do something, and I must obey. I do not believe it is like that between you two."

"What?" I screech in alarm.

I practically throw myself off Darion's lap to put space between us. The tub is deeper than I expect though and immediately my head slips under water. Darion's large hand wraps around the back of my neck and lifts my head out of the water. I sputter as I try to collect my wild thoughts.

"Don't die on me yet, Gemma," Darion says with a soft smile.

"Please tell me you're joking," I say to him. "I'm not going to command you to do anything. You're not a slave!"

"I'm not joking," Darion says with a sigh.

"Jesus…" Christopher repeats.

I immediately try to think of ways around this so that way we're both more comfortable in this relationship. "Then, I command you to never listen to my commands."

Darion's answering smile lacks the contempt that usually comes with it.

"That's not how it works, but I appreciate the effort. I do not expect you to abuse such power. But you can see why we do not share much about ourselves," he tells me. "In any case, I do not think I would have picked someone who is cold and callous. I trust you implicitly, Gemma Thomas."

Well… shit. I guess I have myself a sex slave.

Chapter Seventeen

Tate

I sneak into the office, unseen by the others, to see what all the commotion is about. Unfortunately, too consumed by curiosity to remember to be wary of Darion's power, I'm struck just as hard as the others and become consumed with lust. But I can't give myself away. Knowing I walked in uninvited would piss both Christopher and Darion off. Who knows what Christopher's wolf would do? So, I slip out and jerk off until my dick is so swollen that it hurts to touch myself. I cum so many times that I feel like a dried-up sponge.

Eventually, I pass out.

I now lie on my mattress awake and staring up at my ceiling. I am *lying* on my mattress. The phenomenon of such a simple feat is life altering. Tentatively, I place my hands, palms down, on the bed and feel the soft sheets, amazed that I can do so without any issues. This morning when I woke, I experienced the same thing. I brushed it off as a fluke. When was the last time I've held my physical form this long without any effort?

Never.

Usually, my body shifts into its shadow form, and I sleep against the walls or floors along with the rest of the shadows in the room. So… Why can I hold my form now? Is there some new technology in the house allowing the molecules that make up my physical form to maintain this physical feat? Did Darion pull some strings and find someone who could help me? I want to get up and ask him, but the relief of being me and the fear of losing this ability to be a tangible human being for longer than few minutes keep me on the bed.

I don't know how much time passes, but there is a knock on the front door. I wonder if either Darion or Christopher will answer. Silence follows the knocking. A minute passes before whoever it is outside knocks again. The others are probably still in the midst of their threesome. Darion can get a bit carried away.

I roll out of bed and leave my room. I'm walking down the hallway when more knocking echoes through the house. I'm about to yell that I'm coming when suddenly the door is knocked off its hinges and comes flying into the house. Four men rush in, dressed in all black with ski masks on and guns in their hands.

Fuck.

I shift and rush forward. In an instant, I'm down the stairs, using the shadows in the house to travel from the first floor to the second floor. I come up behind the last man to enter the house. Shifting to my physical form, I grab the man's head and twist it. He falls quietly to the floor, dead. I come up behind the next guy, planning to do the same thing, but he turns and sees me. He brings up his gun and fires repeatedly in my direction.

I shift in just enough time that the bullets pass through me quickly. The others turn around to see who their buddy shot at, but none of them can see me as I move between shadows. I can't attack in this form, though, so I'm forced to wait until it's safe to shift again.

A snarl rips through the house, and suddenly, a large wolf launches itself over the upstairs railing and slams into one of the intruders. The other two turn their attention to the wolf, their guns raised, ready to shoot at Christopher. I leap from the shadows, shift, and tackle one to the ground. I get the upper hand and snap this unsuspecting man's neck. I leap back to my feet just as a gun fires several rounds.

Drywall is hit, and something shatters. I rush the gunman at the same time Christopher leaps at him. I skid to a stop as the wolf's teeth sink into the man's neck. The wolf shakes his head twice. I hear the fatal snap of his victim before the man goes still. Without waiting, the wolf bounds out the door. Instead of following, I rush to the other side of the house through the shadows to see if anyone has tried to enter through any of the back entrances.

When I'm sure they are secure, I run back through the house. I grab a gun and then head outside. Through the trees, I can see a car rushing up our driveway trying to escape. I shift using the darkness of the woods and rush after the car. It's easy to catch up. I pass the vehicle and shift to stand directly in its path before firing at the driver. The vehicle swerves off the road and slams into the tree. I shift again and get close to the wreckage. The driver is slumped over the steering wheel, a bullet wound in his temple.

I circle the vehicle to make sure it's empty before slipping back into the shadows. I'm back at the house in no time. As I step out of the woods, so does Christopher. He doesn't acknowledge me as he rushes back inside the house. Unsure if he heard something or saw someone enter before I arrived, I rush in after him with my gun drawn. The wolf bounds up the stairs and disappears out of sight. I follow him, shifting as I do.

I see the wolf rush into Darion's room. I change direction and head for the guest bedroom that I know Gemma is staying in. I kick open the door in my physical form before immediately shifting back as a shadow as I enter. I check the room. No one is in here. I check the other guest rooms, making sure that each one is secure before heading to Darion's room.

Darion is there, standing just in front of Gemma as a shield, in the middle of his room with his arms crossed over his chest. Gemma has thrown on one of Darion's shirts in a haphazard attempt to be decent, but her hair is soaking wet, as is Darion's. Christopher is pulling on pants as I enter and nods in my direction when he sees me.

"Tate, are you okay?" Gemma asks as she moves around Darion to walk over to me.

Her brows are pulled together in concern. When she stops just in front of me, I take a moment to appreciate how she doesn't cower away from my scowl like many soldiers, hell, even generals would.

"I'm fine," I tell her and step away from the woman to address the others. "I killed the driver, but his car is at the top of the driveway. We should call the cops before a neighbor drives by and notices."

"On it," Christopher says heading towards the door.

The wolf is close to the surface. His eyes are glowing, and his voice is deeper. He is shaking with fury. Hm… It isn't like we haven't had people come after us before for various reasons. He is usually the laid back one, taking everything as a joke. I glance at Gemma and realize she must be the cause. Stupid mating bond.

"There are three dead in the woods, too," Christopher adds grimly as he heads out of the room.

"Are these the guys you were talking about?" I ask Darion.

"They have to be," he responds with a furious scowl. "Why didn't the security system go off?"

"I'll check it out," I tell him. "In the meantime, you need to get someone to come replace the door. Preferably with a steel one."

Darion nods and turns towards Gemma. "Until I'm absolutely certain no one else is out there, I'd rather you stay up here."

I think my brows rise to meet my hair line. There really must be something special about this woman for him to suddenly show enough interest to care about her safety like this. I open my mouth to give some snide remark about his situation, but Gemma beats me too it.

"I'm not a princess that needs to be locked away. Christopher is calling the cops, who should be here soon, and I highly doubt that either Christopher or Tate have left anyone out there to report back to whoever their boss is. I'm going to join Tate."

I scoff, "I don't want to babysit you."

"Perfect, because I don't want a babysitter." She walks by me without another word and leaves the room. Does she even know where the security room is?

"Who the hell does she think she is?" I demand.

Darion's angry expression softens as he stares at the door where Gemma exited.

"She's our woman," he answers before pulling out his phone.

Fuck. He's truly smitten.

***

I think about shadowing myself down to the security room, avoiding Gemma, and not giving a fuck if she finds the room or not. But I have to remind myself that as much as I don't want some stranger around, she'll be in Christopher's life until they're both in the ground. If I want Christopher in my life, then I have to play nice occasionally. So I walk with Gemma downstairs.

She glances at the bodies on the floor. She covers her mouth to muffle a squeak, and I watch as she makes a wide birth around them. I hardly spare them a glance. I wish the sight of bodies still bothered me. Somewhere along the way in my career, I stopped flinching at the sight of death and violence. It has become a way of life for me.

What am I going to do now that I am a civilian? Death isn't normal for them. Darion's offer to work on his team as undercover intel and security will be as close to the life I gave up as I can get in this world. But what about after that?

"What's wrong?" Gemma asks me as we head down the stairs into the basement.

How does she know something is wrong? I scowl at her perceptiveness. Instead of answering, I flick on the light. I hear her suck in a sharp breath. Guess she's never been down here before.

The space is set up like a fancy night club with red satin drapes lining the walls, shiny wood floors, and comfortable seating. There is a small bar that I know is stocked with everything anyone could possibly want. On the far side of the room is a small stage. It's not used for typical entertainment. I smile as I think about how shocked Gemma's face would be if I told her what it's really used for.

In my head a picture of her naked and tied up on display for us to view forms. The image is so startling I stop in my tracks to blink it away. She isn't my type at all. I enjoy a strictly submissive breed of women. Yeah, Gemma's hot, but she would not do well as a submissive.

My abrupt stop causes Gemma to run into me.

"Oof, sorry," she says and steps up next to me to see why I stopped.

"Can you not crowd me?" I ask sharply and charge forward.

"Can you not be an ass for a moment?" she asks, her tone sounds genuinely curious as she follows me again.

I roll my eyes but don't answer. We walk down the hallway, passing doors that, if open, would cause Gemma to run screaming. Finally, we get to the back, and I punch in the code to the security room.

We enter the small room filled with monitors. There is a desk with several computers set up and running but nothing else. I walk over and sit down. The door shuts, and the room is silent. I know Gemma is standing behind me though. Her presence in the stark room is strangely comfortable.

I toggle the computer mouse and begin running a diagnostic. As I work, I use another monitor to replay the last thirty minutes. On the monitor, the car approaches but remains out of sight of the house. The bastards split up, one group to bombard us at the door while the other group tries to set themselves up in bushes to catch us in a crossfire should we escape the first group.

I work for a while on trying to find the problem. When I find it, I grit my teeth in anger. I lean back in my seat and glare at the monitor. I'm not used to sitting in front of screens this long. I pause... It's been a while now since I've shifted inadvertently. Sometimes, I don't realize when it happens, but I am sure Gemma would have reacted if I did. I frown as I wonder what the hell is going on.

"What did you find?" Gemma asks from behind me.

"Someone fried the wiring by the gate. They reran their own wiring and have been watching your comings and goings," I tell her before I start slamming my fingers against the keyboard.

I'm sure whoever is behind this will have detected that I am on to them, but it is worth trying to trace where the new feed is going to.

"Were you in IT during your time in the military?" Gemma asks.

"No."

"How do you know what you're doing right now?" She presses.

"I pick up on things quickly."

The streaming cuts off abruptly. Whoever is watching has severed their connection to us. I swear and lean back in my seat. In one of the monitors, I see several cop cars and an ambulance pull onto our property. I swear again. I'm supposed to be keeping a low profile, not killing people. What am I supposed to do now? If I give a statement, then my name will be in the police system.

"Thank you for saving us," Gemma says, breaking the silence.

"I don't need to be thanked," I tell her sharply as I stand to turn around.

I don't realize how close she is, though, and I bump right into her. I catch her as she teeters backward. Fuck, she probably thinks I did that on purpose. Better make sure she knows it's an accident before she runs whining to Christopher or Darion.

"Sorry."

To my surprise she laughs. "Getting me back from earlier? I suppose that's fair."

Her laughter makes me uncomfortable for some reason. I scowl at her and add, "Maybe if you gave me some space, we could avoid this in the future."

She shrugs and says, "I think we all need a little space." She sighs, turns, and then leaves the room without another word.

What was that about?

***

I make it back upstairs where the police are questioning everyone. When they spy me, I'm pretty much ignored. Confused, I look down to make sure I'm in my physical state. Christopher strolls over to me, swings an arm over my shoulder, and leans close.

"In case they ask, you were upstairs watching Gems while Darion and I took care of the threat," he whispers.

Tension eases in my shoulders as I realize my brothers are watching out for me. When all the statements have been taken, the bodies have been carted away, and the door installation guy has come and gone, it's dinner time. Just as my stomach growls, the smell of steak wafts through the house. I follow the smell into the kitchen where I find Gemma walking in from outside with a platter of steaks in her hands. On the counter are baked potatoes, steaming hot, with all the ingredients out ready to load them. There are also cooked green beans coated in butter. My stomach nearly roars with delight.

"Damn, Gemma can cook!" Christopher says, grinning as he strolls into the kitchen behind me.

His mate looks up and gives him a smile. It's a tight one that doesn't reach her eyes.

"Yeah, well… It's been a long day for all of us. I figure a good meal will at least end the day on a good note," she tells him.

He walks over and kisses her temple sweetly. This time her smile does reach her eyes, causing them to twinkle.

"Are you good?" he asks her quietly. She nods.

"Will someone grab Darion? I need to finish the garlic bread real quick," she says.

"No need," Darion says, coming into the room with us. "Smells great in here."

"Good. You can all grab a plate and start loading them up," she answers and heads over to the refrigerator.

We do as we're told and head over to the large table. I smile fondly at the memories that we've made on top of it. Damn that woman was great to work with... Maybe I'll give Roxanne a call after dinner to see what her plans are this week. It's been a while since I've gotten to use my flogger and ropes.

Gemma brings over garlic bread and several beers for us. When she moves away from the table instead of joining us, Christopher asks, "Where's your plate?"

"I'm not hungry," she tells him. She grabs a glass from the cabinets and pours herself some wine that she pops open. I frown. She sure has made herself at home here already. "I'm actually going to head to bed early. I have work tomorrow. Yes, I'm going to work, Darion. I'm in charge of my own life. *You* can't tell me what to—"

I turn to see Darion shut his mouth at the same time Gemma stops talking, clearly mortified.

"Oh... ah, that's not what I meant," Gemma quickly back tracks. "I'm just saying that I'm going. Please don't try to stop me."

With that, she practically runs away.

We are all silent as we listen to her footsteps fade away.

I turn back to Darion and demand, "Well? What the hell was that about?"

Darion makes a face, and Christopher rubs a hand over his face in exasperation. When neither of them answers right away, my anger spikes.

"What? I'm not worth the time of day to be given an explanation to? Because that was some fucking strange behavior. I haven't seen that woman flustered once, and she walked around dead bodies earlier. So how come all of a sudden she's bolting up the stairs to hide?"

"*That*, my friend, is a complication," Darion says with a scowl in my direction. "And nothing you need to concern yourself with."

"We have all had a trying day," Christopher says calmly as he cuts up his food. He takes a bite and growls his approval. "I'm sure it's all just hitting her now." He turns his attention to Darion. "You're going to add extra security for her, aren't you? I have to get back to work tomorrow."

"Of course. I need to do some shuffling around. I want my most trusted guys watching her," Darion says with a frown.

"What's she to you, Darion?" I ask, genuinely interested but also pissed. I scowl at the incubus, my steak knife clutched in my fist. "I get Christopher is worried about her, but you? This all feels weird."

"That's because it is weird," Christopher grumbles, taking another bite of his food.

I glance at him and understanding hits me. Christopher already knows whatever is going on between Darion and Gemma. What the fuck?

Darion looks at me, his expression going from annoyed to blank in seconds. I know this look too well. He's masking whatever strong emotion he is feeling. When he opens his mouth, he tells me everything. The information he shares... It floors me. I had no clue that was how incubuses are created.

As I listen, I understand why Gemma ran off for the evening. The enormity of what has transpired between them... Yeah, I would be a little freaked out, too. I'm sure master to a sex slave was never one of Gemma's relationship goals. And if she is a decent person, she's going to have to second guess everything that she says so she doesn't abuse this newfound gift. Her words hold power now. That's not something to shrug your shoulders at. When Darion is done, I gape at him.

"So, what she said about you not being able to do anything about it..." I start but trail off, unable to articulate my confusion.

"She probably thought she was giving me some sort of order or felt like she might have come off as my superior," Darion confirms with a nod.

"Was she?" Christopher asks with concern. Darion shakes his head but doesn't elaborate. "Fuck… This is getting messy. I don't want her on edge all the time, man. You need to talk to her."

Gemma's words in the basement swirl around in my head: *Looks like we could all use some space.* Huh, now it makes sense why she chose to come with me instead of staying put. It wasn't because she has any interest in the security around here. She was just trying to give herself a break from these two. She did so knowing I wouldn't be happy with her joining me. That's telling…

"Maybe just give her a little time to come to terms with this," I say gruffly. "It's a lot for me to take in, and I've known you almost twenty-five years."

Christopher nods slowly. "Yeah, Tate's got a point…"

Darion sighs and nods as he cuts into his steak. After taking a bite, he turns to me. "Did you find anything in the security footage or figure out why we weren't alerted to danger?"

I nod and tell him my findings. We discuss changing the security system and what to do in the meantime. After dinner, we clean up, but there's not a lot thanks to Gemma who did most of the cleanup while she worked. I can tell both guys want to go after Gemma, and I feel a sting of jealousy. How did both get so attached to this woman so quickly? What draws them to her and makes anything or anyone else unimportant? Maybe I need to do my own assessment of her. Maybe I'm missing something. But I can fix this.

"Darion, I'll do security detail for Gemma tomorrow," I tell him.

I find the surprise that crosses his face is both amusing and insulting. Does he really think that I wouldn't want to look out for the woman they are both so attached to? Did I make that bad of an impression?

"Are you sure you don't want time off?" he asks me.

"To do what?" I ask with a shrug. "I'll drive her in tomorrow, stay with her in the shadows so it's not too obvious she's being protected, and bring her back."

I guess the least I can do is attempt to get to know her. What better way to get to know someone than by being around them all day? How hard can it be to get to know Gemma Thomas?

Chapter Eighteen

Darion

The lights are still on in the guest bedroom when I knock on the door.

"Come in," Gemma's voice floats through the door.

I open the door and walk in. Gemma's in bed with her back facing me. I shut the door behind me and walk over to the bed cautiously. In all my years of freedom, I never once gave thought to how it would feel to be shackled again. I never thought I would have to go into detail about such an intimate part of my life. So, as I crawl into bed with Gemma, I am at a loss as to how to broach this subject.

"Gemma." I place my hand on her arm that's over the covers then gently rub it. "We need to talk."

Gemma says nothing for a moment. I decide to wait her out. It doesn't take long. She heaves a long sigh before sitting up and facing me. My hand falls away from Gemma's arm. Her frown is deep, and her brows are pulled together with concern.

"You are upset," I start, not sure how to discuss such a sensitive and sacred topic. "But tell me, exactly, what you're upset about? About how permanent things are between us? When you asked me if I could be a part of what you and Christopher have, I'm sure you weren't expecting another—" I pause as I think of a non-threating way to label our new relationship. "—*mate*. Or, are you worried about the power hold over me?"

Gemma's frown grows deeper as she considers my words. She looks around the room as she thinks. I give her the time she needs. This is not a conversation that needs to be rushed. After a long pause, she turns back to look at me.

"I'm not upset about being tied to another person. Though—" She tilts her head as she regards me. "I do wish I had been told up front, by both you *and* Christopher, what was happening. If I didn't want to be with you, I wouldn't have asked you to be in a relationship with us."

She looks down at her hands when she stops speaking.

"Gemma, if I knew what even considering being in a relationship with you could do to the both of us—"

"You wouldn't have put yourself in this position," she interrupts, looking back up at me with a serious gaze. "Would you?"

I pause, taken back by her solemnity and her question. I think about it. Would I have chosen this for myself? I take mental and emotional inventory. I *feel* like myself. Not like before. Before, I was so swept up in my master's needs and wants that I had no thoughts for myself or for anything else. I was quite literally a slave to whatever desires she had. I was so obsessed and devoted to my master that I became distressed or even ill if she was not satisfied in every way. Maybe if I were feeling that way again, I would try hard to fight this. But here I am, sitting in my new master's bed with a clear mind. While I am concerned about Gemma, my mind isn't sickeningly obsessed about every word coming out of her mouth. If I'm myself... there's no need to be upset over what has taken place.

And emotionally? I think I've already been balancing precariously between trying to stay objective and not falling for the woman next to me. With her bright smile and sparkling personality, it is hard *not* to be drawn to her. My body already made the decision of who it wanted to service well before my mind had. It seemed to know that Gemma is someone worth caring for. Out of all the women I have been around, and that is quite a large number, Gemma is the only one who comes across as selfless, sweet, and genuine. Out of all the women I have known, Gemma is easily the best choice to become my master.

I wonder if these thoughts are due to the new bond between us. During my first few years on this Earth, I was sure that I felt love for my master. Am I blinded now? Immediately, my whole body seems to shrink away from the thought that what I am feeling now is fake. No, *these* emotions are different from before. The happiness and wholeness I feel now is nothing like the sick aching and urgent need for affirmation I used to feel.

Thinking back to those times makes me cringe.

"See? You've pretty much had no say in this either. I forced you into this position by demanding your companionship," Gemma says, mistaking my cringe for confirmation. She hangs her head. "And what's worse is that there is some sort of power exchange. I don't want that. I don't want to be your master. So not only have I stripped you of your free will to choose your life partner, but I've gained *actual* power over you. You're not a slave, to me or to anyone else, Darion."

I shake my head even before she's done speaking.

"No, Gemma, you're wrong. Honestly, I have no idea how choosing a master happens. It happens so rarely there aren't even others to ask. But while my body decided that you are its next temple to worship, *I* made the final decision to want to be loyal and faithful *to you*. That's what sealed our fates together. I do not feel any regret or anger in this decision. In fact—" I pause as I assess how I feel. "—there is a peace within me now. This, to me, has been the best decision I could have made for myself."

Gemma looks up to me in surprise. It's clear she expected a reprimand or condemnation from me. But how can I condemn this woman, who is so clearly upset *for me*, when this is my own doing? Quite frankly, *she* should be upset with *me*. She didn't ask to be tethered to someone else. She simply asked if I thought I would be interested in a *normal* polyamorous relationship. She has had zero choice with this new binding between us. Plus, I bestowed upon her an enormously powerful and dangerous gift. If someone with less than honorable intentions were to manage to become a master to an incubus, they could use the power of the incubus to manipulate the people around them. Luckily, Gemma is as far from malicious or evil as one can be.

"Are you telling me the truth, or are you just telling me what you think I want to hear?" she asks as she studies my face. I scowl.

"I would not and will not lie to you, Gemma. Ever," I tell her seriously.

She stares at me a little longer before she acknowledges my promise with a slight nod.

"What if we're not on the same page about certain things?" she asks me.

I frown. "Like what?"

Gemma makes a face like she's embarrassed and looks away quickly. "You know… like important couple stuff. What if I want kids someday in the future and you don't? Or you do but Christopher doesn't? Or what about marriage? What about meeting parents or simply just living together? Because as of right now I have my own apartment. I'm only here because it's safer than being at my own place. It's not like either of you have asked me to move in and that right there is a big conversation.

"I haven't even talked to Christopher about this yet. We're only now just finding our footing with each other, but we should have had this conversation *before* he bit me. There's a lot we, all three of us, just kind of skipped over and now some irrevocable things have happened. How is all of this supposed to work?"

Shock paralyzes me into silence.

Kids? Those things are typically germ-infested nuisances with poor manners. From what I've witnessed throughout my life, they are clearly a lot of work, and I'm not quite sure they are worth the investment. I've never even considered them since free incubuses cannot get women pregnant. But now that I have a master, rules in the biological department are different.

"*Do* you want kids?" I ask her. My voice is strained as I think this over.

"In the future, yeah," She mumbles. She looks up at me curiously and asks, "Can you even get me pregnant?"

There is a short silence as I consider my next words wisely. I answer cautiously. "If our masters want children, our body's genetic make-up changes so that we can start producing viable sperm cells that would impregnate them. They would be normal human children."

The shock on Gemma's face doesn't hide the way she visibly cringes at the word master. I shake my head quickly to dispel her negative thoughts. I reach over and take her hand. Our eyes meet, and I smile down at her.

"Master does not have a bad connotation between us, Gemma," I tell her calmly. "It actually…" I pause as I brace myself to share more of my secret with her. "It actually brings an incubus great pleasure to regard you in such a manner. We were born to serve. My mind and body *want* to do whatever it is you wish."

Surprise ripples across Gemma's face. She presses her lips together in a straight line and shakes her head in disbelief. I sigh, both with frustration and amusement. I can understand her skepticism. If this conversation were reversed, I would have a hard time believing it, too.

"I told you, I will never speak a lie to you," I tell her. "Just thinking about you giving me a command turns me on."

Even as I speak the words out loud, my body grows hard. It is a strange thing, to *enjoy* serving another who has ultimate power over you. When free of a master, the thought of serving another is repulsive and undesirable, but now that I have Gemma the idea feels right. I know she will not abuse her power, and I have great affection for her. With my previous master, there was neither trust nor fondness.

"You *want* me to tell you what to do?" she repeats with incredulity.

"Yes," I tell her without hesitation. When Gemma shakes her head and looks away, I add, "But there is a word you have to use along with your command. It strips us of our free will, but god does it feel so damn good."

She looks back at me with narrow pupils. "A word?"

I nod as I begin to unbutton my shirt. Gemma's eyes fall to watch my hands. I open my shirt just enough so she can see the runes on my skin. I point to the largest one just under her fresh mark.

"This word is what controls an incubus. Only our master is privy to the word, though if someone else says it nothing can happen to us. It is pronounced, *hesirah*." Fuck, I'm hard as a rock right now as I think about Gemma using the word on me. "It means, roughly translated, *desired one*. You would use it before or after your command, and I must comply."

Gemma stares at the rune on my chest then her gaze drops to my erection, which I do not bother to hide from her. Slowly, she raises her eyes to meet mine.

"This really does excite you, doesn't it?" she asks softly.

"What do you think?" I counter, lifting a brow with amusement.

"I think we went from talking about kids to servitude really quick. There must have been a reason for that diversion," Gemma says with smile. I sigh.

"Gemma, if you wish to have children, then so be it," I tell her seriously. Gemma laughs and replies,

"Please, contain your excitement, Darion." She doesn't seem put off, and I'm relieved. Hopefully talk of kids can be put to rest now. "That would be way in the future anyway. I was just pointing out conversations we probably all should have before hopes and dreams are shattered a few years down the line."

"Whatever it is you wish, I will make sure you have it," I tell her, meaning every word.

There is no way I will allow the woman to whom I am bound struggle for anything. Not when I have the means to provide for her. "And as for all those other pesky conversations, we will have them. Just give us some time. It is clear we were all meant to be together. Watch how everything will work out."

Gemma's soft smile melts my insides.

"Thank you, Darion, for talking about this with me. I didn't know how to broach it."

I bring her hand up and kiss the back of it.

"Of course," I murmur.

Gemma scoots closer to me so that her whole side is pressed against mine.

"Can I ask you something?" she hedges. I glance at her face and wait. Her expression flickers from embarrassment to uncertainty to curiosity. "May I use our word this evening? Now that I know that you want me to use it… Maybe we could try now? So I can see and understand what happens?"

My erection grows dramatically harder, so swiftly that I grunt at the sudden tension.

"You do not have to ask permission," I tell her.

As I think about all the different things she could order me to do, I begin to smile. For all these years, I've been in charge of both my pleasure and whoever I am with. Now it is someone else's turn to take charge. The idea is exciting.

"I do," she replies quickly and firmly. "I'm not going to abuse my power."

"How about, when we're in the house, you do not have to ask," I suggest. "This is a safe area."

Gemma thinks about this. When she realizes my offer is fair, she nods. I brace myself, waiting for my first command from my new master. Gemma shifts her position, so she is on her knees staring at me, her expression serious. I can't help but chuckle. My sweet Gemma is so worried I won't enjoy this. She will see soon enough. My amusement seems to ease some of her stress because her shoulders relax.

"Please remove your clothes, *hesirah*," she asks me softly.

The effect is instantaneous. If there were any desire to refuse Gemma's command, it would have been snuffed out. My blood begins to grow hot under my skin, and my cock twitches eagerly. I move off the bed. As I peel off my clothes, electrical pulses start from the new mark on my chest and radiate out into each limb of my body, causing a sense of euphoria to take over. Taking off my clothes has never felt so wonderful.

When each item of clothing lies on the floor, I stand before Gemma with a grin splitting across my face. She's watching me. Her smile is tentative, still uncertain about her new ability. But her eyes have grown darker, and I can smell her desire now.

"Are you alright?" she asks me softly.

"Darling, I'm more than *alright*," I tell her with a shit-eating grin.

My voice has a demonic ring to it now. It's an effect of my master's power when she summons the demon power within me. My erection is uncomfortably hard, begging for attention. I'm excited for her next request. I wait, and the anticipation only makes it more thrilling.

Gemma studies me for a moment. After a brief pause, she climbs out of bed and walks over to stand in front of me. When we're hardly a hair's width apart, she stops and looks up at me with those large brown eyes. Slowly, she rises onto her tip-toes and kisses my chin.

"*Hesirah,*" she whispers as she pulls away. "Remove my clothes. And as you do, kiss me, everywhere."

I growl as a shiver of pleasure slides over my skin. It's every bit as good as being buried between Gemma's legs. Without missing a beat, I start to peel Gemma out of her night shirt. She raises her hands above her head, and I pull it off her. As I toss it to the ground I lean down and take her mouth with mine. Oh, sweet heavens, does she taste wonderful. I don't linger on her lips, though. She has asked me to kiss her everywhere, and I will. I pull away from her mouth and lean down further to kiss her neck.

Her shiver of desire does not go unnoticed as I trail kisses from her ear down to her shoulder. I don't pull away as I reach around and unclasped the bra she still has on in bed. As the straps droop over her shoulders, I allow the bra to fall away. With her breasts exposed, I reach forward to cup them. For as much as she works out, she still has some perfectly sized breasts. A full handful. I kiss both eagerly. Gemma's soft sigh fills the room. My mind begins to grow hazy as the need to fulfill her request causes a euphoria within me. Pleasure is continuously rippling through me as I do as I am told.

I leave her breasts to kneel before Gemma. My hands run down her sides as I kiss her stomach. Reaching forward, I slip off her panties, the only item of clothing left. They are damp with her arousal. My lips skim across her pelvis from hip bone to hip bone, leaving soft kisses in their wake. My hands come around and grasp her ass as I kiss her inner thighs. They then slide lower to grab the back of her thighs. I grip them and pull them apart, causing Gemma to gasp and grab my shoulders.

I take a moment to stare at Gemma's arousal. My cock is so swollen it should be painful. It's not, though. I know soon enough I will be relieved of this ache as I continue to do as requested. I lean forward and slide my tongue through her folds. Gemma's entire body trembles hard. I do it once more to tease her before feasting on the delicacy in front of me.

Gemma's cry of pleasure sends a pulse of ecstasy through me. Her hands leave my shoulders to find their way into my hair. Her fingers grab a handful, and she pushes my face further between her legs.

"Yes, oh god, yes!" Gemma says, choking as her body trembles again.

As her breathing quickens, I let go of one of her thighs and slip two fingers inside of her as I continue to eat. While I stroke her, Gemma's body begins grinding against my face. Her soft gasp and cries are enough to make me nearly burst just kneeling before her. I forgot how good it feels to serve. To worship. To devour… Gemma's whole body stiffens before convulsing as she finds her release.

I lick her clean with slow, purposeful strokes of my tongue, which causes her body to shake. When I'm done, I stand and look down into her glowing face. Gemma smiles up at me.

"Give me another command," I tell her, hoarsely.

My eagerness is almost childlike. The rush and thrill of serving is powerful.

"Hm…" She playfully ponders her next command, and I wait, eager to perform. "*Hesirah,* take me in the position of your choosing."

The order takes me by surprise. While my mind begins to flip through every single position a couple can create with their bodies, my body is already on the prowl. I take Gemma's face in my hands and kiss her. My tongue parts her lips and clashes with hers. Her hands skim down my chest. One hand slides all the way down, and she grabs the length of me. I groan as she strokes me. I walk forward, forcing her to step back. I keep walking until the back of her knees hits the bed. I pull my mouth away from hers and push her backward, adding a little something as I touch her…

As she falls back, I can see the effect of my power as it rushes through her. Her nipples tighten, her eyes roll to the back of her head, and her body convulses as another orgasm ripples through her.

"Darion!" The way Gemma screams my name causes me to grin.

I don't allow her to recuperate. I grab her legs, bring them up and then fold them back onto her. Now her thighs are pressed against her stomach, and her legs frame her face. Gemma meets my gaze through half-hooded lids. Her smile grows wide as I close the gap between us. I grin in response. Without any further preamble, I lean forward and place myself at her entrance.

As I surge into her, a part of me wants to show her all the things I can do with the power that courses through me. Gemma shifts her hips, and I sink deeper into her. It's enough to keep me from adding my power into the mix. I want her to know that I, without all the bells and whistles, can please her. I can make her body sing. I'll use my body to show her that even though she didn't have a choice in this union, she will not regret it. I can make her happy.

Her body grabs me with a death grip. I hiss, struggling to breath as her body strangles me. Her loud, passionate groan crescendos as I continue my impalement. When I'm all the way in, I allow her body a moment to adjust.

"Move, *hesirah*," she commands after she tries to do it herself but can't in this position.

I chuckle, half at her greedy demand and half in delight as the command sends another shot of euphoria through me.

My body begins surging in and out of Gemma. I briefly close my eyes to savor the feeling of being inside her, my new master. I force my eyes open to stare down at her. Her beautiful face is flushed, her lips parted. Her eyes remain closed as she feels everything. I'm halfway on top of her, pinning her to the bed, holding both of her legs up as I thrust into her. In this position, I can get deep, so deep. We're both vocal as we near our peak. As Gemma's body denotates, she clenches around me so tightly that I'm forced to follow suit.

Our cries are loud. Loud enough that the others could hear if they are listening. Neither of us care though. Panting, I withdraw from Gemma and help her lower her legs. I scoot her over and climb into bed with her.

She turns her head to look at me. I can see the concern, and I anticipate her question before she even opens her mouth.

"Gemma, I enjoyed every second of that. I do not feel used or violated," I assure her. She smiles and reaches out to caress my face.

"I enjoyed it, too," she says, and I relax. Hopefully, Gemma will be able to relax, too.

"I do need you to do something for me," I hedge, knowing good and well I'm taking advantage of the situation.

"What is it?" she asks quickly.

"Come back here tomorrow after work," I say. "As you can see, matters are escalating, and I would rather you be here with us rather than on your own at your apartment. In fact, you should plan to stay here for a while, who knows when all of this will be over."

Gemma is silent for a moment as she considers my request. I mean it when I tell her it's for her safety, but I also know that her coming back here means more time together. More time to get to know one another. More time to explore this new connection between us. And more time to figure things out between the two of us and Christopher.

She chuckles, breaking the silence. "Fine, I'll come back here tomorrow."

"What's so funny about that?"

"We were just talking about kids and all those 'pesky' conversations. If you're not careful, you'll accidentally invite me to move in, which would fall under that 'pesky' category."

I think about the conversation I had with Christopher about living arrangements. Gemma moving into our place sounds more and more like a better idea now that things have dramatically changed for the three of us. I keep my mouth closed though. Her chuckle sounded nervous, not amused. We can wait to have that conversation another night.

Chapter Nineteen

Gemma

I'm exhausted.

When I slip downstairs to make myself a cup of coffee and toast the following morning, Tate is there waiting for me. When he tells me that his plans for the day include following my every move, I'm not in the mood nor do I have the energy to object.

I hardly notice the trees and suburban houses flying by as Tate drives me to work. The handsome ex-soldier with his shaved head, wide shoulders, and deep blue eyes hasn't taken his eyes off the road since we got in the car. Occasionally when I look over, I catch him scanning the area in front of us for danger. We've hardly spoken a word to one another since breakfast, but I'm okay with that. I don't need his cantankerous attitude right now.

Mentally, I start making a list of things I need to get done today. I have my laptop on my lap. I itch to open it and get to work. I'm so far behind, and while I managed to get done what I set out to do on Saturday, that only puts me on schedule, not ahead of it. I check my emails on my phone. Two of the three designers that work for me emailed me this morning that they won't be in due to either a family emergency or the cold. Great, more work for me. I have to make sure their clients are happy, too.

Luckily, the stress of work manages to keep my attention off the two men who have been bound to me. Darion had to go to court to file some paperwork this morning. He was getting dressed in his own room when Tate and I left. Christopher was in the shower. Part of me wonders if I should have kissed them both before leaving for work.

No, I need some space from them both. This is too much too fast, and I just can't handle it.

When Tate pulls up to my building, he holds a hand up, indicating that I should wait. I huff in annoyance but nod. Then, he simply disappears. My mouth drops open while the rest of my body freezes. Christopher warned me about Tate, but seeing it with my own eyes... No one can prepare for that. Quickly, I compose myself, remembering Christopher's warning about how touchy Tate is to people's reactions.

It's silent for about five minutes. The parking lot fills with businessmen and women who work in the surrounding buildings as I wait. I tap my foot impatiently. How long am I supposed to wait? Is he going to give me a sign that everything is okay? I don't see any sign of the mysterious Tate Ganger; then, suddenly he is there opening my door.

"All clear," he says softly.

I step out of the car with my purse and laptop in tow. Tate follows me to the door and stands close as I punch in the code. I want to mock him and throw his words back in his face about staying out of each other's space, but I hold my tongue. I may not be a fan of his, but the others are, so I am going to try my hardest to be nice... or at the very least civil. When I enter the building, Tate vanishes again. This time I force myself not to react. I flick on the lights as I head back to my office. When I open my door, I find Tate already inside.

"Nothing appears to have been touched or tampered with," he tells me.

He's standing with his feet set wide and hands clasped behind his back. Not only does he look like a soldier, but he stands like one too. Does the guy ever relax?

"Thank you," I tell him.

I'm sincere in my gratitude. The past few weeks have been terrifying. To know I'm safe in this little space gives me a sense of comfort. Tate doesn't respond. Instead, he vanished out of sight in less time than it takes to blink.

I get to work at once. I work on projects, call clients, contact the local printer, schedule new clients who have projects that need completing, and handle my own marketing needs for my business. I don't stop for lunch. I just power through my day. Twice, I am interrupted by walk-ins. Both times I witness Tate stopping them at the door to search them before they are allowed to enter. I'm so swamped and up to my neck in work that I don't realize how much time passes.

"You know ignoring their calls and texts will only piss them off," a deep voice says from my office door.

I jump in surprise and look up. Tate leans against the door frame with his arms crossed over his chest. His expression is borderline annoyed, but there is a hint of amusement in his eyes. I glance at the time and gasp.

"Oh! I didn't realize it's past eight," I say as I stand. "You're probably starving. I'm so sorry."

"Do you have much left to do?" he asks.

I pull my hair out of the tight bun I twisted it into that morning and sigh in relief as the tension in my scalp eases.

"Only about a million things," I grumble.

"How about I order dinner for us and have it delivered here so you can finish up?" he offers.

I pause my gathering of the paperwork spread out on my desk to look up at him.

"You'd do that?" I ask in surprise. "Don't you want to go home and relax with the guys?"

He shrugs. "I can do that later. I'll order something for us. I hope you're not picky."

He turns to walk away, not waiting for a response. I stare after him, baffled.

I turn my attention back to work. Again, time slips by unnoticed. When Tate walks back into my office with a bag of food, I'm almost positive I didn't blink the whole time he was gone. I rub my eyes, not caring that my eye makeup smears.

"Hm… smells good." I stand up and walk around my desk. "How much do I owe you?" I ask as Tate places the Styrofoam container onto my desk and pulls out a plastic fork and knife.

"Don't worry about it. You can get it next time," he grumbles. I can't help it. I laugh. Tate pulls the chair for clients close to the desk and collapses into it. When he looks at me, he's scowling. "Something funny?"

I pick up the container with my name on it as I answer. "You said 'next time.' What? Was this an exhilarating day for you? You want to do it again?"

Tate says nothing for a moment as he grabs his meal and opens it. Hm… He went with a burrito with ground beef and veggies. It looks amazing. I open mine up, content to have a non-answer from my security guard. Oh goodness, chicken enchiladas with guacamole and sour cream on top.

"This is my favorite Mexican dish. I don't know how you would know that, but thank you," I tell him and lean over to grab my fork.

I lean my hip against the desk and begin to tear into my dinner.

"Christopher and Darion are like my brothers," Tate says, breaking the silence. "I'll do anything for them. You seem to make them happy, so if I want them to stay that way, I need you to stick around. That can't happen if you're dead. If they need someone who they can trust to watch over you, then I'll do it."

A bite of enchiladas pauses halfway to my mouth. His frankness is refreshing, and I'm glad he has Darion's and Christopher's best interests at heart. I capture the bite in my mouth and chew, not sure what to say to that.

"But if you fuck with them in any way, I'll remove you from their lives myself," Tate warns.

Ah, there's the asshole. I swallow my food and wipe my mouth with a napkin.

"First of all, I have no intentions of fucking either of them over," I tell him with a glare. I open my mouth to continue, but he cuts me off,

"Intentionally or not," he snaps, glaring back at me.

"That certainly doesn't leave any room for human error," I tell him angrily. I put down my food so my fists can rest on my hips.

"Sounds like that's your problem, not mine," Tate quips as he shovels food into his mouth.

What a fucking dick. Anger unfurls and collides with my fatigue. I glare at the bastard and lean forward to get in his face.

"You're right, it *is* my problem. Add that to the growing list of problems in my life. Urgh! Why can't I escape any of them?" I yell at him. I'm suddenly feeling everything at once, and I lash out in anger. "I've been bitten by a wolf without my consent who humiliated me in my most vulnerable moment and has now waltzed back into my life wanting to play boyfriend. I save his friend's life, and now, not only am I a target of one of Darion's enemies, I'm suddenly his *master* too! I can't even go back to my apartment to just give myself some space to breathe, because said enemies could attempt to kidnap me again. So, I've been beaten down to agree to staying in a house with two guys who want everything from me and with one guy who hates my guts!"

I stop only to take a deep breath. Then I continue,

"Did you know the other day was the first time I've seen a dead body? And not only did I see one, I saw *four*. How did I end up in this situation? I'm a mate, a master, and a headache." I give him a pointed look at the last title. "So much has happened in such a short amount of time. I'm going insane! So yes, you're right, it is *my problem*. Along with all of these other problems. I'll somehow have to prioritize them. I'm utterly alone and have no one to talk to while the three of you can just chat amongst each other! So, forgive me for ignoring their texts or calls all day. They can be pissy for a moment while I catch my breath!"

"It's not in my job description to deal with your pity party," Tate drawls as he gives me a cold and unmoved glare.

A knot forms in my throat, and tears form in my eyes. Angry that Tate has managed to make me cry, I walk around my desk and grab my purse. I pull out cash, which I toss to the asshole. I shoulder my purse, slam my laptop shut and walk over to my door.

"The code to lock up is nineteen sixty-nine," I tell him over my shoulder and storm out.

"Where the fuck do you think you're going?" he yells after me.

I ignore him and storm out the front door. Tate drove us here this morning in one of the cars that Darion and Christopher own, so without the keys to the vehicle, I'm stuck taking public transportation. I'll have to figure out the closest route to their house once I get on. I head towards the bus station. It's dark, but the streetlamps light the way as I head to the bus stop about five blocks away.

I make it one block from my building when a hand grabs my forearm. Fueled by adrenaline from both fear and my argument with Tate, I whirl around on my attacker and let my fists fly. I land two punches into my attacker's face and am able to bite at their ear before I am shoved away.

"What the hell, Gemma!?"

I'm so hyped up that it takes me a moment to realize who is yelling and that I'm not being assaulted. When I realize it's Tate on the receiving end of my fists, I'm so shocked that the only thing I can do is laugh. The laughter is cathartic. Tears well up, and spill down my cheeks as I double over with laughter.

"Have you gone insane? Why are you laughing?" Tate demands.

It takes a moment, but eventually I'm able to suppress my laughter. I wipe away the tears streaming down my face.

"If I haven't yet, I'm pretty sure I'm at my breaking point." I pause to catch my breath and to allow my heartbeat to go back to normal. "You shouldn't sneak up on people who have gone through traumatic experiences! I could have killed you."

This time it's Tate who finds amusement in the situation. He chuckles as he pulls his hand away from his ear. A lot of blood coats his hand and drips down his neck. Huh, I must have done some real damage there. I smirk at him, and his chuckles stop.

"Tell me something," he says with a scowl. "If you lie to me, I'll make your life a living hell."

I scoff. "You think way too highly of yourself to think that you can top everything else I've been dealing with. But go ahead, I'm still catching my breath, so I have time to listen to whatever offensive question you have for me."

His voice drops to a deep, icy octave. "Are you a government plant?"

The hairs on the back of my neck rise. A government plant? Why would he assume this? Is this some sort of PTSD response to my attack?

"No, I've never worked for the government a day in my life," I answer, baffled and a little concerned by the way Tate is staring down at me.

"Then how come ever since I've met you, I haven't had a lapse in control?" he demands.

"What are you talking about?" I ask him.

His pupils narrow to pinpoints, and he takes a step closer to me, invading my personal space. I don't back up. I meet his gaze and clench my jaw. There's no way in hell I am going to let him intimidate me.

"Ever since I've been home, I haven't had a lapse in my ability, and it hasn't made any sense! But now I realize it's *you* somehow controlling my stability," he snaps. "I didn't even consider that you could be some sort of test or plant until you just walked out of your office, and immediately, I couldn't hold my form. It didn't make sense that they would just let me go… But suddenly you appear around the same time I'm released from duty. This has to be more than a coincidence."

He takes another step forward, bumping me with his chest. This is unacceptable, so I shove at his hard chest. He doesn't budge. Tate grabs my forearm with a bruising grip and leans down so his face is in mine.

"Tell me who you work for!" he demands. Spit hits my face. I try to pull my arm away, but he only grips me tighter. Tate's blue eyes are now wide, his face is red, and his body is shaking. "Who are you working for?" he yells again.

"I told you! I'm not working for anyone," I tell him angrily. "Now get your hands off me, or I'll scream."

Tate's anger twists his handsome face into something ugly. His grip on me tightens for just a moment before he practically shoves me away.

"Then tell me why I'm able to hold my shape around you?" he demands. "I haven't been able to be this solid since…since…"

He breaks off as confusion contorts his face. It's followed by a glimpse of desolation as his shoulders slump, and he sighs. I realize that I'm not the true cause behind his ire. Well, at least not fully behind it. My own anger eases as concern for this man's well-being takes precedence.

"Tate, have you asked for help for this… um, issue?" I ask him. "Christopher told me that you have a problem staying present, but I didn't realize what that meant. I didn't realize you couldn't stay…well, you. There has to be a way to help."

Tate shakes his head in defeat and looks away from me. "No one can help me. They've tried. I've done all the experiments, all the drugs… Nothing helps." He pauses as he turns back to face me. "Well, nothing except you."

"I'm not doing anything, though."

"Well, you just being you is doing something. Since I've been home, you've been around me. Then, I'm with you all day today with absolutely no issue. I can hold my shape and shift to my shadow form and back again with no issues. The minute you're… out of range, I guess, I'm flickering like a lightbulb that's about to burn out. You have no idea what it's like to finally feel… normal. But it's dangerous to get comfortable like I have been. I can't get caught flickering in and out. I was given early retirement on the condition that I remain out of the public eye. Civilians, heck, other countries, can't find out that our government has been experimenting on its own people."

I open my mouth to ask him how this all started, but we're interrupted by the sound of gunfire.

Bullets hit the ground around us as people emerge from the alley between two buildings across the street. Tate lets go of me as I scream.

"Run, Gemma! I'll take out as many as I can," Tate yells.

Then, the crazed man who has just accused at me of being some sort of government spy disappears before my eyes. I'm left alone, and bullets are still flying. I take off down the street. Bullets hit the brick buildings around me and ricochet off the sidewalk.

Two men step out from behind a parked car in front of me with guns raised. I duck between two buildings. I instantly regret this direction. There is a chain link fence at the end of the alley, blocking my way. Instead of slowing down, I rush it, knowing that if I stop, I'm dead. I leap at the fence and start climbing. I'm over it just as men hurry down the alley after me.

I run down this side of the alley, turn, and find myself between another two buildings. I duck behind a large dumpster as three men round the corner, shouting to one another. I listen to their footsteps getting closer to my hiding spot. My heart is beating rapidly, and my hands are shaking. I clutch my purse closer to my side like a shield under my arm. A commotion from somewhere nearby causes the men to stop their forward motion. They yell at each other, and I hear them moving away from me.

I look around me, trying to find a way out of this. I see it in the form of a fire escape ladder. Without hesitation I rush forward, leaving my hiding place to leap up for the bottom step. I make it and pull my dead weight up slowly until my feet hit the bottom step. I send up a prayer of thanks that I compete in obstacle course races. Without that athletic background, I would have just dangled from that bottom step like an idiot.

Someone sees me and yells my location for others to hear. Bullets start flying again. I cringe as some hit close to me. The ladder shakes hard, and I take a half-second to look down and see someone climbing up after me. They are quickly gaining. I double my efforts. When I make it to the top of the building, my feet hit the ground, and I sprint across the roof. Unfortunately, there is nowhere for me to run. The distance between this building and the next is simply too far for me to reach, but I head in that direction anyway.

What else can I do? Get shot?

A bullet wheezes by my ear, and I wince. My feet pound against the stone on the roof, my breathing is loud, and my panic is full blown. I'm feet away from the ledge of the building, and I have to make a decision: stop to face the gunman and beg for my life or take a leap of faith and pray to every single deity that I make it across. My decision is made as a bullet hits just where my right foot had been.

I jump.

Time halts around me as my life, all twenty-eight years of it, flashes before my eyes. There is nothing under my feet but air. My stomach drops, and a scream begins to bubble up as I realize that I'm going to miss the edge of the next building by mere inches. The unfairness of it all feels cruel. A sharp pang of despair courses through me as I think of Christopher and Darion. I have been given *two* gifts, two great men to be with, and I never got the chance to enjoy my time with them.

On the edge of other building, Tate materializes out of nowhere. He reaches out and grabs my outstretched hands just as I start to drop from the sky. My face slams against the side of the building, but I'm not falling. Thank goodness for that. Tate pulls me up and draws me to his chest.

"Hold on to my shirt and don't let go. Hold on as if your life depends on it. And close your eyes, *now*," he orders. I do as he says, my brain too scattered to do anything else.

One moment, we're standing on the top of a building; the next, I'm thrown into a world where time and space mean nothing. There is a horrible sensation of someone ripping out my guts, ripping off my limbs, and reaching into my skull to rip out my brain. The pain is unbearable. I'm dying. Before I can scream, the sensation stops.

I open my eyes to find both Tate and me on the sidewalk blocks away from where we just were. I can't hear any guns going off, nor can I hear people yelling. It's quiet. Enough so that I am aware of my own hyperventilation. I'm gasping for air as my legs tremble hard beneath me. The world is spinning. I can feel the blood drain from my face.

"Gemma, are you alright? Talk to me," Tate demands.

I can't talk. My mind is whirling too fast. My body is humming from pain, but it's not nearly as bad as it had been moments ago.

"Gemma!" Tate yells.

I can hardly feel him take my elbow, and his voice sounds far off. It takes more effort than I thought was physically possible to lift my eyes to meet his, but when I do, I see his expression is petrified. His brows are drawn tight together, his eyes are wild with fear, and every muscle in his jaw is taut.

"Talk to me, Gemma. Tell me you're alright!" He shakes my arm a little. My stomach lurches.

"I'm going to be sick," I gasp.

I turn and throw up the few bites I ate of dinner. My legs wobble. Just as they give out Tate's arm wraps around my waist, preventing me from collapsing into my own vomit.

"Take deep breaths," he commands.

He uses two fingers to check my pulse on my wrist. When he's done, Tate takes my chin with his hand and forces me to look up into his eyes. He looks for something, but I am too dizzy and distorted to focus. The world beneath me seems to shift, and my legs give up trying to support me.

"Fuck," Tate snarls as he scoops me into his arms. "Tell me what you're feeling. Any tightness in your chest? Do you know your name? What year is it? The alphabet?"

I squeeze my eyes closed as nausea rushes through me again. As I try to calm myself, I answer his questions. When I'm done reciting the alphabet, Tate sighs.

"Tell me immediately if you feel anything other than nausea," he tells me sternly. I nod, still feeling weak. "I can't believe you're alright."

The relief in his voice is scary. I open my eyes and ask, "What just happened?"

"We rode through the shadows," Tate says as he checks our surroundings.

He starts walking us through the mostly empty streets. I have no idea where we're going, and honestly, I don't care at the moment. As long as I don't have to walk, I am content.

"It was extremely dangerous of me to do that with you, but we were surrounded. If there was any other way out of that situation, I wouldn't have pulled you into the darkness."

"Dangerous how?" I ask.

I'm trying to keep him talking. I'm afraid that if he stops, I'll have nothing to focus on and faint.

"You could have died."

"How did you know that I wouldn't?" I ask, tensing in his arms, alarmed.

Tate looks me dead in the eye, his expression grim, and answers, "I didn't."

Chapter Twenty

Christopher

Tate texted saying they would be home in an hour. That was almost two hours ago. Neither he nor Gemma are picking up the phone or answering text messages. Gemma hasn't answered any of my calls or texts all day, which already put me on edge. But now my gut is telling me that something is wrong. I shifted twenty minutes ago, unable to keep my wolf calm in my human form. I pace by the front gates of the house, anxious and tense.

I wonder if I should have stayed in my human form. Maybe Darion has heard from them. I don't have my phone on me so if they have called or texted, I am at a disadvantage. Darion is certainly handling this better than I am. The incubus disappeared into his office a while ago, apparently comfortable with the knowledge that Tate will watch out for our woman.

It isn't that I don't trust Tate. I know he will do as he says and watch over Gemma. What I don't like about the situation is how much of an ass Tate has been to Gemma. He is going to make it harder on all of us if Gemma doesn't want to hang around the house. I am used to Tate's ornery attitude. I know how much he struggles with what has happened to him and what our government had him do while he was in the service. Well, I know as much as Tate can share with us. It's hard to be a science experiment gone partially wrong.

But around Gemma, his behavior is the worst I've ever seen. Usually, he has some sort of manners. His cool demeanor is off putting to most, but he's never outright hostile the way he is around her. My wolf bristles as he thinks about Tate and Gemma. He didn't like how our brother treated his mate either. I'm going to have to talk to Tate.

Headlights flash as a car roars up the street. I still and watch as the car approaches. It turns into the drive, and the security guards posted at the gate allow it to come through. I throw back my head and howl in relief. Without wasting another moment, I run in the woods alongside the car. The car skids to a stop behind Darion's SUV, which is parked behind my truck in front of the house, and the headlights turn off. I shift and sprint across the front yard.

Tate gets out of the car and walks around to open the door for Gemma, but I'm already there. I fling the door open and nearly yank her out of the car. Immediately, I smell blood. I hold her at arm's length and take in the scrape across her cheek. A handprint-shaped bruise wraps around her forearm. Her face is pulled taut, and her body is trembling. There are unshed tears in her eyes. My wolf snarls as he pieces together what I have already concluded: Gemma was attacked.

"What the hell happened?" I demand as I clutch her to my naked body.

Gemma throws her arms around my neck, and I hear her breath hitch as her body shudders. My heart squeezes in my chest at her visible distress. I rub my face into her hair, breathing in her scent. Whatever happened, she's fine now, I tell myself.

"They had a crew waiting for us outside when Gemma got off work," Tate answers.

I smell more blood. I glance over to him to see blood has crusted around his ear and dried down his neck.

"Were you shot? You're missing a piece of your ear," I ask, alarmed.

In my arms, Gemma chuckles weakly. Tate's expression sours.

"I was shot at but not hit. This," he says as he reaches up to gingerly touch his ear, "is from Gemma. I accidentally snuck up on her, and she attacked me when she thought I was an assailant."

"It's stupid to sneak up on people," she mumbles into my chest.

"I know that for next time," he says.

"There's not going to be a next time," Darion says behind us. I turn with Gemma in my arms to see him standing at the top of the stairs. His expression is thunderous. "You're not going back to work, Gemma."

Gemma nods, providing no objections. Whatever happened tonight must have been her breaking point.

"You should get her something to eat," Tate grumbles. "She didn't eat much for dinner, and what she did eat she threw up after I was forced to travel through the shadows. I've had to pull over a few times so she could be sick *outside* the car."

Red blankets my vision and a snarl ripples through me, sounding more wolf than man.

"You did what?!" Darion bellows.

My whole body shakes hard as my wolf reacts. I place Gemma away from me, afraid I'll lose control and hurt her as I change. My vision narrows as I focus on Tate. My fingers curl into claws, and I can feel blood in my mouth as my jaw tries to elongate. Darion is on top of Tate before I can settle on which form I am going to take him out with. Darion tackles Tate to the ground and slams his fists against his face.

"No! Stop, stop!" Gemma cries out and tries to jump between Darion and Tate.

But she stumbles weakly. I grab her around the waist and pull her away from the two men brawling on the ground. As much as I want to jump in on the action, Gemma can't get hurt because we're pissed. Anyway, Tate is giving it back as good as he gets.

"Darion, stop! Tate saved me!" Her voice is raspy, so she clears her throat to try again.

"He shouldn't have traveled through the shadows with you, Gemma," I snap, my voice barely audible as I fight back my wolf.

"He had to! We were stuck on the roof and had nowhere to run. If he hadn't, we would have died," Gemma objects, struggling to get out of my grasp.

Darion grabs Tate around the neck, and for a moment, I wonder if he's going to strangle him. Tate has told us about what happens when he takes objects or people into the shadows with him. Inanimate objects make it, most of the time, without getting destroyed. People, on the other hand, rarely ever survive traveling like Tate can.

As angry as I am with Tate, Gemma is standing here alive because of him. I open my mouth to tell Darion to cut it out when Gemma groans.

"I'm going to be sick." Her body lurches forward, and she proceeds to dry heave.

The sound of Gemma becoming sick causes Darion to pause. Instead of strangling Tate, he pushes off him and stands. He turns towards Gemma as she collects herself. She sags against me and sighs.

"Let's get you inside," I tell her and guide her up the stairs. Inside the foyer I hesitate, "Food or bed?" As I say it, I answer my own question. "I'll bring you food in bed."

She gives me a weak smile and nods. I let go of her for a moment to sweep my pants off the floor where I stripped them off earlier and slip them on. Then, I scoop her up into my arms and carry her upstairs. Instead of taking her to the guestroom where she's been staying, I carry her to my room. She gives me a curious look.

"You're staying in my room tonight," I tell her.

I kick open my door and walk in. She looks around with wide eyes, and I grin. My room is set up like a den. The expansive bed is tucked into a large half-cave structure I had custom built. The carpet is a deep green, and around the edge of the room are ornate wooden dressers. Hanging on the wall are pictures of woods and nature.

"You've been letting me sleep in that little rinky-dink guestroom?" Gemma asks as she looks around the room.

I chuckle. "As much as I wanted to throw you in here on the first night, I figured you'd be more comfortable in a space of your own. I'm more than happy to have you move into my room." I place her on the edge of the bed, and she sighs. "Take off your dress, and I'll grab you something more comfortable to wear."

I head into my closet and grab a shirt and a pair of sweatpants for her. When I get back, she is shimmying out of her dress. I pause to watch the show but when her legs begin to shake so hard it looks like she'll collapse, I move quickly to her side. She gives me a grateful smile while I hold her as she peels out of her dress.

"Will you tell me what happened?" I ask her.

She's been through a lot. I know at some point, if this continues, she'll have a meltdown. It's only natural, so I tread lightly. If she doesn't want to talk about it, then I won't push her. I'll talk to Tate later regardless.

When she's dressed, she sighs and answers, "Tonight was all my fault. If I hadn't been so stupid, then none of it would have happened."

"I'm sure it's not your fault," I assure her.

Tate was supposed to check for signs of danger before they left her office. If anyone is to blame, it's most definitely him.

Gemma climbs onto the bed and makes herself comfortable in a sitting position.

"It is, though," she says with a frown. "If I hadn't stormed out of my office, Tate would have done a sweep of the area and realized that people were nearby, and then he would have called for backup or something."

I clench my jaw for a moment, knowing the answer to the question I need to ask, "Why did you storm out of your office?"

Gemma's expression turns from forlorn to nonchalant quickly. She picks at the comforter.

"Tate and I got into a heated discussion." She looks up at me quickly and adds, "But that doesn't give me the right to put both of us in danger."

"He was giving you a hard time," I state.

My anger returns and swirls around in my gut. My wolf's hackles are up. Fuck, why's he being such a dick? I need to do something about this. My hands curl into fists as my body shakes again. His inability to be civil could have cost them their lives.

"Well… Yes, but in fairness, he's just looking out for you and Darion," she says, coming to the asshole's defense. "He warned me to be careful about hurting either of you two. I understand his concern and appreciate that he is looking out for you."

"That doesn't explain why you stormed out," I point out, knowing she is probably heavily editing the conversation. She stares up at me, and I can see how tired she is. My anger eases up. I sit down beside her. "Whatever he said to you, don't take it personally. I don't know why he's being such an ass to you."

She shrugs and responds, "You should talk to Tate about it. Actually, I need to talk to him so I can thank him. I was too sick in the car to say much of anything."

"You can talk to him tomorrow… If he can move his jaw after that beating and what's coming," I add darkly. Gemma shakes her head but doesn't say anything. She leans back until she's lying down. "I'll get you something to eat."

With that, I get up and leave. Downstairs, Tate's nursing his jaw with a bag of peas and sipping on a beer at the counter. He straightens when he sees me. His pupils narrow as he tries to assess my mood.

"You're fucking lucky Gemma needs something in her stomach, or I'd rip your throat out," I tell him as I head to the refrigerator.

"Hey, man, I'm sorry. Gemma and I were talking out there in the dark and—"

"Talking or arguing?" I interrupt.

Tate grimaces and quickly says, "Look, Chris, I took it too far. I shouldn't have touched her, but I'm sure she's exaggerating about everything—"

"You *touched* her?" I shout, slamming the refrigerator shut to face him.

Tate winces. "She didn't tell you?"

"No, she's hardly said anything about what happened. The only thing she's made clear is that she blames herself for putting you both in danger, even though it sounds like you drove her to want to get away from you. She ran out headfirst into danger to get away from you!" I shout.

I'm so furious that I lose control of my hold on my wolf. My body begins to contort as my wolf fights me to get to Tate. He's had enough of Tate's behavior towards Gemma and learning that he's touched her is his last straw.

"I know, I'm sorry. I'll go apologize—"

I'm halfway through the change as he speaks. Another wave of fury crashes over my senses, but this time it stops and reverses the shift so I can respond.

"I don't want you anywhere near her," I snarl when I'm capable of responding. I look at the guy who I've thought of as my brother. It's strange seeing someone I trust so much in a new light. What the fuck is going on with Tate? "It's not like she doesn't have enough on her plate. Don't go passing out lame-ass apologies."

I open the refrigerator again and pull out the leftover soup I bought for lunch. It would sit better in her stomach than something too heavy. I heat it up and toast some bread. Tate sighs and takes a swig of his beer.

"I fucked up, Chris. I'll do better. Hell, I'll *be* better. She's gone through hell, and I'm making it worse," Tate says. He watches me put together dinner and adds, "She'll feel weak for a few days, but—"

"—but it could have been worse," I finish for him with a scowl.

Just the stories I've heard him tell me over the years are enough to never want to even attempt traveling with him through the shadows, despite how incredible the feat is. I am an adrenaline junkie for sure, but I sure as hell know where to draw the line.

"I don't want her to run, Tate," I tell him, my anger deflating as fear overrides it. Tonight may have been Gemma's breaking point. I can understand her need to run away. But even if the events that unfolded tonight don't scare her enough to run, what will? What will push her over the edge? Will it be the constant danger she's always in, or will it be due to the barrage of harassment coming from her mate's friend? Most likely, it will be because of the combination of both issues. I place her meal together onto a plate and look over at Tate. "She will run if this gets to be too much, and I wouldn't blame her. I want you both in my life, but in the end, she's my mate. There is no me without her now. If it comes down to it, if she leaves, I'm out, too."

With that, I leave Tate alone in the kitchen while I head back upstairs. As I enter my room, I can hear Gemma retching in the bathroom. Between heaves, I can hear Darion softly reassuring her. I walk over to the bed and place her meal on the nightstand. A few minutes later the toilet flushes, and Gemma comes out, her expression strained. Darion has his arm wrapped around her waist and is guiding her towards the bed.

She crawls back into bed before giving me a weak smile.

"Jesus, Gems, you look like hell," I say with a frown.

I wait until Gemma is comfortable before handing her the plate with her bowl of soup and toast. I crawl into bed next to her and scoot close so I can help her if she needs it. She gives me and Darion a strange look and then shakes her head slightly, a small smile tugging up the corner of her mouth.

"What?" I ask, curiously.

"It's just… I've never had anyone dote on me before. Now I have *two* sexy guys helping me? I'm not sure how I got so lucky," she says, not looking at either of us as she stirs her soup.

My wolf grins at the compliment. I chuckle and say, "I didn't think I was a doting type either but look at me now. I'm nailing it."

Gemma giggles while Darion snorts and rolls his eyes, but his expression is still dark. I almost feel bad for Tate. Someone is about to get the bluest balls of his life tonight...

"I don't think being attacked again counts as being lucky," Darion says bleakly. "I got a call from one of my men just before you pulled up. I need to follow up with it, but I'll be back."

He glances over at me to, what? Make sure I'm okay with him staying in here tonight? I give him a nod even while I feel strange having to do so. This is new territory we're navigating through. I guess it's bound to be awkward for a while. He leaves the room, still practically trembling with rage. When the door closes behind him, I look over to Gemma who also watched his departure.

She looks at me with a frown and says, "You guys can't stay mad at Tate."

"I don't want to talk about him right now," I snap.

Just the sound of his name sends a flare of anger through me. Gemma nods once then takes a spoonful of soup. She pauses, then smiles.

"This is good."

"It's from a restaurant near work called Caleb's Deli. It's my favorite place. I'll take you there sometime," I tell her.

My chest swells up with pride that I'm able to provide for my mate. It should feel strange. I've never cared to tend to someone else before, but it comes naturally when it comes to Gemma.

She takes a few more bites, and I lean back against the pillows and watch her. After she's eaten about half, she stops to turn to face me.

"You know, before shit hit the fan tonight, Tate was lecturing me about how I need to make things work between the three of us. He was pissed that I wasn't answering your phone calls. I guess you were checking in on me through him?"

I can't tell from her tone if she's pissed or not that I had hounded Tate about watching her. As each day passes, my adoration for the woman next to me grows. With everything that has been going on, I've been anxious about her wellbeing. That's fair… right? I've never been in a relationship long enough to know what is acceptable when it comes to communication etiquette. I've never cared what the women I've slept with were doing. Gemma is so different from all of them. Thank goodness. I open my mouth to defend myself.

Gemma cuts me off with a wave of her hand.

"I'm not upset. I actually want to apologize. After the bomb Darion dropped on me the other day and then the break-in, I just needed some time to myself. I threw myself into work today and avoided coming home because I'm just… overwhelmed. But tonight, I had to throw myself off the roof of a building—"

My breath hitches in my throat as my body locks up in surprise and horror.

She holds my gaze as she continues, "—and as I realized I wasn't going to make the jump to the other roof, I immediately thought about how I didn't have enough time with both you and Darion. So, I'm sorry that I tried to avoid both of you today. I don't want to take you or Darion for granted ever again."

I let out a long breath, relieved to know that she isn't upset. At the same time, my heart grows two sizes.

"Gems, I get it," I tell her. I reach up and stroke her hair as I stare into her beautiful eyes. "I'm trying to navigate my way through this new relationship, too, and I'm sure Darion's feeling the same way. Having people trying to kill the both of you doesn't really make this any easier. We're feeling our way through the unknown, and it's uncomfortable."

I chuckle and then run my hand through my own hair. "Hell, Darion and I never shared a bed when it came to sleeping until you arrived. We've fucked women together in the same bed but usually one, or both of us, leave afterwards. Having him come in here to join us later feels strange, but I don't hate it.

"Honestly, I don't know how to make this easier, for any of us. But we need to be comfortable around each other. So, how about next time you're feeling overwhelmed just tell me? Let me know when you need space. Don't just ghost me, okay? Especially when your life has been at risk multiple times now."

Gemma's look of relief makes me smile and eases the tension that has settled on my shoulders. She nods and says, "Sounds good."

I take the plate off her lap and place it on the nightstand. When I turn back around, I ask her, "You said you weren't going to make the jump, yet here you are. So how did you survive it?"

She raises a brow and gives me a pointed look before answering, "You said you didn't want to talk about Tate."

I reach over and grab Gemma, bringing her to my chest where I crush her against me. My heart is racing as I think about how lucky she, and Tate, were tonight. I kiss the top of her head and breathe her scent in. She tilts her head up and kisses my chin. I lean down and capture her mouth with mine.

She pulls away a little with a grimace and says, "You don't want to kiss me. I've been thr—"

"I don't give a fuck," I snap and kiss her again.

Her giggle vibrates through her body. Her fingers come up and touch my face before racing up into my hair. I can't believe I could have lost her *again.* When is this nightmare going to end? Gemma's soft moan eases the worry in my chest. I pull away from her to nip at her earlobes and kiss her neck. She arches into me, and I feel myself harden as her lips skim across my skin.

I pull away again, wincing as I do, "You need to relax and rest. We shouldn't take this further—"

"I don't give a fuck," she mimics my previous answer with a playful growl and leans back, pulling me with her. I war with myself even as I take her lips with mine again. She should be resting…

My body pins her to the bed. As much as I want to pull away, I can't seem to stop my hand from reaching under the shirt she wears to slide my hand over her soft, smooth skin. I pull my mouth away from hers again to sit up and reach down. I tug off the top she's wearing and place it next to us. Her nipples are tight buds, and the way her breath hitches in excitement causes me to grin. I lean down and kiss her neck. Then, I trail kisses over her skin, down her chest, and plant one over each tight bud.

Gemma's hands are back in my hair. The way she gently tugs and massages my scalp sets a fire in my gut. My wolf is enjoying the simple touch. I trail more kisses down her stomach. I gently tug down the sweats I gave her. When I get them down past her hips, she helps kick them off with a grin. Her arousal is evident, and when I growl with pleasure, I know it sounds more wolf than man.

"Tonight, we're taking it easy. When you're feeling better, I'm going to spank the shit out of you to punish you for putting yourself in danger," I warn her as I peel off my pants. Her eyes widen.

"I've never been really spanked… I like the idea of it though," Gemma's smile turns smug. I chuckle.

"We'll just have to see how much you like it once you have a taste of it," I warn.

I roll off her to grab a condom from the drawer in my dresser. I toss it next to her and climb back on top. I nip at her nipple and then take one hand and slide it between her legs. With my fingers, I stroke her folds, and Gemma quivers. She closes her eyes as her body relaxes. As I slip two fingers inside of her, I lean down to kiss her stomach. My lips skim across Gemma's body as I stroke her insides. Her inner walls clench around my fingers. My erection twitches, jealous of my fingers.

As Gemma's breathing hitches and her body clamps down tighter around me, I slip my fingers out. Her huff of annoyance causes me to smile. I reach over, grab the condom, and rip open the packaging. I slip on the rubber and position myself between Gemma's legs. I lean forward, both hands on either side of her face and kiss her again. I press into her entrance and shudder as her body accepts me greedily.

Gemma lifts up her legs and wraps them around my waist, which causes me to sink further into her body. When I've been completely accepted, I pause, gauging Gemma's reaction. I don't want to hurt her. After what she's been through, I'm not sure what her body can handle. As if she can read my concern, her eyes meet mine, and she reaches up to touch my cheek.

"I need this, Christopher," she says softly. "Please."

"Tell me if you're in any pain," I tell her.

She nods and smiles. "So far so good, babe."

I chuckle and move as requested. I grit my teeth as I force myself to go slow. We fit perfectly together. There have been so many women before Gemma, but none of them felt as good as she does. Nothing comes as close to this sensation, of perfection, of everything righting itself in my world, when I'm with her. As I surge back and forth with long slow strokes, I thank the moon goddess for this gift. I haven't talked to her since my teenage years when I had once needed guidance. Since I left the pack, there has been no need to talk to her. She failed me.

Or so I thought.

Maybe leaving the pack was necessary for me to find Gemma. If I never left, I would have married another wolf shifter, had kids, and never met the woman beneath me. The thought shakes me to my core. Gemma is everything I could want and everything I didn't know I needed. She's funny, smart, driven, and sexy. This has to be the moon goddess's doing. So, I send up another word of thanks as I feel my body coiling, ready to snap.

Gemma arches her hips forward, meeting each stroke. I can feel her body gripping me tightly as she grows closer to her release. I reach between her legs and circle her clit, knowing I won't be able to last much longer.

"*Yes*," Gemma hisses, and I feel the moment her orgasm strikes.

Her body grabs mine so tightly that I immediately follow suit. We both cry out in ecstasy, both trembling as pleasure ripples through us.

When my orgasm subsides, I withdraw from Gemma and take care of the condom. Once I've tied the thing, I toss it into a wastebasket across the room and collapse next to her. She turns into my chest and snuggles closer. I smile and wrap my arms around her.

"Thank you for taking care of me," she mumbles into my chest. "In every way."

"Always, Gems," I promise into her hair. "Always."

Chapter Twenty-One

Darion

"We have reason to believe that Jacob's brother has quietly taken over," my head of security tells me.

Ian stands on the other side of my desk, ramrod straight. His buzz cut is fresh, his suit immaculate. He wears an earpiece in his ear and dark shades. While the shades complete the look of an agent, that's not what they are for. Those are to protect the vampire's eyes from the sunlight.

"He has a brother?" I ask with a frown.

Mentally, I flip through all the information I know about Jacob. I'm sure I would have known he had a brother.

"His name is Pierce, and he's older. He doesn't work in the limelight like Jacob did. He coordinates and oversees the darker side of the gang. From what I've heard, that includes sex trafficking and selling organs they take from their victims. Unfortunately, Pierce is very good at his job, so this is just hearsay. Jacob was just the drug dealer of the family, but he pretended to be the leader to keep the attention off Pierce."

"What are you guys doing about this?" I ask as I lean back in my seat.

"I have my men scouring the area, looking for Pierce. If we find any of his, or Jacob's, men we're pulling them into interrogation," Ian assures me. "We'll accumulate as much information as possible on Pierce and his whereabouts, and then we'll take care of this issue."

I nod once, pleased with Ian's work.

"On another note," Ian continues, "The decoy plan worked this morning. The car you typically take to work was followed by an unmarked white van. My men followed it, but the van noticed and tried to escape, which led to a fiery car explosion after my men chased after them for about ten miles. No survivors. We cleaned up the mess."

"How fortunate for them you did not catch them," I say grimly. I shake my head, unconcerned for my own safety. "How's the crew at the house? Any activity?" I ask him.

Ian shakes his head.

"No activity this morning. The second shift should get there just before the doctor arrives. We'll frisk her down before she can enter. Would you like someone inside with Miss Thomas while the doctor conducts his examination?" Ian asks.

"No need, Tate will be with her," I tell him.

This morning Tate intercepted me on the way out to apologize again. If he were *anyone* else, the man would disappear and never be seen again. I'm not sure the last time I've felt my emotions get so out of control, but last night I was murderous. My master almost died because my friend does not have the ability to keep his stupid mouth shut. Ian's expression does not change, but I can almost feel his displeasure.

"Do you have something to say?" I ask him, my voice cold.

I may have a problem with Tate, but I'll be damned if my security, or anyone else, has a problem with him.

"No, sir," Ian says.

"Good. Keep me posted on Pierce," I say just as my phone lights up with a text from Christopher.

Ian nods and leaves my office. I glance at my watch. It's seven in the morning. I read the message from Christopher who is letting me know he's left for work.

I left over two hours ago confident that with both Christopher and Tate home, along with my security staff, Gemma will be safe. I left the house early to make sure my less than legal activity is taken care of before my regular work schedule begins. With my men prowling the city and state, I know the inner workings of the criminal activity almost all the time. It helps to have eyes and ears everywhere. It makes finding dirt on the criminals I put away easy. The fact that I can just *happen* to find a witness who would be more than happy to incriminate the criminal I'm prosecuting makes my work easy.

After last night, I have my reservations about Tate and his ability to watch over Gemma. But when he met me at the front door, I saw the regret and guilt eating at him. Tate has hinted at the things he did for the government. Every time he comes home, I can see the shadows in his eyes. When I picked him up from the airport a few days ago, I saw even darker, blacker shadows haunting him. But those were nothing compared to what I saw in his face this morning.

His request to watch Gemma again today was sober. I know Tate better than most. He's a good guy. The best. We are close for a reason. If it hadn't been for his quick thinking, both he and Gemma would have died up on that roof. After all is said and done, I trust Tate, so I agreed to his request to watch over her.

I think past my conversation with Tate to earlier in the morning and smile.

I awoke with Gemma practically on top of me. When I went to bed last night, she was sleeping soundly, curled around Christopher's body. Sometime during the middle of the night, she replaced Christopher's body underneath hers with mine. Gemma's unconscious need for contact is endearing, and this morning, I bathed in contact. When I realized I was running late, I tried to slip out of bed without waking her. I failed. The moment I moved, Gemma only clung harder to me. When I tried again, she woke with a pout.

Then, we made silent, sweet, love with Christopher sleeping soundly next to us. Gemma's soft moan in my ear, the way her body gripped me as she came, it had been perfection. The sexual energy we created together was more intense and fulfilling than anything I've ever eaten before. The power that normally courses through me feels more intense, more frenzy-like. I like it. I also like Gemma. A lot. So much so it's startling but in the best way possible.

A knock on my door jolts me from my thoughts.

"Come in," I call, standing to greet whoever stands just beyond the wood barrier. Phillip walks in with a frown.

"Darion, I knew you'd be in early. Good, we need to talk," Phillip says as he shuts the door behind him. "Gemma told Aaron she's staying at your place."

"Is this a problem?" I ask with a raised brow.

Phillip, typically a good-natured fellow even in court, scowls.

"It is if she doesn't want to be there. She can come stay with us," he tells me.

I walk around my desk slowly, eyeing the young lawyer.

"Did she say something to make you believe she's not happy with her current situation?" I ask curiously.

"No, but it sounds like she really didn't have any other option," Phillip tells me. "Now that we're back, I had Aaron let her know that our door is always open. I appreciate you taking her in, but maybe it's too soon for her to be moving in with her mate. They should probably get to know each other before just jumping into things. And I'm sure you don't want two newly mated people around. It must get terribly annoying, even with your disposition towards sex."

Anger flares white hot in my chest. Phillip doesn't know me well enough to assume anything about me. He's never tried to get to know me.

He is a lawyer in my firm, that is all. In fact, Phillip and I have never even had lunch together to discuss cases. He might be a good lawyer to have in my firm, but we know nothing of each other.

It also annoys me that Gemma has not told her friend, who I am sure would tell his partner, that we, too, are together. It annoys me less than Phillip's assumption of my attitude towards Christopher and Gemma, however. In fact, I should be slightly relieved Gemma has not said anything. The three of us should figure out how to be a… a throuple before other people can voice their opinions on the matter. Not that those opinions will do anything. It will just make it easier between the three of us to know where we stand. Then maybe it will be easier to let friends and family know about our situation.

Family… Christopher has a family, although they hardly speak and then Gemma has her parents. I wonder how Gemma's parents will feel about this arrangement. The thought amuses me as much as it concerns me. Will they accept the three of us together? How will they take the news that their daughter is my master? Would they be repulsed? Horrified? Or is it possible they would accept us? Me? How strange I sudden seek the acceptance of two people I've never met. Mentally I shake off these thoughts and turn my attention back to Phillip.

"If Gemma wishes to leave, then she can. Neither Christopher nor I are holding her prisoner," I tell the man. The relief in Phillip's face and the way his body relaxes amuses me. "What? Concerned she had become one of my sex slaves?"

Phillip flushes. As I examine his expression, it hits me that that's exactly what he thought. I take a deep breath to breathe through my anger. In my most contemptuous tone I can muster, I say,

"No one is coerced into having sex with me. Your prejudice is showing, Phillip. It would be wise to reevaluate your assumptions of me if you wish to continue at this firm."

Phillip manages to compose himself enough to stand up straighter.

He meets my gaze and says coldly, "If making sure my friend is comfortable in a situation that could be considered to some *difficult* puts me in a situation where I may be fired, so be it."

With that he turns and leaves the room, slamming the door behind him. My anger eases as I realize Phillip is just being a good friend to Gemma. He has every right to step in and make sure she is safe. I sigh and run my hand over my face. I push away from my desk and walk back to sit behind it. I think back to my time with Gemma this morning and puzzle over all of it.

I can still smell Gemma's sweet scent clinging to me even after my shower. I wonder if I will wake like this every morning. Wrapped in her arms, or legs, and covered in her scent. If so, I look forward to it.

My first master never slept with me.

Casabella... I haven't thought of her in so long. The woman was my creator and my master. My life with her consisted of only service. Looking back, I shudder at my time with her. She used me and abused me. At the time, I thought that was how it was supposed to be.

To find myself locked to another woman for the rest of her life... It should terrify and sicken me. To know that I can now only have sex with one woman, that I can be controlled and abused once more, should cause me to lash out in anger at the hand I have been dealt. But I am no longer the one-track minded incubus of my early years. I have not reverted to those times, nor will I.

This new master, this new woman who my body has chosen to worship and cherish is courageous and selfless. Gemma didn't hesitate to save me when those gunmen came at me that faithful evening. Since then, she has been harassed and almost murdered several times. Yet, she hasn't once blamed me for this situation. Anyone else in her position would. Instead, she stays driven to succeed. Her work ethic is admirable. The way she stays strong in the face of danger is humbling. Gemma's concern for me because of this new situation between us is touching. I did not lie to her when I told Gemma that I trust her. Hell, I may be in the early stages of even loving her.

If that is actually possible for an incubus.

I shake my head and turn my attention back to work.

One thing at a time.

Chapter Twenty-Two

Gemma

"Whiplash, huh?" the doctor, Candice Wilson, repeats.

She's pretty with dark hair, clear skin, and thin lips. I wonder how Darion knows her and why she would drop everything to come check on me this morning. She shines a light in my eyes, and I squint.

"Why didn't you go to the hospital after the car accident?" she asks as she takes a look into my ears. She jots down notes on her tablet.

"It was late, and it takes forever to be seen in the emergency room," I tell her. "I felt a little sick and dizzy last night, but I feel okay this morning."

"You could have a concussion. Do you realize coming home and going to bed was the worst thing for you to do?" Dr. Wilson scolds with a severe scowl.

"I told her that," Tate says. He's leaning against the wall by the bathroom door. His expression is unreadable, but the way his arms flex then relax tells me he's stressed. "She never listens to me."

"That's because he's an ass. Falling into a coma out of spite seemed like a good idea at the time," I tell her without looking at him.

This is so awkward. I can tell Dr. Wilson doesn't believe our story, but she is professional enough to play along. Tate refused to leave the room, arguing that it is his job to report the doctor's diagnosis back to Darion. After a shouting match between the both of us, I gave up and allowed him to stay.

Dr. Wilson checks my reflexes, my pulse, looks inside my mouth, and draws blood. All the while, she asks me questions about my overall health. We go through typical eating habits, physical well-being, and sexual activity. This is already awkward enough, having a doctor I don't know poke and prod at me. It's even more awkward when your incubus's and wolf shifter's best friend who hates you is standing in the room watching and listening to everything.

When the doctor is done, she tells me, "Lie down today and take it easy. Your vitals look good, and everything else appears alright. If you have any questions call me, or have Darion call me."

I nod. I lean against the counter as Tate walks the doctor to the front door. When he's out of sight, I try to stand up straight, but I'm hit with a wave of vertigo. I hold onto the counter and close my eyes to try to stop the spinning. I woke up dizzy, but the spells seem to be happening less and less. This is just one of them, and they go away pretty quickly.

Several deep breaths later, I test my balance and find that I can stand without swaying. Pleased that I am doing better, I leave the bathroom and head to the kitchen to make breakfast.

After toasting some bread, grabbing some jam, and pouring myself a glass of juice, I sit down at the large dining room table and begin eating. I answer the texts from Aaron. Also, doing my part to be a better mate and master, I send a text to both Christopher and Darion letting them know how I hope they have a good day and that the doctor thinks I'm fine.

A few minutes after I have taken a seat, Tate walks into the open space. He pauses as he scans the large kitchen, living room, and finally the dining room where he spots me. I continue eating as he walks over to me. When he stops just a few feet away from me, I brace myself for a snide remark.

"How are you feeling?" he asks.

I look up from my toast and stare at him suspiciously.

"You heard the doctor. I'm fine."

"Just because there's nothing obviously wrong doesn't mean you're alright," he says stiffly.

I take another bite of my toast, still staring at him, wondering if this is some type of test. When I'm done chewing, I say, "I'm feeling okay."

"No more nausea? No headache?" Tate pushes.

"Nope and a small one. Nothing some Advil won't cure," I tell him honestly.

The tension in his shoulder eases dramatically, and he sighs. "Good."

"Can I ask you something?" I ask cautiously. Any minute Asshole Tate could show up. I need to brace myself.

"You want to know what I did." Tate figures out where I'm going before I can ask. I nod. He sighs again before pulling out a chair and sitting down. "I shouldn't tell you anything. It's top-secret government information. Telling you could get me killed."

"Well, since you think I'm part of the government as some sort of spy already, wouldn't that mean I already know? Maybe I'm just testing you," I say sourly.

Tate doesn't respond, and his face remains impassive. He looks away from me, and I think our conversation has ended before it began. I go back to eating.

"I don't think you're a plant," he says with a scowl.

His jaw clenches so tightly I'm sure he is about to break his teeth. He looks down at the table before looking back at me. His glare is so intense I know that if looks could kill I'd be dead. Taken aback by such loathing, I lean back in my seat with a frown, trying to figure out what I did to deserve this.

"It is just a weird coincidence that somehow my life gets a little easier when you're around," he tells me.

"I'd believe you if you weren't staring daggers at me," I tell him.

Surprise crosses his face before the tension lessens in his expression. "Sorry," he grumbles.

I roll my eyes but say nothing. If this is how he acts when life gets easier for him, I'd hate to see him when he thinks life has it out for him.

"What I do... It's called shadowriding. Or, at least, that's what I call it. Back when I enlisted in the marines, I opted into a special program. They told me they were trying to create super soldiers. Being young and naïve, I agreed to opt into this program. I signed the paperwork without any hesitation. I didn't even bother reading the fine print. I saw the dollar signs and the ability to travel, and I was in. They started experimenting on us almost immediately. There were about two hundred soldiers in the program. By the end, by the time they found the right ratio of super soldier serum to deadly poison, there were only four of us left."

I stare at Tate. My mouth is hanging open, I can feel it, but I'm too stunned to close it. Tate doesn't seem to notice. He's staring at the table again as he continues his story.

"When I first learned what I could do, become a shadow and travel through them, it was horrifying. For months I had absolutely no control when I was sucked into the darkness or when I became solid. And, in the beginning, the transition from solid to transparent was agonizing. I thought I was going mad. Then finally, after countless trial and error, I figured out how to hold my shape. It's not for long periods of time, but enough that I could pretend to be a member of society."

He pauses. As he collects his thoughts, I remember to close my mouth. I realize that I'm leaning towards him, so I lean back in my chair again and stare at the ex-soldier in front of me. His expression shifts to disgust.

"I became the super soldier our government was looking for. I can melt into shadows and become practically invisible," he tells me, lifting his blue eyes to meet mine. "I can travel through them quickly and undetected. Gravity and space don't apply to me when I'm in that state. I can walk on ceilings, slide under doors, slip through cracks in the floor."

I snort in both shock and amusement. Tate gives me a strange look, so I explain my reaction, "There's no mystery why those abilities are important. You're probably the best spy in the world."

Tate stares at me for a moment before cracking a small, tight smile. "Yeah, I was. Imagine being able to grab top secret documents, laptops, or take pictures of weapons and draw up blueprints of an enemy's, or even an ally's, military base. The things that happen in the dark, the things that our people don't want to know... like how we torture innocent people or how we turn a blind eye when our soldiers need help, I know it all. I've witnessed it."

We stare at each other. I try to digest what he's telling me. Picturing all that he must have seen, the secrets he has to keep, and the burden of being unable to be a functioning member of society... It is becoming clear that Tate isn't an asshole. He is lonely and scared. Maybe this crappy personality is how he keeps himself from feeling anything for anyone so he doesn't become attached to someone he can never be himself around.

"But while their experiment on me and the other three soldiers wasn't a complete bust, I wasn't a success story either. I've been in for almost fifteen years and still can't hold my form for longer than a few hours here and there. It's a headache for the government trying to shuffle me around without people learning what I can do. When I asked to get out over a year ago, I was sure they were going to deny the request. In all that paperwork I hadn't bothered to read, it says I'm the government's property for the rest of my life. But, for whatever reason, they agreed."

I frown. "But if the experiment happened to you, how come you could drag me into the shadows? Does it affect everything that you touch?"

Tate shakes his head. "I have the ability to manipulate the things I touch to become a shadow. But if I don't want it to happen, it won't. It's risky and difficult to pull a person into the shadows with me. Usually, I do it to people I have to kill. The shift in your molecular structure is unparalleled to anything else on this earth and almost impossible for most people to handle.

I grab people, and if I don't physically pull them out, they can never come out because their cell structure has been destroyed and is trapped within the shadow world. It's easy enough to hide a body that way for your government."

Again, my mouth pops open.

Tate nods once stiffly and continues, "I've only tried a handful of times to travel through the shadows with someone. It's only been successful, as in that person not dying, a few times. Even then, it really messed that person up. Like... We're talking multiple strokes and massive heart attacks right afterwards. It's a risk I don't take lightly or try often."

I grimace, wondering if a stroke or heart attack is waiting just around the corner. Trying to suppress my shudder, I turn my attention back to breakfast. Darion and Christopher's anger makes sense now. If they already knew this information, their reactions are a little justified.

"I wouldn't have tried if I thought there had been another way," Tate says after a few minutes of silence.

I look up at him to find Tate staring at me. His brows have pulled together again, and his mouth is turned down in a frown. The emotions in his eyes unnerve me. No longer do I see hate or anger but genuine regret.

"I know I've been an asshole, but I'm not *that* big of an asshole. I wouldn't do that to an innocent person or to the guys'… significant other, or whatever you are to each of them," he tells me.

We stare at each other for a long moment. I'm not sure what he's looking for as he searches my face, but as I search his, I realize I can no longer see him as an asshole. I can feel my heart soften towards him.

"If Christopher and Darion trust you, then so do I," I tell Tate slowly. I may not like the guy, but I don't think he'd risk killing me. "Thank you for saving me."

Tate immediately shakes his head and says, "I don't want your gratitude."

"Then what do you want from me?" I ask curiously.

"Answers," he replies quickly. The sudden brightness in his eyes and the color coming back into his face tells me this is what he has been waiting for.

"What answers?" I ask him.

"Do you have any non-humans in your family tree?" he asks me.

I shake my head. "Human through and through. Why?"

"I'm trying to figure out how you made it through the shadows unharmed. Whatever the reason is has to be the same reason why I can hold my form around you," Tate explains. When he meets my gaze, his expression changes to pained. "I can't go *anywhere* without working extremely hard to stay solid. No bars, no restaurants, no dates… I can't do shit without mentally straining myself. And if I slip up, people freak out, and a government secret is exposed. I can't risk it. It feels so good not straining to stay seated in this chair. I could stay a shadow, but I don't want to be too comfortable in that form."

"Oh," I say lamely.

I try to picture being unable to go out and be *normal*. The stress behind accidentally blowing a government secret this huge would be enough to give me a pulmonary embolism. Struggling to stay in the moment, to be me and present with the ones around me, would just add to the pressure. There is no way I can completely understand what he is going through, but now I can empathize with the man just a little.

Is there a way to make his life a little easier? Is there something about my family that he might find useful?

I tick off information for Tate. "Well… Most of my family is A-positive blood type. My mom's side is French Canadian; my father's side is from Cameron. I'm about the average height of most of my family members. I'm terrible at math, as is most of my family, but we're all pretty athletic."

I give him a half-smile, and after a long minute, he smiles back.

"None of that is helpful," he tells me. I shrug.

"That's all I got for you right now," I say apologetically.

I push away my empty plate and look past him into the living room.

What if I keel over before the others get home today? Would I know it's coming, or would I just blink and then find myself dead? The thought is unnerving and sends a cold chill down my spine.

I glance at the clock on the microwave. I need to start working. I can't fall behind and piss my clients off any more than I already have. But as I think about work, I realize that's the farthest thing from what I want to do.

I glance at Tate. The tension in Tate's body language tells me that he is far from relaxed. He seems wound up, as if sharing his secret with me only made his guilt worse. With everything that he has shared, with all this worry about my health, and with his own guilt about failing to watch out for the both of us last night, it's clear that we're both not in the frame of mind to sit around today.

So, pushing the thought of work aside, I lean towards Tate.

"Do you have anything to do today besides babysitting?" I ask.

Tate looks up at me and shakes his head.

"Want to go do something?"

"It's not safe, Gemma," he reminds me. "And the doctor said you need to lie down and rest."

I roll my eyes.

"I feel fine, Tate. And we can go somewhere no one will think to look for either of us," I tell him. "We'll let security, Darion, and Christopher know where we're going, and we'll be safe. Let's get out of the house and leave all this bullshit behind for a bit. Please?"

Tate starts to shake his head, but I push before he can protest.

"I need to stop thinking about what happened last night, and you need to unwind. Relax and just *live* for a few hours."

"I can't just go out in public—" Tate abruptly stops talking.

I watch as realization dawns on his face. He *can* go out in public as long as I'm there with him. The wonder and surprise that moves across his face shift to relief and excitement. When he grins, I'm struck by how handsome he is.

"Alright, let's get out of here," he says.

I smile back at him. "Let's go have some fun."

Chapter Twenty-Three

Gemma

Five hours later, Tate is driving the golf cart off the greens towards the restaurant attached to the clubhouse. The sky is overcast, but the weather is warm, and golfing has been, surprisingly, a blast. The first hour I constantly had to assure Tate that I could see him. There were multiple times I caught him looking down at his hands to see if he'd turned into a shadow.

When he finally relaxed, a grin stretched from ear to ear and hung around for the rest of the game. His hits got better, too. I am no professional golfer, but for the first nine holes, I was in the lead. The course got harder, and Tate's constant playful jabs became distracting. By the eighteenth hole, the scorecard was embarrassing to look at. Tate made a comeback and won.

It is strange seeing the tension and the hate missing from Tate's expression. He is actually funny and has plenty of stories to share that are wild and unbelievable. He tells me about how he and Christopher met when Christopher freelanced for the government as a contractor. Then, Tate goes on to share his favorite places he has traveled. I can tell in his voice that his condition made the trips a little less fun, but the happiness in his face tells me that what fun he could have, he did.

I've learned a lot about the handsome soldier over the past few hours, and I'm beginning to enjoy the person behind the angry façade.

Tate parks the golf cart with the other empty ones, and we walk up to the hostess desk where a pretty blonde-hair woman waits for us. She openly eyes Tate, who is suddenly tense again.

"Two this afternoon?" she asks him.

He glances at her, then down at his hands, then back at her.

"Ah, yeah…" he says slowly.

She beams at him, grabs two menus, and directs Tate to follow her. She approaches a table in the middle of the restaurant. Next to me, Tate slows, and I hear his breath hitch. His sudden apprehension warns me he's no longer comfortable. I understand his concern immediately.

"Do you mind if we have somewhere a bit more secluded?" I ask her just before she places the menus down.

She looks at me as if I suddenly appeared out of thin air.

"Oh, ah, yes. Of course, this way please."

We follow her to an outside table halfway surrounded by thick bushes. It's shaded here, which is only enhanced by the clouds overhead. Only a handful of patrons in the restaurant can see us here. I can see Tate's shoulders relax, and his hands, which had curled into fists at his sides, unfurl.

"Thanks," Tate mumbles into my ear as we sit down, and the hostess walks away.

I ignore his gratitude. Of course, I'll do what I can to make him feel comfortable. The waitress walks over, takes our drink order, and disappears, giving us time to look for something to eat.

"Hm… Should I go with a salad? But that spicy chicken sandwich is calling my name…" I mutter.

Something touches my arm, and I glance over to see Tate's hand wrap around my forearm. I look up at him and find him staring at me, panicked and wide-eyed. Alarmed, I drop the menu onto the table.

"What is it? What's wrong?"

"We need to go, I think I'm about to shift," he says, his voice tight.

I nod and start to push my chair back.

"You can feel it coming?" I ask him as I glance around us to see if anyone is paying us any attention. Tate stands slowly, still holding onto me as if I'm his lifeline.

"No, but it's been so long. It's bound to happen," he tells me.

I pause at his words.

"So, you're just worried it will happen. Not that it *is* happening," I clarify.

His eyes are getting wider as they dart around us, and he's beginning to breathe hard. I turn my whole body towards him and place my hands on the side of his face. The contact surprises him, and he looks at me.

"Tate, shh. Take a deep breath for me. Good, now let it out," I instruct calmly. "Now do it again. Perfect. Listen to me. You haven't vanished once since we've been out. Is this the longest you have gone without issue?"

Tate nods. His grip on my forearm is borderline painful, but I don't pull away.

I mimic his nod and continue quietly, "Then what makes you think you can't go longer?"

"I just… I just can't risk this any longer," he says, his voice strained. "There are too many people here. Out on the greens, we were pretty much alone, but here…"

"If you want to leave, we'll leave, Tate," I tell him calmly. "But not until you've taken another few deep breaths. I'm sure you've heard panicking is the worst thing that you can do when you're scared or think you're in danger. I want you to make the decision to leave when you've had a moment to collect yourself, alright?"

His blue eyes are frantic. I pull his face down so instead of looking around, he's forced to look at me. Our eyes meet, and I smile.

"Deep breaths, Tate," I tell him calmly. He does what I ask, and I can see when it starts to help. "Here, let me do something real quick."

I let go of him and step around his body to pull his chair practically into the bushes. No one would see him in any direction unless they are standing right in front of us. I guide him back and request him to sit. When he does, I pull my seat closer on his right so I become another barrier people will have to look past to catch a glimpse of Tate.

Tate's deep breathing stops as he looks around and realizes what I've done. His shoulders are stiff, but the panic begins to fade from his expression. Just as he becomes calm, the waitress returns with my mimosa and his water.

"Have you guys decided what you want to eat?" she asks.

She stares straight at Tate, oblivious to his discomfort. I wait a second to see if Tate will order himself, but he's still not quite ready. His hands are gripping the armrests so tight that his knuckles are white.

"Do you want to leave?" I ask him softly. "We can if you want."

Tate shakes his head once. Okay, he wants to stay. I wait another second to see if he'll speak to place his order. When it's clear he has no intentions of talking to this waitress, I take the reins.

"I'll have the spicy chicken sandwich with salt and vinegar chips, and my friend will have... the swordfish with a side of roasted brussels sprouts."

The waitress glances at me and gives me a tight smile. "It'll be right out."

With that, she disappears, and we're alone again. I turn back to Tate and give him a half-smile.

"I hope you're not picky," I repeat the words he said to me only the day before.

This seems to snap him out of the rest of his panic. His blue eyes search my face while he clenches and relaxes his jaw. Finally, he lets out a long sigh.

"Thanks for waiting out my panic attack."

"Of course," I reply as I lean back in my seat. "You know, you may still have a chance to get with her if you actually *say* something to her when she comes back."

Tate looks at me with confusion. He looks toward the waitress inside placing our order on a kiosk, and I watch as understanding lights up his blue eyes.

Tate chuckles darkly, "Yeah, I can't just pick-up women, Gemma. Darion usually has to hire the type of women I like, and they are paid to stay quiet if they see things they aren't supposed to witness."

I blink in surprise at his words. "Darion hires women to have sex with you? But you're... you know, good looking enough to pick up whoever you want."

Again, Tate chuckles, this time with a little more amusement. "Careful, flatter me any more, and I'll think you're hitting on me."

"Trust me, that will never happen," I assure him with a dry smile. "But be nice to me, and one day maybe I'll be your wing girl so you can pick up whoever you want. I bet it would be nice to not have to worry about ordering your next fling. Maybe give yourself a challenge."

Tate's amusement disappears as surprise flickers across his face. This time it's my turn to chuckle. Bet he wasn't expecting that offer.

He's not stunned long. Tate leans forward and says quietly, "Dear Gemma, you couldn't walk into a room full of the woman I like without blushing. While your offer is appreciated, unless you have some submissive friends who enjoy the BDSM lifestyle, I'll make my own way."

I gasp in shock. He's staring at me with a smug smile on his face. He's pleased he surprised me. My sex life is *very* vanilla, or at least it was, before I met Christopher and Darion. What I know of the BDSM scene is limited to the romance novels I read. For a moment, I try to picture Tate in a position of dominance, but instantly regret it. I do not need to picture Tate naked, telling me what to do. I quickly look away from him as my cheeks warm up.

"The weather turned out nice today, didn't it?" I say, purposely trying to redirect the conversation.

Out of the corner of my eye, I can see Tate throw back his head as he laughs at my discomfort.

"Yes, it is a nice day," he says mockingly nonchalant.

For the rest of the afternoon, the conversations stay on *safe* topics.

Chapter Twenty-Four

Christopher

As I walk into the house that night, I'm braced for drama. According to the texts I got throughout the day from Gemma and Tate, both *willingly* went out together to golf. They even sent a picture to the group text with Darion and me to prove neither of them have killed one another. I texted Darion on the side to confirm that security has kept them both in sight. At Darion's confirmation text, I was sure something was up. No way had Tate gone from asshole to friendly to my mate in less than twelve hours.

I walk deeper into the house and find Tate settled on the couch watching some football rerun. He looks up and flashes me a grin.

"Hey, man, work alright?" he asks.

"Yeah, just the same old grind," I say as I head over to the refrigerator.

I'm scanning the room for Gemma. I can smell that she's been in here recently.

Tate notices and says, "She's on the back porch stretching. I think she wants to go for a run, but I said she'd have to wait until you or Darion get home. I'm not running miles for fun."

The idea of going for a run perks me up, but I hesitate. I've hardly spent any time with Tate since he's been home. I need to figure out a way to balance my time. I grab a beer from the refrigerator and head over to where he's sitting. I glance out the back window, and there she is. Gemma uses the handrail on the deck to stretch. She's facing the backyard and unaware I'm here. I smile as I flop down on the couch with Tate.

"So, how was golfing?" I ask and wait for the eye roll, scoff, or the snide remark.

Instead, Tate's grin is genuine. "With a little bit more practice, I'll be better than Darion in no time."

I sip my beer before answering, "There's going to be more golfing? Whose idea was this? Yours?"

"It was Gemma's," Tate says. "She wanted to get out of the house and suggested it. And before you ask, I was on my best behavior."

"Did you have any issues?" I ask with a frown.

Tate's attitude right now is strange. He's rarely ever in a good mood, and after a night like last night, I was sure he'd be in an even worse mood.

Tate's smile doesn't falter as he says, "Not a single slip."

"Not a one? You were out for hours," I say, confused.

"I know, it's crazy," he tells me.

"Were you risking exposure to make up for last night? Tate, you know you don't have to do that. I'm sure if you told Gemma no she would have understood," I say with concern. I frown. "I hope you didn't overextend yourself."

Tate sighs dramatically.

"I'd be lying if I said it was all me keeping myself in check." Tate shoots a fugitive glance out the back window at Gemma. When he turns back around, his smile has faded. "Since I've been home, I haven't flickered once, Chris. Not a single time. I've been able to sleep on my bed instead of floating around on the walls and ceilings. Everything I've held stays in my hand instead of falling through it randomly."

"What?" I yelp, getting to my feet. "That's great! How is that possible? Why haven't you said something to us?" When Tate makes a face, my excitement fades, knowing that look. "What is it?"

"The other night, when Gemma ran out of her office, I flickered *hard*. I could hardly shift back. It was terrifying. Then I realized I've been around Gemma this whole time and haven't had an issue with shifting. The moment she was far enough away, I instantly got hit with the inability to stay solid. That was enough to send me into an angry frenzy. I went after her, with no thought for either of our safety and when I caught up to her, I called her a government spy. A plant. In my panic and anger, I thought she had been sent here by one of my superiors as a test. I don't know. It sounds crazy now that I'm level-headed, but I was sure she somehow knew how to keep me from flickering."

I don't know what to say at first. Part of me is pissed that he accused Gemma of something she isn't capable of being. But the rational part of me can understand Tate's thoughts of conspiracy. He's a government experiment walking freely through the streets. None of us thought that an early retirement was in his future. I can understand his suspicion of Gemma if he can suddenly maintain his human form after his entire career in the field being unable to.

"Did you figure out how she helps you?" I ask after a long silence.

Tate shakes his head and says, "No. Honestly, it could just be a fluke in her genetic make-up that counteracts whatever fucked up drugs they put in my system. I don't know how that would work, why her, or anything like that. All I know is she's not a plant, so I'm good with that."

He stops talking and looks back out at Gemma again. This time when he talks, he doesn't look at me.

"Do you know what it's like going almost half my life unable to just walk down the street without constantly staying present? The mental strain I've gotten used to over the years has been lifted without me realizing it. It's so easy being *me* again. That's because of Gemma. Who the fuck knew the cure to my problem would come in the form of your mate?"

I glance at Gemma, who turns towards the house. Our eyes meet, and her face lights up. The grin that spreads across her face makes my heart swell. I smile back.

I look down at Tate and tell him, "I'm glad you're able to hold your shape. I know how hard this has been for you. Maybe soon we can all go out one night."

"Yeah, Gemma offered to be my wing woman," Tate says with a snort of derision. "As if I'd need her help to pick up a woman."

"I don't think that's what she was offering. If she's around you can *finish* what you start, if you catch my drift," I tell him with a smirk.

Tate's expression changes from scorn to surprise, which makes me laugh.

"Go get your girl," Tate grumbles. "Before she comes in here and tries to talk me into running, too."

I chuckle as I place my beer on the coffee table and head out back. Without breaking my stride, I walk over to Gemma, bend down, and lift her into my arms. Her laughter is music to my ears, and the stress of the day dissolves with her in my arms. I place her on her feet, take her face in my hands, and kiss her. She steps out of my arms, breaking the kiss quickly. Surprised, I study her face, making sure everything is okay.

"I've been thinking," she starts, her smile disappearing. "I think I've been making this a little too easy for you. You sleep me with, kick me out of your room, and ever since then, I've been in danger, so I haven't put up much of a fuss. I think tonight, you have to work for it."

My eyes narrow on her.

"What are you thinking?" I ask. She takes a step backwards, then another.

"If you want another kiss or *anything* else, you're going to have to catch me," Gemma tells me as a grin spreads across her face.

Before I can say anything else, she whirls around and rushes off the deck towards the woods.

Even without the enticement, I would have chased her. My mate wants to *run* from me? My wolf will not allow such a thing. Besides, one should never run from a predator. I give her a few seconds head start as I strip out of my clothes right there on the back porch, not caring if Tate sees. Then, I shift and the race is on.

Gemma has already made it to the woods as I bound across the yard. The animal in me insists I chase and take down my prey, but I forced my wolf to hold back, to stalk only. No need for this to end quickly. I gallop through the woods, weaving close and keeping her in sight. I yip and bark when she looks for me, letting her know I'm close. Her giggle makes me grin. She tries to outwit me. Zigzagging through bushes, swinging on lower limbs, but her scent is in the air. The two times she is able to get out of sight, I easily catch up to her by following her scent in the air.

My wolf is having a blast. He loves the run, and he loves that his mate is enjoying it, too. But while we have fun, I use my wolf's ability to hear, smell, and sense danger. When Gemma gets too close to the property line, I nip at her heels again to turn her in another direction. I don't pick up any new or unusual scents in the area, but that doesn't mean danger isn't nearby. Eventually, as it grows dark, I start herding her back towards the house. Just as we break through the woods into the backyard, Gemma comes to a stop.

I walk up behind her and rub my body against her, making sure my scent covers her completely. Her hand comes down, and her fingers weave through my fur.

"Thanks for running with me," Gemma says softly.

I glance up at her face and find her smiling as she stares at the house. I take a deep breath before I shift. When I'm human, I wrap my arm around her waist, tug Gemma to me, and kiss her. Her arms wrap around my neck as she kisses me back, and I hold on to her tighter. I breathe her scent in. Its familiarity is comforting, and my heart expands in joy.

"If I ever say no to a run, it's not me," I assure her with a grin as I break the kiss.

I take her hand, and we head back to the house.

"How was work?" she asks me.

"The same old bullshit, just like every day," I say, rolling my eyes. "How was golf?"

"I thought I was better than I was," she says grimly. "I'm pretty sure Tate cheats. I just can't figure out how you cheat at golf though."

I laugh. "Tate's good at golf. He doesn't need to cheat. I'm surprised he's not gloating."

"He was, but then I threatened him, and he stopped," she says and laughs.

I shudder as the sound wraps around me. My whole body feels lighter. The tedious tasks and meetings I've dealt with all day become the farthest thing in my mind. Her laughter is like a dose of serotonin shot straight into my veins, and I find myself truly happy. Why did I fight being with Gemma for so long? This feeling of rightness is incomparable.

I'm grinning like a fool as I walk up onto the deck. Quickly I pull my clothes back and we head into the house. Darion is home and leaning against the kitchen counter checking his phone, and Tate is nowhere to be seen. Darion looks up and pins Gemma with a look so intense that *I* am shaken by the emotions he is projecting. He walks over to us, meeting us halfway to the kitchen. The incubus takes Gemma's face in his hands, leans down, and kisses her.

Gemma's hand never leaves mine. In fact, she squeezes my hand while her free hand comes up and wraps around Darion's neck, and she stands on her toes to get better access to his mouth. I check my wolf. He's content and even pleased with the situation. When Gemma pulls away, she's smiling but shaking her head.

"This is weird," she tells us. "But I don't hate it."

Darion laughs as he drops his hands away from her.

"I agree." He tells her. He steps back and says, "I had a visitor today in the office."

My stomach sinks. Darion had trouble at work? He has almost ten guys watching him at all times. How did someone slip by his security? Gemma must come to the same conclusion because she tenses.

"What happened? Are you alright?" she asks before I get the chance. Darion raises an eyebrow.

"Phillip came in wanting to make sure you were not some type of sex slave for me while you're coming to terms with having a shifter as a mate," Darion tells her and then glances at me with a smirk.

Both Gemma and I heave a sigh of relief.

"Jesus, way to scare the hell out of us," I tell him with a scowl.

"I hope you told him that's exactly what I have become," Gemma scolds playfully. "That may be more acceptable to him than learning that we're all a thing now."

Darion snorts and rolls his eyes. "I assured him you are free to come and go as you please. You may want to contact your friend to confirm this before I get slapped with a kidnapping charge."

Gemma lets go of my hand and steps around Darion.

"I'll video call him now. Someone's about to get a real earful…" she grumbles and leaves the two of us as she goes to get her phone.

"Everything else go smoothly?" I ask once Gemma's out of sight. Darion nods and then proceeds to tell me about Pierce.

"Should you and Gemma get out of the city for a while until your guys find this Pierce fellow?" I ask, concerned that there's a whole organization out there looking for blood and has Darion and Gemma in its sights. Darion frowns.

"My men have the house and my office completely secure. To move locations would put us in jeopardy while they familiarize themselves with a new place."

I can hear Gemma's voice and her footsteps coming back down the stairs as she talks to Aaron on the phone.

"Do you have anyone watching her apartment?" I ask Darion,

lowering my voice so she can't hear. No need to worry her without anything substantial to tell her about.

"Yes, but nothing notable has happened…yet."

"Should we just have her move here permanently? Our fates are pretty much tied together now. Wherever one goes, we'd all follow. Our house is certainly big enough for one more person, and you're both safe here. Why not make this the real thing?" I ask.

While I didn't plan on having this conversation tonight, it's one I have been thinking about broaching sooner rather than later. Moving Gemma here seems like the most logical course of action. With both of us irrevocably attached to her and needing to be near her, along with the ability to protect her from the danger of Darion's enemies, it feels like a no-brainer.

I watch Darion's face to see how he takes the offer. His poker face is immaculate. It's no wonder he wins whenever we go out and gamble. Suddenly, it cracks, and a smile appears. Before he gets a chance to respond, Gemma's back, holding her phone out in front of her showing Aaron the inside of the house.

"See? I've been let out of the sex dungeon for a bit. I get fresh air and food occasionally, too," she tells her friend.

She keeps walking past us and out the back door where she continues to talk to her friend privately.

"I can't wait to see her face when she finds out we actually do have a sex dungeon," I say with a grin.

Darion chuckles. He looks around the room before turning towards the kitchen. As he opens the refrigerator, he says, "I'm happy to have her move in with us. But maybe we should show her the house and then talk to Tate before extending the offer. He should get a say about an additional roommate since he lives here too. We should also talk about sleeping arrangements."

Before I can respond, Gemma walks back in, her phone slipping into her legging pockets. She pauses, looking from my face to Darion's.

"What is it?"

I look over my shoulder at Darion before turning back to ask her, "We were just talking about how you haven't seen much of the house since you've been here. Want a tour of the place?"

"Oh, yeah, sure. Let me put the pot pie in the oven first," she answers.

As she walks into the kitchen to prepare dinner, Darion and I exchange looks. First, let's see if Gemma can get past what's downstairs. If she doesn't want any part of that, we can get rid of it, or if Tate wants to keep it, we'll let him have it.

I take a deep breath as excitement brews within me. Whether Gemma wants to move in or if we get our own place, with or without Darion, I can start enjoying the next phase of my life: mated and happy. Just thinking of the past few years of my life, the constant hookups, long nights out drinking, gambling, partying… Nothing in me longs for that lifestyle anymore. I'm *happy*, and none of that really ever brought me the joy that Gemma does.

When Gemma's ready, I show her the rest of the first floor. I have a small office that I hardly ever use, and there is a billiard room and a library that she hasn't seen. Then, I take her downstairs.

"So, you hire local bands or singers and host private performances?" she asks curiously as she wanders around the large space. "I saw this when I came down here with Tate to check the security cameras, but he wasn't feeling all that chatty, and I was in shock, so I didn't get a chance to ask questions."

I honestly have no idea how Gemma is going to react, but I don't hold back. "No, the stage is for a different type of performance. Usually, sex acts are performed for a handful of people to watch. Darion feeds— *fed*," I correct quickly, "off the energy, and Tate gets to enjoy viewing his fetishes performed for an audience."

Or participates. I leave that out though. Tate's sexual activities are for him and his partners. Gemma doesn't need to know about them.

Gemma freezes. She is standing by the stage gazing around at the set up when I drop this information. It takes her a full ten, silent, seconds to process the information.

She looks up at me and says, "I'm assuming that if Darion and Tate are down here enjoying the show, so are you."

I nod. I was definitely a part of those wilder nights. Gemma says nothing, but she does start moving around the room again. When she's done exploring, I take her over to the first door on the right. There is a code I have to punch in for the door to open. I hesitate when the door unlocks.

I'm nervous. I've never had any reason to be ashamed or uncomfortable about what I do sexually. The escort service Darion uses hires only sophisticated, beautiful women who are open to having a good time. I always made sure to wear a condom, I always made sure the women were consenting, and then I fuck them however I pleased. I saw nothing wrong with that. But my mate might. My mate could be repulsed by how sexually active I've been, and behind this door she will see how truly dirty things got. I've never cared about people's opinions of me before. But that's changed. There is one person's opinion I do care about.

Before I open the door, I turn to Gemma who's watching me curiously. I take a deep breath.

"I'm showing you all of this now because I would like you to consider moving in with us. Even after everything has died down, I want you to stay with us. We can make this our home. I like coming home to find you here, comfortable, and happy. Darion and I need to talk to Tate about it, too, but… we think maybe you should see the whole house before you make a decision. If you don't like what's behind this door, we can move somewhere else together."

Gemma's expression is concerned as she meets my gaze.

"Okay, you're kind of scaring me," she says quietly.

"Don't be," I assure her quickly. "I just want you to know everything about us before you make a decision."

With that, I push open the door, reach in, and flick on the lights. I step aside to allow Gemma to walk in. Her gasp makes me wince. I stare into the room, trying to see it with new eyes. The room itself is painted in a deep navy blue with soft lighting accenting certain features. The bed in the middle of the room is the focal point. There is a sling hanging from the four-poster bed frame, attached with chains. Dangling off the corners of the mattress are thick, padded restraints. The mattress has no bedding on it, but it does have pillows used for propping up the body in various positions.

On the left side of the room is a spanking bench, a bondage couch that has multiple metal hoops to attach a submissive to, and a personal favorite: a hanging stockade. On the right side of the room is a large metal X-shape cross that is attached to the wall. Again, another favorite. Next to it is a dresser full of toys and a wall full of different flogging tools.

All in all, it's a pretty timid room for those into the BDSM scene. Well, according to Tate. While I enjoy this occasionally, I prefer a little less dramatic flair. I have to admit, though, it is fascinating to see him work in here. Watching his submissive get off is fucking incredible. Add Darion into the mix with his ability to keep things going, and we've ended up down here for days.

Gemma walks into the room slowly. I turn and watch her face as she takes everything in. Her mouth is pressed into a tight line, and her eyes are wide. She walks over to the bed and then walks around it, studying it. She pauses when she makes it to one side. She's not staring at the bed but what's next to it. I walk further into the room to see what she's looking at. Oh… the cage. It's practically a fancy crate for a dog, with a flat wooden surface on top placed strategically next to the bed like a nightstand.

Her gaze darts to me in surprise. I wait for her to speak, but she doesn't. Instead, she pulls her eyes away from me and walks over to the pillory. I picture her head and hands attached into the wooden piece while her naked body stands there, exposed and vulnerable. She'd be unable to see what is coming when I approach her, especially if I decide a blindfold is needed. Immediately, my dick hardens.

I pull my eyes away from the pillory as she moves from it to walk across the room to the cross. She reaches out to touch the large metal frame but stops herself. Gemma continues her tour around the room. When she's done exploring, she simply stands in the middle of it looking lost.

"You okay?" I ask her, anxious to hear her thoughts.

Gemma opens her mouth but then shuts it. She looks around the room again. When she meets my gaze, she says, "I thought my fuzzy pink handcuffs were kinky. This is…"

She flounders for the right word but gives up with a shrug.

"It's a lot," I agree and step towards her.

"You like this stuff?" she asks, her voice is strained. I shrug.

"Occasionally, I'll dabble in it. It's more of Tate's scene, but if the opportunity arose, and the right woman came along then I was down to play," I explain.

I watch her throat as she swallows hard.

"Do you want to do this stuff to me? Is that why you wanted to show me this room?" she asks, her voice almost nonexistent.

I close the distance between us and tell her the truth: "Only if you wanted to explore. Like I said, this isn't exactly my scene. But I don't want to hide anything from you. I'm trying to be completely transparent for you. I want you to see all of me. Including this."

Gemma nods.

"So, Aaron really should be worried about me being trapped in a sex dungeon…" she says looking around her one more time. I chuckle, relieved that she is making jokes and not running from the house. "Is Darion… into this?"

"Darion's an incubus; he's down for whatever," I say dryly. Darion's pretty much willing to try anything since he can control the outcome in any instance. "But he won't try anything like this with you if you don't want it either."

"Why didn't he join us down here for the tour?" she asks me curiously.

I shrug. "You'll have to ask him."

"I should probably go check on dinner…" she says, looking past me towards the door.

Shit, she's not running, is she? I reach up and cup her face.

"Hey, really, how are you feeling about all of this? I can show you the other rooms down here—"

"You have more sex dungeons?" Gemma squeaks in surprise.

"No, just a home gym," I assure her quickly. She sighs in relief. "And you've seen the security room. I'll give you the access code in case you ever need to get in there. It works as a safe room, too, should something ever happen."

"No, I really should go make sure dinner isn't burning," she says. Her light brown eyes search my face for a moment. "I'm fine, Christopher. Just surprised. I don't think I'll be participating in most of the stuff in this room, but maybe we can start with handcuffs and just work our way up."

I let out a relieved breath and nod. "We don't even have to do handcuffs if you don't ever want to try them."

She laughs. Though, it's a bit breathless. "I bought them when I was with my ex to try to spice things up, but he wasn't into it. I think his reaction to seeing them is the same way I feel about all of this."

I chuckle.

"I'm glad things didn't work out with him," I tell her with a grin. She rolls her eyes.

"Me too," she agrees and steps around me. "I'll meet you upstairs."

She practically runs out of the room, leaving me alone.

"She reacted much better than I thought she would," Tate's voice says from somewhere in the room.

I roll my eyes and look towards the darker shadow in the corner of the room. He steps out of the darkness with an amused grin.

"Why are you here?" I ask suspiciously.

"I heard your conversation with Darion and wanted to see how this would play out. She's so… *vanilla*. I was sure she was going to run screaming from the room. I would've put money on it," he replies and then laughs.

"If you heard the conversation, then what do you think about her staying here?" I ask him.

Tate frowns.

"Let me think about it," he says after a moment. "In the meantime, let's go get dinner."

Chapter Twenty-Five

Tate

In the next few days, a routine begins to take shape. Each morning, I get up before everyone else to slide through the shadows in the house and around the property and then check in with the security detail standing by the front gates. After speaking with them, I head back into the house where I find Christopher or Darion, sometimes both, getting ready for work. By the time they head out of the house, Gemma comes down dressed, looking either freshly fucked or showered.

She makes breakfast for the both of us before getting to work on her laptop. Earlier on in the week, Darion had his guys bring her desktop and another monitor from her office and placed them in Christopher's unused office where she works most of the day. While she works, I monitor the security cameras, oversee each security guard change, and sweep the woods for any signs of trouble. I check in on Gemma often, and each time, I'm greeted with a dismissive wave of her hand if she's on the phone or an amused roll of her eyes if she's simply working on the computer.

Gemma has made it her job to make sure dinner is on the table by the time the guys get home. After we all eat together and talk about our days, it's time to lounge about together for the rest of the night. Nights include movies, enjoying cold beers around the firepit outside, billiard games, and whatever else we can get into. Eventually, the three of them all slip away. Some nights, they go one by one, other times two go upstairs together, and some nights all three of them disappear together upstairs, and I'm left to my own devices.

I don't mind their disappearances. Gemma has been pretty gracious about sharing her time with Christopher and Darion. While we hang out, sometimes she leaves us alone to give the three of us space to hang out together. Those times are great because it's the three musketeers back together again. Minus the women who used to be a revolving door every night, things feel normal.

"Hey, you need to relax," Gemma says as reaches over to stab a fork into the pot sticker sitting untouched on my plate.

"Easy for you to say," I tell her through gritted teeth.

"And it's easy for you to do if you just breathe," she responds and then pops the pot sticker into her mouth. "Oh, these are my new favorite appetizers."

The way her face lights up as she reaches for another one off my plate reminds me why I agreed to take her to lunch.

As days turn into weeks with no disruption in security either at the house or at Christopher's or Darion's workplace, I began to notice Gemma's restlessness. With the inability to leave the house, she was starting to get a little stir crazy. So, I spoke with the guys the other night, and we agreed that if I take her somewhere in the complete opposite direction of Boston, we'll probably be safe going out to lunch for an hour or so.

"Your food is getting cold," she points out as she twists her fork into her noodles.

"I'm not hungry anymore," I grumble. "You can have it."

Gemma frowns. "Come on, we get this one day of freedom. Let's enjoy it!"

"Gemma, I—" I pause, looking around the Chinese restaurant. There are a few businessmen and women scattered about, but it's not overly busy. "I could shift at any moment. How am I supposed to relax?"

"Because I'm here," she says as if it's obvious.

She has a point. It's been almost a month now, and I haven't had a single issue with her around.

"Yeah but—"

"How about this?" Gemma says, cutting me off. "Eat your food, and then we can go do something that *I'm* uncomfortable with so you can tell me to relax? Fair enough?"

"We shouldn't stay out long. I told the guys—" I warn, but Gemma waves her hand dismissively.

"Live a little, Tate."

I huff, and she giggles as she rolls her eyes. Her giggle does something to me. My chest feels lighter, and I can't help but smile. Sometime within the past few weeks, I find myself coaxing a smile from her whenever I can. I'm not sure why, but it steals my breath away. Her laughter makes my legs tremble, and my knees become weak. Somewhere along the way, during our time together I have gone from despising her to... whatever this is. I think it started during our golf outing. The panic I felt was so real, but Gemma was there, calm and understanding. There was no judgement or impatience as I worked through the new reality I face. Because of her, I *can* 'live a little.'

"Fine," I tell her. "But whatever it is you have planned, it better *really* upset you."

"Want to see me upset, huh?" Gemma asks with amusement. "Oh, I'll show you upset. You're going to see some real, pure unadulterated, unreasonable amount of uncomf-y."

I chuckle at her mocking. We eat quickly, talking as we do. When we finish, Gemma, against my objections, pays for lunch, and we leave the restaurant. Instead of getting back in the car and heading home, as the original plan calls for, we head a few miles up the road to a mall.

"You're taking me shopping?" I ask, appalled. "What happened to doing something you're uncomfortable with?"

"Tate, trust me. I'm not taking you shopping," Gemma says.

I groan as she leads the way through the mall. There are more people here, and I find myself even more worried about a lapse in my ability to hold my physical form than I was back at the restaurant. Luckily, we don't end up going far. We stop at a large simulation ride that is planted right in the middle of the walkway. From the graphics on the side of the machine, it looks to be a simulation of a ride through space. The ride is currently occupied and is tilting left and right, front and back. It spins rather slowly all the way around, and I can hear the adolescents inside the machine squeal with fear and joy.

"We're here," Gemma says.

The tone of her voice catches me off guard. I look down to find her staring, wide eyed at the ride. All amusement has drained from her expression and has been replaced with trepidation.

"*This* is what scares you?" I ask in surprise. "This measly little ride?"

"Well, all rides scare me," she admits. "But for some reason, this type is next level terrifying for me."

I throw my head back and laugh.

"Oh, we're definitely doing this," I tell her as I walk over to pay the college-age attendant.

When I return to her side, I find she's actually trembling. She's wringing her hands and is watching the ride warily.

"I can't believe you're actually scared of this thing. Look at it! It's hardly tipping ten degrees in any direction," I tell her, still chuckling.

The machine comes to a stop, and the people occupying it are helped out by the attendant.

"Come on, it's our turn," I tell her and walk over to the entrance.

I'm about to climb in when I realize that Gemma hasn't followed me. I turn around to find her eyes so wide I can see the whites all around her irises. She has taken a step back, as if to turn and run. Her trembling has turn into full blown tremors now. It's becoming quite clear that this isn't a game. Gemma is actually terrified of this ride.

"Hey, you can't back out now," I tell her, though I wonder if I should let this go.

She pulls her gaze from the ride to me. She gives me one tight nod and walks over to where the attendant is impatiently waiting for us. We climb into the simulation ride, and the kid straps us in.

I'm grinning. When was the last time I've done something like this? I look around the machine. It's pretty basic. Pictures are plastered all around to make it look like we're in a spaceship. I look over to Gemma, who's frozen in terror. She has a white-knuckle grip on the harness strapping her into the seat. Her foot is tapping rapidly against the floor, and her breathing comes in rapid gulps.

"Gemma, you're going to be fine," I tell her as I suppress laughter. "We're not actually going to space."

She looks over at me and says, "I think I'm going to pee myself."

I throw my head back and laugh just as the ride starts. Gemma's squeal of terror only makes me laugh harder. The ride is only three minutes long, but as it comes to an end, I know it has been the best three minutes of my life. Gemma's unholy screams of terror as we jerk around causes tears to run down my face. Her fear is completely and utterly unfounded, which makes it all the more hilarious to see her so truly scared.

By the time we both step out of the ride, I swear Gemma is ready to puke.

"Don't tell the others I'm scared of rides or I'll tell them you were equally as scared at eating lunch in public," Gemma threatens as we head to the car.

I grin over at her and find her grinning back. Getting into the car, I send up a small prayer that there will be more days like this, with Gemma, in the future.

Chapter Twenty-Six

Darion

I've missed dinner.

It's not mandatory to be home for the meal, nor is it expected that we all sit together. But as I open the front door and walk into the house, I feel guilty. Gemma has a full-time job running her own business, but she has taken it upon herself to make sure dinner is warm and ready for each of us when we get home. The fact that she's started this habit of making sure we have eaten at least one good meal a day is… well, its touching. The gesture is sweet, and it means more to me than she can possibly understand. I hate that I couldn't enjoy it right when it came out of the oven or off the grill. I'm also disappointed. After the shit day that I've had, I looked forward to sitting down with everyone and blowing off steam over a good meal.

I sigh as I walk to the back of the house where Christopher and Tate are hanging out and watching a game on TV.

Tate looks up as I enter. "Hey man, long day?"

"You have no idea," I grumble and run my hand over my face.

I walk over to the refrigerator and open it. I reach for a beer but stop when I see a plate covered in foil. A post-it note sits on top of it with my name written in the middle of a hand drawn heart. I grab the plate, forgoing the beer, and shut the fridge behind me. I take off the cover and find curry chicken on a bed of quinoa, a piece of naan bread, and some steamed vegetables plated for me. I stare down at the meal while my heart does a funny flip in my chest. I reach up and touch my chest where it hides and rub at the spot.

"You good?" Christopher asks.

I look up to find both Tate and Christopher staring at me curiously. I drop my hand and walk over to the microwave and set my meal inside.

"Yeah, just tired," I tell them.

"Any... *problems*?" Chris asks. I can hear the concern in his voice.

I look over at him and frown. "No, thankfully. Today was uneventful except for the lousy case dropped in my lap. Sorry I stayed late to get work done."

Both Tate and Chris exchange looks.

"Why are you apologizing?" Tate asks, baffled.

He's right, why am I apologizing? I've never apologized for staying at the office late before. Why have I started tonight?

"Shit, I don't know," I grumble as the microwave dings. Before I grab my food, I reach into the fridge and grab that beer I wanted. "Where's Gemma?"

"She just headed upstairs before you pulled up to soak in a bath," Chris says.

A bath? That sounds nice. I think I'll join her. I grab my food and drink and head upstairs. I expect to find her in the bathroom attached to the guest room she's been using as her room, but she's not there. Frowning, I head to my room to eat dinner and change. Inside, I hear Gemma's soft voice humming from my bathroom. I grin and head in that direction.

The door is open a crack already, so I use my foot to push it open the rest of the way. Gemma's back is facing me, her head leans over the edge of the large tub, and her eyes are closed as the steam clings to the air around her face. Her arms are doing gentle circles in the water in front of her, jostling the bubbles she has poured into the water and let build up over the surface.

"You look comfortable," I say, interrupting her humming.

She flinches hard at the sound of my voice and immediately turns around to face me. As she does, I catch a fleeting glimpse of fear before it melts away when she realizes it's me. At once, I regret startling her.

"Sorry, I didn't mean to scare you," I tell her. The things she has gone through the past few weeks would put any normal person on edge.

"It's fine," she assures me before sending me a large warm grin. "You should eat that before it gets soggy from all this steam."

"It'll be fine," I assure her. "Mind if I join you?"

She waves a bubble covered arm over the top of the water and says, "I'd like that. There is more than enough room for the both of us."

Yes, the tub is huge. It is built into the floor and was made to accommodate many people after, or during, an orgy session. I don't tell her this as I place my meal and drink on the counter to undress. She watches me with hooded eyes and a smile. I walk over with my meal and place it on the floor as I get into the water. I don't use the available space of the tub. I make it a point to slide into the water right beside her. I turn and take her mouth with mine. The moment our lips meet, the tension from the day unravels completely.

I pull away and look down at her. "Sorry I missed dinner."

Gemma appears breathless, and it takes her a moment to find her voice. I smile, feeling smug knowing that I can do that to her.

"You don't have to apologize, I understand," she says after a moment. She resituates herself in the tub and leans her head back onto the tile floor.

"Yes, I do. I should have texted to let you know I wouldn't be here," I tell her with a frown. I didn't think of that while I was at the office, but now I know to do it in the future.

Gemma chuckles. "Really it's okay. I made sure you had a plate for when you got here in case you didn't get a chance to grab something to eat on the way home."

I grab the plate in question and bring it around as I lean back against the tub. I want to tell her how much I appreciate the meal. It may mean nothing for her to go through the hassle of cooking for us, but to me...

"My previous master... She never cooked for me. In fact, I don't think she knew I ate regular food," I tell Gemma. My voice is soft as I admit this piece of information. I don't talk about my past with Casabella. Not with Christopher. Not with Tate. No one in this world knows about her. Anyone who knew about my past has long since passed away. "To know that you think about me... that you *care* enough about me to make dinner every night... It means a lot to me. I don't want you to think that I don't appreciate dinner when I can't make it home on time."

Gemma's eyes are wide as she stares at me in surprise. I don't think she expected me to mention Casabella. Slowly, a smile spreads across her face.

"I do care about you, Darion," she says. "Don't ever think otherwise."

I lean over, kiss her cheek, and turn my attention to dinner. Silence hangs between us as I eat a few bites. It's delicious. I wonder when she learned to cook. Does she enjoy it? Is it a way for her to unwind? Part of me has always been interested in taking cooking classes. Maybe we can take some together.

Gemma's hand slides onto my thigh under the water. I look over, and she's still staring at me, but the surprise has faded and been replaced with a warmth I don't understand.

She tilts her head to the side and asks, "May I ask you about *her*? Your previous... um, master?"

Internally, I sigh at her uncomfortable use of the title. I'm going to have to somehow prove to Gemma that the word 'master' has no bad connotations between us, but I let it go for now.

"You may," I confirm after I take another bite and a swig of my beer.

Gemma hesitates, biting her bottom lip as she considers her next words. Her hand absentmindedly strokes my thigh. The motion does not go unnoticed by me, and I try hard not to let it distract me.

"What was your relationship like with her? Why wouldn't she know if you ate or not?" she asks finally.

I think back to Casabella and wonder again how often I compare that life to what I have now. Things were so… bleak back then. Yet during my time with her I would never have described my life in such a way. I take a few bites of my dinner, finishing it, and clear my throat by chasing the food with beer. I place the plate and bottle behind me. With my hands free, I reach one under the water and grab the hand stroking my thigh. I bring it up out of the water to kiss her knuckles.

"I believe, before she gave me life, that she was a genuinely good woman. I think losing the person she loved destroyed anything good about her. The way people around her acted… It was like they were meeting a whole new person. Like they couldn't believe she had become this twisted evil human being. When I knew her… She was a selfish, rotten human being. She only thought of herself and only interacted with people when she knew she had something to gain by the connection. I thought her pigheaded, haughty attitude was Queen-like back then. She didn't take shit from anyone, and I admired that about her. At the time I thought I loved her," I pause as I think back to the cruel woman.

She killed for pleasure, laughed at others' pain… How did I think that was okay?

"But you didn't love her? Being someone's incubus, you don't feel…" Gemma hesitates as she struggles for the right word. "*Compelled* to have feelings for your master?"

I stare at the steam rising in front of us as I mull over her question.

"No, I didn't love her," I answer firmly. *That* I know for sure. But for the other question… "As for being compelled to feel anything for anyone we're tied to… Honestly, I'm not quite sure."

I look over at Gemma and find her frowning. Her brows are furrowed as she stares at the water. I squeeze her hand, and she peeks over at me.

"With Casabella... She was my first master. I was new to the world, new to my powers, and even new to emotions in general. With her, there was this frantic need to please her in every sense of the word. In or out of the bedroom, I *had* to do what she wanted, or I would fall into a terrible depression that only she could relieve me from by commanding me to do things for her," I explain softly.

I shudder as I think back to those times. To those dark moments when I thought I had failed Casabella in some way. Those memories fill me with dread, and it takes a moment to push the darkness aside. When I can speak again, I continue,

"When she died and I was freed from her hold, I instantly felt the change. It was like coming up for air after nearly drowning. My life no longer revolved around Casabella. I was in charge, and I learned how to be... Well, I was going to say *human*, but I guess as human-like as possible. That included learning how to feel and express emotions properly. I now know, looking back, what I felt for Casabella was simply a sick obsession."

Gemma nods slowly. I'm not sure if she understands, but I can see her considering my words. She looks away again, and for a moment, we're both silent.

"You don't seem...I don't know, out of character now that we've become something," she says thoughtfully as she turns to glance back at me. "I know I don't know you well enough to assume anything, but... It doesn't sound like what you had with Casabella is similar to what we have."

I nod and say, "You're absolutely right. I haven't lost myself and become the pathetic incubus I used to be. When I'm with you, it feels like I've stepped out of a musty, dark cave and into the sunlight where I can breathe fresh air and bathe in the warmth. I feel lighter, happier... My life feels like it has a purpose and meaning again. This feels right."

As I speak, the certainty of what I am saying solidifies. This does feel right. I feel like I belong here with her. Gemma's answering smile is soft and understanding. My heart swells as I stare down at her. I lean over and kiss her mouth swiftly. As I pull away, I scoot closer to her so that our arms touch.

"For years, I struggled with who and what I was. I was Casabella's slave, so she never thought to teach me to read or write. I had to teach myself those things, but it took time. I lived in poverty for years while I struggled to learn the ways of the world without a master. During that time, I got myself into a lot of trouble with the gangs and crime lords that ran the streets. Eventually, I managed to pull myself out that hole, and I worked hard to get to where I am today.

"I'm not perfect, Gemma. I am able to afford the things I have not just because I'm a prosecutor but because I do some… shady things here and there to get the bad guys off the streets. I've seen all the harm that they can do during my own time on the streets, and I know that sometimes the law needs to be bent in order to catch the worst offenders. But all in all, I'm proud of what I have accomplished and who I have become. And for someone as kind-hearted and selfless as you are to care for me, I feel like it's a confirmation that I'm doing something right."

A weight's been lifted off my shoulders. I can feel the shift as I speak. Talking about my past, parts that not even Christopher or Tate know about, is cathartic, and a chuckle slips out. It tumbles out of me and gets louder, turning into a full-blown laugh that echoes throughout the bathroom. By the time it subsides, my stomach hurts. I turn my attention back to Gemma and find her staring up at me in wonder.

"You're magnificent when you laugh," she says softly as our eyes meet. Her compliment takes me off guard, and I am instantly humbled by the sincerity I see in her eyes. "As for what you've told me, that's a lot to unpack. But it sounds like you had it rough in the beginning. I can't begin to imagine what life was like for you even though you've given me some insight. I don't want you to ever feel like that again."

Emotions choke her, and she stops talking as her face turns pink with… embarrassment? What does she have to be embarrassed about? It's strange to wonder about the feelings of others. Besides Christopher and Tate, I don't particularly care to dwell on what others think and feel. But with Gemma... I want to know everything. For her to feel comfortable sharing what she feels with me, it is only fair that I do the same with her.

"Despite having people wanting to harm us, I'm happier than I have ever been," I tell her solemnly. "I awake with a smile on my face every morning, and I go to bed with a smile because of you. You make me laugh and keep me on my toes. You care for me, and I find myself caring, very much, for you. I have never felt this way before with anyone else, so I'm almost a hundred percent sure it has nothing to do with the bond between us and everything to do with who you are as a person."

Gemma's mouth pops open in surprise. I chuckle at her reaction but wonder at it. Did she not believe I cared at all for her? The thought seems ridiculous, but I understand insecurities. Even though Gemma comes off as confident, maybe she does question how I feel about her. It's not like we've talked about it before. Until now, how else would she know how I felt?

Gemma closes her mouth but opens it right back up to say, "I feel the same way, Darion. I'm glad to know that what we have is much different than what you've experienced in the past. I want you to know we're partners in this. If you ever start to feel like you did with Casabella, tell me immediately, and we'll figure out a way to work through it okay? That goes for anything in life moving forward. If I'm ever doing something that doesn't sit right with you, tell me. If I can do something to make your life easier, tell me. Together, with Christopher, we'll grow together and always have each other's backs."

Partners? Grow together? Her consideration for me, and for *us*, is astounding. I sigh and shake my head. Gemma frowns, confused by my reaction. I smile at her as my heart continues to swell to new sizes.

"Oh, Gemma, what am I going to do with you?" I ask wearily.

"What do you mean?" she asks as her brows come together in confusion.

"When you say stuff like that, it makes me want to have one of those pesky conversations you mentioned," I tell her with a mocking frown.

"Oh? And what pesky conversation would you like to discuss?" she asks curiously.

"The one where I ask if you'll move in with me," I inform her. "Well, with *us*. I know Christopher has already brought it up, but now it's my turn since you haven't given anyone an answer yet."

"What?" Gemma gasps in surprise. She scoots to the side to put some distance between us. I don't like it. Not at all. I haven't yet let go of her hand, so I use it to pull her back to me.

"Well, how else are we to grow together or be the partners you speak of when you live in an apartment in the city, and we live here?" I ask her. I make sure to add a teasing note to my tone, but I'm serious. Has she truly not considered Christopher's offer?

"I'm not opposed to the idea," Gemma starts slowly. She huffs, and her cheeks turn pink again. "It just feels like everything is happening so quickly. And while you and Christopher may want me to move in, I don't know how Tate feels about all of this. Have you asked him?"

Tate… He's been a mystery lately. Ever since the incident that caused him to take Gemma into the shadows, his attitude towards Gemma has changed. I'm not sure what is going on, but I've noticed the coldness towards her has thawed, and I catch him watching her when he thinks none of us notice. He hasn't complained about her presence in the house, nor has he mentioned how much time he has to spend with her throughout the day. It's very un-Tate like to be decent around a person for long periods of time. With the way he first treated Gemma, I was sure this living situation was going to be tricky.

"I don't think Tate has any objections to you moving in, or he would have made them astoundingly clear right off the bat," I tell her after a moment. "But I'll run it by him again just to make sure. If he objects, either we can find a new place to live once it's safe to start looking, or he can pack his bags. Either way, I want you with me and Christopher."

Gemma studies my face. I wonder what she's thinking. Does she want to move in with us, or does this feel like an obligation due to our circumstances? I don't want her to feel pressured, but I want this badly, and I know Christopher does, too. Whatever issues arise from her moving in, we can deal with them as they come.

"Alright, I'll move in," Gemma says finally and grins up at me.

My heart feels too big for my body. I beam down at her and ask, "That conversation wasn't too bad, was it?"

"One pesky conversation down, only about a hundred more to go!" she says playfully.

I lean over and take her lips with mine again. She leans into me, and my dick begins to stiffen. She places her free hand on my chest, and her tongue demands entrance into my mouth. I allow it, and I groan when she shifts her body to straddle mine. I drop her hand to hold her hips. She pulls away after a moment and looks down at me with hunger in her eyes.

"Can I show you how much I care about you?" she asks. As she speaks, her hips lean forward so the junction between her legs presses against my erection.

"Absolutely," I tell her and place a swift, hard kiss against her lips. I pull away again and say, "You may have to show me over and over again."

"*That* I can do," she assures me with a smile.

Chapter Twenty-Seven

Tate

"Open your legs a little more. Yup, just like that," I tell Gemma as she adjusts her stance.

The target attached to the hay barrel blows in the breeze a few yards away. Darion and Christopher stand there, watching as Gemma stares through the scope on the rifle.

"Remember to breathe," I remind her. "And lift up that elbow a tad. Perfect."

My dick twitches as Gemma listens to my commands perfectly. I try to ignore it, as I have been for weeks now, but damn, if she doesn't look like perfection standing there in that outfit, holding a gun, and listening like a good submissive would.

I breathe through the desire as it surges forward and say, "Whenever you're ready."

A few seconds tick by before Gemma pulls the trigger. She misses the bullseye, but she hits the target in what would be a fatal shot if it were a person. Another few seconds tick by. She pulls the trigger again, and this time she does hit square in the middle of the target. She lowers the rifle as she yelps in delight. She spins to face us, and a large grin splits her face. I struggle to take a deep breath.

Being around Gemma as much as I have lately, I find myself struggling to breathe a lot. Since she moved in two weeks ago, I'm constantly reminded of her presence whether she's in the room with me or not. With little personal belongings everywhere, the sound of her laughter ringing throughout the house, and the sweet treats she bakes almost daily, there is barely a moment in the day that I'm not thinking about her.

"My turn!" Christopher says eagerly.

He takes the rifle and eyeglasses from Gemma and steps forward to shoot next.

"Pay up," I tell Darion, who is also grinning at his woman. "I told you I could get her to hit the bullseye in a week's time."

Darion pulls out his wallet and hands me a hundred-dollar bill.

"Treat yourself to something expensive," the incubus says.

I laugh at his mockingly sour expression.

"Don't be a sore loser," Gemma reprimands Darion playfully as she comes over and kisses his cheek.

I look away when their eyes meet. A surge of some hot emotion wells up in me whenever I witness Gemma's affection towards either brother now. I've been spending most of my time with her throughout the day, and I love every minute of it. Lately, at night I've found myself dreaming about Gemma giving *me* those same looks. Touching me the way she touches them...

How could I have ever conceived the notion that Gemma would be annoying to have around? She's literally the whole package, and more. I've been spending much more time with her lately. During lunch we talk and laugh. Sometimes, I hang out with her in her makeshift office while she works. The few hours we allot ourselves out of the house during the week have been some of the most enjoyable times in my life.

Gemma calls them mini dates to tease the others whenever we do make it out of the house, and secretly, I love it. I know she does it to taunt them to take her out, and I know they want to, but both Christopher and Darion are still concerned for her safety. I don't blame them. I don't want anything to happen to her either. But those are *our* time together. While I might not be her actual boyfriend, when we're alone together I like to pretend…

Gemma's phone rings, and she steps away from Darion,

"Oh, it's my mom," she mumbles.

When she frowns, Darion asks, "What's wrong?"

"She's going to start asking about holiday plans soon," she says with a sigh.

"What's wrong with that?" Darion pushes.

Gemma grimaces. Instead of answering Darion, she answers her phone and starts to walk away towards the house.

"Hey, Mom."

Darion stares after her with a frown.

"I'm going to take a wild guess and say that she hasn't told her parents about seeing two guys at once," I say, taunting the incubus. "It's going to be hard to explain to her mom to put *two* extra places at the table."

Darion turns and gives me an appraising look but says nothing. His frown deepens. Hold up, did I actually just get under his skin? I open my mouth to backtrack.

Christopher interrupts with his back turned to us as he looks through the scope at his target. "I just talked to Mrs. Thomas the other day. She knows we're coming."

"*What?*" Darion and I say in unison.

"Yeah, Gemma formally introduced me to her parents as her mate on video chat the other night when you were on the phone with your client, Darion," Christopher lowers the rifle to look over his shoulder at us. "I don't think I've ever been that nervous. I practically pissed myself."

"She told her family about me?" Darion pushes. I glance over at him, confused by his anxiousness.

"She told her parents that she has another special friend coming, too. Her parents didn't ask any questions, just nodded and let it go," Christopher says.

"Special friend…" Darion repeats slowly, testing the title. Does he… Does he *want* her parents to know about their situation? That seems like a horrible idea, but what do I know?

"Better than introducing you as her sex slave," Christopher says with a grin. "That may have made it a little awkward."

Darion's shoulders relax, and he chuckles.

"You're probably right," the incubus admits.

"Fuck, that sucks for you guys. You'll have to suffer through a boring holiday meal dodging awkward questions for hours. Sounds terrible," I grumble, pulling my own pistol from the holster on my hip.

I take a step towards the target Christopher is ignoring and shoot off several rounds. I hit the middle with every shot.

"Don't pretend you're not jealous that you're not going," Darion says when I stop.

I scoff but don't look at him. I fire a few more shots at the target.

"I'm not jealous. I'm relieved honestly. *I* don't have to deal with the questions from the parents of the piece of ass I'm fucking," I tell him.

"Don't call Gemma a piece of ass. She's more than that, and you know it. Show her some respect," Darion says, his voice dropping an octave. "And cut the shit, Tate, I know you've been thinking of that same piece of ass for weeks now."

I look at him in surprise as Christopher shoots me a dark look.

"What?" he demands.

I shake my head in denial and tell Darion, "I don't know what you're talking about."

"Every time Gemma gets fucked, you start jerking off. I'm an incubus, Tate, remember? I can sense sexual energy, and it pours off of you and fills the house while the three of us are together," Darion says. "I even heard you moan her name the other night when we were doing it on the pool table, and you were right outside the door."

"*What?*" Christopher repeats louder, a scowl appearing. "Why didn't I know he was standing there?"

"Because you were face deep in between Gemma's legs," Darion tells him with a calm smile.

I stare at my two friends who stare accusingly back at me. I brace myself, ready to defend myself, but then I hear Gemma's laughter, and my gaze is redirected towards her. My chest swells at the sound. She's up on the patio with her back facing us, leaning against the railing, oblivious to the conversation.

"See? Can't keep your eyes off of her, can you?" Darion pushes. "You've had an erection ever since we set these targets up. Seeing her holding a gun really gets you going, doesn't it? Or is it because she's listening to your orders? You do love a good submissive woman..."

Damn, Darion really knows me well. Maybe a bit too well. I make a face and sigh. There's no point in denying any of this. What I've been feeling for Gemma has evolved from a friendship to something else quickly. What can I do but accept what I'm feeling and just hope that my brothers won't hold it against me?

"You're right," I say, letting my shoulders sag. "I am attracted to Gemma."

Darion nods. He has clearly put this together already. Christopher, on the other hand, scowls as he stares at me.

"How long?" he demands.

"I think it started after we went golfing," I admit.

Both guys trade looks of surprise with one another before turning their attention back to me.

"That was weeks ago," Christopher says, confused. "I thought you were just trying to play nice after almost killing her."

"Yeah, I was playing until… until I wasn't anymore," I tell him.

They are both silent for a moment as they mull over my words. Christopher turns his back to me, lifts the rifle and shoots off a few rounds. Hm… Maybe I should have admitted my feeling about Gemma when he doesn't have a gun in his hand. Darion turns and looks back towards Gemma, who is heading inside to keep talking without competing with the sound of gunfire.

Time ticks by, and I find myself holding my breath. What are they going to do? What are they going to say? I'm nervous. My palms are sweaty, and I'm holding my breath. Is this how nervous Christopher was when meeting Gemma's parents? Is this even comparable? Me, declaring my feelings to her lovers and hoping that… that what? What do I want from them?

"Okay," Christopher says after a few minutes to no one in particular. He looks over at Darion who nods. He looks over at me and says, "You're my brother, and I trust you. If you like Gemma, and understand that this isn't like the women in the past, I… I can be open-minded about this situation. My wolf accepts and trusts you, too."

"I can share Gemma," Darion says slowly.

I'm floored at what I am hearing. Gemma is their *everything*. With how I treated her in the beginning, I would bet a million dollars if I brought this conversation up myself, they would shut down the idea of me being included in what they have in a heartbeat. It's humbling that they are able to overlook my past indiscretions with their woman to see that I'm no longer like that around her.

Christopher holds up his hand to halt the conversation. "You need to speak with Gemma about your feelings to see if they are reciprocated. It's obviously going to be her decision whether you get to join what we have."

I nod. The movement feels jerky, and my heart starts to race. How am I supposed to broach this subject with Gemma?

"On another note, now that Gemma is out of earshot, I want to give you an update on Pierce," Darion says after a moment of silence.

"You found out something?" Christopher says with surprise and relief. "Please tell me it's good news."

Darion looks at both of us.

"I've received a tip about where he is and where he's going to be." The incubus grins. It's an evil one that sends a shiver down my spine. "Ready to take this bastard out?"

Chapter Twenty-Eight

Darion

"I rule in the favor of the prosecution. The plaintiff will not be allowed bail at this time," the judge calls and slams her mallet down as the decision is made.

The thrill of winning my cases has long since diminished over the years. But as I hear the verdict, a zing of pleasure ripples through me as I complete Gemma's orders that she gave me before I left, "*Hesirah, do your best to win this case and put this asshole behind bars.*"

My cock twitches as another wave of pleasure ripples through me. I can't wait to text Gemma about the victory. God, this is the type of life I can certainly enjoy forever. Life is certainly much more fun now that I have her in it.

As the audience begins talking, I move around the desk to approach the bench.

"Thank you, Your Honor," I tell the judge.

"Impressive handling of the case, Mr. Nightshade," she says with a polite nod.

I turn and head back to the desk. As I do, I shoot the other lawyer a cocky grin. He turns red and glares at me. The criminal next to him has his shoulders slumped and is glaring at the table. Pathetic idiot.

I collect my files on the desk and leave the courtroom. Three of my security guys are waiting just outside the doors and walk with me while we stroll down the hall. I check my phone. It's just past four in the afternoon, and I have several texts from clients, Phillip, and another lawyer in my firm, but the only ones that matter are from Gemma. She has sent several texts letting me know about her day and a picture of just her cleavage with a suggestive message under it. I grin.

My grin disappears as I read her last text: *Headed to some secret destination with Tate. Will text you when I know where I'm going.*

I sigh and shove the phone back in my pocket. Tate is about to shoot his shot with Gemma and is taking her to some Fall Festival in Salem. He overheard Gemma talking to her friend Aaron about being bummed not to be able to go this year, and he ran with the idea that this will be as good a time as any to tell her how he feels. Both Christopher and I agreed and noted that it would also be a good time for her to be as far from the city as possible. Now that I have an idea of where Pierce is hiding, I am going to make a move. I don't want Gemma anywhere near Boston while things go down.

Outside, the press is waiting for me on the stairs that lead up into the courthouse. I answer their questions and allow a few pictures to be taken. Once the press conference is over, I head down the rest of the stairs and climb into the SUV waiting for me filled with my security team, and we pull off. I pull off my tie and jacket as I mentally prepare to remove another piece of scum from this Earth.

I could let the law handle this. I have plenty of evidence against Pierce that would put him away for life. It would probably be smarter to just make a call and let the police handle it. But the thought of taking out the piece of scum that has been terrorizing the people around me sounds much more satisfying.

"Sir, our sources say Pierce has been seen entering the warehouse about an hour ago. No activity otherwise," Ian says from the front seat.

"Are your men ready?" I ask.

"They have surrounded the building, and we have snipers in place."

"And Christopher?" I ask.

"Waiting a few blocks away with some of my team," Ian responds.

I say nothing as I unbutton the sleeves of my white shirt and roll them up. The excitement and pleasure of winning my trial has passed. Now on to real business. It's been a while since I've taken on a large group like Pierce's. The last time was about eight years ago. It's typical to get threats from family members of those I put behind bars. Sometimes, things escalate to more than threatening notes or a punctured tire.

Usually, I find the threat on my life exhilarating. I suppose Gemma was right during our first conversation; I am bored. Why else would someone find some excitement in such a dangerous situation? In any case, I make sure to handle said threat appropriately. All evidence of my involvement is wiped clean by my crew, and no one is the wiser.

But this time is different. I have someone worth living for, and her life is now at risk. Not only hers, but Christopher's as well. My security has managed to take out every tail Pierce has placed to follow Christopher, but there will be a time when they are too late to act. We've kept this from Gemma, knowing it will only scare her, but Pierce has been trying to close in and take away everything that is important to me. When we finally got a break and found out he's been staying nearby, I knew it was time to act.

Tate's upset he isn't going to be involved with this hit, but Gemma needs to be kept unaware. Pulling him from watching over her would draw too much attention. While his ability to get in and out of places undetected would be helpful, there are other ways to handle this. The drive is silent as we approach our destination. Soon, we're pulling up behind another black SUV. Christopher steps out of the dark alley next to it. His body trembles, and his eyes are shining.

I get out of the car and approach the furious wolf shifter, who has been my friend for years.

"You going to be able to handle this?" I ask him calmly, as I take in his hyped-up state.

He bares his teeth at me.

"Take out the scum going after you and my girl? Hell, yes," he growls. He flashes me a predatory grin and adds, "Just like old times."

I chuckle. "We'll need to get in and out fast. Less bloodshed this time, please. We're supposed to be meeting Tate and Gemma around six."

"Don't put limits on me. I'm going for blood," Christopher snaps, but he grins again.

I sigh. "Let's take care of this then."

Ian hands me an earpiece, and I stick the thing in my ear.

While Christopher is visibly amped up for this, my excitement and need for blood boils within me as well. I smooth back my hair unnecessarily, taking the moment to calm myself down. Christopher steps back into the shadows while I turn towards Ian who is leaning inconspicuously against the SUV. He glances at me and raises a brow. I nod, and he touches his earpiece and sends a message to his crew. Christopher steps out as his wolf a moment later, and we exchange glances. He nods to let me know he's ready.

I shove my hands into my pockets and begin to walk towards the warehouse. Christopher disappears down a side street while Ian and the rest of the security team that came with us melt into the minimal foot traffic in the area. It doesn't take me long to make it to the front of the warehouse. Two men stand there, pretending to be casually loitering outside the abandoned industrial building.

I don't even let them react to my presence. With just a thought, both men's eyes glaze over before they roll into the backs of their heads. They reach into each other's pants and begin to jerk each other off. They'll be like that for a while. No need to worry if they'll raise the alarm.

Taking the handles of the large door in my hand, I yank it open without much effort. Even before I step foot into the building, I let my power surge forward. Guns drop from the hands of the guards from the second floor and clatter to the ground around me. The guards just beyond the door collapse as they thrash around on the floor. Orgasms are all fine and dandy, but when they don't stop, they're painful. Any testicles and ovaries will eventually begin to explode the longer I'm in the room. Most of them will die of heart failure soon enough.

Cries of pain begin to echo around me like music, and I smile.

Outside, I hear a round of gunfire. There is a pause, followed by another few rounds.

"Sir, four down. On the first floor. I can see people coming up from the basement. Christopher has made it in. We'll take them out as they continue to come up the stairs," Ian's calm voice says into my ear.

Doors open within the warehouse, and people come running out from wherever they have been hiding with guns raised. The second they are in the vicinity, they react to my power. Some keel over while others grab each other looking for relief. I'm completely forgotten as I tour the warehouse. I hear the sound of windows shattering as my team takes out an unseen threat somewhere in the warehouse. Downstairs, panic ensues.

I'm on the second floor when I hear screams, a wolf's snarl, and a few more gunshots.

I keep moving, knowing Christopher will find me shortly. On the third floor, I find what I'm looking for. There are five guards, armed and waiting for me. The first two fall, thrashing about on the ground as their bodies begin to turn themselves inside out. The next two seem unaffected by my power and raise their guns. I'm on them instantly, moving with supernatural speed, and their bodies hit the floor almost simultaneously. The fifth guard manages to get two shots off, both missing me. His neck is broken quickly and effectively.

I yank open the double doors just as Christopher bounds down the hallway. I tone down my power, so he is not affected. In his wolf form, he is less inclined to feel my power, but there's no reason to take a chance that this time may be different.

Inside is a grand office space with that same industrial feel of the rest of the warehouse. Lights filter in through the tinted windows, the desk is immaculate with no paperwork or files out, no fine layer of dust, or a pencil unsharpened in the cup.

Pierce comes here a lot. He should be here now. So where the hell is he? Christopher snarls as he sniffs around the room.

"Did you really think it would be so easy to catch me?" a voice breaks the silence. Christopher's hackles rise as we look around for where it's coming from. "I'm smarter than Jacob. I know how to cover my tracks and take care of issues without getting caught."

I walk around the desk and see Pierce's face on the monitor. His face tattoos look identical to his brother's. His grin is shiny with the gold teeth that glint in from the light around him.

"Ah, there you are Nightshade," he preens happily. "I assumed your furry friend would be there with you. Is he?"

"Why these games, Pierce?" I ask. My tone is calm, but inside I'm furious. I've been tricked.

"What games?" the gang leader asks innocently. "A game implies there is something to win, but I've already taken the thing you love the most. I've already played, and won, this game."

"What are you talking about?" I demand, scowling.

Pierce gestures to someone offscreen, and his image disappears, only to be replaced by a sea of people laughing, conversing, and eating. The cameraman is right dab in the middle of a crowded area. People are bumping into him, unaware of the criminal lurking next to them. The video shakes as he's jostled, but it steadies a moment later. The camera zooms in on two people a few feet in front of the cameraman.

My heart stops.

Tate and Gemma are walking through the festival, unaware of the danger behind them. Gemma points to something, and both venture in that direction. The cameraman hums happily as he follows them.

Fuck.

Christopher snarls in fury while my fingers twitch towards my pocket where my phone is kept. Before I can pull out my phone, Ian's voice is in my ear.

"A man just got out of a car with a bazooka,"

Christopher hears Ian's warning, and his snarling stops as he freezes. I glance towards the window just as a gunshot rings out.

"The threat is eliminated," Ian says.

"Nice try, Pierce," I tell the computer screen.

The gang leader is still not in sight, but I know he can hear us.

"Oh, no problem," Pierce says.

Not a second later does the cameraman pull a gun out and point it towards the unsuspecting Tate and Gemma.

"Enough!" I bellow, my heart in my throat.

Suddenly, the cameraman is hit sideways by someone, hard. The gun goes off, and chaos around the festival ensues. I can no longer see Tate or Gemma.

"If the gunman doesn't get them, and the bomb doesn't kill you, don't fret. I have a backup plan. They won't make it home," Pierce says before the computer screen goes blank.

The hair on the back of my neck raises as Christopher and I exchange panicked looks. We're both rushing towards the wall of windows in the same breath, and as we break through the glass and plummet the two and a half floors down to the sidewalk, the building explodes. Both Christopher and I are blown forward by the blast. Glass and heat beat at us. I twist and grab Christopher just before I hit the ground.

I pull the large wolf into my body and then tuck and roll, taking the impact of the fall. Not only are incubuses fast and strong, but we can take a beating. A wolf… not so much. The breath is knocked out of me as I hit the ground on my side. I let go of Christopher to let him roll as I skid to a stop.

I can feel blood trickle down my face, and I can feel the burn of the blast against my back, but miraculously, I am able to get to my feet.

My ears are ringing as my head spins. I grab my head and take a deep breath as I try to head back towards the car.

"Shit, Darion, are you alright?" Christopher asks with concern.

He puts his hand in the middle of my back and guides me to the waiting cars.

"Fine," I manage to get out through gritted teeth. I reach into my pocket, but find my phone is smashed beyond repair. "We have to get to Tate and Gemma."

Ian and a few of his men are waiting for us at the SUVs. He opens the back door and practically shoves both of us into the vehicle before rounding it and climbing into the driver's side.

"Gemma—"

"We heard. My men have taken out the gunmen, but there was a group of Pierce's men waiting in ambush by the car, and everything has gone silent, sir," Ian says.

The SUV peels away from the sidewalk, and Ian guns it towards the highway.

"Have you tried Gemma's or Tate's number?" Christopher asks as he grabs the sweatpants laid out for him in the third row.

"Neither one is answering," Ian says grimly. There is a short pause. "The tracker on their car says they are heading back towards the house. Quickly. No reports from any of my men."

"No way Pierce managed to take out everyone," Christopher says in hushed disbelief.

"Ian, we have to intercept Tate and Gemma, make sure they're alright and aren't being followed," I tell my head of security.

"On it, boss," he says and guns it.

Chapter Twenty-Nine

Gemma

(Two Hours Earlier)

"Okay, the suspense is killing me. Where are we going?" I ask Tate with a huff.

"We're almost there. Hold your horses," Tate grumbles as if he's annoyed, but when I look over, I can see the way one half of his mouth tugs up into a smile.

"I'm dying of curiosity," I tell him. "Like I can feel death descending upon me. Everything feels so cold..."

"You're so dramatic," he chuckles.

The chuckle, the smile—They're a wicked combination. As hard as I try not to think about it, Tate Granger is a handsome guy. At some point during the few weeks together, I have gone from dreading being around the guy to hoping he'll appear out of thin air in my makeshift office just so I can see those handsome, dark blue eyes stare back at me.

I mentally shake my head at myself. You're shacking up with his friends; you don't need to think about him! I scold myself.

A few minutes later, we turn into a lot labeled "festival parking only." Around us, people are getting out of their cars and heading down a cobblestone street decorated with arches of dried corn stalks and lined with pumpkins. The security SUV parks first, and I watch as five people dressed in black exit the vehicle and disappear into the crowd. We park next, and I notice another black van behind us parking nearby. Another five people, also donned in all-black attire, disperse into the crowd.

"I can't take the suspense. What is going on?" I ask Tate as I unbuckle my seatbelt and climb out of the car. Tate comes up next to me, sliding on a pair of sunglasses.

"I heard you on the phone a few days ago talking to Aaron about being unable to risk coming out to Salem's fall festival this weekend," Tate tells me, guiding me towards where the rest of the crowd is heading. "So, in an attempt to take you on a real date, I've made it happen."

"A real date?" I repeat, surprised.

"Yeah, a *real* date. You deserve more than those brief moments that you consider mini-dates," Tate explains with a smile.

"You don't have to take me on a date, Tate," I tell him even as my eyes begin to take in all the fall and Halloween décor adorning the area. While I'm baffled by this sweet gesture, I'm excited to be here. The fact that we're taking a risk coming here in broad daylight tells me this is more than just a typical outing. There is something going on. "You know I just call our outings that to get the others all worked up."

There are tents everywhere filled with handmade crafts or food. The smell of pumpkin, cinnamon, and apple twist through the fresh air, and I'm struck by the cozy feel of the festival.

"Yeah, I did," Tate says, slowing his gait. I look over at him, and he gives me a tentative smile. "Because that's what people do when they want to court someone. They take them on real dates."

I freeze mid-step at his words. My heart flutters wildly in my chest as I process what he is saying. Before I get a chance to say anything, Tate takes a step towards me, and takes my hands.

"Gemma, you're an amazing woman," he says. "Being with you all day, laughing and joking, having the ability to share secrets and interests... I love that. You've given me the ability to enjoy life again. Before, when I got home from deployments, I'd have my fun with the guys, but it always felt like I've been trapped in a hell of isolation and loneliness. I guess I grew to accept it and found it normal after a time, but since you came along, I realize feeling that way isn't normal. You've turned my world upside down. Even on the days when we don't go out to do something, just spending time with you is like tasting freedom."

Tate stops to take a deep breath. As he does, I'm trying to find a way to exhale. All this time together, enjoying one another's company... I've never once suspected that Tate feels like this. We've had a great time together these past few weeks, and I'd be lying if I said I haven't at least *thought* about Tate joining the three of us in bed. But that was just a fantasy, I can't actually believe this is what he wants... right?

"Lately, I've realized that I want more than just this friendship, Gemma," Tate says quietly, as he pulls of his sunglasses. I'm falling into the depths of those dark blue eyes as he pushes forward. "Gemma, I've fallen for you, and I want you to look at me, to touch me, like you do the others."

I open my mouth to say something, anything, but I find I'm speechless. People walk by us as I process this news. My heart is pounding wildly in my chest as I try to gather my wits. *That* organ is completely onboard with this, but there are other things I have to think about before considering what Tate is offering.

Finally, I muster up the ability to force out, "Have you... spoken to the others about this?"

Tate chuckles. "Darion was the one who called me out on it. I didn't realize my infatuation was so obvious until he said something. Christopher was surprised for sure," he admits. "But both are open to it if you are."

"Oh..." I say lamely.

"Look, I know this is kind of coming out of left field. If you don't feel the same way, if there isn't a chance that we could be... together, I'll drop this and never bring it back up. We can go enjoy the day as if I never said a word. Chris and Darion both are going to meet up with us after they get off work. All you have to do is tell me: Are you interested? Even a little?"

I bite my lip cautiously. I'm not seriously thinking about this, am I? Is it crazy to add a third person into my already crazy love life? Maybe if it were a stranger, it would be easy to say no. But this is Tate I am thinking about, not some stranger. I stand there considering all the wonderful possibilities that would come from Tate being a part of what Christopher, Darion and I share. I smile up at him.

"I'm interested, Tate," I tell him softly. A wide grin splits his face, and for a moment, I forget what I'm saying. I blink away the stupor and continue. "But let's take this slow. Let's all sit down and figure things out together, and we can go from there, okay?"

Tate grins. "Understood."

With that, he leans down and kisses me fully on the lips. This kiss is nothing like Christopher's, which is full of hunger, or Darion's, which promises so much pleasure. No, Tate's kiss is much different from theirs. *This* kiss is full of command. He is telling me that he's in charge, and he'll do what he pleases. I sigh against his lips, ready to relinquish all control to him. I may have once detested him, but over these past few weeks, things have changed, and I'm ready to see where this goes.

Tate pulls away first and beams down at me, and I grin back up at him. Casually, he throws an arm around my shoulders, as if he's been doing this forever and says,

"Let's go enjoy our first real date together."

***

The day speeds by in a blur. It's late afternoon as I drop a piece of apple fritter into my mouth.

"Here, you have to try this, it's amazing," I tell him as I break off a piece.

I hand it to him, but he makes a face and says, "There's powder sugar getting everywhere. Just put it in my mouth so my fingers don't get sticky."

"Alright, bend down," I tell him and then place a piece into his mouth. I watch as he closes his lips. The look of surprise that crosses his face makes me laugh. "I told you it was amazing," I say smugly.

"Jesus, that's the best thing I've ever had. Give me another bite," he demands after he's swallowed, and I laugh again.

Overhead the clouds are growing darker, and it's getting pretty cold out. I hardly notice due to the amount of alcohol in my system, but Tate does and at some point produces a sweatshirt for me to wear.

In my hands are multiple bags full of handmade crafts from the local vendors. Tate has a tote full of locally crafted beers in one hand and is playing with the new knife in his other. We have gone pumpkin chucking in a nearby farm, gorged ourselves on maple-flavored cotton candy, a massive turkey leg, and nearly two large bags of kettle corn. An hour later we approach a dense crowd. People are cheering and laughing as they watch something.

"I found it! Here's the axe throwing," I tell Tate and drag him closer to the line.

My hard apple cider sloshes around in the plastic cup I'm holding. I may have had one too many over the past few hours, but it feels good to be out and enjoying myself.

"Lead the way and brace yourself for some major ass whooping," Tate says with a large grin. I giggle as I enjoy his playfulness.

"*Oh please*, get ready to have your ass handed to you," I tell him, rolling my eyes as we approach the fall festival worker to sign up to try our hand at axe throwing.

Before I get a chance to give him our name, a loud gunshot pierces through the festival. My initial reaction is to duck down. My throat squeezes shut as panic spikes through me. The last time I heard gunshots, people were after me. Around us, the crowded festival turns into a stampede. People are screaming and running in every direction.

"Come on," Tate yells in my ear as he grabs my arm and tugs me towards the parking lot.

Three more gunshots go off as we follow the crowd of people.

"Do you think they're after us?" I ask him when we get to the car.

Another gunshot goes off, and this time the bullet hits the hood of the SUV we took here.

"Get in!" he shouts as he opens the passenger door for me. The moment I'm in, he disappears and reappears next to me in the driver's seat.

"You shouldn't have done that! We're in public!" I tell him.

I'm hoping that because it's dusk and there is so much panic ensuing around us that no one has noticed his little trick.

Tate doesn't respond. Instead, he turns the car on and throws it into reverse. We narrowly miss pedestrians as we peel out of the parking lot. The screen on the dashboard lights up, and one of the security people that works protection detail comes into view.

"Sir, it's Pierce's members. They're coming for you. They took out four of my men before heading to their cars. We're trying to follow you, but it's chaos out here. Get out of here as fast as you can, and we'll catch—"

Suddenly, there's an explosion somewhere behind us, and the security guard's image goes blank. I slap my own hand over my mouth as I scream in terror. Tate's hand lands on my leg, and he gives it a squeeze.

"We'll be okay," he assures me grimly.

The minute we hit the highway, Tate floors it. I'm flung back in my seat as he takes off and weaves through traffic. We drive in tense silence. My body trembles with fear, and my breathing sounds loud in the quiet car. I continuously check the side mirrors to see if anyone is following us, but I can't tell. At one point, I reach into my pocket to call Darion or Christopher to warn them not to go to the festival but find my phone dead. I fling it to the floor of the car and let out a sigh.

Tate abruptly gets off at the next exit. Confused, I glance at him then behind us. Without having to ask, I know they've caught up to us. I can see a truck speeding after us, a member hanging out the window with a gun pointed in our direction. I want to scream again, but instead I keep my mouth shut. I hold on to my seatbelt with a grip so tight that my knuckles turn white.

Tate whips down random streets, not bothering to slow down as he takes them. After a few minutes, we lose them, and I let out a sigh of relief. Tate gets back onto the highway, and for a brief moment, I think we're in the clear.

"Give me your phone. I want to call the others," I tell Tate. I watch as his jaw clenches and relaxes.

"You can't call them right now. They're busy," he says after a moment.

"What do you mean they're busy? I thought they were supposed to meet us at the festival," I ask him. I glance at the dash's clock; it's just now past five. They should be on their way.

"I haven't gotten a call from them saying that they finished the job they're working on," Tate tells me.

His knuckles are just as white as mine as he grips the steering white hard, but that's the only sign that he's bothered by any of this.

"They're working on something together?" I ask, confused. "Since when?"

Tate sighs, rather dramatically, before saying, "They got a lead to where this Pierce guy was and went to… handle it. But they were supposed to text or call me when the job was over."

"By 'handle it' do you mean… kill him?" I ask breathlessly as the blood drains from my face.

Tate makes a face. That's all the confirmation I need to know that's exactly what Darion and Christopher are going to do… or have done.

I gape at Tate. Darion and Christopher were going to go *kill* Pierce? Dread blossoms in my gut. Did they succeed? Is this just the gang coming after us because they're upset their boss is dead? Or did Darion and Christopher fail? Did Pierce kill *them*? Is this guy coming after me and Tate just to tie up loose ends now? Oh, god, they can't be dead. I can't lose the two men that I love. No, not like this.

The thought brings me up short. Love?

Do I love them?

My heart flutters in my chest as I picture both Darion and Christopher. Yes, there is no doubt that what I feel for both men is love.

"Do you think… Do you think they're okay?" I ask, my voice hardly a whisper.

"I'm sure they're fine," Tate says firmly. "They're probably just busy cleaning up after themselves."

"Why wouldn't they contact you? And why didn't anyone tell me? Is this why you brought me out here? To distract me? To make everything seem all hunky dory when in reality they planned to murder someone?"

Before Tate can answer, the back window shatters as bullets come flying through the SUV. I scream and cling to my seat as Tate jerks the wheel. We take the nearest exit towards the house. It doesn't take us long to get onto the two-lane backroads. Our SUV winds through the woods now. The truck behind us is trying to keep up, but Tate is fearless as we take the twists and turns.

For a while, I can't see them behind us, but I'm not so stupid as to think we've lost them. Not back here. We fly around another corner and come to a straightaway with a stone bridge just ahead of us. My heart stops when I see a truck similar to the one chasing us parked on the other side of the bridge blocking both lanes. Someone is standing in front of it with… I lean forward and gasp in horror.

A bazooka gun is pointed straight at us.

"Tate!" I scream just as smoke shoots out of the large gun.

Tate jerks the wheel hard. The SUV swerves out of the way, and we miss the missile by inches. Unfortunately, as Tate slams on the breaks, we skid, much too fast, into the railing of the bridge. The stone gives way, and our SUV topples over the edge. I scream as we plummet to the water below and then fall into darkness.

I awake to the sound of rushing water and a horrible frigid cold surrounding me. My eyelids flutter open, and I scream. The SUV is stuck vertically in the river, and the water is coming through the dashboard. My legs are already submerged, and the water rises quickly to my waist. I look over to find Tate, slumped over, unconscious. The airbag is slowly deflating, and I can see blood pouring from his nose.

"Tate?" I call his name. When he doesn't move, I yell again, "Tate!"

I reach over and shake him, repeating, "Please don't be dead, please don't be dead!"

The soft groan he makes gives me a moment of relief before I start to panic again. Okay, I have to get us out of here. I struggle against my seatbelt, which is the only thing that kept me from being thrown through the windshield into the river water.

The seatbelt is locked. It won't move.

"Tate! Tate! Wake up!" I scream his name as I struggle with the belt.

Giving up on my own seatbelt momentarily, I turn my attention to him. I reach over and try to unclick his belt from the lock, and to my relief, his seatbelt retracts. Tate's body slumps over into the water. I curse and yank his head up by his short hair he's been slowly growing out. Still, he remains unconscious.

"Tate!" I yell his name again.

I look around me for anything that can help me escape. My heart races, and my body is trembling violently from the cold water. If we escape this, we'll still have to deal with hypothermia. But one thing at a time...

There! Floating near Tate's leg is the new knife he just bought. I grab for it, unsheathe it from the leather holster, and cut away at my own restraints. The water is up to the middle of my chest now, and it's so cold the muscles in my chest feel restricted. The moment I'm free, I lower myself further into the water until my feet touch the floorboard. It takes up precious time, and a great deal of energy, but I am able to finagle Tate's body into the backseat.

I climb back there with him, but just as I do the SUV sways and collapses onto its side. Windows break as the pressure of the river water comes crashing down on the already cracked glass. Water pours in, and I scream Tate's name one more time before we both are trapped in a submerged car.

My mind is racing, and I know we don't have a lot of time. I grab Tate's body and push him out the broken window. The current grabs him, and I pray I'll be able to catch up to him before he drowns. I swim up after him, and the current sweeps me away from the vehicle just as quickly as it did with Tate.

I pop up for air and suck it in before being dragged under. A moment later, I am able to break free from the strong current to come back up for air. This time when I do, I look around for Tate. I see his body, his back specifically, floating a few feet ahead of me. Instead of trying to fight the current, I use it to swim towards him. It takes me much too long to get to him. I can hardly feel my body as the biting cold numbs my limbs. When I get to Tate, I grab him with all of my might, praying I can keep my grip on the man, and yank his head up as we fly down the river.

As I try to get my arm around him so I can tow him to shore, I'm tossed around by the strong river water. My back slams into a rock, and then we're both sucked under as another current underneath captures us. We pop back up a moment later. After what seems like forever, I swim us to the edge of the riverbank and am able to wedge us between two larger rocks. Using my back and my legs, I push off from the rocks to the stony riverbank and, to my relief, manage to get us there.

I climb out, wedging myself under Tate's arms, and drag him towards the tree line. Glancing in the direction we came from, I can't see the bridge anymore, but I know we can't be too far from it. If Pierce's men decide to do some investigating, we could still be in trouble. Gently, I place Tate on his back and check for a pulse.

"Shit, Tate!" I cry out softly when I realize how slow his pulse is.

I check his breathing and find that he isn't. I start CPR. I don't know how long I should do this for, but my mind is utterly focused on saving his life. Tears stream down my face as nothing happens. Times slips by, and I call his name as I do chest compressions, but there is no response. Just as I am about to give up, Tate suddenly coughs and sputters. I cry out in relief and more tears fall as I help turn him onto his side. He throws up an impossible amount of water. I rub his back and quietly reassure him everything is okay as he struggles to breathe.

Just as his coughing subsides, I hear something in the woods behind us.

"Gemma, what—"

"Shh!" I hiss and press my hand against his mouth.

His eyes go wide as he realizes we're not out of danger yet. I indicate with my finger to my mouth to stay quiet, and he nods. I look over my shoulder, and my eyes search the woods. It's dark now, and all I can see are shadows. I can't tell if they are Pierce's men or just trees, and it scares the crap out of me.

There is another, distinct snap of a stick somewhere nearby. My frantically beating heart nearly stops in horror. Whoever it is, they are close. I lean down to whisper into Tate's ear.

"Can you run?"

He shakes his head and whispers back, "I think my leg is broken. I can heal it if I shift, but my head is spinning, and I can't focus hard enough to do it right now."

I look behind us again, searching for whoever is in the woods. I can hear the shuffling of leaves as they walk. Whoever it is, they aren't trying to be quiet. I lean back down.

"If you don't have to focus on shifting, you could heal yourself?" I ask him.

Tate gives me a confused looked before understanding dawns on him. "No, Gemma, don't do anything stupid."

"If they get any closer, they'll see us both. If I lead them away from you, you can shift easier," I tell him in a hurried whisper. "If I don't make it and you do, tell the others I love them and that I wish we had had more time together."

Tate's shaking his head with wide panicked eyes as I talk. "Gemma, don't—"

"Stay quiet," I warn him. I kiss his forehead and send up a prayer that we'll both be okay. Then, with my heart in my throat, I jump up and yell, "Tate? Tate! Where are you?"

Without hesitating, I take off into the woods. My feet are so numb I immediately stumble, but I find my footing and run.

"There! I see her! Get her!" I hear a voice yell.

Gunshots ring out, and bullets hit the trees around me. I scream and cover my head with my arms as I run. I keep to the shoreline and pray that if I can get away from these men, when I double back, I will be able to find Tate.

"Tate! Tate, where are you?" I scream again, hoping to draw them further away from where Tate is lying.

"Get back here!" a man's voice yells. "Get back here, and we won't kill you!"

I scream again as more bullets rain down around me.

"Quit shooting! Your aim is terrible. You're just wasting bullets!" I hear someone yell.

Their voices are drawing closer. My legs aren't moving as fast as I need them to go. I've lost most of the feeling in them, and it's hard to breathe. It's just so cold. Out of nowhere, a deep, bellowing roar echoes through the woods. I stumble in horror.

A shifter.

I hear the footsteps of a large animal charging through the woods towards me. I try to pick up the pace, but I can't move any faster. I debate heading for the water again, but my body is so tired, sore, and numb that I am sure I would drown at this point. I can almost hear the pants of the beast coming towards me. Would drowning be preferable to being mauled? Another roar rings out through the woods.

Two shifters.

The first one I heard is on me after a few more yards. I scream as I'm tackled to the ground by a large grizzly bear. I struggle to get away, but it pins me down with a foot. I feel a rib crack underneath the sheer weight of the animal. But I'm more focused on the large paw swiping through the air at my face than the pain in my chest. I squeeze my eyes shut and brace myself for a gruesome end.

The weight of the bear suddenly vanishes as if it was never there. I gasp in surprise as my eyes flutter open. I look around, and it's gone.

"Run, Gemma!" Tate says, appearing from the shadows.

He collapses on his side holding his leg.

"Tate, come on!" I yell, scrambling to my feet and trying to help him to his.

"No, I'm not healed enough to run yet," he says through gritted teeth. "Keep going. I can follow through the shadows in short bursts."

I hesitate but, he pushes me away when I try to crouch down next to him.

"Go, Gemma!" he snaps just as more bullets whiz by.

He disappears, and I'm left on my own. I stumble to my numb feet and take off again.

"Where the hell is Gerald?" a man shouts behind me.

"Fuck, did she kill Gerald?" someone else asks. "There she is! She's running east!"

"I see her!"

There is no out running them. There are too many, and I'm starting to see stars. My feet stumble, and I slow. Breathing is getting hard; the cold air in my lungs is painful. I'm used to endurance running, but this... This is a whole new extreme. Some irrational part of me is disappointed in myself. At my prime, I might have been able to live through this. Maybe out-run the bad guys. But being injured, freezing, and frightened is far from prime level, so I'm sure no victory is in sight for me. I hear hard breathing. Whoever is behind me has caught up.

"Get back here—" I hear him grunt, and I'm sure he is reaching for me, but then, his footsteps stop.

I look over my shoulder to find no one there. I turn my head straight again and keep running.

I make it another hundred yards before someone shoves me to the ground. I roll onto my back, ready to fight him if I need to, but Tate appears behind him, and they both disappear into the shadows of the woods. I scramble back to my feet but trip, and my head hits a rock. The world swims around me. I struggle to get to my feet and am again unsuccessful.

I feel like I'm going to be sick. But I would rather be sick than dead, I tell myself. So with that positivity coursing through my veins, I force myself to my feet. Hurrying as fast as I can through the dark woods, I try to keep low. I can hear angry yelling, and I hear another roar of a shifter as they look for us. I move closer towards the riverbank. Drowning is most definitely preferable to being mauled, I decide as the river comes back into view.

I trip again before I break the tree line, and this time, I don't get up right away. My breathing comes in heavy gasps, and my body is shaking so hard that my vision isn't clear enough to see straight anymore. Somewhere in the distance I hear a howl. Fuck, a wolf? They'll find me in no time. I groan in defeat as I crawl on my hands and knees towards the water.

A pair of hands grab me from behind, and I'm picked up and tossed onto my back. Three men stand over me with their guns pointed at my face. Defeated, I sigh and stare back.

One smiles and says, "Buckle up princess, you're about to take a trip straight to Hell."

Another man crouches over me. Before I get a chance to fight him off, his meaty fist comes swinging at my face, and everything goes dark.

Chapter Thirty

Christopher

The fire truck and police lights are striking in the dark as we approach the stone bridge. As Ian slams on the breaks, I've already thrown open the door and hurried over to the scene. My heart is frantic as I scour the area looking for Gemma and Tate's SUV. Their tracker stopped working right here fifteen minutes ago. They have to be here somewhere.

"Sir, you can't be here," an officer says coming up to me.

I ignore him as my eyes find the destroyed railing of the stone bridge. My heart jumps into my throat as I hurry past the officer over to the gaping hole. Stopping just at the edge, I look down. Nothing but the side of a black SUV can be seen sticking out of the rushing water.

"GEMMA!"

I move to jump, not caring that the water is cold or that the current could sweep me away. All that matters is that I get to her and Tate.

"No! Stop!" the officer who tried to stop me before yells and grabs the back of my shirt. "There's no one in the car, sir!"

"What do you mean? Where are they?" Darion's contemptuous tone demands a response.

I whirl around to see him a few feet away staring at the officer. I can see the incubus's hands trembling; it is the only sign that he is upset.

"Our shifters have detected two scents appearing a little way down the river. Whoever was in the car must have escaped and been pulled by the current to a calmer area where they managed to pull themselves out of the water," the officer said.

"Where are they now? Did you find them?" I ask.

"I cannot disclose any more information at this time. Do you know who was in this car?" the officer asks.

"My mate and my friend!" I tell him.

"And you are...?" the officer asks.

Before I can respond, Darion says, "Chris, let's go."

Go? I have to find them... The urge to shift and search for their scent myself is almost overpowering. I'm trembling in the effort to keep my human form as my wolf shoves to the front. I look over at my shoulder and see my phone in Ian's hand. It's lighting up, and Darion is reading the messages coming in.

"Is that them? Is that Tate and Gemma?" I demand, hurrying over to them. I left my phone in the SUV that Darion's people picked me up from work with, and they must have retrieved it with my discarded clothes.

"Let's go," Darion growls as he pushes me back towards the car.

"Wait! If you know what happened here, we need to get a statement from you!" the police officer demands.

"You'll get one later," Darion snaps as we climb back into the car.

Ian climbs into the driver's seat while Darion and I sit in the back and read through the messages from an unknown number.

555-1239: *This is Tate.*

555-1239: *Stole a phone from one of Pierce's goons. Will text when it's safe.*

Ian backs the car up, and we head back towards the city. My heart is back down in my chest. It's still fluttering painfully, but at least I know there is a *chance* that Gemma and Tate are alive. The screen lights up again, and both Darion and I stare at the screen.

555-1239: *They're taking Gemma into Boston. Will send address when I have a location.*

555-1239: *We changed cars.*

"Do you think it's really him?" I ask Darion as I dare to hope.

Darion stares down at the screen, his face as hard as stone. His hands have stopped shaking, but I have no doubt in my mind he's just as worried as I am.

"I don't know," Darion says.

"Let's test him," I say. I take the phone from the incubus's hands and text: *If this is Tate, tell me our favorite part of our trip to Spain three years ago.*

Darion snorts in derision but says nothing as we both wait for the response. It comes two minutes later.

555-1239: *That redhead who liked wearing that ridiculously cheap bejeweled butt plug.*

This is no time for laughing. Once I know he and Gemma are safe, then I'll laugh. So instead, I lean back in my seat and let out a sigh of relief. Okay, Tate is with Gemma. If he can text, then he's probably in hiding. He will watch over her until we get to wherever they are.

I text him back: *Are you both ok?*

It takes a while until I hear back from Tate. I exchange looks with Darion, whose expression darkens. Has Tate been compromised? Is something happening?

555-1239: *273 Bridgeton Ave*

That's the whole message and nothing further. Darion shouts the address to Ian, who guns the gas pedal. My fingers curl into claws, and I can taste blood as my teeth try to lengthen. My adrenaline pumps through me as I think of my friend and mate in danger. Ian is speaking on the phone with the rest of the security. I hear him pulling men from whatever jobs they are doing and directing them to get to the address Tate has provided for us as Darion and I sit there in silence.

"Christopher," Darion says after a long moment.

I grunt. It's all I can muster. Words are not manageable while I fight the change as hard as I currently am.

"I've told you what Pierce's job in the gang is, right?"

My wind whirls as I think about the conversations we have shared out of ear shot of Gemma. I know about the gang and what Jacob's involvement was. But Pierce? He is the silent one. One that Darion had no information on before. With his men combing the underground crime scene, Darion was able to assess that Pierce's job is to…

"*No!*" I roar.

It's more a gargled noise rather than a verbal cry of denial due to my vocal cords being in the process of shifting, but the sentiment is understood. Darion nods sharply once.

"We need to get to Gemma quickly. If she is placed with any of Pierce's other… merchandise, we may lose her altogether. We're lucky Tate is with her, but his lack of response to your question about their wellbeing concerns me. He may not be able to do much in his current state except stick with our woman. Our mission earlier was to kill Pierce. This one is simply to make sure the people we both care for get out alive. In and out, do you understand?"

"I will murder every last one on my way in and out," I tell him.

"I understand your desire for blood, Christopher, truly I do but…" Darion trails off and shifts in his seat uncomfortably. "But Gemma comes first. If she and Tate are injured, they'll need us both. Bathing in the blood of our enemies will take up precious time."

I growl in annoyance at his practicality. Of course, my mate and my friend come first, but if I could kill just a *few* people…

Since we were already on our way into the city, it doesn't take us much longer to pull up a few blocks away from the address Tate gave us. I text him where we are while Darion and I slide out of the SUV. I take a deep breath of the stale air here. We're just a few blocks away from the shipping docks. There's no hint of Gemma in the air. A whine escapes from my wolf before I can tamper it down. I take a deep breath to settle my nerves, but knowing that Gemma is close makes that impossible.

What is happening inside the building? Is Tate looking after her? Are they separated? Are either, or both, hurt? What monstrosities are both of them dealing with? All the different possible things they could be seeing or hearing or enduring flicker through my head like an old-time movie reel. I feel ill.

"Where is he?" Darion asks, more to himself rather than of me or Ian, who has exited the car.

"Sir, your men are scattered about taking note of every entryway and exit," Ian says softly.

"Do they have eyes on Gemma or Tate?" Darion snaps.

"No sir, not yet," Ian replies.

"I'm here," a weak voice says from a nearby shadowy alley.

The three of us whirl around to find Tate sitting on the ground, his back against the brick wall of an abandoned building, trembling hard. I reach him first and crouch down in front of him. Tate's clothes are soaking wet, blood has stained one side of his shirt, there are bruises along his face, and the exhaustion on his abnormally pale face is frightening.

"Jesus, you look like shit," I say and pull off my shirt. "Here, let's get you out of these clothes."

Tate shoves my shirt out of his face as he shakes his head.

"We need to get Gemma," he croaks.

"Where is she?" Darion asks, kneeling next to me.

"Upstairs on the third floor in a back room with no heat. They knocked her out before they took her, and she hasn't woken up yet. Her shivering has stopped, too. I've checked her pulse, and it's there but weak," Tate says through chattering teeth.

"Fuck," I growl. "Okay, we'll barge through the front door like we did this afternoon and take everyone out that way."

"No, they're expecting you to do that," Tate says. "There are explosives attached to most of the doors that would kill you the moment you open them. The first floor windows are also rigged with explosives."

"Alright, I'm assuming you took note of places we *can* enter," Darion says in exasperation.

"They missed one window in the back of the building, but there are about fifteen men holed up in that room with guns," Tate warns.

I nod slowly, thinking of the different ways to divert these men away from the room. "We'll set off one of the explosives, which I'm sure will draw attention. Someone will come to investigate."

"I can have some men who look like you two approach the front doors to set off the bombs and get out of there quickly," Ian offers.

"No, I'll do it. I can trigger the bombs and make it into the shadows before I get hurt," Tate says quickly. "That way no one else gets hurt."

"*You're* staying here with the car," Darion says grimly.

"Over my dead body," Tate responds before shivering violently.

"That may very well happen," Darion snaps. "What's wrong with your leg? Shouldn't you have healed up by now if you've been hidden in the shadows?"

I glance down at Tate's leg and can see Darion's issue with Tate coming with us. Both legs are splayed out in front of him, but one is strangely twisted.

"I am healing. It is just... taking a little longer than usual," Tate says through gritted teeth. "And every time I come out of the shadows, like to send a text, I interrupt the healing. But it doesn't matter. I can still move through them. I'm just a little bit slower than before."

"Can you take us through the shadows into where Gemma is, and we can work our way from there?" Darion asks slowly.

I shoot him a surprised look. It was Darion who pummeled Tate when we heard that he had traveled with Gemma through the shadows. The risks certainly outweighed any good that can come from getting to Gemma that way. Before I can object, Tate shakes his head.

"With how slowly I move through them, for you that would mean longer time in the shadows, which only increases the risk to you. If I thought I could grab Gemma and get her out safely, I would have done so," Tate says with regret.

"Alright, so let's get a diversion going and get Gemma out of there," I growl.

"I'm going to set off two of the explosives: the front door and a rear side window," Tate says. "I'll meet you inside and stop what attacks I can."

"I don't like you getting into trouble in your state," Darion grumbles. He looks over at Ian and says, "Have your men ready to pick off anyone who isn't us. If you get Pierce in your sights, take him out, but once the four of us are out of the building, pull back."

Ian nods and walks away to call his men.

"Any sign of Pierce inside?" I ask Tate.

"I didn't see him, but his people have been communicating with him via walkie talkies. He's got to be close," Tate says.

Darion nods and stands. "Alright, let's go get Gemma."

***

An explosion shakes the entire building. My ears twitch as I listen to the sounds of shouting and footsteps. In my wolf form, I can hear and smell much better. I bare my teeth in a grin as another explosion rocks the night. More footsteps move about nearby inside the building. I crouch down so my belly is on the ground and watch the window I am about to enter. Next to me, Darion stands, unmoving, staring at the same window. I strain my hearing to listen for signs of Gemma, but there is nothing.

"Six remain in the room, go now!" Tate's voice hisses at us through the darkness.

Darion moves like lighting towards the window and uses his body to crash through it. I'm right behind him. I grab the nearest moving gang member and go in for the kill. His neck snaps, and he goes limp in my mouth. I take two more down at the same time Darion kills his three.

"The other side of this door is clear for now. There is a set of stairs about a hundred yards to your right," Tate's voice says from all around us.

Darion swings open the door, but I barrel out first, intent on finding Gemma. I can hear Darion follow, and I know that Tate is following in the shadows although I cannot sense him. We find the stairs, and I bound up them. Just as I reach the top, a gang member turns the corner to descend the steps. Before he gets a chance to raise his gun or to cry out, Tate's hand comes out from nowhere and yanks the poor bastard into the shadows. I rush through the spot where he stood and sniff the air. I can smell humans and shifters nearby.

A moment later, a door down the hallway opens, and people begin to spill out. I howl, furious that they would try to keep me from my mate. I turn my attention to them, but Darion leaps over me and shouts, "Go find her, Christopher. I got this!"

Slowly, I back away from the incubus, with my hackles raised and teeth bared. I don't want to leave him, but Darion can take care of himself. It's only a handful of men. He's taken on more.

"She's this way, Chris," Tate says.

I turn towards his voice and run down the hall. I can smell drugs. Have Pierce's men been enjoying themselves while they hang out waiting for us? I also smell sex in the air. My stomach turns. Pierce oversees sex trafficking in the area. The poor women who find themselves in his possession…

Gemma will not be one of them.

"Over here, take the stairs," Tate directs.

I do as I am told, and when I reach the top, I freeze. Gemma's scent is in the air. No longer needing Tate, I rush down the hallway. As her scent gets stronger, so does the smell of blood. No, no, no, a cold rush of fear trickles through me as I weave through the halls of the building. Just as I round another corner, I smell a shifter. I skid to a stop just as a leopard slams into me, appearing from a connecting hallway.

Claws sink into my sides as the leopard latches onto my back. Thinking fast, I slam my body into the wall, bucking and snarling. The large cat lets go and jumps away, crouches, and then lunges for me again. This time I'm ready, and I meet it halfway in midair. Claws and teeth collide. Blood splatters around us. Roars and snarls echo through the halls. Finally, I manage to get my teeth into the creature's neck, and I shake until I hear the death rattle that comes with its last breath. The leopard goes limp in my mouth. I let the body drop, and I sniff the air for Gemma's scent again.

When I find it, I take off towards the smell. I round a corner and find two men with guns guarding a door. Gemma's behind it. I just know it. Before I can attack, Tate appears in front of them, grabs both men by the neck, and yanks them forward. All three of them disappear into the shadows of the hall.

I bound down the hall and stop in front of the door. Shifting quickly, I reach for the handle and throw open the door. The first thing I see are three men in the middle of the room. They're armed and standing in a semi-circle. In the middle of that circle is Gemma. Her arms are bound behind her, her feet are zip tied, and there is a bag over her head taped around her neck. Her body weakly tries to thrash about as she suffocates.

I roar and charge forward, shifting as I do. I hit the nearest guy first and use my teeth to tear away his nose before clawing out his eyes. Without pausing, I leap off the dying gang member to the next one who has raised his gun and it pointed to my head. He's not fast enough to pull the trigger; I grab his wrist in my mouth and break it. His cries of agony are ignored as I jump up and rip his throat out. I whirl around to find the third man pointing the gun to Gemma's head. Her body is eerily still. Before I can act, Tate appears behind him and grabs the guy's head. He disappears and so does the gang member's head. The rest of the body crumples to the floor.

Skirting Fate | 281

Without hesitation, I shift, grab the bag around Gemma's head, and rip it open. I note how tight the duct tape is around her neck and rip at it as well.

"Gems? Gemma!" I call her name.

Gemma's eyes are open but staring unseeing ahead of her. I note how blue her lips are. Swearing profusely, I reach down and untie her arms. I break the legs of the chair to free her ankles, place her on her back, and start CPR. As I blow air into her mouth and start chest compressions, I'm sending up prayers to the moon goddess. She wouldn't give me a gift only to take it away, would she? What type of cruelty is that?

Tate appears on the other side of her and watches quietly as I try to breathe life into Gemma's still body. Somewhere in the building another explosive goes off. It shakes the floor. Off in the distance outside I can hear sirens. None of it matters. All that matters is Gemma.

Finally, after what feels like an eternity, Gemma sucks in a sharp, albeit short gasp of air. I pull away as her eyelids flutter.

"Gems, can you hear me? Gemma, it's me," I call her name, gently shaking her shoulders. She moans, but that's the only response I get.

"Come on, we need to get her to a hospital," Tate says through gritted teeth.

I glance up at him and note that he is even paler than he was outside. Our eyes meet.

"I'll be fine," he insists. "Let's go before the cops get here. None of us need to be caught here with all of these bodies around."

I scoop Gemma up off the ground, and we make our way back into the hallway. There is someone at the end, and for a moment I freeze, bracing myself for a fight. When I see who it is, I relax a little.

"Is she...?" Darion starts as he hurries towards us, fear and worry marring his features.

"She's alive," I say grimly.

"Give her to me," Darion demands and reaches for her, but I pull her to my chest and snarl at him.

"No! Let's just go," I snap.

Darion glares at me, but I ignore it and move past him.

"Where's Tate?" Darion demands as we take the stairs downstairs.

"I'm here," Tate's strained voice says around us. "Let's get out of here."

We make it out of the building without any more issues. Ian streaks down the street in the SUV and comes to a screeching halt in front of us. The sound of sirens are growing louder. Darion opens the back door for me to climb in with Gemma and then climbs in with us.

"Tate?" I call out.

"Don't worry. I won't let you leave me behind," he answers from the third row as Ian pulls away.

"Don't die in the shadow world, Tate," Darion orders.

"Don't plan on dying. Period," Tate says. His voice is strained and soft. "Not when Gemma promised to give me a chance."

I glance down at Gemma, who has made no other noise than her gasp earlier. She looks beaten and ashen. Her breathing is raspy, and her skin is freezing. Her wet clothes aren't helping her condition. Darion must have realized this at the same time as me because as I rip them off her, he grabs his suit jacket off the floor to cover her with it. I pull her closer to my chest, hoping my body heat will help warm her.

"Hang on, Gems," I whisper to her.

"Ian, get your men to set off the rest of the explosives," Darion orders.

"Right away," Ian answers and pulls out his phone.

I stroke Gemma's hair and try to hold one of her hands to warm her. She's gone through so much... Will she recover from this? Will she want out of what the three... now four, of us have? Honestly, I wouldn't blame her for wanting space.

"Sir, I have news about Pierce," Ian says, looking back at Darion through the rearview mirror. "My men located him down at the warehouse with a shipping container full of women. I had them call in an anonymous tip to the authorities about the women, and Pierce himself has been… taken care of."

    The three of us are silent as we process this information. Part of me is angry. I secretly hoped that one of us would run into him inside and take care of him ourselves. But mostly, I'm relieved that the bastard is gone. Now we'll all be safe.

Chapter Thirty-One

Darion

I bark orders to Ian the entire trip to the hospital. By the time we get there, Dr. Candice Wilson, who checked over Gemma after her trip through the shadows with Tate, is waiting for us, along with another car filled with my security men. I take Gemma from Christopher while he pulls on pants, and I slide out of the car.

"Tate, go with Dr. Wilson," I order as I hurry through the glass doors into the emergency room. "I need help!" I bellow to the nurses behind the counter.

There is a flurry of activity as a bed rolls out and doctors appear to take Gemma back. I try to follow, but a nurse places her hand on my chest to stop me.

"Sir, you can't come back here," she says.

"I'm her fiancé!" I yell, thinking quickly. "I need to be with her."

"We need to run tests, get some x-rays, and then once we get her settled in a room you can join her," she says firmly but becomes flustered as I glare down at her. She gulps and says, "You need to fill out some paperwork for her, so we know her medical history."

"I'll do it," Christopher says coming up next to me.

The nurse looks over to him with confusion. "Who are you to our patient?"

"I'm her mate," Christopher growls.

The nurse's brows fly upwards as she looks between us and asks, "A mate *and* a fiancé…?"

"It's complicated," both Christopher and I say in unison.

The nurse's expression turns disapproving, but she says, "Well, in any case, both of you need to wait out here. We'll do what we can for your fiancée, uh, mate… her."

"Fine," I snap. "We'll be right here."

The nurse disappears, and I whirl around to look around the surprisingly sparse waiting room. I don't bother to go sit down. I'm way too anxious to hold still and do nothing. Christopher heads to the front desk to fill out information for Gemma as I storm back out of the emergency room to find Dr. Wilson, with the help of an aid, moving Tate onto a stretcher. It's clear he isn't doing well. I walk over to them and stop next to Dr. Wilson.

"Remember, we need discretion," I warn her softly.

"Always, Mr. Nightshade," she says with a nod. "I'm going to see what type of injuries that Mr. Granger here is dealing with and that way he and you will know what to keep an eye on while he recovers from them."

"What did they say about Gemma?" Tate asks. His grimace speaks volumes about his condition.

"They're going to help her," I tell him grimly. "Worry about getting better before worrying about anyone else."

"No point getting better if the person I've fallen for dies," Tate says with a sigh and lies back on the stretcher. Dr. Wilson's aid pushes Tate through the doors, and the doctor follows.

"Sir," Ian says as I come back over to the SUV.

"What is it, Ian?" I ask.

Ian turns his back to the hospital and unlocks his phone. He shows me the picture of Pierce's head in a box. It pleases me. I nod once.

"Make sure his brother just happens upon that picture in his cell," I say softly.

"Yes, sir," Ian says, shoving his phone back into his pocket. "My men have brought you all a change of clothes. You have a new phone that's been set up, and we have details from the police report of Mr. Granger's and Miss. Thomas's accident. It is being emailed to you now."

I thank my head of security and busy myself for the next few hours while I wait for news on Gemma's condition.

***

Hours have passed. I have done everything that I can do at the moment, including getting us something to eat and talking to the police about the strange explosions downtown at one of Pierce's known hangouts and about the scene down by the docks. When everything is said and done and everything that can be done has been, I am stuck pacing the waiting room with Christopher.

The new rune on my chest aches. It's been aching since the tracker on Tate and Gemma's car suddenly stopped working. It's a warning that Gemma's condition is serious. The fact that the ache has not yet eased up is making me sick. But that's not the only thing that aches. My heart feels like it's been through the ringer. The pain in my chest is so great that I find myself absentmindedly rubbing the area on my chest where it hides.

I try not to think about how still Gemma was the entire drive here. Or how much blood stained her face from a wound on her head. Moisture keeps blurring my vision as I pace the length of the waiting room. It's a strange and irritating phenomenon.

Dr. Wilson comes out first. I leave Christopher in the waiting room while I follow her outside to discuss Tate. We don't go far. I can still see the doors the doctors would use to come out into the waiting room.

"Mr. Granger's left leg is completely shattered. It's amazing he's been able to put any weight on it whatsoever. It must have been the adrenaline. Even with his ability to… ah, heal quickly, he'll be bedridden for at least a week or two. He also has some intense bruising from the seatbelt, which is usual for someone who has been in a car accident. I put a cast on his leg and warned him not to do any strenuous activity. Unfortunately," she says with a disapproving frown, "he has ignored my orders to take it easy and disappeared on me."

"I'll make sure he follows your orders," I say darkly.

I'd be damned if I allowed my friend to disregard a doctor's order. Dr. Wilson hands me a prescription bottle.

"Once the adrenaline wears off, he's definitely going to need these," she says. "Do you need me for anything else?"

"No, that's all. Thank you," I tell her, grateful for the woman's discretion. She nods and heads off into the parking lot. I head back inside. Just as I walk through the doors, an older doctor comes out.

"Who is here for a Miss Gemma Thomas?" he calls.

"I am," both Christopher and I answer in unison. The doctor looks between us.

"Are you the mate and the, uh, fiancé?" he asks, checking his notes.

"Yes," I say confidently.

"Alright, follow me please," he says, and we do.

The doctor leads us back to the room they are keeping Gemma in. I barely step into the room before I freeze. Gemma in a hospital gown, lying motionless in bed. There is a monitor next to her bed beeping, keeping track of her vitals. She is hooked up to a breathing machine with a tube shoved down her throat. Her face has been cleaned of the blood that dried there, and there are at least ten stitches along her forehead. Now that she's been cleaned up, I am able to see a massive bruise along her chin and the smaller cuts on her cheeks.

She looks so… lifeless.

Christopher runs into my back with a huff. He steps around me and sees Gemma. I can hear his sharp intake of surprise. The shifter walks slowly further into the room while I stand there stunned by Gemma's condition.

"Most of her injuries were clearly sustained from the car accident Mr. Rogue here informed us about," the doctor starts. "There was severe bruising where the seatbelt caught Miss Thomas and a severe sprain of one ankle. She does have a fracture along her rib cage, but this is minor. There are scratches across her chest, which looks like an animal attack, possibly a shifter. Though, that's just speculative and minor. The concerns we have are the injuries to her head. She has a pretty serious concussion, and there was bleeding in the brain. We managed to get it to stop, but I'm also concerned with these markings."

The doctor points to her neck, and I take a few steps further into the room. That's when I notice the raw ring of skin around her neck.

"This indicates that she may have been strangled…" the doctor says with a deep frown. "So if that's the case, we need to consider that there may have been a lack of oxygen to the brain for an undetermined amount of time. With all of these factors and the first signs of hypothermia, Miss Thomas's condition is critical. We've placed her into a medically induced coma to allow her brain to recover. We will attempt to wake her up in twenty-four hours, and if she wakes, that will be the start to her recovery."

A strangled noise comes out of Christopher as he moves over to Gemma's side. He takes her hand and visibly swallows. I force my eyes away from Gemma to look at the doctor and ask, "And if she doesn't wake up?"

"Then her family needs to decide what they think would be best for her. But I'm optimistic that Miss Thomas may wake up. She's a healthy young woman, and I think she knows she has people that love her who are rooting for her, so she'll fight," the doctor says with a smile.

I nod slowly.

"There is a small couch for one of you to stay with her if you wish, but she'll be resting for the next day, so if you want to go home, we can call you to—"

"We're staying," I cut him off firmly.

The doctor nods. "Alright. Well, the nurses will be in shortly to check her vitals again and to make sure she's comfortable." He pauses to check his watch. "The cafeteria just started serving breakfast if you want to go down to get something to eat."

I nod again, and the doctor leaves us alone with Gemma. I walk over to Gemma's other side. Each step feels heavy, but eventually, I make it over to her and grab her free hand. The ache in my heart grows sharper and more acute as I stare down at the beautiful woman who has become so much to me in such a short time.

I know without a doubt that I love her. I have never felt anything so strongly, so powerfully before. Weeks ago, I wondered if love is something an incubus can actually feel. Since then, my affection for Gemma has flourished as we grew to know one another. Now, I'm so choked up with emotions I cannot even consider that this is anything other than love. I love my master. I love Gemma.

I cannot, I *will not*, lose her.

"What happened to you guys?" Tate's voice asks. I turn to find Tate sitting there on the couch with his bad leg up. He looks exhausted and filthy. "You were supposed to kill the bastard, not antagonize him."

I sigh, grab his medication out of my pocket, and toss it to him. He catches it with one hand, pops the top off to take two pills, and throws the bottle back.

"He anticipated our arrival. He purposely made an appearance so my men would see him, and he lured us into a trap," I tell him. "Just before he blew up the building with us in it, he showed us that one of his guys was with you at the festival. Once we escaped, we headed your way and used the tracker on the car to follow you. Then, we found your car in the river…"

My voice fails me as I think about the scene we had pulled up to.

"How did you survive that crash?" Christopher asks, his voice barely more than a whisper as he looks over his shoulder at Tate.

Tate sighs heavily and shakes his head as he closes his eyes.

"It was all Gemma. She kept saving my life," Tate says through clenched teeth. "She somehow got us out of the SUV before we drowned, she gave me CPR after swimming with my dead weight to shore, and then because I couldn't put any weight on my leg, she started yelling to draw Pierce's guys away from me. No one has ever put so much effort into keeping me alive before. Our fucking government has left me to fend for myself countless times.

"I tried to help her. I tried to move as fast as I could through the woods in the shadows after her. I managed to keep most of them off of her, but then my leg finally couldn't take it anymore. Three of Pierce's men descended on her, knocked her out, and all I could do was grab onto one of their shadows and stick nearby. She never woke back up... I was terrified she was dead. While I waited for you guys, I kept checking her pulse because she was hardly breathing."

We all fall silent as we think about how horribly wrong the previous day went. This is my fault. It was my idea to go after Pierce. I should have just let my men deal with it. I wipe my hand down my face as exhaustion and dread beat at me.

"I'm sorry," I tell them both.

"Not your fault," Christopher mutters as he turns his gaze back to Gemma's face. I look over at him and find his eyes red rimmed. He struggles to keep his breathing even as he looks up at me. "This is Pierce's fault. He was pissed you put his brother behind bars and came after you. You were doing your job," he says grimly. "This shit comes with the territory when you're a prosecutor."

"What do we do now?" Tate asks.

"We wait for Gemma to wake up," I answer grimly.

Chapter Thirty-Two

Christopher

Gemma has been taken off the breathing machine, and she's been breathing on her own for four hours, but still she hasn't woken up. I feel physically ill. I pace the room in my wolf form because while he is just as upset, the way he feels emotions is easier to handle than the way my human form does.

Tate is passed out on the small, uncomfortable couch. At some point during the day yesterday, he managed to get into clean clothes and grabbed something to eat to help him keep down the medication Dr. Wilson gave him. He looks worse for wear with new bruises appearing along his arms and neck.

Darion is unable to do nothing. He's been on his phone all day with various people. I pay him no mind. I get that he needs something to do.

The police come in to check on Gemma's state. They also try to pull more information from us about our whereabouts during the previous day. I'm sure they believe, at the very least, Darion is connected to the explosions, but without any evidence, all they can do is try to get us to trip up. Darion and I have our stories down pat. The police leave unsuccessful.

It's just past two in the afternoon when Gemma's hand twitches. My peripheral vision catches it. I freeze and turn my attention toward Gemma, unsure that what I saw is real or if it is in my head. It happens again, and I shift quickly. I grab my clothes off the empty chair next to Gemma's bed. As I pull on my shirt, Gemma moans. It's so soft that it can hardly be considered an audible noise, but with my shifter senses I hear it. I take her hand and squeeze it, hoping to reassure her as she wakes.

"Gemma? Gems?" I call to her softly. "Can you hear me?"

On the couch, Tate jerks awake as I break the silence. I ignore him as I stare down at Gemma. She doesn't move or make another sound for a long stretch of time. The brief relief I am feeling fades. Tate moves to sit up but groans.

"Gems?" I call to her again.

A moment passes when suddenly her hand squeezes mine. My heart leaps for joy at the same time her eyes flutter halfway open.

"Chris?" her voice is so hoarse I wince, knowing her throat must hurt.

"Gems," I sigh in relief. "Oh, thank god, you're awake."

"You're alive," she whispers.

Taken back by her statement, I squeeze her hand and ask, "Of course, babe, why wouldn't I be?"

Her eyelids flutter shut as she sighs. Her brows come together, and she frowns as a groan slips past her lips. She doesn't answer my question, and after a moment of silence, I'm sure she's slipped into unconsciousness. I wait, my heart still pounding wildly, thrilled she's talking. Her eyelids crack open again after a long stretch.

"Darion? Tate?" she asks softly.

"They're here, too," I assure her.

"I'm here, Gemma," Tate says as he tries to push off the couch.

"Stay there, Tate," I snap at him. He's going to hurt himself and hinder his recovery if he tries to stand on that leg. "You'll hurt yourself."

"Fuck off," Tate grumbles.

"Stay, Tate," Gemma whispers as her eyes close.

To my surprise, Tate listens. He murmurs his displeasure about being told what to do but settles back against the couch. He turns his body towards the bed so he can see her.

"Do you need anything? Water? Food?" I ask her, anxious to do something, *anything* to help.

"A blanket," she whispers. "I'm cold."

I move quickly, leaving the room and walking over to the nurses' station. The nurse looks up, and I note how she bats her eyes at me. I ignore the look and tell her, "Miss Thomas has woken up and would like another blanket."

"Oh! I'll send a nurse in right away with a blanket and to check her over," she says.

"Will she be able to come home tonight?" I ask.

"That's up to the doctor. We'll call him right away."

I make a face but decide not to push the issue about taking Gemma home. I leave the station and head back to her room. Gemma's eyes are closed again, and a little shiver of panic that she could have died while I was outside crawls down my spine.

Coming back over to her side, I tell her, "The nurse will be in shortly with a blanket. She wants to check you over and then the doctor will be in."

"Hm," she says without opening her eyes. "Thank you."

"Oh, Gems, you don't have to thank me," I tell her as relief floods me. Emotions well up so strongly I'm choked by them. "I'm so happy you're awake. I thought... I thought we'd lost you. I can't ever lose you, Gemma."

"I thought I lost you, too," she says, opening her eyes. "All of you."

"Gemma!" Darion calls in surprise as he hurries into the room. He glares at me. "You should have told me she woke up!"

"She just woke up," Tate says from the couch.

Darion comes over to Gemma's side, grabs her face in his hands, leans down, and kisses the top of her head.

"How are you feeling?" Darion asks.

"Sore," Gemma responds.

"The doctor should be in shortly," I assure her just as a nurse walks in.

"Miss Thomas, so glad to see you awake and talking!" the woman says cheerfully. She looks at us and says, "I need to get to Miss Thomas to do a thorough check over."

Both Darion and I hesitate, not willing to leave Gemma's side but knowing it's for a good reason. Gemma squeezes my hand and looks up at me then over to Darion.

"Don't leave," she pleads.

"Of course not, we'll be right here," I tell her quickly.

"I'm not going anywhere," Darion promises solemnly.

"Love you guys," Gemma says softly as her eyes slide shut. "All three of you."

My heart soars at her words.

"I love you too, Gems," I tell her, unable and unwilling to stop the grin that splits my face. My mate loves me. Once she's home and comfortable, I'll show Gemma how much I love her.

Chapter Thirty-Three

Gemma

"Oh god, I look like a corpse," I say as I stare at my reflection in the bathroom mirror in horror.

It's the first time I've been up on my own in over a week and a half. I've been drifting in a fog from my pain medication, and this morning I finally refused to take them. While I'm aching, it's worth it to not feel sick from them. It's also nice to have a clear head. I can't *think* when I descend into the fog.

"You said it, not me," Tate says from the bed. "Now get back to bed before you fall over and hurt your ankle."

My face looks flush, and I can tell I've lost some weight. The dark circles under my eyes are from the nightmares that plague me at night. I grimace as I look away from my reflection and hobble over to the shower. The pain in my ankle is making it hard to want to do anything other than get my weight off of it.

"I need a real shower, not another cloth bath," I grumble. "I can smell myself, and it's grossing me out."

"It grosses me out, too, but I'm not complaining," Tate tells me.

I chuckle at his orneriness as I turn on the shower. By the time the water gets hot, I'm leaning against the wall, too exhausted to get in.

"Come on, you got this far. Might as well get in," Tate says, suddenly behind me.

His hands land on my hips, and his breath trails over the back of my neck. I shiver at the contact. I'm *almost* distracted from the slippery floor of the shower. I look over my shoulder at him.

"*You* should still be in bed," I tell him. "What if you hurt yourself helping me?"

"*I'm* nearly as good as new," Tate says with a smug smile. "I just stay in bed to keep you company."

"It's not fair you get super healing abilities," I grumble.

"If I didn't, I couldn't help you shower," Tate points out.

I nod and take a deep breath. Reaching down, I untie my robe. Tate reaches up and slides it off my shoulders. The robe falls to the floor. I shiver as cool air touches my naked body. This is the first time Tate has seen me completely naked. Perhaps if I weren't covered in horribly disgusting bruises that only appear to be getting worse not better with each passing day, I would be more excited about this moment with Tate. But now I feel self-conscious.

I reach out and test the water with my hand as Tate's hands come back to my hips.

"Don't hunch your shoulders in shame," Tate commands softly in my ear.

"The bruises are so ugly," I tell him, making a face.

"Those bruises are battle marks. They tell me you're a fighter," Tate says firmly. "And I used to have similar ones. Did they disgust you?"

I shake my head at once.

"No, not at all," I tell him honestly.

There is absolutely nothing disgusting about Tate's body. He's been far from modest since our arrival home. He hardly wears shirts anymore while he lies in bed with the three of us, and I've awakened to his pajama bottom hanging so low I can see his butt, and there is nothing soft about it.

"Good," he murmurs near my ear. "Now let's get you into the water before it gets cold."

With Tate's steady hands, I step into the shower. The hot water hits my body, and immediately, I'm relaxing.

"Place both hands against the wall and lift your injured ankle up to get the weight off of it while I undress," Tate orders.

I do as he says and let the water cascade down my back as he removes his pajama bottoms. I sneak a peak of his naked body and freeze when I see how sculpted he is. There is nothing soft about his body... anywhere. When I see his erection, I gulp and look up at him.

"Don't get excited Gemma, I'm helping you shower. I'm not a creep," he warns seriously.

I sigh dramatically and look away. It feels like forever since I've had some good old fashion dicking. I mean, Darion needs to eat, so luckily, I get to be devoured and fingered, but no one seems to want to do more than that with me. Ever since my one-night stand with Christopher, I've become this sex-crazed woman. And since the night I pushed Darion out of the way of the gunman, I've gotten exactly the kind of sex I desire. But since I came home from the hospital, I've been feeling... unsatisfied.

Tate chuckles as he steps in behind me.

"Lean your head back to get your hair wet," he tells me.

"I can wash my hair. I have hands," I tell him while I comply with his demand.

"Well, I want to do it for you. Keep your hands on the wall," he says.

He pours shampoo into his palms and begins to wash my hair. I groan as he scrubs my scalp. He washes it out and proceeds to add conditioner into my hair. To my surprise, he twists my curls up into a bun and grabs the loofa.

"How'd you know you're supposed to let the conditioner sit?" I ask him with amusement.

"I know women, Gemma," he drawls as if it's obvious. "I've picked up a few things around them."

I chuckle and then sigh as the soapy loofa makes its way around my body. Tate is respectful as he washes me. I should be thankful that he's more worried about my wellbeing than sex, but I'm not. My nipples bud, my breathing catches in my throat, and I know I'm wet. When he commands me to turn around, he helps me turn to face him. His eyes meet mine, and we stare at each other. Staring into those deep blue eyes, I see a fire burning there. I catch my breath and hold it.

I will him to kiss me. I want to touch those lips and feel his hands on me. Instead, he moves the loofa over my front and turns me back around. As he hangs the loofa up, I brace myself against the shower wall with my hands as first instructed and lean my butt backward, so it's nestled right at his hips suggestively. His erection settles between my crack.

"Gemma," Tate growls a warning.

"Tate, I want you to touch me," I plead. "Please."

Tate says nothing and does nothing for a long moment. I groan in frustration. His hands appear at my hips, and his grip is punishing.

"You've listened to me very well," he says slowly. "I will reward your obedience once I get the conditioner out of your hair. Do you understand?"

Excitement spikes through me, and I nod.

"I asked you if you understood, Gemma. When I ask you a question, you answer it," Tate states firmly.

"Yes, I understand," I say and grin.

"Good."

Tate reaches up and grabs the showerhead. He pulls my hair out from its bun and washes out the conditioner. I swear he is purposely going slow now. Teasing me. I groan in frustration, and Tate chuckles but says nothing.

Finally, when my hair is clean, he braids it slowly. When he's done, he lets the braid drop, and his hands come back to my hips. He leans forward and kisses my neck.

"You're fucking gorgeous, Gemma. Do you know that?" he asks me between the kisses that he is trailing down my neck onto my shoulder. "And you listen so well…"

His right hand travels from my hip to between my legs. There, his fingers part my folds, and I gasp softly as he explores me.

"Oh, sweet hell… You're so wet," he groans.

His fingers slowly slide into me, and he strokes me.

"Tate," I hiss as I arch my hips into him.

I need more; I need him. I've had the others, claimed them with my body. But I haven't had a taste of Tate yet. I want it now. Tate's fingers withdraw from between my legs, and I open my mouth to protest, but suddenly Tate lifts me by my hips and turns me around. I gasp and reach out to place my hands on his shoulders as he places me down. His mouth crashes down on mine, and I kiss him back greedily.

Tate breaks the kiss and says, "Wrap your legs around me."

He lifts me up, and I do as he asks. In the same motion, he impales me. We both cry out as my body accepts him greedily. When he's as deep as he can go, he holds me there, letting the water crash over us as we catch our breath.

"I've wondered what this moment would be like for weeks, Gemma," he tells me as he leans forward to kiss the base of my throat. "It's better than I could possibly have imagined."

"Please, Tate," I whine as the urgency to move grows.

He chuckles and says, "I've told you before, babe. I'm into a certain lifestyle. *I* tell *you* what to do. Do you understand?"

I nod frantically. Then, I lean down and kiss him. I slip my tongue into his mouth, needing as much of him as I can get. He kisses me back, just as frantically. His fingers dig into my skin, and it hurts, but I ignore the pain as I devour him.

"Tell me something, Gemma," Tate asks, pulling away from my lips. "At the hospital, the day you woke up, you said you loved all three of us. Is this true?"

I nod. "Yes."

"Do you really love me?"

"Since I saw the real you at the golf course," I tell him, panting.

My body clenches around his erection as I think about how quickly my affection for Tate has grown since then.

"We started off on the wrong foot," he tells me through gritted teeth. "But god, I have fallen so hard for you. I love you, too, Gemma. Now, put your arms around my neck."

My heart explodes with joy, and I do as I am told. The moment I do, Tate begins moving his hips. The friction is exactly what I need. I cry out as he slams into me, filling me perfectly. Pleasures builds swiftly, and I can feel myself teetering on the edge of an orgasm. I'm panting, crying out Tate's name, pleading for more. Tate leans forward and bites my nipple. The sharp pain is my undoing. I cum hard around him. He thrusts in me two more times before finding his own release.

"Oh god," I groan. "I never wanted that to end."

"Same," he agrees through his panting.

"That can be arranged," Darion's voice drawls from the door.

Tate jerks as his softening erection grows hard in me again. Darion saunters over to the shower, stripping off his own clothes. I grin and reach out to him. He takes my hand with one hand, kisses it, and then grabs something from the counter with the other.

"Fuck, Darion, too much... I already have to bust again," Tate growls through his gritted teeth.

Darion chuckles. "You're fine."

"Easy for you to say. I'm still inside Gemma, and god, does she feel so good," Tate gasps and jerks his hips, unable to fight whatever effects Darion has placed over him.

I groan as he hits that special spot inside of me. Tate begins thrusting like never before, and it feels fabulous. Darion steps into the shower with us and begins to kiss the back of my neck. I look over my shoulder and take his lips with mine. His hands travel over me, and I shudder under the contact. My body is hot, too hot. The water is growing cool, but it does nothing to slow down the heat burning inside of me. A familiar haze begins to descend over my senses.

"Darion," I groan his name as his hands trail down my body.

"You'll tell me if you're in pain, right?" my incubus says.

"Yes," I lie. My hips begin to move of their own accord as Tate continues to push in and out of me.

I could be dying, but as long as I'm in their hands, I'll die happy. Darion chuckles as his body presses up against my back. His hands trail down my back, along my butt crack, and then he pulls my cheeks apart and pressed his finger against my back door.

The shock of the touch causes me to gasp and still for a moment.

"Have you ever explored this type of sex before?" Darion quietly ask into my ear.

The sexual haze he cast over us makes it hard to think, but I try. With a deep breath I tell him, "I have a plug I used to play with…"

My body begins to grind against Tate, who groans.

"Oh, god, I want to see you with a butt plug," Tate pants. "Just thinking about it is going to make me lose it. Jesus, Darion, I can't—"

"I won't let you cum. Not until I've had my fun," Darion snaps, cutting Tate off.

I can hear his grin in his voice, and when I look over my shoulder at the incubus, I see it.

"Bastard," Tate says as he thrusts into me harder.

The tight coil of pleasure is growing in me, but I know I'm stuck at the same precipice as Tate. As much as my body is ready to go, Darion has us both in his grasp. I whine as I arch my hips against Tate, hoping to find release.

"Please, Darion, join us," I plead.

"Don't mind if I do," Darion says, removing his hands from my body.

I hear the pop of a bottle top opening. I glance over to see him lubing his thick erection. Watching him fist himself is so hot that I lick my lips. I could get off just watching that. Tate leans forward and pulls my attention away from Darion's dick as he takes my nipple into his mouth again and toys with it with his tongue. Darion's hands grab my butt and begins to spread my butt cheeks again. He inserts a finger first and I shudder with delight as he works it in. A moment later he withdraws it only to replace it with his erection that he presses against my back entrance.

"If you don't want this, tell me now," Darion growls into my ear.

"Darion, *hesirah*, fuck my ass," I cry out.

Darion's chuckle is deeper, more demonic. His teeth scrape across my neck.

"Relax and bear down while I enter you," Darion tells me.

The sexual haze deepens, and my nipples become hard points. Each stroke of Tate's erection threatens to send me over the edge. I need to let go, oh god, I'm so close, but I know I need more if I'm going to find this release. As Darion gently surges forward, I bear down. As he slides in, I see rainbows and stars. The pressure is absolutely incredible, indescribable.

When he's all the way in, I'm panting. Oh god, this feels fantastic. So much so that I can't think. All I feel in this moment is pleasure. I can hear myself yelling for more, for release. I'm pleading, I know I am, but it sounds like it's far away. Darion is moving, Tate is moving, both moving in and out of me at different times. I feel the wave of pressure building, reaching the peak. Just as I'm sure I'm going to pass out from the intensity of pleasure, the wave crashes.

I scream as I cum, hard and long. My body grips both of them. I hear their cries as they succumb to their own throes of passion. Tate takes my mouth with his, and we both sigh into the kiss. Darion's lips skim across my neck, and his hands hold my sides.

"Jesus, that was the hottest thing I've ever seen," Christopher's voice says.

I'm too exhausted to be startled. I look over to see him holding his own dick in his hand. Our eyes meet, and we both grin at each other. He grabs a hand towel off the counter and cleans himself off.

As Darion's sexual haze begins to evaporate, Darion pulls out of me first, slowly. Tate is next and helps me to my feet. I can feel every ache and pain in my body now that my arousal has been satisfied. I brace myself against Tate's chest and hold my ankle up off the ground.

"So much for not touching Gemma until she's better," Christopher says as he grabs a towel off the hanger. Tate hands me off to Christopher who wraps the towel around me. He helps dry me off, and when I'm done, he swoops me up into his arms. My shifter leans down and kisses me, and I kiss him in return.

"I insisted," I explain with a wicked smile. "A woman has needs you know, and I have three fabulous men at my disposal. I didn't want any of them to go to waste."

The three guys laugh.

Christopher carries me out of the bathroom and places me on the bed. Since our arrival home, the dynamics of the four of us have changed immensely. Christopher and Darion changed out the queen bed in my room and replaced it with two king size beds placed directly next to each other. It was a given that I would be placed on the bed, but I was surprised, and pleased, to see them help Tate into the new bed set up as well. Thankfully, neither Christopher or Darion seem upset or bothered by the decision to allow Tate into our relationship. Since then, the four of us have shared this room together.

According to Christopher, the renovations to the house will start soon. In just a few months, we'd all be sharing a large room together. While we will still have our own private rooms to maintain some semblance of privacy, it will to be nice to convene together in the evenings in one room that will fit us all.

"Gemma, you're hurt. None of us want to see you any more injured than you already are," Christopher tells me.

"I had aches that needed tending to," I tell him matter-of-factly with a grin as I relax into the bed. "Darion and Tate were very attentive nurses."

I feel like I'm floating on cloud nine. My eyelids flutter shut as a smile spreads across my face.

"Next time, I expect you to be a part of it, too," I mumble to Christopher as sleep pulls me under.

Chapter Thirty-Four

Gemma

"Oh, please," I beg as I arch my back against the seat of the car.

The small vibrator nestled inside of me is going crazy. I reach over and grab Christopher's leg as a hard shiver runs through me. He covers it with one of his and grins mischievously at me.

"Please what?" Darion asks from the driver's seat.

"Please guys, just let me—" I plead but the vibrating stops.

"I don't know what she's asking, do you?" Christopher asks Darion innocently.

"I have no idea," Darion shrugs.

"Urgh, you guys are killing me," I huff breathlessly from desire. "Are we almost there?"

"A few more minutes," Darion says.

I look out the window as I shift in my seat, looking for relief. It's hard to relax though. With the guys taking turns with the remote to the vibrator, they're driving me mad. That and the fact that ever since the accident two and a half months ago, being in a car causes me to become anxious. I think this game is to help distract me as they take me to some secret destination.

Per their request, I have dressed in my favorite sexy dress and managed to tame my curls. Normally, I would don some sexy heels, but my ankle isn't strong enough for that just yet. It's been three months since Pierce was taken care of. I hoped to be further along in my recovery, but according to the doctor, I have a few more months to go before I'll be completely healed. I push away the annoyance at myself for not healing faster to focus on what the guys are up to.

I'm curious and excited to know where we're going. Lately, we've all been going out a lot more together, and each time it's an adventure. Now that we're free from Pierce and his gang, we've taken advantage of that freedom. Tonight is just another adventure; I'm just the only one who doesn't know what that adventure is yet.

"Has anyone texted Tate yet to let him know we're almost there?" I ask.

Tate left with Darion for work this morning to talk to Ian, Darion's head of security, about some job they are working on and then stayed late while Darion came home. According to Darion, Tate is just finishing up some loose ends. Whatever that means.

"Tate is probably already there waiting for us," Christopher assures me. "You know he's a stickler with time."

"Do you think he's okay on his own?" I ask, knowing his aversion to being out in public. "I hope he's not stressing out."

"He's fine, Gems," Darion says and makes it a point for me to see his eye roll in the rearview mirror.

At the same time, the vibrator turns back on. I squeeze my legs together, trying to suppress a moan. I fail. Christopher suddenly leans over, turns my head in his direction with his hand, and kisses me. His tongue slips into my mouth, and I welcome it. He tastes fantastic. I unclick my seatbelt, hike my dress up, and straddle Christopher. His deep chuckle unfurls something wild in me as I continue to kiss him.

He uses one hand to hold me around the hips, and the other one creeps under my dress to push my panties aside. His thumb rubs against my clit. My moan is even louder than the first, and I open my legs wider for him. With his ministrations and with the vibrator going, which has been edging me the entire car ride, my release comes swiftly. I pull away from his mouth and throw my head back as my orgasm crashes through me. Christopher kisses my neck as I come down from my high.

"We're bringing this thing everywhere with us," I tell them both as I slide off Christopher.

Both of them laugh as I reach between my legs and pull the toy out. I plop it into my clutch and sigh, feeling at ease.

Darion parks the car a short time later, right outside of a swanky restaurant. He climbs out and opens the back door to help me out. Christopher slides out after me while Darion throws the keys to the valet attendant. Darion takes my hand, and Christopher takes my other. They lead me through the doors into the restaurant.

I'm not sure what I expect when I walk in, but a completely empty restaurant is not it. Almost all the tables have been cleared away. There are rose petals lining the floor to the only table in the room, which is draped in a white tablecloth and set for four. Next to the table, Tate, wearing his best suit, stands there with his hands clasped in front of him. He is tall, dark, and handsome and every bit a sight for sore eyes.

My mouth drops open in surprise, and I stop to take in the sight. I don't have long. Both Darion and Christopher gently pull me forward. My eyes are glued to Tate as we approach. For whatever reason, my heart is pounding wildly in my chest. When I'm hardly a foot away from Tate, both Darion and Christopher let go of my hands and step away to stand on either side of Tate.

I look at all three of them in astonishment. What the hell is going on? What is all of this?

"Gemma," Tate starts. "When I came home from deployment, I

knew I was walking into trouble. I had heard about you from the guys, and I instantly thought you were here to break us apart. I hated you without even laying eyes on you. Little did I know that you would be the best thing to happen to not only Darion and Christopher's lives, but my life as well. Every day I wake up thinking life can't get better, but every day you prove that it can."

Tears spring up in my eyes and blur my vision as his words unravel me. Tate unbuttons his jacket and pulls a small box from his inside pocket. I gasp as he drops to one knee and opens the box, in which a massive diamond ring is nestled.

"Gemma Thomas, would you please do me the honor of being my wife? I promise to love you and look after you until my dying breath," Tate asks me.

I can't talk. There is a knot in my throat and tears spill down my cheeks. I look up at the others, who both wear large grins. There is no jealousy or resentment in either of their faces. They're all in on this. They knew what Tate planned and kept me in the dark just for this moment. It doesn't matter if I marry Tate. I'm Christopher's mate, and I'm Darion's master. I look down at Tate and nod.

"Yes. Yes, I'll marry you," I manage to say.

Tate moves so swiftly I hardly have time to brace myself as he picks me up and twirls me around. I giggle in delight, and when he puts me on my feet, we kiss. We kiss so passionately it steals my breath away.

"Alright, it's my turn to kiss the bride to-be," Christopher says.

Tate and I break apart, sharing wide grins. I'm trembling with excitement and nerves. I look over to Christopher who steps forward.

"Congratulations, Gems," Christopher says warmly as I step over to him.

He leans down, and we kiss just as fully as Tate and I had. When he breaks the kiss, the room is spinning. I try to catch my breath, but I'm pulled in another direction as Darion comes forward, and I am swept into his arms where we embrace for a kiss.

When I step back from Darion, it's only his support that keeps me on my feet.

"Gemma, you are the love of my life. Don't you ever fucking leave us," Darion tells me.

I laugh, a little breathlessly. I look around at the three of them beaming back at me.

"I love you all so much," I tell them when I find my voice. "I can't wait to spend the rest of my life with you."

"Gemma, you are the love of *our* lives. Without you, there is no life to live," Christopher says warmly.

Darion turns, grabs a bottle of champagne off the table and pops it open. He grabs the nearest flute and pours a glass. He hands it to me and begins to fill the others for himself and his brothers.

When we all have a glass, he turns to me and says, "Here's a promise from all of us Gemma: we will love you unconditionally and forever."

"Unconditionally and forever," both Tate and Christopher repeat.

I grin and stare at the three men who I love. I couldn't be more excited to share a future with them.

The End

Dear Readers-

Thank you so much for taking the time to read Skirting Fate.
I truly hope you enjoyed it. The best way to let me know how
much you loved (or hated!) this novel is to leave a review on
either Amazon and/or Goodreads. This way I know what to do
for the next book. I love hearing from people so look me up on
social media and let's contact. Keep an eye out for my newsletter
(that you can sign up on my Facebook page) to see when my
next reverse harem will drop.

Best Wishes,

Salem Cross

Salem Cross is an avid writer who finds inspiration for her stories in even the smallest details in her life. She lives on the coast of North Carolina where you will either find her lounging on the beach or curled up with her three dogs on the couch while she reads a good book. She enjoys travelling, running, and woodworking. Visit her website at www. salemcrossauthor.com to find out more about Salem Cross.

Made in the USA
Middletown, DE
12 July 2021